One Thing
After
Another

Neive Denis

Merivale Retirement Village series Book 3

Cataloguing-in-publication data
Creator: Denis, Neive, author

Cataloguing-in-Publication details are available from the National Library of Australia
www.trove.nla.gov.au

ISBN: 978-0-6454907-8-7 (paperback)
ISBN: 978-0-6454907-9-4 (eBook)

Cover: T A Marshall, Mackay, QLD, Australia.

Disclaimer

This novel is a work of fiction. All characters and events are the product of the imagination of the author. While some of the characters might remind you of people you know, they are fictitious and any resemblance to anyone living or dead is purely coincidental. Although some locations also may seem real and familiar, most places referred to in this work constitute a collage of places the author has known and are fictitious. Any resemblance to an existing location is coincidental.

Chapter 1

"Okay, you lot, how did we manage to be on the brink of World War III?" Cilla Longhurst demanded as, still looking back over her shoulder, she strode into the recreation room. "Sorry; good morning all. Apologies for being a bit late today. I was delayed by having to take evasive action to sneak past the bowls club safely. What the hell is going on over there?"

Standing closest to the doorway, Rod Maguire gave her a piercing hard look and hissed, "Later…," as he accompanied her to join the group of mahjong players still indulging in pre-games morning tea. "Coffee, Cilla?" he asked, ignoring Cilla's question.

"Eh? Oh, yes, please, Rod." Then, addressing the rest of the group, she continued, "I suppose all today's teams have been drawn up by now, but I wondered whether there might still be a team in need of a player."

"Welcome back," Janet Furlong called back. "There's a spare chair at our table. How was Sydney?"

"Sydney was Sydney. Tell you about it later. I don't want to hold up proceedings more than I already have."

Handing Cilla a mug of coffee and shoving the remainder of a plate of scones at her, Rod again suggested, "Later, not now….", as he slid his eyes towards Bernard Stuart-Parnell, striding into the Recreation Room.

Cilla raised her eyebrows at Rod and murmured, "Not only late, but primed and ready for combat, I see. What could possibly have gone wrong today? Marion, fill me in, please. What has happened, Marion?"

I could only echo Rod's 'later' comment but, as it happened, she didn't have to wait long to find out anyway.

"The cheek of some idiots…!" Bernard exploded as he approached the group.

"Which idiots would they be?" Alice Logan asked innocently.

"Women…! Women trying to take over the bowls club. I can't even begin to imagine why they were allowed to play in the first place."

"Probably because they are both residents and people," Alice retorted. "And that's all they need to be to play bowls here."

Bernard was not about to be silenced by logic and continued as though nothing had been said. "Lawn bowls is a man's game. It requires more than just skill. Tactics and game strategies are a major part of the sport." He ended with a disgusted snort for emphasis.

"Like cricket?" Cilla asked.

"Yes, exactly. It's about more than an outing for a giggle and a cup of tea. It is a sport far too complex for women to master, and dress standards apply to the sport. The Merivale women's dress standards – or lack thereof – are bringing the sport into disrepute. As you say, Cilla, it's like cricket."

"Hmm…," Cilla murmured as she appeared to ponder Bernard's comments. "That's why there are so many women's cricket teams playing nationally and internationally, I suppose … and often with better spectator support than some of the men's games. Women even attract big money now in their own international competition."

"Shall we suspend discussion of cricket – and bowls – for the moment?" Rod asked a touch tartly. "We are here this morning supposedly to play mahjong, and I believe that is something suitable for both men and women. May we get on with it, please? …Or, we could all go home again, if you would prefer?"

A flurry of activity followed as people rinsed mugs and headed for the tables already set up for the morning's games. Armed with coffee and a scone, Cilla eyed off the other players as she made her way beside Rod to her table. Cocking an eyebrow at Rod amidst the scraping of chairs as players took their places, Cilla murmured, "Hmm… now isn't that interesting, eh?"

"That's for later too," he answered cryptically, "much later, perhaps."

The morning did not go well for Cilla. Not only had she arrived late and was part of a different team from her usual one as a result, but she played worse than a raw beginner. It earned her more than one angry glare from her playing partner, Alice Logan, along the way.

Cilla almost heaved a sigh of relief when mahjong ended, and chairs were being pushed back from the tables again. She hoped they would all leave straight away. It was not to be. A couple drifted off as soon as they left the tables, but the rest opted for another coffee before heading home.

As the only female member of the bowls club management committee, Cilla felt obliged to look into its current kerfuffle. And, as the next committee meeting was scheduled for the following day, she needed to come up to speed quickly on the matter.

At last, only Cilla and the usual four others remained in the Rec Room. As they busied themselves with cleaning and putting everything away, she had her chance to ask questions.

"Right. Now we are alone, I want to know more about this bowls club issue. This isn't about me being nosey. If I'm to represent Merivale's women bowlers at tomorrow's committee meeting, I need to know the whole story. And, since when did Bernard become so passionate about bowls? He was one of the strongest opponents of the establishment of a bowling green here."

"Ah, yes," Maria Lancini began. "Most of the time, it feels as though nothing ever happens here. Then, you look away for five minutes and can't recognise the place when you look back at it. You've been away a few weeks. Perhaps not much else happened in that time, but Bernard did take up playing bowls… probably soon after you left."

Cilla grinned broadly and, tongue in cheek, said, "I didn't realise my presence in the Village inhibited Bernard from playing bowls."

"There are other changes too," Alice added with a cheeky grin, "but now I think on it, they seem to revolve around Bernard as well."

"Yep, I think I noticed one of them earlier today as we all took our places at the tables," Cilla agreed. "Bernard and Marjorie were not at the same table, and I sensed a certain frostiness between them."

"Probably safe to say Bernard and Marjorie are no longer an item," I suggested.

"Well, our esteemed volunteer librarian, Marjorie Bosworth, certainly wasn't fawning all over Bernard as usual. What happened there?" Cilla glanced around the group as she finished speaking, but no one met her gaze, not at first anyway. Then Alice found her voice.

"James happened… Let's call it like it is: James happened, and Bernard's attention is now firmly focused on James." No one responded, so Alice addressed the group. "Am I right or not? Or, out of some intrinsic need to be polite, are we going to pretend that's not the case?"

"Forgive me if I appear a little slow today, but to me, *James* sounds like a bloke's name," Cilla said.

"Oh, you know how it is, Cilla," I reminded her. In Bernard's opinion, we are blind and stupid, and can't possibly be aware of the relationship that appeared to develop almost overnight between James and Bernard."

"O-kay … so, if Bernard loses his trousers again, it's likely he's left them at this James's place instead of at Marjorie Bosworth's unit this time?" Cilla asked, cocking an eyebrow.

"That's about the size of it," I agreed.

"Right, but I need to bury that thought for the moment and focus on the bowls club problem. Alice and Maria, are you available to join me for afternoon tea at three o'clock?" Both women nodded, and Cilla continued. "If there are another three or four women bowlers you think would be worth joining us, please invite them along."

"We'll be off then," Maria announced and added, "Alice, you can phone a few of the women while I make lunch." Moments later, they were gone.

"Am I invited too?" Rod asked.

"Not unless you've changed gender while I was away." Rod looked a little put-out but just shrugged in response.

"Cilla, I wouldn't mind being there, if that's okay. I'm not one of the most dedicated bowlers, but I am interested in women's rights," I told her. "And I'll bring something for afternoon tea … unless you already have something."

"Thanks, Marion. That would be wonderful. All I had to offer them was old cheese on stale crackers."

"In that case, I'll be off to have lunch and do some baking. See you at three o'clock, Cilla, and I'll see you at your place for happy hour this evening, Rod."

"Hang on a minute while I lock up, and then we can all walk back together," Rod suggested.

"I heard you drive in last night. I didn't think you would bother with mahjong this morning," I told Cilla as we waited for Rod.

"Mahjong is the best way to catch up on what's happened while I was away. And I would have been here on time, if it weren't for whatever is going on at that bloody bowls club."

Chapter 2

About twenty minutes before the appointed hour, I found Cilla madly dashing about her dining room, trying to have it 'looking civilised', as she put it, by the time the others arrived.

"Where do you want me to put these cupcakes? And, is there anything else I can do to help you be ready for your meeting?" I asked as I marched into her dining room.

"Oh, thanks, Marion. Please take them to the kitchen and see if you can find a suitable plate or something to put them on."

"Do you know who or how many are coming?"

"Haven't a clue; I was hoping Alice or Maria might fill me in before the hungry horde arrived, but I haven't heard from them. I doubt there will be many, so we'll play it by ear as it happens."

A few minutes later, Alice and Maria arrived. "Alice and I tried quite a few numbers, but not too many were home," Maria apologised. "So, in the end, we know only four are coming."

"I don't know where everyone was this afternoon, but Stella, the one we really wanted, is coming," Alice added.

Some quick mental arithmetic told me that making the cupcakes smaller than usual had resulted in fourteen instead of twelve. That would be enough for eight not-too-greedy people.

"What's so special about this Stella person?" Cilla asked.

"Stella…? Of course, you haven't met her yet. She only moved into the Village while you were in Sydney.

Stella is a gun player who has competed at state and national levels and often won. After arriving in the district about eighteen months ago, she was a member of several local clubs before she moved here. She knows people in just about all the women's bowls clubs in the area. We thought she might be useful." Maria raised her eyebrows at Alice for confirmation as she finished speaking.

"Yeah, that's right. And Stella has run a few clubs in her time," Alice confirmed. "She is one of those people who are a bit of a force to be reckoned with."

"Sounds like Stella might be just what we need," Cilla agreed.

After the other four women arrived and coffee and cakes were doled out, Cilla didn't waste any time explaining why we were all there.

"If I am to use my position on the bowls club management committee effectively, I need to know the cause of the current tension within the club. Will someone please try to explain why the women members are so cranky at the moment?"

"Maybe you should be asking the men," Sandra spat out.

"That is not helpful, and if that's the best you have to offer by way of explanation, you might as well all go home as soon as you finish your coffee." Cilla's rebuke caused some to squirm on their chairs. Maria stepped in to head the discussion in the right direction.

"You might not be aware, Cilla, but despite all the agreements made before the first bowls were rolled, the men have bulldozed their way into having more green time than the women."

"When I joined," Stella began, "I was told the women had Mondays and Wednesdays for competition games and Tuesdays for social women's games. The men had Thursdays and Sundays for competitions and Fridays for their social games. Saturdays were for mixed games."

"Yes, that's the agreement we finally reached before the green was opened for play," Cilla confirmed. "So why is there a problem now?"

"Let's start with Tuesdays," a woman with blue hair began, "for a while now, a few of the men have been muscling in and forcing women off some of the rinks on Tuesdays. And that was only the start of the rot."

"Now they've started an interclub competition, and every week, a team from one of the other district's clubs comes here to play competition games," Maria told us. "And…."

"And that's only part of it," Sandra interrupted. "A few of us turned up yesterday, and four blokes came out to meet us. They wouldn't let us go anywhere near even the clubhouse. They just blocked us and stood there hurling abuse at us.

Maisie left her hat in the clubhouse on Monday and said she just wanted to go in to get it. As she went to walk past one of the blokes, he gave her an almighty shove, well, something between a punch and a shove. It caught her on the shoulder, and she fell to the ground. While she was lying there in pain, he stood over her, calling her dreadful names. She has her wrist in a splint and was to have it x-rayed today."

"Has she taken any action over the matter?" Cilla demanded. "What happened constitutes common assault and, more importantly, it's physical assault on an elderly person."

Stella cleared her throat before looking directly at Cilla. "We tried telling her that, but she was frightened and said she didn't want to say anything unless they came after her. She is now considering finding somewhere else and moving out of the Village."

"Well, we are not going to let that happen," Cilla snarled. "Although I have to admit, taking action of any sort will probably end up in a situation of 'he said/she said', and it could get messy."

"Perhaps not," Stella said, a sly grin sliding across her face. "I was a bit late arriving yesterday. I stopped and dug out my phone when I was close enough to see what was happening. I've been taking snaps of the weekly prize winners and pasting the images on our Facebook page. Anyway, I checked my phone last night, and I have a clear video of the whole incident."

"You're my kind of girl," Cilla exclaimed. "Could you send me that video, please?"

A little more discussion about Maisie's injury was allowed before Cilla saw fit to bring it to an end.

"Right, ladies, it is time for action, but it needs to be sly and quietly executed as only we women know how.

Although I didn't know the exact nature of the problem, I did a bit of thinking after mahjong this morning. The plan I devised still holds true now I know what we are dealing with here."

"Is what you plan legal, and are any of us likely to get hurt?" Sandra asked quietly.

"Definitely legal, and no one is going to get hurt, but there is work to do before tomorrow's bowls club management committee meeting."

"We're up for it," Stella assured Cilla as heads all around the table nodded in agreement. "What do you want us to do?"

"The first thing – and I think this job might fall to you, Stella – is to contact other women's teams at the various bowls clubs in the area to see if they are interested in establishing an interclub competition similar to the men's."

"Yep, I can do that," Stella confirmed, "and I know there is quite a bit of interest out there in setting up something like that. What else needs to be done?"

"Maybe we need to establish a Merivale Bowls Club women's subcommittee."

"O-kay," said the blue-haired woman whose name I still hadn't heard. "Why do we need one of those? We seem to be managing all right as we are so far."

"As you are now, you don't have any clout. Don't worry about it; just make it happen. For the moment, it will remain informal and confined to the realm of the women bowlers here. But it is part of a bigger plan ultimately designed to have another woman representative on the management committee."

"Nothing that's been suggested so far is beyond us, is it?" Stella asked and received unanimous agreement. "Okay, so yes, we can do that, but does it have to be in place by tomorrow's meeting?"

"Probably not, but it wouldn't hurt if there had been some move towards establishing it by then."

"What's this subcommittee supposed to do, apart from getting us more representation on the management committee?" Sandra asked.

"Let's see…I think it would look after drawing up the competition roster for our local club games, organising prizes as and when needed, and have a major role in organising and scheduling the women's interclub competition matches."

"We do all that already, except for the interclub stuff," Sandra argued.

"I know that, but it is done unofficially by volunteers. The work needs to be recognised and given proper standing within the overall function of the management of the bowls club.

Trust me. Tomorrow will not be about charging in with all guns blazing. It will be about going slow and being *devious.*" Cilla explained. And we will need as many women bowlers as possible to be observers at tomorrow's meeting … when, hopefully, I will launch our cunning plan."

Excited, rowdy conversation filled the room for the next ten minutes as the group discussed everything Cilla had laid out. Cilla let it run on for as long as she thought necessary before bringing it to a halt.

"Ladies, as much as I enjoy your company, you have work to do and not much time to do it before tomorrow's management meeting… And I have a plan to refine. So please don't consider me socially inept when I ask you all to go home."

The silence after Cilla dismissed them was deafening, but excited conversation soon resumed and was accompanied by the scraping of chairs as everyone drifted outside and away. I remained behind to clean up and to ask a few questions of my own. Cilla could read me like a book and knew she was in for a barrage of questions.

"Save those questions you want to ask for a bit longer, Marion. Ask them tonight if you must. By then, I might have the answers you're looking for."

It was soon after five o'clock when I drifted down to Rod's place. I knew it was early for happy hour, and I'd be the only one there. I wanted some time alone with Rod before the others arrived. I had intended to take a platter of chicken bits for people to nibble with their drinks but, as I was going to be there so early and the chicken would be cold by the time the others arrived, a platter of crackers and two types of cheese accompanied me instead.

"Come in, come in. I was hoping you might be a little early this evening. I noticed you were one of the mob at Cilla's this afternoon. Being the wrong gender to attend, I now await your full report." As Rod finished speaking, he gave me a 'gimme' gesture.

"Well, you might be a bit disappointed. I didn't take minutes, but I suppose I could give you an executive summary of the proceedings. Anyway, I suspect Cilla will have more details to share with us all tonight. And, unless my instinct is way off beam, I suspect she might also lobby our group for support."

As we sat perched at Rod's kitchen bench for the next few minutes, I gave him the key points from this afternoon's discussions. His reaction to news of Maisie's injury seemed to mirror my own.

"This can't be explained away as something other than what it was. People need to be accountable for their actions, and I would go so far as to say that anyone guilty of such an act has no place here at Merivale Retirement Village. I'll mull this over until tomorrow, but I will do something about it."

"Rod, whatever you do is up to you, but please be aware that Maisie is terrified they might come after her if she makes a fuss about it. She is now talking about moving out."

"Really…? Well, we'll see about that. Now, come on, give me a hand to finish setting up before the others arrive."

After the first few minutes of chatter as everyone arrived, Cilla called for their attention. She delivered a brief but concise report of SOME of what was discussed at this afternoon's meeting. I was disappointed. I had expected to hear a bit more about what she hoped to achieve and how she planned to go about it. That wasn't forthcoming. The most she shared was that she would use the excuse of 'catching up on recent news' since her recent return to the Village to deliver belated praise for the establishment of the men's interclub competition.

Like me, the others remained silent, waiting for more details – that were not forthcoming. And, despite judicious coaxing, they remained withheld. But Cilla was happy to discuss one other matter.

"There is something you can all do. If you're interested in assisting, turn up as observers at the management meeting tomorrow, and invite any of your friends, who also might be sympathetic to the cause, to come along too."

As it turned out, the rush to have those initiatives in place before the next afternoon proved unnecessary.

An early Friday morning phone call advised Cilla the management meeting scheduled for that afternoon had been cancelled and would be rescheduled for sometime in the next week or two. It appears three of the leading lights of that committee were not available. One was on holiday, and the other two had other engagements that clashed with the meeting time.

Although an announcement of the meeting cancellation was to be posted on the Village's Facebook page, Cilla opted to call some of those from yesterday's meeting to let them know and to ask them to tell anyone else they'd spoken to about the change of plan.

My call came as I was making breakfast. For a brief moment, as I listened to Cilla, I wondered whether the management committee had gotten wind of whatever Cilla was planning. She said she believed that unlikely.

"After all the work to have things in place for today, you must be disappointed it's not going to happen as planned," I commiserated with her.

"Not at all; it gives us more time to ensure everything is set and ready when the meeting happens. I need to work on my motorbike, Black Bess, and I didn't want to make a start and then have to leave it to go to the meeting. Now I've got a whole day to get on with it. So, as the adage goes, it's an ill wind...."

No meeting today suited me fine as well. It allowed me a leisurely morning to check supplies for tonight's pizza and karaoke night.

It was becoming a regular thing for me to doze off in front of TV after lunch. Despite my best efforts to watch the news broadcasts, today was no exception. It was almost three o'clock when the sound of Black Bess being taken for a test ride through the village woke me from a deep sleep.

Then, later, as I prepared to head off a little early to the Rec Room to do some work in the kitchen before the others arrived to set up for the pizza night, I heard the sound of the Village's only motorbike returning along the street. It did not sound like a happy, well-tuned Triumph Tiger motorbike, but more like a second-hand lawnmower. It looked as though Cilla's 'tuning' had not gone well today. One thing was sure. She would not be in a good mood tonight as a result.

While I worked alone in the Rec Room kitchen before the others arrived to help set up, my mind was on other things and not pizzas. In amongst it all, Cilla occupied a large part of my thinking. Thoughts of Cilla only reignited my curiosity about her intriguing plan for the bowls club meeting.

It didn't take me long to realise that, no matter how hard I thought about it or from what angle I came at it, for the life of me, I couldn't work out how Cilla could change the culture within the bowls club management committee.

To my mind, it would take nothing short of an epidemic to kill off a few of the 'old brigade die-hards' before any change was possible. Further adding to my frustration, while we slaved away in the kitchen to meet the demands of a full-house pizza night, Cilla refused to discuss any aspect of yesterday's meeting or her plan for the management committee meeting.

As we cleaned up and put everything away after the pizza and karaoke mob left, I heard Ted having a word to Rod. "It was good of Bernard to have something better to do again tonight than to help out here. He never does much, but it does ease the strain a bit when he is here. These 'no shows' are becoming a regular event on his part."

"It might interest you to know that I did query Bernard about his absences. I asked if something had upset him and made him decide not to come along to these nights anymore. He told me it was personal and that he was free to choose what he did with his Friday nights. And, just because he has missed a couple of Friday nights, it shouldn't be construed as its having become a permanent arrangement."

"Well, good for Bernard," Ted snarled, "but I don't think I'll count on his assistance again any time soon."

Just as I was about to wander out to ask about Bernard's spending so much time recently pursuing 'other interests', the moment was lost when Rod called out to ask how much longer before we finished in the kitchen. The men had finished with the rest of the building and were keen to go home.

We left the building in two groups to walk home. Frank, Luigi and Steve headed towards the new section of the Village, while Rod, Cilla, Maria, Alice, and I took the shorter route to our houses close together along the same street. Although not technically a resident, Alice Logan, who lived in a concrete and glass monstrosity on the other side of the park from the Village, always stayed with Maria rather than walk home after pizza night.

For some reason, most of our group was busy on Saturday night, so the next happy hour at Rod's place wasn't until Sunday night.

With nothing else on my calendar and no need to rush home to get ready for a Saturday night happy hour, I opted for a long afternoon walk that morphed into a leisurely stroll through the park that borders the Village, followed by a wander through the Village's newer residential area. Then, on my way home along our street, I did a double take as I passed Rod's place. Rod was standing, hands on hips, in his front yard and scowling at something hidden from view. He looked fierce.

"Rod, what's happened? You look as though you are about to kill something."

"I thought I had killed it. Maybe I did, and now it's back to haunt me."

"Hmm, I'm not much of an exorcist, not much good with ghosts. Would a sharp stake and a string of garlic help? Anyway, what are we talking about here?"

"Bloody weeds… I cleared this bed, and it looked beautiful two days ago. Now, nutgrass and other weeds are popping up everywhere. Tomorrow, the war begins in earnest. I have been avoiding the weedkiller in my shed, but tomorrow, it joins the battle.

Anyway, standing here scowling at these weeds won't make them disappear. I know we decided there was no happy hour tonight, but could I interest you in a drink, although there will only be the two of us?"

A cosy drink with Rod … Just the two of us … What's not to like about that? Of course, I'll stay for a drink. And, who knows, I might get lucky, and it will stretch to include dinner.

My vision of a cosy interlude was shattered as he poured our first drinks. Cilla's voice accompanied a knock on his front door.

"Although I knew there was no happy hour tonight, I thought I might join you for a drink before dinner. May I come in?"

While I struggled to restrain myself from yelling 'NO', I told myself this was Rod's house, and he could welcome whoever he pleased to have a drink with him. Besides, as soon as Cilla called out, he had rushed to usher her into the kitchen to join us. So, I bit my tongue and tipped a packet of nuts into a bowl. As an alternative to being antisocial, I tried for a neutral comment.

"I heard you returning from taking Black Bess for a test ride yesterday. She didn't sound too happy. Have you had a chance to do any further tuning of the old girl?"

"Argh, Friday's efforts were a bit of a disaster. My tweaking might have fixed the original problem, but it upset something else. It's taken me all day to sort out what I might have upset. I'll put her back together in the morning and see how she runs then. She wasn't running all that badly before I started fiddling with her. But she wasn't quite right, and I do like it when she runs perfectly."

"What seems to be the problem? I mean, the original problem that made you start working on her in the first place?" I asked, hoping I sounded as if I knew something about how motorbikes ticked.

"Well, I thought it would be a simple fix, but it seems I was wrong. She was running a little rough, and I needed to see if I could do something with her suspension. It's a bit too stiff for my liking, especially on some of the not-so-smooth bitumen you find around here. But I haven't even looked at the suspension yet. I'll look at it tomorrow after I put her back together and before I take her for another test ride."

It was a pleasant night, so we took our drinks out onto Rod's back deck. Our glasses were barely empty when Cilla's phone demanded her attention. After checking the caller ID, she excused herself and took the call out in the kitchen. Returning a couple of minutes later, she again apologised for having to leave so suddenly. The call had been to do with her advisory contract with the New South Wales police's special task force.

"They called to tell me they had set up an urgent Zoom call in about ten minutes. No rest for the wicked, eh?" she chirped over her shoulder as she picked up her empty glass and left it in the kitchen on her way out.

If there had been anything resembling 'a moment', it was now gone, and I felt compelled to follow Cilla's example and bid Rod goodnight. As I strolled the short distance past the couple of houses to my front door, I considered the state of my relationship with Rod Maguire. Yet again, I wondered if there actually was any romantic connection. Over the last couple of weeks, and based on any evidence to the contrary, my doubts about us being in a relationship had increased.

Chapter 3

There's nothing quite like an early morning caller ringing your doorbell on a Sunday morning before you've managed to kick your brain into gear. Being gracious is a difficult ask when they arrive before you've had coffee, and all they have come for is to drop off a book they promised to lend you about a month ago. Somehow, I managed not to be rude … at least, I think I did.

A friend who has a small hobby farm was on her way to market with a van loaded with fresh produce.

"It's a new market I heard about recently that's held on the Esplanade at Sandy Cove on the last Sunday of the month. I was coming this way and finally remembered the book I promised to lend you. I've thought about it plenty of times but always forgot to bring it whenever I was coming past."

"What about your regular stall at the weekly markets in the city? Are you still doing those as well?"

"Yep, I was there yesterday and sold everything I had on my stall. The Sandy Cove market is just an extra one I'll attend whenever I have excess produce. Since I built that big shade house last Christmas, I can produce early vegetables that are being snapped up at the markets.

The only problem is, when they are ready for picking, they are ready. You can't tell them to hang about until next week's city market. If they are ready, it's a case of pick them now or have them fall on the ground. Yesterday, after my stall, I found a lot of vegetables ready for picking. So, I'm off to try my luck at the new beach market. You should think about getting a stall to sell some of that baking you do."

"That's a thought, but probably not. Thanks for the book." As she drove off, I considered her suggestion about a stall to sell baked goods.

"No way…" I told the universe as I prepared my coffee. "I'd have to be up baking in the wee hours of the morning to sell freshly baked stuff on my stall." Besides, I told myself, I don't need the extra cash – and I certainly don't need the hassle.

While waiting for the coffee, I stared out the kitchen window and saw Frank and Luigi drive past in Frank's car. Frank Risdale and Luigi Giordano were among the first residents in the new section of the Village, and both are exceptional gardeners. They were the driving force behind the establishment of the Village's community gardens that have kept other non-gardener residents supplied with fresh vegetables during the season.

I remembered the men talking about checking out the Sandy Cove markets as a possible outlet for any surplus produce they might have. Seeing them drive out of the Village so soon after my friend left suggested they would be checking out the new beach markets today.

An extended breakfast with the weekend newspaper saw it almost mid-morning before I became mobile again and faced the question of what to do today. Of course, there was always housework, but a walk through the park on a glorious morning held more appeal. Come to think of it, walking barefoot through Hell would have more appeal.

While lacing on my boots, I heard Cilla go past on Black Bess. Her motorbike sounded a lot happier this morning. Cilla might have chalked up another victory in having Black Bess running better, but I wondered if she had corrected the problem was with its suspension.

Cilla's return around mid-afternoon again roused me from my after-lunch snooze in front of the TV. As I coaxed my neck upright and flexible again, I blinked blearily at images flashing across the TV screen. How had some Canadian ice hockey match managed to invade my lounge room? Never mind; it's time to think about other things.

A stew would be nice for dinner tonight, and if I put it in the slow cooker about now, it would be perfect by the time I returned from happy hour at Rod's this evening. Once the stew was happily doing its thing on the HIGH setting, it was time to think about nibbles to take to happy hour. As I wasn't planning on going early, a platter of hot, crumbed chicken bits was possible. After a quick shower, I dressed while the chicken bits were cooking.

Ted and Janet Furlong disappeared through Rod's front door as I strolled towards it. As I was about to open Rod's gate, Cilla bounded across the road to join me.

"Black Bess sounded good this morning. Looks like you might have had a win there, eh?"

"One down and one to go." Cilla's reply caused me to give her a questioning look. "Oh, I now have her running okay, but I still have to do something about her stiff suspension. That will be tomorrow's challenge, I fear."

Luigi, Maria and Alice caught up with Cilla and me at Rod's door and walked with us. Frank arrived a couple of minutes later and reported that Steve was on his way. Cilla asked a question never usually heard at such gatherings.

"Does anyone happen to know if Bernard is coming this evening?" she asked loudly but casually.

"Depends what James wants to do, I suppose," Frank muttered beside me.

"Bernard…? Since when have we been interested in whether Bernard is coming?" Steve asked. "After all, he's not what you might call a regular attendee."

"No, Bernard will not be coming tonight," Ted told us. "I ran into him earlier, and he mentioned that some visiting academic is presenting a guest lecture at the university tonight. You know how Bernard is about anything happening at the university. He believes he is obligated to support it, even if it is of no relevance to his area of expertise or interest."

"Is James going with him," Janet asked her husband.

"Dunno, but I suspect not."

"So they are not actually joined at the hip then?" Frank quipped.

As soon as the banter ended, Cilla announced that the cancelled bowls club management meeting had been rescheduled for Friday. She asked us to remind all our friends about attending what could be the most interesting committee meeting yet. And she was pleased Bernard wasn't here, as she wouldn't have been able to mention it in front of him – given his sudden passion for lawn bowls.

While I suspected there had been some private discussion between Cilla and Rod before Sunday night's get-together, Cilla still refused to discuss her plan with the rest of us. As usual, after everyone left, I stayed behind to help Rod clean up and put things away … And to try to coax out of him what he might know that I didn't. It's amazing how he can make a lie sound so plausible! As I walked home on Sunday evening, Friday afternoon seemed a long way off.

Monday morning saw me out of bed and out walking earlier than usual. The reason for the hustle and bustle this morning was a nine o'clock appointment with Bianca at the Village's hairdressing salon. Bianca's grandmother, Mavis Grimshaw, who lives on my street, delights in telling me how well the new salon is doing. I discovered how well it was doing when I tried to make an appointment for one day last week. Nine o'clock this morning was the earliest one available.

Mavis was out deadheading her roses as I walked home after my haircut. I had hoped to say good morning without stopping to chat, but it wasn't to be. She was up for a chat and, when she noticed my haircut, was keen to regale me with tales from Bianca's salon and Bianca's ex-husband, now doing time for attempting to rob her blind while living quite a life with a variety of young, good looking, women.

After about fifteen minutes, an escape was possible when her phone called her into the house. "You had better grab that. Bye, catch you next time," I said as I hurried off.

That's when I saw Rod approaching along the street from the opposite direction. He was on his way home from his morning run. We both reached his gate at almost the same instant.

"Are you available for a coffee," he asked.

Silly question; of course I was, and we were soon relaxing on his back deck with our mugs of coffee and enjoying that special kind of silence that can exist between close friends. All too soon, the blissful moments were shattered by the sound of Cilla's motorbike.

"Sounds like Black Bess was taken for a spot of early morning exercise, too," Rod observed as we listened to the bike drawing nearer.

"It sounds as though she is coming along that dirt track behind us, the one that runs along the other side of the Village's perimeter fence. Why would she want to ride along that rough track?" I asked.

Rod shrugged, and we both sat listening as we waited for her to pass behind Rod's place. I suggested something was wrong when she didn't appear after a few moments.

"I think she has stopped. I mean, I can hear the bike is still running, but I think it is stationary. It doesn't sound any closer than when we first heard it." Rod nodded and agreed something didn't seem right.

We rushed to peer over his back fence and back along the track to where we could hear the bike. Cilla was off the bike and appeared to be fiddling with some part of it. After a moment, she stood up and, seeing us at the fence, waved to us before throwing her leg over Black Bess and cruising up to us.

"Top of the morning to you two… and is that coffee I smell?"

"Another cup might be possible if you would care to join us," Rod responded. I cursed silently.

"Start the coffee machine. I'll ride around and be there by the time the coffee is ready," Cilla said as she dropped the clutch and eased off along the track again.

Damn… How will I ever know whether Rod and I are still an item if we never get to spend time alone together? Lately, it seems as if the whole group is programmed, if not to keep us apart exactly, then to make sure we aren't left alone.

True to her word, as the coffee machine finished doing its thing, Cilla strode into Rod's kitchen in her trademark grease-stained green overalls. Moments later, the three of us were settled on Rod's back deck.

"Things not quite right yet with Black Bess?" I asked.

"Eh, why do you say that?"

"We noticed you were stopped a little further back on the track. I thought something must have been amiss with your bike."

"Nah, not really; her suspension is pretty good now I've adjusted it. I hopped off back there to see if I could tweak it a little more, but I needed a spanner to do it. After I finish my coffee, I'll go home and have another little play with it before taking her for another test ride."

"Why test it on that rough dirt track when there is plenty of good bitumen around to ride on?" I had seen the cloud of dust she kicked up as she rode the last part of the track before coming around the front to Rod's place.

"There's no point testing the suspension on smooth bitumen roads. Something rough is needed to tell you whether you have it set right to guarantee a comfortable ride. So, after another quick tweak, you will be able to watch me flying along that track again."

"Is your health insurance up to date?" Rod asked. "And do you have hospital cover?"

"Very droll, Rod. I've never come off a bike yet. Came close a couple of times, though – but not with Bess."

As soon as she finished her coffee, Cilla was on her feet and heading for the door. "If this final adjustment does what I want it to, I'll be able to put my feet up for the afternoon or maybe look at some of my contract work that's crying out for attention."

"Could you go another coffee, Marion?" Rod asked as we heard Cilla ride Black Bess across the street and into her garage.

It seemed like only minutes later when we heard the bike start again and roar off along the street. A speed limit applies on all Village streets, but I'm not sure Cilla's car or bike can travel at 20 kilometres per hour. Or, maybe Cilla has never noticed the speed signs. In any case, she didn't think it applied today.

Long before we finished our second coffee, we heard Black Bess tearing along the dirt track again.

"She doesn't pamper it, does she? I mean, it's an old bike, and I would have expected her to be nursing it along, not going flat out all the time," I said as I stood up. "I'm going to stand at your fence to watch her come along the track."

"Sounds like she's stopped again," Rod commented as we strolled across his backyard.

"I hope she hasn't had an accident, fallen off or something," I replied as I felt my pulse quicken. It wouldn't be easy to get an Ambulance along that track.

"Not only has she stopped, she's turned it off now," Rod muttered. "What the hell has happened now? I'm almost not game to look."

But we had reached the fence, and, of course, we had to peer back along the track. Black Bess leaned over on her sidestand in the middle of the track and roughly behind my house.

"I can't see Cilla," I croaked. "What's happened to her? Has she been thrown off into the long grass or something?"

"No, I don't think so. We should be able to see her if she came off the bike. Come on, let's go and look over your back fence. We might have a better view from there."

At first glance, there was nothing more to be learned from peering over my fence than from Rod's.

"I still can't see her. Where is she?" I was starting to feel frantic, although Rod seemed calm enough about the situation.

Suddenly, he let out a yelp. "There… I think I just saw her out there in that paddock." He indicated an area in the now long-abandoned cow paddock on the other side of the dirt track.

"What the hell's she doing in the paddock … and why can't I see her?"

"She's crouched down or bending over, I think. I can't see her now either, and I only caught a glimpse of her green overalls anyway."

"Should we call out or something? Ask if she is all right or if she needs help?"

"Nah, I don't think so. You know Cilla as well as I do. She would not appreciate us making a fuss over her. Let's be patient a bit longer and see what happens."

"Well, I thought, if we called out, she might stand up or give us a wave. Then we would know everything was okay." Despite Rod's apparent lack of concern about the situation, to me, doing nothing did not feel right.

"Marion, if she were injured, she would do something to attract our attention, like wave to let us know she needs help.

Anyway, she didn't have an accident or come off her bike, so she is unlikely to be injured. Mind you, whatever she is doing in that paddock intrigues me."

"How do you know she didn't come off the bike?" I demanded in a voice a bit sharper than I intended, but Rod's superior attitude was starting to grate.

"The engine has been turned off, and the bike is on its sidestand. If she had come off the machine, the bike would be lying in the dirt, and so would she. The engine would still be running, and we would hear it cavitating as the fuel leaked out of it."

Okay, maybe he did know more about such things than I did. But, if Cilla wasn't hurt, what was she doing in that paddock?

"Rod, I think I'm inclined to climb over this fence and fight my way through the grass and weeds in that paddock to see what she is up to."

"Might not be such a bad idea. I'll fetch a chair from your back deck to help us climb over the fence. No point in injuring ourselves in our quest for knowledge."

There is nothing to recommend old age… and it definitely is not an advantage when climbing over a fence. Nevertheless, we both made it safely to the other side – the exercise proving easier for my fitter companion. As we dusted ourselves down and prepared for our trek into the wilderness of the former cow paddock, a depressing thought occurred to me. Although I didn't share it, the thought of having to scramble back over that fence later, without the help of a chair on this side, did not thrill me.

We hadn't waded more than a couple of metres through the grass in the paddock when Cilla suddenly stood up and started back in our direction.

"Stay there," she yelled. "Don't come any further."

Her words riveted our feet to the spot. I raised my eyebrows at Rod in alarm. My mouth was hanging open in fright, and it had become so dry, I couldn't speak. After a bit of effort, it was moist enough for me to croak, "What's going on? Are we safe here?"

"Your guess is as good as mine about what's happening, but I'm fairly sure we are safe. Whatever Cilla found there doesn't seem to have terrified her, or she wouldn't be walking out now as calmly as she is."

By then, Cilla was close enough for Rod to shout at her. "What have you found over there? Is there something we need to do?"

"Nope. We should probably all go home and wait for the coppers to arrive. I've called the local lads. Come on, let's all go home. I'll tell you about it as soon as I've dealt with the police."

Rod and I elected not to climb back over my fence, opting instead to walk along the track to the end of the fence and then come back into the Village and back to Rod's place along the street ... Much more dignified and less strenuous.

We were at Rod's gate when Cilla, on Black Bess, led a police vehicle to where Bess was recently parked on the dirt track. The police dealt with, she came back to Rod's place and joined us in a long glass of iced tea.

"Look, I know you're both dying of curiosity, but I have a phone call to make. I suggest we all do our own thing for lunch and then reconvene at your place, Marion, as it probably provides the best view of what's happening in the paddock. I'll tell you the whole story then."

"Can't you give us even a clue now?" I wailed. "I don't know if I can wait much longer."

But Cilla was already on her way to the door and responded over her shoulder without breaking her stride or looking back. "Think about those clothes that went missing from clotheslines here late last year. Part of the mystery of their disappearance might be solved." And then she was crossing the street to her house.

"Well, if that was supposed to be helpful, it wasn't," I snarled. "What are you doing for lunch, Rod? Would you like to come to my place?"

"Tempting, thanks, Marion, but no, I can't. I'm supposed to participate in an online chat in a few minutes, so I need to stay here and get set up for it."

I marched home alone, thinking sour thoughts about a couple of supposed friends.

Chapter 4

Although I knew there was no point in hurrying lunch, I did. And, no, it didn't make the other two arrive any sooner or help me find out any sooner what was happening in the paddock behind my house. Wandering out onto my back deck about every five minutes to check on the action didn't help either.

It was close to two o'clock when Rod and Cilla arrived. For the previous hour, it was all I could do to stop myself calling to hurry them along. To add to my frustration, now they were here, nothing had changed. I still didn't know any more than when I came home for lunch.

"Right, Cilla, that's it. I can't wait any longer. What is the story about over there?" I demanded as I made a sweeping gesture toward the paddock – in case the others didn't know where it was!

"Okay, let's sit on your back deck to watch what's happening while I tell you about my discovery this morning."

Armed with long glasses of iced tea, we strolled out onto my deck. Activity appeared to have stepped up a notch since I last checked. After the usual faffing about getting settled, Cilla launched into her story.

"Well, I guess the story really started earlier this morning when I took Bess for that first test ride along the track. It happened when I stopped to see if I could adjust her without having to go back for a tool to do it. When I realised I couldn't, I stood up and had a swear about the situation.

That's when something over in the paddock caught my eye. Although I dismissed it then as nothing, I knew I would investigate it sometime in the future. Then, after I adjusted it, the suspension seemed perfect when I went for a test ride. When I was about here along the track, I remembered the thing I'd seen in the paddock."

"I must admit, I was concerned when I saw your bike abandoned in the middle of the track, and you were nowhere in sight.

Sorry, I shouldn't have interrupted. Please go on with your story." I apologised and reminded myself to keep my mouth shut until Cilla finished telling her tale.

"Yeah, I suppose it might have looked a bit strange, but there wasn't a problem. I didn't expect anyone to come along the track, so I left the bike there and fought my way through the grass and weeds towards where I thought I had seen something.

As you probably know, the paddock used to be fenced until the grass and vines growing up through the fence pulled it over. I became caught up in the wire as I tramped over it. That's how I know the paddock once was fenced. Anyway, it's just as well I was wearing my oldest pair of overalls. I'd be cranky if they were newer ones that were torn."

She indicated a tear near the hem of one leg of her overalls. I don't know how she knew they were an old pair. All the ones I've seen her wearing look the same: green and grease-stained. Rod picked up on her mention of the fence.

"Of course, there was a fence. I'd never thought about it before, but it used to be a cow paddock until the property was abandoned. Nobody associated with the place was still around to remove the fence, so it was left to become overgrown," Rod told Cilla.

"Is there a bit of a story attached to the property?" Cilla asked. "I had wondered why such a prime piece of real estate was allowed to become derelict."

I was pleased she asked. I didn't know the paddock's history and often wondered about it. Rod was happy to share his knowledge, so I sat and listened.

"It's a bit of a sad story … and a bit hard to buy if you don't believe in coincidence, bad karma, Divine comeuppance, or the like. I heard it used to be an outstanding stud cattle property in its day, but it had already looked a bit neglected when the Village's first residents moved in here. At one time, I heard that the Merivale directors had tried to buy it to develop as a future Stage 2 of this place, but they were given the clear message that the place was not for sale."

"Shame to see it looking like it is. Who owned it, and what was his story? If the owner was so attached to it, he must have had a plan for if anything happened to him or he dropped off the twig," Cilla suggested

"He was very much a recluse, although there was one woman he was friendly with in town. As the story goes, if he ever had to overnight in the city for any reason, he always stayed with her, and she sometimes came out to do a bit of housework for him."

"Housework… is that what they were calling in those days?" Cilla chuckled.

"Well, I don't know what it was, but they were both getting on a bit and then something happened to the friend. I don't know what it was, but she died. The romantics among us would have you believe the old bloke died of a broken heart after pining for her for some time afterwards. Without being too insensitive, I think he simply reached his 'use-by' date with the usual consequence."

"Perhaps, but it's a good story. It would make a ripping yarn. Was the journalist in you never tempted to follow up on it?" I asked, forgetting I'd decided to remain silent.

"Nah, it's not the sort of thing I write these days. But, come to think of it, if there is more to the story unfolding over there in the paddock, I could find myself interested in writing something about it."

"Did the old bloke never marry or have any family to take over the place after he passed away," Cilla asked.

"As far as I know, that remains a bit of a mystery. I believe a couple of people came forward claiming to be extended family members, but the estate's executor was sceptical about both claimants. From the various stories I heard, it appears the two claimants were locked in a struggle to prove which one was a true family member and the other an imposter.

The battle for the property raged on for a couple of years. People thought the problem was sorted out about three years after the old man died. One of the claimants was killed in a light plane crash. Everyone thought it left the door open for the other claimant to walk in and take over, but the executor had other ideas. He instigated something akin to a witch hunt to establish whether the remaining claimant had any real family connection or not.

About six months later, nothing had been resolved, but word filtered out that the remaining claimant was dead. I never heard what happened to him."

"Rod, does that mean the property still awaits probate?" Cilla asked. "It's obvious the place has been abandoned. The fences are down, there are no cattle on the place, and I've never seen anyone wandering around over there. I can't believe such a valuable property has just been abandoned."

"Well, whatever now has the place swarming with police might shed some light on the property's current situation.

So, now I've told you what I know about the history of the place, how about you bring us up to speed on what happened today to have the place swarming with the police's scientific investigation team?"

"Oh, yes, that's what I was going to tell you about. Well, as I came down the track, I thought I saw something move over in that paddock. It wasn't just that something was moving over there that intrigued me. The flash of colour I saw made me stop and investigate.

Remember how this morning looked like such a beautiful day, and then the weather changed soon after breakfast? I thought we were in for a squall. Pitch-black clouds rolled in, and the wind got up. I was determined to take Black Bess for one more test ride and figured if I didn't go then, it was about to bucket down, and I wouldn't be able to go for a ride. So off I went."

"Was that your first test ride this morning?" I asked.

"Yeah, that's when I decided Black Bess needed more adjustment. It was while I was stopped on the track trying to fiddle with the suspension that I thought I saw something moving in the paddock. Anyway, after we had coffee and I adjusted the suspension, I took it for another ride.

By then, the breeze had really come up, and I was sure it would start raining, but I remembered that thing I thought I saw on my first ride. So, I slowed down as I approached roughly the same spot on the track. And then it happened again. But this time, because I was stopped and deliberately looking for something over there, I saw what it was. There were no two ways about it. I had to investigate and charged off into the paddock on foot."

At that point in Cilla's story, a shout went up from somebody over in the paddock. We all tensed and waited to hear what came next, but there was nothing more. It appears the shout was simply one officer calling a colleague to look at something he had found. We all eased back on our chairs when we realised nothing more was about to happen.

"Come on, Cilla, please get on with your story. You left us dangling at the point where you marched into the paddock, but you still haven't told us what you saw from the road or what you found over there."

I knew I was being impatient and a bit rude, but I couldn't help nudging Cilla to get on with the story. We'd been sitting on my back deck for some time now, and we still didn't know why the police were swarming all over that paddock.

"Okay, okay, don't get your knickers in a twist. What I saw was something green – the same sort of green as my overalls. I didn't think it was my overalls, just something of a similar colour being buffeted about by the strong winds. Nevertheless, my curiosity got the better of me. I had to know what it was.

What I found just about blew my mind. It *was* my overalls. Do you remember that fuss late last year when some clothing went missing off the Village's clotheslines?"

"How could we forget after all the fuss Bernard kicked up about his missing trousers? And, as I remember, Ted lost a shirt … and you lost a pair of overalls. I can remember us joking about what a strange-shaped person it must have been who was nicking the clothing," I recalled. "Are you saying what you found over there in the paddock was your missing overalls?"

"Yes, that's exactly what I'm telling you. But, not only did I find my overalls, I also found what I believed to be Bernard's trousers and Ted's shirt."

"That's intriguing," I muttered. "Why would someone steal that clothing off a clothesline only to dump it in a neighbouring paddock? It doesn't make any sense to me. Did the fuss Bernard kicked up make them realise they had to get rid of the stuff, or what?"

"No, I don't think that's what happened. As I told you, at the time, that squally wind was belting through the place when I saw this 'thing' in the paddock. It helped me realise that there is something of a 'wind tunnel' effect created by the way the buildings are laid out in our part of the Village.

Wind from the east, and even the southeast, rips through my backyard, past my house, and then down through a created corridor between Ted's house and the block of units where Bernard lives.

It had been windy for a few days back then, and I believe it blew the clothes off the clotheslines at various times and deposited them in the paddock. The low-flying clothes probably became tangled in that particularly tall patch of weeds."

"Surprising, there were only the three missing items we know about," Rod commented. "When you said you found them, I half expected you to tell us there were other items there as well."

"Only *special* people's clothing was selected, it appears," Cilla quipped.

"While that is quite a story in itself," I began, "I wouldn't have thought three lost items of clothing warranted a police investigation, particularly now they've been found and a probable explanation for their disappearance established. I'm not a Law expert, but I don't see any crime involved in this story. Am I missing something?"

"You're right about no crime involved in the disappearance of the clothing, but what else I found out there does constitute a serious crime." Cilla had become serious again, and I saw Rod sit upright at the mention of a serious crime.

"Do you intend to tell us about this serious crime?" he asked.

"Eh? Yes, of course. I was just lost in thought there for a moment. Let me think… What was the sequence of events? Telling you about it will help me get it straight in my head before I give the local coppers a detailed report of this morning's events.

Right… after I found our three bits of missing clothing, like you, I thought other stuff probably had become tangled in the weeds, too. So, I had a bit of a scratch around through the grass. I didn't find any more clothing … but I did find a body."

"A body! Christ! Hang on, Cilla. I need to get my head around this. Before you go any further, take me back to where this event started. What was the thing you saw from the road that lured you into the paddock in the first place?" I asked. "Whatever it was led you a long way across the paddock."

While I didn't want to interrupt the story, I felt as though I needed to have a firm handle on the sequence of events before we progressed to details of the body.

"What? Oh, the thing I had seen moving, the green thing? Yeah, it was a sleeve of my overalls. The wind must have loosened it from the weeds, and every time there was a gust, the sleeve waved in the air. Then, once the gust passed, the sleeve flopped down out of sight again."

"Good; now back to the body, please," Rod demanded.

"Sorry about the interruption, but yes, please, back to the body," I echoed.

"Uhmm, the body… well, it was that of a male. It was well dressed and didn't look like a down-and-out who was using the place to doss down."

"What? Was it just lying there out in the open?" I stammered.

"Yes… Well, no, not really, but it had been there for a while by the look of it. I've been trying to work out how long it might have been there, but without much success so far. How long has it been since we had rain?"

"Rain… What's rain got to with anything?" I demanded. Rod was more polite.

"Are you talking about our wet season rains or rain we've had recently?" he asked, and Cilla confirmed she was interested in recent rain.

"Recent rain, I think. It looked as though the body had been buried. No, that's not right. It wasn't buried as such. The body looked as though it just had a layer of soil thrown over it. Since then, much of the dirt has been washed away by recent rain," Cilla explained, and Rod endeavoured to answer her original question.

"After the wet season appeared to be over for the year. We had no rain at all for about a month. Everything dried out to the point where the swimming pool contractor thought it safe to make a start on our new pool. Then, about two weeks ago, a real downpour came out of the blue, and the ground was soaked again. After that lot dried out a bit, there was another bit of a shower a week ago last Friday and another one a couple of days ago, but there wasn't much in that one."

"Thanks, Rod. Right, so the last rain was about a couple of days ago… And the weather is fairly mild now. Has it been like that since that last shower of rain?"

Rod and I conferred briefly before confirming the weather had been mild.

"Ye-es, that would be about right then, I think. I'd say, at a rough guess, that it is likely the body I found was dumped in that paddock sometime during the last fortnight and more likely the last week."

"Is that possible?" I queried. "Surely, we would have noticed any activity happening in that paddock – not to mention the smell. Anyone using that track during the day would have caught our attention – as you did when you rode Black Bess along it. And, if they had dumped it at night, they would have needed lights of some sort. We definitely would have noticed those."

"Whoever dumped that body were not rank amateurs. They would not have announced their presence or alerted people to what they were about. The fact that it was covered probably masked any smell." Cilla's reply was a touch patronising, but I let it go by unchallenged. "Damn; I should have investigated a wider area. I was so concerned about not messing up a crime scene, I didn't check for any tracks leading to the dump site."

"For which the local plod will no doubt thank you," Rod added.

"I think I'll make coffee," I chirped. "Is anyone else interested in a cup?"

Both Rod and Cilla volunteered to come and help… which amounted to sitting at the kitchen bench watching me make our coffees. We needed the coffee to help wash down the now slightly dry, two-day-old leftover blueberry muffins.

As we finished our afternoon tea, Rod started making noises about needing to go home for some reason or other, and Cilla agreed we weren't going to learn much more about what was happening in the paddock by watching from my deck. They were both on their way home a few minutes later, and I felt greatly relieved. Neither of them had seemed remotely interested in going home before I made coffee.

Since they arrived earlier this afternoon, I was concerned that they would still be here this evening, and I would feel obliged to ask them to stay for dinner. There was nothing unusual about that except, today, everything I had in sufficient quantity to feed three people was in the freezer and would never be thawed out in time to cook for dinner.

Through the long twilight shadows stretching across the paddock, the police scientific investigation teams trudged back to their vehicles parked on the dirt track. They drove off one by one, leaving only the two clearly marked police vehicles. There appeared to be a brief discussion between two uniformed officers before one of those vehicles executed a tricky turn and left in the same direction as it arrived.

I didn't see the second police vehicle leave, but I heard a vehicle on our street a few minutes later. From my kitchen window, I watched it park on Cilla's driveway.

It had been agreed at last night's happy hour that there would be no happy hour tonight. I can't wait for tomorrow and the possible opportunity to catch up with Cilla to find out what the cops told her before they drove off about half an hour after they arrived at her place.

Chapter 5

Luck was not with me this morning. It was Monday morning, and I was out of the house early for my walk. About halfway through the park, I realised I was too early. I had hoped to 'accidentally' catch up with Cilla on my way home from my walk. While I knew she would be up and about already, it was too early to expect her to be out in her garage or front yard and, therefore, too early for me to 'casually' stop for a chat.

My frustration endured until almost ten o'clock when a phone call brought relief via Cilla's invitation to both Rod and me to join her for morning coffee. A quick check on my fridge revealed that about half of a passionfruit cheesecake still lingered there. It would accompany me to Cilla's to help loosen her tongue if needed.

Within minutes of our arrival, we were sipping coffee and devouring cheesecake, accompanied by only sporadic light conversation. I was grateful when Cilla didn't allow that situation to drag on.

"Right, down to business," she announced. "I thought you might welcome an update on yesterday's events. A couple of the senior officers working the scene called here as they were leaving. There was nothing in that. They just wanted me to go through my story again.

I didn't bother flashing my credentials as they do not need to know who or what I am. But after they left, I wanted to speak to a senior officer and called a former colleague from way back. I asked Richard to keep me updated and to send me fingerprints and DNA results as soon as they were available."

"Richard…? Do you mean our local top cop, Richard Wilson?" I asked.

"Yeah, we collaborated on a couple of cases back in the day, and before that, we were in uniform together south of the border."

"Did he agree to make their test results available to you?" Rod sounded sceptical.

"Of course… Why wouldn't he? Anyway, I might be able to identify the victim for him. I sent an image of the body to my special task force team. We might have an open case involving the victim. If he is who I think he is, I've asked for pertinent identification details to be sent to me today for comparison purposes. Richard is dropping by for a drink after work, so I might have more to report later … Oh, and I might not make it to happy hour tonight."

"Anything else we should know in the meantime?" I thought it wise to ask.

"No… Ah, yes. Throughout today, the coppers will be interviewing residents along this street. It's just routine stuff to establish if anyone saw or heard anything relevant to what happened over in that paddock. As they know of your involvement already, they probably won't interview the pair of you, but if you think of something you want to tell them, feel free to accost them while they are working the street."

"Do they think it happened in the paddock?" I asked, and then realised my question required clarification. "I mean, do they think the person was killed in the paddock or dumped there later?"

"As it is early days in the investigation, that remains unclear," was Cilla's curt, professional reply.

With little else to say about the case now centred on the neighbouring paddock, the conversation moved to other lighter topics before becoming contentious. For me, there was a whole lot more that hadn't been said, but something suggested I should leave it that way, at least for now.

"Rod, what's the latest on the swimming pool?" Cilla demanded. "I see an area over by the community gardens has been pegged out and has materials and equipment strewn around it. Is that the site for the pool?"

"That's where the pool will be," Rod confirmed. "Work was to commence about two weeks ago, and then we had that storm the night before they were to start. If there is no more rain, they are supposed to arrive on site tomorrow, and things should start to happen after that. I was a bit nervous yesterday when it looked like we might be in for another storm, but so far, so good."

"How long will it take them to finish the project?"

"Not long; a week or two at the most. There might be a bit of subsidiary work to complete later."

"I was a bit intrigued by some aspects of how the site is pegged out. It looks like there are some extra footings for something outside the pool area," Cilla commented.

"Uhmm…I think you're referring to the footings for the poles that will support the shade sail."

"A shade sail! Jesus, what will that cost us, and can we afford it? I thought our discrete fundraising for the pool only gave us enough to cover the contracted price of the pool and a little extra for contingencies."

"You're right, but we did have a fair bit extra to play with. It's an ill wind and all that… The current cost of living crisis has seen a slump in the demand for pools. As a result, the supplier has opted to slash his prices to the bare bones to keep sales happening and to be able to retain his workforce. When the contract price was reviewed, we found that we could afford a shade sail over the most critical areas for a couple of thousand dollars over the original price. And, before you ask, yes, there is enough cash in the bucket to pay for it."

"And I don't suppose the board of directors has seen fit to put their hand in their pocket to help pay for any of it?" Cilla added with a contemptuous sniff.

"No-o, not as such, but discussions are ongoing."

"Intriguing… Am I allowed to know more?" Cilla asked. I almost applauded when she posed the question. I also wanted to know more about whatever Rod might discuss with the board.

"Nothing to share at this stage. As I said, discussions are ongoing."

What is it they say about blissful ignorance, I wondered… but it didn't matter anyway. There is nothing blissful about my level of curiosity.

By then, all matters relating to the body in the paddock and the new swimming pool having been discussed, there wasn't much else of importance to say. A few minutes later, we were on our way out, having been reminded we might or might not see Cilla at happy hour tonight.

Happy hour proved a fairly subdued event. The police interviews were the cause. Speculation was rife about why the police wanted to know whether anyone had seen or heard anything happening recently in the neighbouring paddock. Nobody did, of course, and nobody was told why they were being asked about it.

A subdued gathering made for an early night. Rod and I exchanged a look as he walked me to his gate. A strange car remained parked on Cilla's driveway.

"Looks like Richard has been invited to stay for dinner," I murmured as Rod opened the gate for me.

It was Wednesday morning when several of us gathered at the site of the new swimming pool to watch work begin. Rod, of course, had to be there. I stopped to watch on my way back from my walk. Frank and Luigi, on their way to their garden beds in the community gardens, paused to see what was happening, and Cilla was there out of sheer curiosity. Apart from Rod, it didn't take the rest of us long to realise that watching a piece of heavy machinery going about its business soon loses its appeal.

Despite everything that happened along the way, somehow, between Sunday night and the following Friday, life managed to go on as normal – well, at least, it did for me. But I knew Cilla had been busy.

Friday afternoon was when the rescheduled bowls club meeting would be held. In the intervening days, big slabs of Cilla's time had been taken up with online meetings with various personnel from the police special task force, as well as, I suspected, with several meetings with Stella to discuss the Village women's bowls situation. For fear of even a whisper leaking out about her strategic plan, Cilla – and Stella – remained tight-lipped about any such discussions.

The 'observers' gallery' at the bowls club management committee meeting was filled to overflowing, requiring latecomers to scrounge extra chairs from wherever they could find them. It didn't go unnoticed by committee members and caused comment when the meeting opened.

"We seem to have an inordinately large audience today," one of the 'old brigade' committee members drew to the chairman's attention as soon as the meeting was declared open. "As this is a management committee meeting, I'm wondering if we shouldn't clear the room before we begin the business of the meeting."

"Why would you want to clear the room?" Cilla asked. "I was unaware we had any top-secret business to discuss. If we have, I'm afraid I haven't read up on it prior to the meeting."

"Well, yes, I suppose it is a committee meeting and not a public event," the chairman began. "Perhaps we should consider…"

"Mr Chairman," Cilla barked, "perhaps we have lost sight of the fact that we are a *community facility* erected and paid for by the Merivale Retirement Village community members through its many fundraising ventures. It is not the management committee's bowls club.

We, the committee, have simply been charged with overseeing its running and sound management. I am concerned that excluding community members from observing the meeting might give rise to speculation about this committee and what it might be up to behind closed doors. The community has a right to observe, and those here today merely exercise that right. This committee must operate with complete transparency."

A large round of applause rang out from the gallery. The chairman, whose face was becoming redder by the moment, called for silence.

"The Chair recognises the community's right to observe, but it must not interrupt the business of the meeting in any way unless called upon to do so. Now, may we proceed with the rest of this meeting, please?"

But Cilla remained on her feet and chose to interject again at that point. "Mr Chairman, if I may…," she began. A hush fell over the room.

"At this point, and before we move to the business of the meeting, I would like to express my congratulations to the committee and any others who may have been involved in initiating a men's interclub lawn bowls competition. I feel it deserves recognition as a remarkable feat for such a small and new bowls club."

Committee members' heads were nodding, and a barely audible 'aye, aye' went up from the gallery. The chairman's chest expanded by at least a shirt size as he thanked Cilla for her kind words in acknowledging the enormity of what had been achieved.

"It has been a time-consuming, and at times difficult process, but worth the effort and the ongoing work that will be required to keep it rolling along."

"Hmm… yes, it's that effort that concerns me. The Games Committee already had a lot to do, and now the interclub competition will add to the heavy load. Are we asking too much of our volunteers? Oh, I know they all willingly give their time and effort, but do we risk burn-out amongst the Games Committee members by adding to their workload?" Cilla's voice, face – everything about her – demonstrated her deep concern.

"Ye-es, that's a valid point you make. We don't want to work people into the ground. There needs to be a way to share the load a bit more. While the club has plenty of members, the management committee is small by comparison. Do you have any thoughts on how the situation might be improved?"

Cilla began tentatively. "Well... this is off the top of my head, as you can probably appreciate, but... yeah ... I think it might work...."

The chairman asked her to share her thoughts on a possible fix, no matter how abstract they might seem.

"My thinking involves a subcommittee to look after everything concerning the interclub competition. We don't want to expand the management committee, so this new subcommittee could comprise one existing management committee member and three or four regular club members who are not on the management committee. The member from this committee would be a two-way conduit between management and subcommittee and would report on subcommittee matters at our regular meetings."

"That sounds pretty good to me," the secretary said with some conviction as he looked up from his notebook.

"Your suggestion would make it possible to involve more of the membership without further burdening the management committee or increasing its size," the chairman agreed. "Please note the suggestion as a motion," he instructed the secretary. "Right then, we've all heard details of a suggested interclub subcommittee, and it's likely make-up. So, perhaps we should have a show of hands as to whether to proceed with such a committee or not. All those..."

"Uhmm... excuse me, please, Mr Chairman, but could we hold the vote for a moment to allow us to explore a technical matter first?" Cilla rushed in to ask.

"What sort of technical issue?" The chairman barked.

"As I recall, when this club was established, the club members approved the constitution, the establishment of the management committee, and the games committee. I'm wondering if – constitutionally – setting up an interclub competition might also require the approval of the club members."

"Call another members' meeting…? That would simply delay an outcome for God knows how long while they all argued about when to hold it so they might all be available.

"True, but I would hate for us to institute something worthwhile, which later might be challenged as being illegal.

But, as you pointed out earlier, the gallery is full to overflowing today. It is likely there is a good cross-section of members present. Might the approval of those present be sufficient for our purposes? Oh, I suppose we need to know if they are all members.

Would anyone not a current Merivale Bowls Club member please raise your hand." Cilla left no one in doubt she was in control of this meeting. After allowing a few moments for hands to be raised – and none was – she continued.

"Well, Mr Chairman, I would further suggest that we ask the members present whether they believe they are sufficient to approve the establishment of a subcommittee comprising one management committee member and three ordinary members."

The chairman asked the crowd if they believed they could approve such a request. A resounding 'Aye' went up from the gallery. The chairman cleared his throat and attempted to regain control of the situation.

"Right then, having heard the details of the possible subcommittee, I'll call for a show of hands from the members in the gallery. Those…"

Rod sprang to his feet. "Mr Chairman, before you proceed to a vote, I would suggest an amendment. Committees function better when they are comprised of an uneven number of members… as when a casting vote is required. So, to that end, I suggest amending the membership to FOUR ordinary members."

With the amendment endorsed by all present, the chairman finally put it to the vote. The establishment of the new subcommittee was carried unanimously. An audible sigh of relief went up from the top table before the chairman gushed generous thanks to Cilla for having made an outstanding contribution to the club's business.

"Others should receive praise for their achievements, not me," Cilla said coyly. "But I will share with you something of a conversation I've had since my return last week. Our interclub competition is held in such high regard that women from many of the area's bowls clubs have contacted us to have a similar competition established for female players. I believe it highlights the position our small club has achieved in the area's lawn bowls community."

"A women's competition!" the chairman spluttered.

"Yes, and there has been so much interest, our women have established a working team to deal with it. As I understand it, their next move was to contact the men's committee to see how their competition runs, to ensure uniformity and avoid reinventing the wheel, so to speak."

"We would need to know more about this before they progress further. How do they think they can do this without prior approval?" exclaimed one of the management committee members, who had remained silent throughout the meeting to that point.

"I'm sorry, Mr Chairman. I don't have all the details, but I thought it a positive step and good for the club's image. As for my fellow member's comment about 'prior approval', I have one question: *prior approval from whom? This committee did not seek the approval of the women players – or of any other members – before instigating their interclub competition. The women have no such need either.*

Cheering and clapping erupted from the gallery. The chairman almost shouted himself hoarse calling for silence. When things finally quietened down and he realised their predicament, he asked Cilla for details of what had been done to date.

"As I indicated earlier, I only learned of it in casual conversation. Nevertheless, I believe the group managing the process has a spokesperson. Perhaps she might be asked to provide us with details." Cilla raised her eyebrows at the chairman, who squirmed on his chair before agreeing to the suggestion.

"Good. Stella Winters, I believe you are the women's spokesperson. Perhaps you might give us a rundown on progress to date."

Stella stood and thanked the chair for the opportunity to address the meeting before giving an impressive account of the level of interest and progress to date and closed by echoing Cilla's remarks.

"In attending this meeting today, I had hoped to discover who we should speak to regarding how the men's competition runs so we could ensure the women's competition runs along similar lines."

After naming a committee member to confer with, the chairman again directed his attention to Cilla.

"It appears this now has created another problem for the management committee. If the women are to run this competition, do they expect one of our management committee members to be involved? Or, as the only female committee member, do you intend to be this committee's representation on their subcommittee?"

"Good Lord, no. I am often absent from the Village and am not a regular player when I am here. But I take your point. The women's subcommittee does need a Management Committee representative on board … and one of our male members will not do. It must be a woman."

"So, Ms Longhurst, how do you propose we manage this problem?"

"Hmm… well, Mr Chairman, it might not be as complicated as it first appears. When this management committee was set up, it was to include two female members … but, to date, it has only ever had one. Therefore, there remains a vacancy on this committee for another female member. I would propose Stella Winters, as she already is the group's spokesperson, be appointed to the management committee.

Oh, and now I'm not sure, but does such an appointment require the approval of the club members?"

The chairman heaved a sigh of resignation. "I suspect it does. Again, I will ask the gallery to vote on the matter by a show of hands…. Record it as carried unanimously, please, Mr secretary."

Then, turning his attention to Stella, the chairman asked, "Exactly when might we see the first women's interclub games played here at Merivale?"

Stella beamed at him. "We are excited to announce our first interclub games will be played next Wednesday. A busload of women players from western clubs travelled north to play in the recent bowls carnival there and, on their way home, are playing at various greens along the way. Instead of our usual Wednesday competition games, half of the busload will play here next Wednesday, while the other half plays at one of the inner city greens."

"They can't play here on Wednesday," the otherwise silent committee member bellowed. "We have that day booked."

"Well, you will bloody well have to make other arrangements," Cilla responded. "Wednesdays have been allocated to the women members, and you have no right to them. You will have to arrange to use one of your men's days for your interclub games, either your Thursdays or Sundays. Alternatively, you could scrap your Friday afternoon social games in favour of Friday, being interclub competition days."

Angry debate raged for a few minutes before Rod stood up and yelled for silence. He remained standing and glared at each of the committee members in turn until silence reigned.

"Now, gentlemen, it appears you have adopted an authority you do not have and, in so doing, have demonstrated your inability to manage appropriately and legally. The matter will be referred to management and the board of directors. In the meantime, I believe the appropriate action would be to call for the resignation of the male members of this management committee."

A roar went up from those men, and one shouted, "Well, that ain't going to happen."

"That would be unfortunate – for you, that is. It was your chance to jump before you were pushed. As you have been happy to accept the gallery here as representative of the club's membership, the same will apply in all matters.

I believe the matter before the members at this time is the dissolution of the present management committee and the creation of a caretaker committee to manage the club's affairs until the election of a new committee.

A motion to dissolve the management committee is before you," he said, addressing the gallery. "By a show of hands, please, those in favour." Hands shot up everywhere. "Those against...." Only two hands were raised, one of which was Bernard's.

"The matter will be referred to the manager at the close of this meeting, and her input – and that of the Board – will be sought in establishing an interim arrangement.

Thank you all for your participation, and I now declare this meeting closed." With that, Rod resumed his seat.

Stunned silence followed for a few moments before anyone made a move to leave.

"That's the shortest time I've ever served on a committee," Stella Winters murmured to Cilla as they left the building. "What happens next?"

"No idea, but I'm sure all will become clear in the next day or so. In the meantime, proceed as if nothing has changed regarding the visiting teams next Wednesday and all your other routine events."

Chapter 6

Cilla wasn't naïve enough to believe it was the end of the story and that everything would sort itself out before next Wednesday. She made a beeline for Rod as he and I walked to the Rec Room to prepare for pizza night.

"Rod, what are we going to do about the visiting team next week? What I mean is, what *can* we do? Those old buggers probably already have plans for others to play here on Wednesday. And it's now Friday afternoon. You won't be able to see the manager before Monday at the earliest, and that doesn't allow her time to talk to the board, or to do anything to resolve the problem before Wednesday."

"Well, I pre-empted there could be a problem and spoke to our esteemed manager earlier in the week. I believe she has discussed the matter with the board chairman, but I haven't heard where that ended up. I do know Tanya was in favour of issuing a formal notice of dismissal to the Bowls Club Management Committee, but in the end, it comes down to what the board wants to do."

"Whatever they choose to do needs to be done quickly and, more importantly, it needs to be enforced. My concern is that our busload of visitors will arrive on Wednesday to find the men have hijacked our greens. I guess the big question then is, what do we do in the event of such a situation?"

"There is little more I can tell you, Cilla, other than to say that the 'old guard' committee members would be extremely foolish to ignore the dissolution motion passed at the meeting. All right, I'm not saying they will ignore it. But you know as well as I do that they believe they are a law under themselves."

Until that point in the discussions, I had managed to keep quiet, but I felt it was time to add my thoughts.

"I share Cilla's concerns, Rod. It would be embarrassing to have our out-of-town visiting players arrive only to find the men had commandeered the greens and women had no chance of a game. Apart from that, it would mean we can kiss goodbye any chance of running a women's interclub competition." Rod's shrug in response told me the discussion had ended.

We had reached the Rec Room by then anyway, so there was no opportunity to further berate Rod about something that was clearly out of his control. Without further conversation, we split up. Cilla and I went to the kitchen while Rod joined the men setting up the tables.

Janet and Alice were already hard at work folding the pizza boxes while Maria fiddled with the pizza oven to have it ready for what looked like another big night. A subdued atmosphere prevailed. Apart from a nod or grunt of welcome when we arrived, nothing more was shared as Cilla and I set about lining up the various containers of pizza fillings.

The heavy veil of silence persisted almost to the end of the night, but it didn't matter anyway. We were all too busy for conversation… And probably still a bit shellshocked after the bowls club meeting. The evening passed without incident in the kitchen. If anything untoward happened for the men out front, we remained unaware of it. But, like all good things, the night eventually ended, and tradition was adhered to when we all gathered in the kitchen for a drink before going home.

It took a few sips of wine before conversation started to flow slowly after Ted heaved a sigh of relief.

"What a night! I don't think we've ever been so busy. Bernard certainly knows when to have a night off," he complained.

"Did we know Bernard wasn't coming to help tonight?" Cilla asked.

A glance around the room showed all the men shaking their heads before Rod answered for them. "No, no one's heard anything from him, but that's becoming a habit lately. He doesn't bother to tell anyone and just doesn't turn up."

"It's all down to that James fellow," Alice said. "It's as though we have a different Bernard since James arrived. Poor Marjorie; how is she coping with what appears to be complete abandonment by Bernard?"

"Good question, Alice," Maria replied. "I thought that pair had a bit of a thing going, but I must have been wrong. Since Bernard seems to have become joined at the hip with James, I have to ask whether there was ever anything between Bernard and Marjorie."

"Yeah, that's an interesting point," Luigi added. "There has to be more than a love of chess that has the pair of them almost inseparable these days."

My eyes were becoming heavier by the moment, and the call of my bed was strong. I was relieved when Cilla suddenly stretched and stood up.

"Well folks, party on if you like. I'm off home to bed," she announced. "See you at happy hour tomorrow night, Rod?" She asked almost as an afterthought.

"Everyone right for a happy hour tomorrow night?" he asked and received positive responses. "Okay then, six o'clock tomorrow night at my place. I'm also off now, so I'll see you all then."

That effectively brought the evening to an end. As the others headed off as a group, Cilla and I stayed behind to wait for Rod to lock up before the three of us walked home together. There wasn't a lot of conversation as we walked, and what there was consisted of vague speculation about what the week ahead might bring. Whatever the week brought, there was a fair chance it would be less interesting than this week had been.

As I plodded down our street after my morning walk on Monday, I encountered Rod on his way home from an early morning run.

"Good morning, Rod," I chirped. "What does your day and week look like? Any exciting expectations?"

"Depends on your interpretation of 'exciting', I suppose. I intend visiting our manager, Tanya Jellicoe, sometime this morning – if she will see me. I'm hoping there's some positive course of action mapped out regarding the bowls club management committee and that it will be implemented before the end of today."

"At least sometime before Wednesday would be good. And it probably won't help Cilla maintain her sanity if the Merivale women bowlers become nervous and expect her to fix things for them."

We were about to move off on our respective ways home when Cilla bounded across the street to join us. She had a look about her that intrigued me. Was she excited, stressed, or what? For some reason, today, I couldn't read Cilla at all. After the usual pleasantries were finished, I couldn't resist asking a question or two.

"Well, what's happening in your life on this fine Monday morning, Cilla? The most exciting event I've heard about so far is Rod's anticipated visit to Tanya Jellicoe's office."

"I don't know about exciting, but a meeting with our manager today would be useful. As for me, I didn't have anything on my agenda at all … until Richard called first thing this morning."

"Richard?... Oh, our top cop … Have they had a breakthrough about that body in the paddock?" Although my question was innocuous, I felt my pulse step up a notch or two.

"Maybe Cilla should tell us all about it over a coffee at my place," Rod suggested.

A few minutes later, the three of us were equipped with coffee and store-bought muffins and parked in Rod's lounge room. After allowing us barely time to settle, Rod took charge.

"Right, Cilla, you have the floor. What have they discovered about the body… Oh, and do we know who he was for a start?"

"Uhmm… This is still a little tricky, but here goes. I'll see if I can manoeuvre around the facts without getting into trouble.

In response to your question, Rod, I can say the body has been identified – and, for the time being, we will call him 'Ralph'.

"Doesn't anyone in your world have a real name like the rest of us mere mortals?" I snapped, still fresh in my mind having met Cilla's 'Significant Other' at Christmas and being told to call him 'Joe'. No surname, nothing else, just Joe.

A blind man on a galloping horse would have worked out his name wasn't Joe, and the fact that he sometimes failed to respond to it tended to confirm it was a name he had been given just for the occasion.

I looked up to find Cilla glaring at me in indignation. "What?" I demanded.

"No, Marion, that's my question," she retaliated. "What was that smart-arsed comment about? But, if you must know, of course, he has a real name *that is being kept under wraps for now*. So, to simplify any discussions we might have, he will be called Ralph."

Okay, that's me put firmly in my place. I probably deserved it, I suppose, but it does grate a bit when we are treated as both loose-lipped and not too bright. It would be nice to think she trusted Rod and me not to divulge anything sensitive to anyone, but obviously, that's not the case. Before I could comment, and probably to prevent my antagonising Cilla further, Rod stepped in.

"Right, Ralph, it is," he confirmed, glaring at me. "So, Cilla, bearing in mind that we are aware of the sensitivity of an ongoing case, is there anything we are permitted to know about Ralph? I'm surprised they established an identity so soon, given the condition of the body."

"Yeah, it wasn't in great condition when we found it. Still, despite the deterioration of the face, I thought I recognised him. In the spirit of collegiality among law enforcement personnel, I asked my special task force to send me everything they had on the bloke I thought it was.

Any relevant stuff, I passed onto Richard the other night when he came for a drink. Then, it was a case of waiting for the DNA results and fingerprint matches from the local technical investigation people. They came through last night, and Richard's call this morning confirmed my thoughts on the identity of the body."

"If you needed to obtain information from New South Wales for identification purposes, does that mean the person had only recently travelled to this state?" I asked.

"That's something yet to be established. It's possible he might have been here, or somewhere in this state, for years, but he could have arrived as recently as last week. We kept a file on him for many years, and Victoria also had him on their radar. The trouble was, whenever we were getting close to closing-in on him, he disappeared – sometimes for a number of years."

"Does that mean he somehow kept reappearing on your special task force's radar? How would you locate him again after he disappeared?" I was curious about how the police might be able to track someone for so long despite his disappearances.

"Every so often, a crime with all the hallmarks of his handiwork would occur. Eventually, our work would confirm he had emerged from the wilderness at about the right time and probably had carried out the 'job'. The problem was that he had disappeared again by the time we confirmed that information and started closing-in on him once more."

"On this occasion, by way of a change, it seems he was the victim and not the perpetrator," Rod observed. "I imagine that means the police in a few states can now cross him off their 'most wanted' lists and not have to worry about him practising his skills again."

"You would think so, wouldn't you? But now the question is: who did for the bloke who did for a number of others in the past? It's never good when the baddies fall out among themselves."

"Cilla, is there anything we should be aware of?" I almost hesitated to ask. "I mean, there isn't any sort of gang warfare or something similar about to breakout around here, is there?"

"I wish I knew, but it might be more a case of covering one's tracks rather than anything resembling gang warfare.

Anyway, whatever happens, it will be nothing for the residents of Merivale Retirement Village to worry about."

For one fleeting moment, I hoped Cilla's assessment might be true. Although I was sceptical, there wasn't time to ponder it before Rod asked an important question.

"And what about Cilla Longhurst?" Rod asked. "Does she have anything to be concerned about?"

Deftly sidestepping the question, Cilla moved the conversation to progress on the new pool.

"Given the current fuss and bother at the bowls club, is the swimming pool likely to be another monster we are creating for ourselves?" she asked.

"I don't imagine we'll have to worry about allocating specific swim times to the various groups who might want to use the pool," Rod replied. "In fact, I'm not sure what proportion of the resident population will even be interested in using the pool. Anyway, if interest is greater than I anticipate, I'm sure it will self-regulate fairly quickly."

A couple of questions occurred to me as he shared his thoughts. "While I don't want to make things difficult, I was wondering about a couple of things. The first of those is about dress standards. Do we need to have a set of dress standards drawn up for people wishing to use the pool?" I asked and hoped the question would be taken seriously.

"What… in case someone decides they prefer skinny-dipping?" Cilla demanded. "Surely none of us 'wrinkly' residents are likely to be inclined to 'show all'."

Although Rod was chuckling, he managed to comment. "Again, I think any such behaviour might be self-regulating. Anyone daring to indulge in such behaviour, or any other antisocial behaviour involving the pool, would soon be made aware of the other residents' displeasure. It would take a game person to ignore being put in their place by some of the old girls in this Village."

"True, they would soon sort out any behaviour deemed unacceptable," I agreed. "But, I wasn't just thinking about behaviour in the pool. What about people sunbaking around the pool, or holding a bit of a get-together in the pool area – say, to celebrate someone's birthday?"

"Oh, yes, that could get interesting, particularly when someone has to tell them to amend their ways." Cilla sounded genuinely concerned – until she continued. "And I can't help but wonder who that *someone* might be. Somehow, I can't see Tanya Jellicoe taking on the role of Village Morality Officer. So who else is there?" As she finished speaking, she fixed Rod with a hard look.

"Not going to happen…," he said. "We're all grown-ups here, and every one of us is capable of fighting his own battles – and enlisting others if needs be.

Marion, you said you had a couple of questions. Let's not pre-empt problems with dress and behaviour standards and move on to what else concerns you."

"It's not so much a concern as just a thought. Will the pool be for the exclusive use of residents, or will 'outsiders' be allowed in as well? And, if outsiders are allowed in, will it be free for them to use, or will they have to pay a fee of some sort?"

"And who would be responsible for collecting the fee?" Cilla added.

"God, you're all for making things difficult, aren't you? Here's my final word on the subject. When the pool opens for use, it will be for residents only, and we will let it sort itself out after that," Rod declared.

"…Until World War III spreads from the bowls club to the pool, that is," Cilla added.

Rod's voice was becoming sharper as our discussion continued. I decided it might be wise to change the topic before the situation degenerated much further.

"Has anyone told Bernard about Cilla finding his missing trousers?"

"I don't think I've had any conversation with Bernard over the last few weeks, so I haven't mentioned it to him. I image he might have heard about it, though," Rod replied.

"He might not know about it," Cilla said. "It isn't common knowledge yet. In fact, I doubt anyone other than the three of us knows about it. After all, we don't actually have the missing items of clothing yet, although I don't think the police will want to hold them for much longer."

"Why did the police take them in the first place?" I asked. "The clothes weren't related in any way to the body you found and were in that paddock long before anyone decided to dispose of a body there."

"Standard procedure…," Cilla told me. "The area where the body was found is a crime scene, and everything in that area needs to be examined and tested. There's always a chance something from the site that looks completely irrelevant might somehow have picked up a vital piece of evidence. I don't believe our clothes did, but they will be tested before they're returned."

"Speaking of Bernard…," Rod began, "has either of you spoken to Marjorie lately? She is conspicuous by her absence from mahjong for some time. I assume it has something to do with Bernard's having found a new interest."

"Well, I thought I might have a word to her when I returned a book late last week, but she was busy going through a box of new books and didn't come out front. It seems being dumped by Bernard has hit her hard," I commented.

"What she ever saw in him is a complete mystery to me," Cilla admitted. "Although he treated her badly, I suppose he was someone she could fuss over.

I did ask one of the library volunteers how Marjorie was coping. She assessed Marjorie as devastated and throwing herself into her position as the librarian for solace."

"Are we a bit remiss in that, as her friends, we haven't said or done anything to support her?" I asked.

"What can we do?" Cilla demanded. "By staying away from us as she is, it seems she is letting us know she wants to be left alone. She wants her privacy … and not our sympathy and support."

"It's such a shame she has no real friends, no close friends. One way or another, Bernard saw to that. Marjorie is such a mousey little thing, she was an ideal target for Bernard. Someone he could dominate and belittle while demonstrating his superior academic qualifications," I said as I thought about what an existence Marjorie must have had under Bernard's influence.

"You sell her short, Marion," Cilla reprimanded me. "Think back to last year when Marjorie and Bernard fell out over something. I think it was just before his trousers disappeared off the clothesline. Marjorie was a different person then. She showed she had a lively personality when out from under Bernard's influence … and demonstrated she was quite capable of standing up to him."

"Yeah, you're right, Cilla. I do remember that brief period last year when Marjorie was fun to have around." I had forgotten about the change until Cilla mentioned it. "Perhaps it's embarrassment. I mean, maybe Marjorie is so embarrassed by what has happened, she doesn't feel she can face us."

"So, what are you going to do about it?" Rod asked.

"No, Rod, what are WE going to do about it?" Cilla corrected him. "Maybe Marion, Janet and I could make the first move, but the rest of you blokes need to be involved as well. Is tomorrow too soon to launch Operation Rescuing Marjorie?"

"Why would it be too soon?" Rod asked.

"Tomorrow would be an ideal time to try helping her. On our way to the Rec Room tomorrow morning, Cilla, you and I could call at the library to try to persuade Marjorie to come to mahjong with us. What do you think?" I asked.

My companions both agreed tomorrow morning was as good as any other time to have a go. For a brief moment, I felt panic-stricken. What was I thinking when I suggested such an approach? I didn't even want to think about how or why it could go wrong, but it seems that, by opening my mouth when I did, I was now committed. By the time I was home again, I knew I was extremely nervous about tomorrow morning.

Chapter 7

Maybe Marjorie won't be at work today. There's a bout of colds and flu doing the rounds at the moment. I secretly hoped she might be unwell and wouldn't be at the library when we arrived.

Since it was agreed Cilla and I would call at the library this morning to try dragging Marjorie to mahjong, I had been a pack of nerves. So much could go wrong. Perhaps we were too presumptuous about what was best for our librarian, and she might resent our intruding on her privacy. Our excursion could end up being both awkward and embarrassing.

Then Cilla pounded on my door and asked if I was ready to go. I grabbed the container of cupcakes I'd baked for morning tea, locked my door, and strode beside Cilla to the library.

"I can't help feeling this exercise is doomed to failure," I told Cilla as we approached the library.

"What's the worst that can happen?" she asked. "No one will end up dead as a result of it."

Somehow, that was not comforting or in any way reassuring. Then, as if to confirm my fears, when we reached the library's front door, it remained firmly locked. I checked my watch.

"Should have opened almost an hour ago," I told Cilla. "Do you think everything is okay? Even if Marjorie isn't here yet, at least one of the volunteers should have the place open and be on duty."

"Only one way to find out what's going on. Rod gave me his Rec Room key as I was leaving this morning. We'll let ourselves into the Rec Room and then enter the library through the interconnecting door. Come on. Don't stand out here worrying about it. Let's just do it."

She was right, of course, but now I was even more nervous about what might await us. But Cilla charged on without me and

60

unlocked the Rec Room door. I rushed to join her. Entering the building together, we strode down to the interconnecting door to the library.

"Let's just hope Rod's key still unlocks this door," Cilla murmured as she tried the key.

Moments later, we were in the library and dazzled by the bright array of fluorescent lights overhead. My head swivelled from side to side like a spectator at a tennis match as I searched for any sign of a human presence.

"Someone has to be here," I commented. "The lights don't turn themselves on, so someone has been here."

"Marjorie… Marjorie, are you in here?" Cilla bellowed, and silence responded.

"Well, if she was here, it seems like she is not here now," I whispered. "What do we do? Do we return to the Rec Room and try again later, or lock the door on our way out and leave it for another day?"

"We are not going anywhere until we make sure everything is all right in here," Cilla said with a touch of irritation in her voice. "Whoever is here might require assistance. Come on, let's check out the back."

While I knew it probably was the right thing to do before we left, the thought of what we might find caused a swarm of butterflies to launch in the pit of my stomach. I tried easing my nervousness by telling myself Cilla was with me and that she was used to dealing with difficult situations. Somehow, that thought was less than reassuring. Although I dragged my feet a bit, I felt obliged to accompany Cilla on her expedition into the library's nether reaches.

Cilla strode out ahead of me towards the doorway leading into the back room. She stopped suddenly and unexpectedly. I crashed into her back. For a moment, we were in danger of ending up in a scrambled heap on the floor.

"Wha…," I exclaimed in surprise, but that was all I managed to get out before Cilla's voice cut across whatever else I was going to say.

"Marjorie! Are you okay?" Cilla demanded. "I called out. When no one answered, I became concerned about the situation here. Is everything all right?"

"Yes, I heard you. I happened to be busy and didn't need an interruption."

Yep, my suspicions were confirmed. Marjorie was not impressed with our intrusion. I remained silent, determined to let Cilla extricate us from this mess as best she could. But, perhaps my thoughts of aborting our mission were premature. When Cilla responded to Marjorie, her voice sounded absolutely neutral – as though nothing untoward had happened.

"Oh good, that's a relief. We didn't want to interrupt anything important, but we thought we would drop in to ask if you were coming to mahjong today. We've missed you lately and were concerned that we might have offended you somehow. If it's just that you're too busy to join us, that's fine, and we won't worry about you."

"Argh, it's not that I'm too busy. It's just that I…."

Whatever Marjorie had intended to say was left unsaid. At that point, she burst into tears. Cilla looked panic-stricken as she made a 'what do we do now' gesture towards me. I'm not much good with blubbering females, but I'm probably way better than Cilla.

Although wrong-footed for a few moments, I eventually managed to pull myself together, walk up, and put my arm around Marjorie's shoulders. She collapsed into me. I felt her body shuddering against me as her tears gave way to deep, heart-wrenching sobs. The little voice in my head kept telling me to 'say something'. The question was, say what? With no idea what words such a situation required, I plunged in and hoped I didn't make things worse.

It took a few minutes of mindless soothing words and sounds before Marjorie's sobbing eased to sniffles. Cilla then assessed it as safe for her to re-enter the encounter.

"Come and have a cup of coffee, or tea if you prefer, and tell us how we might help with whatever the situation is that has upset you so badly. Come on, we can't leave you like this.

You don't have to stay and play mahjong if you don't want to, but come and have a cuppa while you tell us about it."

"Thanks, but I don't think there is anything anyone can do. I know I'm being a silly old woman, but I can't help it."

By then, the three of us were in the Rec Room kitchen, and Cilla was clattering about making coffee. I noticed Marjorie looked on the verge of dissolving into tears again. I felt obliged to try to intercede before the waterworks became established.

"Marjorie, tell me to mind my own business if you like, but does all this have anything to do with Bernard?" I asked and then held my breath as I waited for her reaction to the question.

"As I said, I know I'm being a silly old woman, but it has everything to do with Bernard. Oh, I won't go into details, but I feel so stupid, so embarrassed… I can't even stand to show my face in the library these days. People must be having a good laugh at my expense."

"What on earth would they be laughing about?" Cilla demanded. "You haven't done anything in the least bit hilarious that I'm aware of, or did I miss whatever it was? Tell us what you are feeling embarrassed about?"

Then, words tumbled out, replacing the tears that had tumbled down her cheeks. In a series of disjointed and sometimes unintelligible sentences, she detailed how Bernard's recent shunning of her had sent her world into a tailspin. It appears there had been no words on the subject between them. He just cut her dead and hasn't spoken to her since he found his new friend, James.

"I was such a fool," she croaked. "I called Bernard and told him I was really happy he had found another chess player of comparable standard, and that I understood that he and James shared other interests as well.

Everything became clear when I asked him to call at the library to discuss the list of the new books I was putting together. He told me it was my library, and he had found better things to do with his time."

"There is no getting away from it. That is a radical change in the man," I conceded, "but I'm not sure whether it is for the better. I must confess this James-thing he has going at the moment intrigues me. I mean, suddenly, chess is the most important thing in Bernard's life? Given this newly found devotion to chess, he must have found our mahjong mornings barely tolerable."

"That reminds me. I should get back to the library before the others start arriving for mahjong. I don't want to be here when Bernard arrives," Marjorie said.

"No need to worry about that," Cilla announced with a hint of satisfaction in her voice. "Bernard has been a non-starter at mahjong in recent times. Perhaps, as Marion suggested, now he has chess in his life, Bernard doesn't need to bother with the likes of we mahjong players."

"Ah well, if that's the case, and he doesn't turn up again this morning, reserve a seat for me at one of the tables, please."

While it sounded like a positive step forward, Marjorie remained nervous about the possibility of encountering Bernard. She asked if one of us would mind calling her from the library when play was due to begin, but only if Bernard was not here. Cilla undertook to do that. I think both Cilla and I sent a silent prayer to the gods to ask them to keep Bernard away today.

Our prayers must have been heard. Bernard again was a no-show, and Cilla retrieved Marjorie from the library as promised. Not surprisingly perhaps, Marjorie appeared nervous and tentative when she joined us, but she soon loosened up. By the end of the morning, we were again seeing the bright, bubbly woman we had glimpsed briefly last year following her tiff with Bernard.

Marjorie's return to the fold was one of the main topics of conversation as Cilla, Rod, and I walked home together at the end of the morning. But, to differing degrees, other topics also occupied us, including progress on the new pool, and tomorrow's visit by out-of-town lady bowlers.

The latter topic gained further impetus that afternoon when the manager and chairman of the board held an emergency meeting with the former bowls club management committee. But, as we walked home, we were still unaware the meeting had been called. In fact, I was unaware of the meeting until I received a call from Cilla during lunch.

"Did you get an invite?" was her opening gambit.

"An invite to what?"

"Oh, I see. So you weren't invited to the management committee meeting this afternoon?"

"No-o, but I wouldn't expect to be. Why would I be invited to a bowls club management committee meeting when I'm not on the committee?"

"Bugger. I had hoped they had invited you. I know Rod's been asked to attend. Never mind, maybe I'll have lots to share with you at happy hour this evening."

Damn, I wouldn't mind being at the meeting this afternoon – even just as a fly on the wall would be good. Now, I'll have to keep my curiosity in check until this evening. For the rest of the afternoon, my mind insisted on keeping itself busy with imagining what the committee might be told at that meeting, and what the board thought it could put in place to sort out something that, in reality, was a chronic problem and not merely an acute one.

It goes without saying, I had every intention of arriving at Rod's place early for happy hour this evening. As it turned out, so did Cilla. We three found ourselves with a good half hour to spare before the rest of the crew arrived. In his usual fashion, Rod wasted no time taking charge of the situation.

"Cilla, I'm sure Marion is dying of curiosity about this afternoon's meeting. Should we use the time available before the others arrive to put her out of her misery?" Rod asked, tongue in cheek.

"Talking through what happened might help me to sort it out in my mind as well," Cilla agreed. "It's a shame you weren't there, Marion. You would have loved every minute of it – as did Stella and I."

"The executive summary of proceedings goes something like this," Rod began. "The board chairman, a board member, and our manager were there. The chairman chaired the meeting."

"You should have seen the old-guard members when they arrived," Cilla chuckled. 'They marched in, all bustle and indignation, and slunk out battered and defeated."

From the report I received, it appears the old-guard committee members were soundly taken to task for their behaviour, the chairman pointing out several times that it was 'not their bowls club or their committee'. He went so far as to ban those men from ever serving on any committee associated with the Village in the future.

While the chairman did acknowledge the interclub competitions and the members' efforts in establishing the initiatives, he was critical of the men for attempting to bully the women out of their playing day. Apparently, he delivered a lengthy lecture on gender equality, what it meant here in the Village, and how he was determined it should be preserved at all costs.

I waited for the 'punch line': how did the meeting end? What were the outcomes of the meeting? Whatever they were, both Rod and Cilla appeared pleased with the results, and I suspected 'pleased' might be an understatement. As the other two seemed to be delighting in taking their time to reach the bit I wanted to hear, I spurred them along.

"Come on, you two. People will arrive shortly, and you still won't have told me what measures are now in place."

"Oh, all right, but we thought you would want to know all the juicy bits too," Cilla apologised. "I suppose we can share those with you at any time later. So, how do things stand now? Rod, you might like to summarise for Marion, please."

"Okay, the most important thing is that the ladies will have the greens to run friendly games with their visitors tomorrow. The original allocation of playing days has been reinstated, and the fear of God has been put into anyone who took it upon themselves to change them. What else was put in place? Let me think…"

"What about a management committee?' I asked. "What's to happen in that regard since the community did move to dissolve the existing committee?"

"Uhmm… that is a bit of a mystery to me, too," Cilla confessed. "I know what we were told at the meeting, but I'm unsure how effective the new arrangement will be."

"Sounds intriguing… Why the concern? What bothers you, Cilla?" I asked.

She asked Rod to outline how things were to operate going forward.

"Well, in effect, there is to be an interim administrative committee to oversee the general operation of the bowls club. Who the committee members will be wasn't spelled out, but it will include our manager, Tanya, and the board chairman. It was put to me that I might like to be on the committee, but I haven't said yay or nay yet."

"Do you need anything else to help fill in your time?" I asked.

"Not really, no, but I don't think I would have much to do. I think it's intended that Tanya will do whatever is required, and she will undoubtedly allocate responsibility for it to one of her staff.

Also, for the next little while, the men's and the women's games committees – or subcommittees, if you would prefer – will be responsible for organising themselves, their games, and any interclub visits for their respective members.

And that's about it for now. As I said, these are supposed to be interim arrangements. How they progress to become a more permanent arrangement is anyone's guess, as far as I can see. Maybe all will become clear after the dust settles in the next few weeks."

"Cilla, as a former management committee member, how does all this sit with you … and with Stella too, I suppose?" I asked.

"It is fine by me. I'm happy to have one less thing to worry about and one less meeting to attend. Stella seems happy enough as well. The new arrangement gives back their autonomy to the women players via their subcommittee. All things considered, everyone should be happy … unless something major administratively occurs."

Voices coming up the path told us the others were arriving for happy hour. Discussion of the bowls club meeting was abandoned and, as nobody asked about it during the evening, it wasn't discussed again. But my short walk home after happy hour gave me plenty of time to ponder what the new arrangements meant for the bowls club's continued operation.

What if scenarios wriggled through my mind like tadpoles on speed. What if there were disputes about manning the bar, using bar proceeds, maintaining stock levels for the bar area, and regularly maintaining and cleaning the bar area and equipment? It wouldn't take long for some of these issues to manifest. I was pleased they wouldn't be my problem when they did.

As I crawled into bed, I consoled myself with the thought that if no one else was worried about the possibility of such problems occurring, why should I worry about it? Nevertheless, I will be at the bowls club tomorrow morning to help welcome the visiting players and assist in any way I can to help ensure the day is a success.

Our visiting players arrived on time this morning and were welcomed by a large contingent of our resident lady bowlers and a few others like me who are occasional players at best.

I was horrified to see four of the old guard members of the former management committee arrive with set jaws, stony-faced, and breathing fire. They pushed through the crowd to where Stella and another woman had welcomed the visitors and were about to usher them into the clubhouse for morning tea before they took to the greens.

As the men strode out through the front ranks of the gathering, they were brought to a sudden halt by what confronted them. Striding around the corner of the building in the opposite direction came our manager, Tanya, accompanied by the chairman of the board of directors. Unfortunately for the men, they hadn't seen the latecomers until after the former president of the management committee fired his first foul comments at Stella and the group of visitors.

Top marks to the chairman and Rod, who had caught up with him. The chairman stepped in front of the belligerent president and his men and unceremoniously bustled them off and out of sight around the side of the building. There was no shouting or screaming. Just the dull growl of a lone voice floated to me as I lingered outside the clubhouse after the others went in to morning tea.

After a couple of minutes, only silence emanated from somewhere behind the building. I hesitated. Was the show over? Should I go inside now, or wait a bit longer in case 'Act 2' would follow? Then, while I stood dithering, Rod poked his head around the corner of the building and gave me a thumbs-up signal.

Although unsure of what he was signifying, I decided whatever it was probably meant the show was over, and I could go inside to join the others in coffee and scones.

Morning tea was delicious, but the players were focused on the reason they were there. Soon, games were in progress on all rinks. As I watched the first bowls roll down the rinks, I breathed something of a sigh of relief. We had been saved from an even more embarrassing confrontation in front of our visitors, but I couldn't help but wonder what the aftermath might be.

I felt sure those old-guard blokes would not lie down quietly. But, frustrating as it was, I would have to wait until later today – possibly until happy hour – to hear details of how the 'right' people managed to arrive at the 'right' time, and what took place behind the clubhouse.

Chapter 8

Relief for my frustration came mid-afternoon in the form of a phone call from Cilla.

"Come and join Rod and me for coffee. We thought you would want to know about this morning's interesting bits. I'm about to put the kettle on, so come as soon as you like."

Rod was already seated in the lounge room. I had the distinct feeling he hadn't just arrived, but had been there for some time. He looked weary when he gave me a wan smile and pointed me towards another chair. A moment after I collapsed into the chair, Cilla trotted in with a tray loaded with coffee and muffins.

"Muffins…" I exclaimed. "Cilla, you didn't go to all the trouble of baking for us, did you?" I heard Rod chuckle.

"Baking…? What's that? A place in Asia or something?" she quipped as she distributed the mugs of coffee. "Why would I bother when the bakery in town does a much better job than I can?"

Little time was wasted on small talk before Rod moved to what I wanted to hear about.

"Well, most of us survived, so I suppose yesterday and today weren't complete disasters, despite their potential to end up that way."

"Yeah, it was good to see the cavalry arrive when it did," I admitted. "I must confess, though, I wasn't sure how effective it might be. Our board chairman is proficient at smiling at people he's trying to impress, but I don't remember him running up too many points in sticky situations."

"Ah, well, you might be selling him short," Rod replied with a knowing nod. "Today, he was magnificent, unflinching in battle. Not that it was too much of a battle, though. It was more like a minor skirmish. Anyway, the good guys won, and a couple of residents – soon to be ex-residents – have been left to rue their bravado in taking on this place's authorities."

"Don't stop there, Rod," Cilla encouraged him. "Remember, I also don't know the full story of what went on behind the clubhouse today. So, come on, tell us the story."

"As I said, our chairman was magnificent. He took the old duffers head-on. Without raising his voice above a low growl, he acquainted them with a few facts of life – and the folly of their actions. By the time he was finished, even those of us who were mere spectators felt as though we had been run over by a steamroller."

"So, our erstwhile chairman pinned their ears back, eh?" Cilla giggled. "I wish I had been there to see it. But I guess the question now is, what happens next? Those old blokes are not going to react too kindly to being taken to task like that, particularly in front of a gaggle of women. I'm concerned about what repercussions might result."

"Oh, I doubt there will be repercussions. The most belligerent of the old guard present at the time have been given their marching orders. They have limited time to find other accommodation, but regardless, they will be evicted if they are still here in a month's time. You'll know who I'm talking about. It's the same two who created all the problems within the management committee.

The other two old blokes there this morning have been given stern warning and are unlikely to lift their heads above the parapet again anytime soon."

"Wow, so the chairman does have a backbone after all. I feel a bit sorry for Tanya. She will be left to ensure all the chairman's threats and promises are carried out and to clean up the residual mess from this event." I don't usually have too much sympathy for our manager, but I feel for her on this occasion.

"I don't think she will have too much to worry about," Rod assured me. "By making an example of two of the old guard, the chairman probably has ensured the others won't step out of line again, and no others will be tempted to try anything funny in future."

Cilla appeared troubled by something. I felt compelled to ask if she disagreed with the chairman's actions.

"No, I don't disagree with what he's done. It required a firm stand so people would understand the consequences of trying to take over the place. My only concern is whether the chairman has the right to take such action. I mean, could those two old blokes he evicted challenge the decision in court?"

"You are not the only one who had that thought. I raised it with the manager. She assured me the chairman had sought legal advice before taking the action he did. So, I think we are unlikely to see any legal ramifications as a result."

After Cilla reported that this morning's games with the visiting bowlers were proclaimed a howling success by all involved, there was little else to discuss regarding the morning's events. It seemed an appropriate time to move the conversation onto something else I wanted to discuss.

"Rod, moving away from bowls for the moment, where are we with the new pool? It looks almost ready for use, but I see work continues on the site."

"Today's advice from the contractor is that all work on the pool itself is now finished. Only the shade sail and the pool surrounds remain to be completed. I've suggested to the manager that we don't fill the pool until all the work is finalised. That way, no one will be tempted to have an early dip before we are ready for it. We do have to put some water in the pool, but it will be less than half full."

"How much longer will it be before people can start using the pool?" Cilla asked. "Oh, and have we confirmed whether it's for residents' only use, or whether outsiders might be allowed to take advantage of it as well?"

"So far, the powers that be appear adamant that it will be a residents-only facility. That's probably because of the logistical nightmare of outsiders using the pool," Rod said.

"Yeah… Would they be charged to use the pool, and how would they pay for it? Who would collect the money? And what about insurance should one of them be injured or worse while using the pool?" I commented.

"They are questions wiser men than I must grapple with… And I think that's why they decided on the 'no outsiders' rule. It was too hard to have it any other way," Rob chuckled.

As there didn't seem to be much else to discuss, I made noises about going home and meeting up with them again at happy hour later. Then Rod announced he had something else he wanted to mention – but not in front of the others tonight.

"I'm sure you will be aware I've exchanged plenty of words with the manager and the chairman over the last week. While most of it was about the bowls club, the chairman brought up something else that was interesting.

He asked how much contribution we expected the board to put towards the cost of the pool."

"Bit late, don't you think?" Cilla snarled. "They made it clear they weren't interested from the moment we started talking about a pool."

"True… And I did remind the chairman of that fact. Apparently, since then, the board has realised they erred badly when they advertised a pool in the new development prospectus and then didn't provide one. It seems they have now developed a guilt complex about it." Rod looked decidedly smug as he shared that gem with us.

"So they should," I snapped. "So what did you tell them?"

"Do we need any additional cash to complete the pool project?" Cilla asked before Rod could answer.

"No, we are more than cashed-up enough to pay for the pool. When I explained that to the chairman, he asked what our next project might be."

"Are we planning another project so soon?" I blurted out in surprise… tinged with horror.

"Hopefully not…." Cilla added. "A quiet life for a while would be good. Since my return from Sydney, it has been just one thing after another."

"Your enthusiasm astounds me," Rod giggled. "Anyway, much to your relief, I imagine, I assured him we had no new projects planned for the future. That's when he dropped the bombshell.

I'm not sure how it has come about, but it appears there has been some discussion at board level about a bus."

"Does he think we will fundraise now to buy a bloody bus for this place?" Cilla growled. "It's bad enough when the residents think they're entitled to some additional facility – and we should provide it for them. We don't need the board adopting that same line of thinking."

"Perhaps the notion that the Village requires a bus came from the residents in the first place. I don't know what has prompted the board's interest in acquiring one, but I do think there is some merit in the idea. I don't think we should have to fundraise for it. And, I assure you, I made that clear to the chairman."

Ignoring the risk of being howled down by the other two, I tentatively suggested, "A small bus might improve the life of some of the residents who otherwise have to rely on taxis every time they want to leave the Village."

"Hmm… Yeah, I can see the idea has possibilities," Cilla added. "Apart from taking residents into town to do their shopping or whatever, other outings using the bus could be organised. A morning at the beach, a day trip up the road to the next town, or even something longer, would contribute to the quality of life of some of the residents."

"Still, what does a small bus cost these days?" I asked.

"I have no idea," Rod admitted, "and I don't think the board of directors knows either. But, while I do agree such an acquisition would be a good idea, I'm not at all convinced paying for one should be our problem. And, as I said, I pointed that out to the chairman.

Now, don't get too excited just yet, but the look he gave me suggested our having to raise funds for it might not have been part of their thinking. I guess it will be a case of 'watch this space' for a while yet."

"Best we don't mention a bus to the others at this point, though," I suggested. "Let's wait until we know a bit more – and the pool is open and being used – before we cause them renewed indigestion by mentioning another expensive project."

My suggestion didn't cause any argument and, with that topic also exhausted for now, I again started making noises about going home.

"Are you in a hurry for something, Marion, or can you stay a bit longer?" Cilla asked. I assured her I had no reason to rush home, and she continued.

"Good… If you both can stay a bit longer, I would like to talk about the body-in-the-paddock situation and where that investigation is at now."

We opted for another coffee before we embarked on what could prove a long and heavy discussion. Once the coffee arrived, this time accompanied by a platter of crackers and cheese, Cilla eased into the conversation she wanted to have.

"Richard advised that all the test results are in and have confirmed the body was that of the bloke I thought it was. Over the last few days, I have received copies of all the material in the New South Wales police files. The bloke in question has been on their most-wanted list for a number of years. Because the file was so extensive, I had the most relevant stuff for Richard emailed to me on the day we found the body. Copies of the rest of the material in the file arrived safe-hand by courier yesterday."

"Was the entire file necessary once you had enough to confirm an identification?" Rod asked.

"Well, yes, it was. You see, there's more to this case than simply closing the file now the man is dead. You need to know something of the bloke to appreciate why that is, and my problem is how much I might need to share for you to understand the situation."

"If you aren't certain after all this time about how secure the information you share with us might be, you haven't gotten to know us well at all, have you?" I snapped.

"It's not about any concern regarding your confidentiality. It's about your safety. The less you know and the less you are involved, the safer the pair of you might be."

"*Might be…*? Why could our safety possibly be jeopardised?" I demanded. "It's a body. He's dead. Why should we worry about him?"

Rod sat staring off into the distance as I spoke and showed no inclination to participate in the discussion. Silence reigned for a couple of moments before he 'rejoined' us. Drumming his fingers on the table, he glanced from Cilla to me and back again.

"Perhaps we do need to know the whole story so we know what we are up against." He gave Cilla a hard look before focusing on me. "As you say, Marion, the man is dead and poses no threat whatsoever, but that raises questions. Why is he dead? And how did he come to be dead?

Maybe the answers to those questions will tell us why we need to be concerned about being too close to this case… although I fear we already are."

"Okay, maybe it is best if you do understand something of the victim's background. I'll try to be as concise as possible without leaving you wondering what I'm talking about.

The victim – let's continue to call him Ralph for now – had a long career on the wrong side of the law. We suspected his involvement in a number of major crimes but were unable to find enough evidence to bring a case against him. Nevertheless, we were sure of one thing. He was an assassin, a killer for hire and generally to the highest bidder."

"So, knew no loyalties, eh?" Rod quipped, and Cilla shrugged.

"If you knew that, why wasn't he caught and locked up?" I couldn't understand how that wasn't possible.

"Knowing something and doing something about it are worlds apart. Ralph was a particularly slippery customer. He would commit a crime. We would establish without a doubt that he was the perpetrator, but he had disappeared. And, he would remain 'disappeared' until his next piece of handiwork brought him to our attention again."

"So, he continued to enjoy life at large and remained on your most-wanted list. How long was this scenario in place … before he turned up dead nextdoor?" Rod asked.

"Let's just say that was the case for a number of years. It's too embarrassing to try to work out exactly how long."

"Well, it looks as though you and your copper mates can now cross him off your list and breathe a little easier after this," I suggested.

"No. That's just the point. The situation has escalated. Someone has eliminated Ralph. Who and why? Has there been something of a turf war between killers for hire and, therefore, is there a new target for police to worry about? Or, did Ralph do the wrong thing by someone somewhere along the line and now has paid the price?"

Cilla looked deep in thought as she spoke. It caused an involuntary shiver to run down my spine. Then logic stepped in. I put it into words before giving it much thought.

"Correct me if I'm wrong, but as I understand what you have told us, an unpleasant gentleman, who might have considered you a threat because you might recognise him, is now dead. Unless there is something about his killer you haven't shared with us, I would have thought any risk to your life has been removed. And, as Rod and I were not a part of this saga, surely we can be in no danger." It still sounded perfectly logical when I said it.

"That's not how the murky world of this type of crime works. The perpetrators remain at large for much longer than they should because they don't take risks, don't leave anything to chance.

At this stage, they probably don't know who found the body and whether that person knew anything about the victim and his career. A lesser person might think that unlikely and believe that some unsuspecting community member was unfortunate enough to stumble across the body."

"Yep, I think that would be a fair enough assumption," I agreed.

"Right, but as I said, in the killer's world, that would be an unacceptable risk they couldn't take. That assumption of nothing-to-worry-about-here might prove true … but what if it wasn't? What if I did recognise the body and I knew the history attached to it? What if I knew, or suspected, something that might help focus attention on, or raise suspicions about, the identity of the killer?"

"Are you suggesting that you are now in danger and, by association, so are we?" Rod asked.

"Perhaps… and that is the best answer I can give you for now. My concerns might prove unfounded, but it is best not to risk complacency in the murky world I work in. To do so could result in paying a high price."

"So, what do you suggest we do to minimise our risk?" I demanded. "Do we lock ourselves in our houses and never come out so as to avoid any possible risk? And, for how long do we have to lock ourselves away or get used to looking over our shoulder?"

"All I can tell you now is that I am working with my Special Tasks Unit to gather as much information as possible that might be floating about south of the border. And I am working and liaising with Richard on the local front. The hope is we will have sufficient details, and early enough, for us to do whatever is needed to keep ourselves safe."

"Might this be a good time for Rod to disappear off to visit his son wherever he might be, rather than risk hanging about here?" I suggested.

"I'm not going anywhere," Rod barked. "In case you have forgotten, I still work part-time as a journo. I have a couple of articles to write in the next week or so, and I haven't even started them yet. So, I'm too busy to be going anywhere, regardless of whatever else might be happening."

"Marion, the short answer is, none of us should think of going anywhere for a while. "Flitting around the countryside would just make you a better target than if you stay tucked away here." Cilla sounded weary as she said her piece, but she continued. "I doubt the two of you have any cause for concern, but you do need to be aware and keep your eyes open. I will keep you informed as things happen – if anything does happen."

While there was little more to be said, we had plenty to think about. Again, Rod and I made noises about going home. Cilla didn't argue but, at her front door, she stopped abruptly and turned to Rod.

"What are your real thoughts about this bus idea? I mean, would a bus be likely to spend much of its time sitting around like a white elephant, or do you think it will see enough use to justify its purchase?"

Cilla's question was a valid one and one that had been rattling about, trying to take form in the back of my mind since Rod mentioned the board's interest in a bus for residents. Rod took his time answering. I guessed he was weighing up whether to brush the question aside and continue out the door, or if he should indulge in a detailed answer that might see us return to the chairs we had just vacated and further delay our departure.

The look Cilla pinned him with didn't allow him much wriggle room, so he heaved a sigh and gestured for us to return to the lounge room.

"Okay, I know purchasing a bus for Merivale Village is something worth discussing at length. But I should say that, so far, I'm not privy to the board's thinking on this matter other than to say they seem to think it's a good idea. They haven't told me how they see the bus being used other than 'for outings'."

"Yes, but what sorts of outings? What do they have in mind?" Cilla demanded. "After all, if they do acquire a bus, I don't doubt that, by some strange process, our group will be lumbered with managing its use."

"It's getting late," Rod said, "and I did want to be home a bit before everyone arrived for happy hour. As I suggested, this could develop into a major discussion, and it is one I believe we need to have. There's a fair chance the chairman will seek our group's opinion before the Board makes a definite move to proceed.

I also think it would be better if we three discussed it before taking it to the rest of the group. Whatever comes out of our discussions could help direct the group's thinking in the 'right' direction on whether they support the idea or not. So, will the world end if we don't discuss the bus until another day?"

As usual, Rod's suggestion made sense, and Cilla and I enthusiastically agreed to leave further discussion in abeyance.

Chapter 9

During the fortnight since the *Battle of the Bowls Club* (as it was now being called), life in the Village appeared to settle back into its normal pace and routines. One major difference was the now apparent distancing by the male members from any administrative functions of the bowls club.

In a major display of community-mindedness, the women members rallied to ensure the club continued to operate as near as possible as previously. Women volunteers now manned the bar area to serve drinks and morning and afternoon teas. They liaised with Linda, the contractor running the kitchen, to have lunches available on major playing days, particularly on both men's and women's interclub days.

While the club's men appeared to be sulking over recent outcomes and restricted their time at the club to actually playing bowls, the women seemed perfectly happy to pick up the reins to maintain normal operations.

The big question for me, and I suspect for many other residents, was the matter of what was to replace the former Bowls Club Management Committee. Nary a word had emanated from the powers-that-be on the matter, not officially anyway. I suspected Rod had engaged in discussions with our manager and various board members. I doubt the current situation would cause any sense of urgency amongst those in charge. While the women ensured the club continued to run smoothly, our manager had little to do, and the chairman had little to concern him.

As another week slipped by since the bowls club kerfuffle, the entire event and its outcomes faded from residents' minds. To an interested onlooker like myself, everyone involved appeared happy with the way things were and content for them to continue in that way. So, it came as a surprise a couple of weeks later, when it was announced that something more official was required.

An announcement on the Village's Facebook page raised a few eyebrows, including Cilla's and mine. It had the predictable effect of becoming the subject of much debate at our subsequent happy hour. All those present admitted to being blindsided by the announcement. Everyone except Rod, that is, who made a good show of being as surprised as the rest of us. I don't know if the others saw through his performance, but I did. Of course, he was aware there would be such an announcement. He probably wrote it. And I didn't doubt he knew more than that as well.

There it was – nicely laid out and in bold type – the announcement of the board's intention to hold an election of a new management committee for the bowls club. The announcement called for firm expressions of interest from any residents interested in serving on such a committee. The timeline for nominations was short.

It shouldn't have come as a surprise, I suppose. We knew the present arrangements were only an interim measure until a new committee was in place. Nevertheless, the announcement coming out of the blue like that did stun some of us. Not surprising, perhaps, was speculation about who was likely to nominate… and whether any of our group were interested.

Cilla admitted to feeling obligated to put her hand up. As a member of the previous committee and having been largely responsible for its dissolution, she felt something akin to needing to make amends. Her reasoning surprised me, and I wondered whether there was more to it than just guilt.

"Geez, Cilla, after all you experienced as a member of the previous committee, I thought you'd run a mile rather than put your hand up to be elected again. Forget about obligation. Are you sure you want to do this?" I asked when we were alone in the kitchen.

"Yeah, I know it looks as though I have a masochistic streak or something, but it's that old rule about putting your money where your mouth is. I mouthed-off often enough about the previous committee's shortcomings and how the club could have been run much better. They would be so many hollow words if I didn't appear committed to what I said.

No, I don't particularly want or need to be on the management committee. My hope is there will be so many other nominations that I will have no problem pulling out of the race and letting those more dedicated to the cause take on running the club."

"Do you think Rod might nominate?"

"Hmm… I doubt it. He has more than enough going on in his life. He doesn't need the hassle of running the bowls club. Still, if he did nominate, he'd be certain of being elected.

If you want my opinion, it would be in our collective interests if he didn't end up on that committee. As something of a residents' spokesperson, he seems to have the ear of those in charge. They appear to seek his advice and hold him in high regard. It would be best if he continued in that role as a free agent.

As a management committee member, he might be constrained by the requirements of his position on the committee, rather than focused on the interests of the rest of the residents."

"So, if we become aware he is considering nominating, we should endeavour to change his mind?"

"That would be the way to go … if we did get an early whiff of something like that. But, knowing Rod, he would not give us any warning."

Cilla's comments made sense, and I agreed with her assessment of the situation. If Rod decided to nominate for the management committee, he would be unlikely to discuss it with us beforehand. I've gotten to know Rod well, but he runs deep. Unless he intends otherwise, we are unlikely to gain any clues about his intentions.

Another thought occurred to me as we were about to rejoin the others on Rod's back deck.

"Cilla, we haven't heard anything more about a bus for Village residents. I suppose, with the Board preoccupied with establishing a new bowls club management committee, there hasn't been further discussion of a bus."

"I had forgotten about the bus. As far as I know, the subject is still restricted to just us three. Perhaps we should wait until the others leave tonight and ask Rod for an update."

While Rod farewelled the last of the group, Cilla and I remained seated on the deck. Rod looked surprised when he returned and found us still sitting there.

"Ladies, am I right in assuming you wouldn't say no to a nightcap before you leave?" he asked, waving a bottle of port at us.

"Thank you. A glass of port would be most welcome," Cilla replied for both of us.

We waited until Rod had settled back on his chair before we opened the conversation we wanted to have.

"Rod, it has occurred to us that we haven't heard any more about the idea of a bus for Village residents," I said to open discussions. "Do you have an update to share with us?"

"Ah, I might have known something was afoot when you two ladies were still sitting out here after everyone left.

Now, about the bus… Well, there isn't much to report. The board is still keen to pursue the matter, but I am unaware of much, if any, progress having been made. The last I heard was that they were investigating what was available and at what cost. Once they have that information, I believe they intend to talk to me about whether its potential use warrants such a purchase.

Is there something in particular that has you asking about a bus now?"

"No… Well, yes. Given all that's been happening with the bowls club lately, it occurred to me that maybe the Village could do with a bus," I suggested before pausing to search for the words I wanted to use.

Wanting more information and thinking I had said all I intended to, Rod held his hands out to Cilla in an entreating gesture for her thoughts.

"For goodness sake, Rod, we're concerned about the interclub bowls competitions. While other clubs will be coming here to play, our members will also be expected to play at other clubs. And that applies to both the men's and women's teams. A bus would be handy to transport bowlers to those other clubs."

"Ah, yes, I hadn't thought about that need. It will be a pain, and the competition could fall in a heap if players have to rely on private vehicles to travel to games outside of the Village. I have to admit, initially, I was sceptical about the need for a bus. But since the board asked about it, I've thought of all sorts of reasons to support having our own bus."

Cilla appeared deep in thought for a few moments before nodding to herself and then rejoining the conversation.

"Yeah. Rod, I think it might be worthwhile initiating further discussion about a bus as soon as possible. The interclub bowls competition is too good an opportunity to waste. If you don't run with it now, the advantage will be lost.

See if you can stir up the chairman and the board to act on the matter as soon as possible."

"Okay, okay, I will. But now that you two ladies were kind enough to stay behind tonight, I also need answers to a question.

Cilla, is there anything more we should know about the body in the paddock? It's been a few days since we last heard anything. I'm sure Marion is just as keen as I am to know if we are now safe and can stop constantly looking over our shoulders."

"Argh, I wish I could give you a definitive answer, but I can't. The last I heard from Richard yesterday was that they were about to drag in someone for questioning. When I say 'they', I don't mean our local coppers. It appears whatever is happening or about to happen is confined to the state's southeast corner. I can also tell you the boys in blue from the other side of the state line are also close to dragging in someone to 'assist with their enquiries'."

"Does that mean you'll need to head off to Sydney again?" I asked.

"No. Why would you think that?"

"Well, I just thought that if your Special Task Unit was about to interview someone, you might need to be there."

"O-oh, I see. No, my team is not involved – not yet, anyway. So, for the moment, I don't plan on going anywhere. Regarding our safety, I would counsel continuing to be vigilant for a while longer. As soon as I know something positive, I'll let you know."

Nothing in Cilla's update on the body in the paddock was reassuring. If I'm honest, as nothing remotely suspicious had happened since they removed the body, I had relaxed a bit. But as I walked home from Rod's place, I felt as nervous as the day Cilla found the body. A while later, that feeling was to intensify.

The 'something positive' Cilla had mentioned came a couple of days later. A call from Cilla inviting me to coffee that morning was a surprise. She hadn't mentioned coffee while we were at happy hour the previous night or as she and I left Rod's place together afterwards.

Something was not right. When I arrived for coffee, the Cilla who opened the door to me appeared to be…. Appeared to be what? Preoccupied? Nervous? Whatever it was, I detected it in her voice when she told me Rod also had been invited for coffee.

"He said he might be a bit late, depending on whether his meeting dragged on longer than expected. I was unsure whether we should have a coffee now or wait for him to arrive."

Who was this woman? She looked like Cilla but didn't sound or act like her. I studied her in stunned silence for a moment or two before offering a suggestion.

"Cilla, perhaps we might indulge in coffee and chat while we wait for Rod. I'm sure neither of us will say no to having another cup with him later.

Now, if you don't think me too rude, what has happened to make you so tense? If it's something personal you don't want to discuss, I will understand."

"No, it's nothing personal, and I didn't know I seemed tense. I'm not really; I'm just preoccupied. But, if you don't mind, I would prefer to wait until Rod arrives to discuss it."

Having assured her that was fine with me, I was at a loss as to what to talk about. Cilla seemed to suffer the same affliction. We sat in a silence punctuated only periodically by odd comments about the weather or our last mahjong games. It was almost an overwhelming relief when Rod arrived. He was like a breath of fresh air entering the room.

"Good morning to you both, and my apologies for being late. Am I too late to get a cup of coffee? I hope not because I sure could use one."

"Was your meeting so bad that it has you desperate for coffee?" I asked to tempt him to tell us about his meeting.

"Huh, I haven't decided yet whether it was good or bad. In all fairness, I think the outcome might be both good and bad – depending on your point of view. But that's not why we are here this morning.

Lovely as your invitation was, Cilla, I suspect you didn't intend this to be a social occasion. So, Cilla, it's over to you. What are we here for apart from coffee?"

"Yes, you're probably right. I invited you for coffee after I received an early morning call from Richard…."

"Richard Wilson, our local top cop?" I interjected

"That's the one. He called to give me the latest update on their investigation. Marion, you recently asked whether it was safe to relax our vigilance. I can give you a definite answer to that question now: NO."

Rod raised his eyebrows in surprise as he said, "Cilla, the last we heard was that somewhere in Brisbane, someone was helping police with their enquiry into the body in the paddock. Your comments now suggest that interrogation went nowhere useful."

"Argh, that might be one way of describing it. A 'person of interest' was interviewed in Brisbane. While he wasn't particularly helpful, and police believe he knew more than he was saying, they also realised he was not the key person they sought.

As a result, they had nothing to hold him on, and he was allowed to leave. And soon after met with an accident, a fatal accident."

"Are we to take that to mean that the man they want to interview made sure the man they did interview could not suffer a moment of weakness and reveal the main suspect's whereabouts?" Rod asked.

"Nobody else I know except a journo would use so many words to sum up an obvious situation," Cilla replied sarcastically. "Yes. As I told you previously, this bloke has stayed ahead of the law for so long because he does not leave anything to chance. The police who interviewed the now-deceased interviewee did not believe he knew anything that would help their investigation. But the killer was not so sure and took what he saw as a necessary precaution.

So, I suppose the big question is, what does that mean for us? While nothing is clear yet, it is fair to assume the killer might embark on a serious clean-up campaign. If that should occur, we will need to be extra vigilant. Although none of us knows anything about the event that resulted in the body in the paddock, we were involved in its discovery."

"That seems a bit extreme," I blurted out. "Surely the killer can't see us as any threat. We don't know anything." It sounded lame even to me as I said it.

"There's no point in adopting a position of denial, Marion," Cilla snapped. "This bloke hasn't been able to ply his trade unhindered for so long by taking chances. Of course, it's a possibility we might know something, and if that's how he thinks, we could well feature on his list of cleaning-up requiring attention."

Firmly put in my place, I opted to sit back and sulk for a bit. While Rod, who had been studying his hands clasped in his lap for some time, finally found his voice and joined the discussion.

"Should we take your comments further?" Rod began. "I mean, is the killer likely to focus on the three of us and the role we played in the body's discovery and removal from the paddock? Or, is he likely to consider any of the residents along this street a potential danger? If, as you say, he leaves nothing to chance, he is in for a busy time cleaning up the potential threats posed by the Village's residents."

"Although no one knows anything…?" Cilla added. "Yes, you probably have a valid point, but at this time, we have no way of knowing what the killer knows or thinks. Given that situation, it's up to all of us to stay alert for anything out of the ordinary happening around us."

My sulk hadn't improved my outlook on life, and Cilla's information had me feeling belligerent and generally put-upon by something I had nothing to do with. My frame of mind was evident in my response. What wasn't obvious, I hoped, was my decision to continue not to mention something I had remembered.

"Right, Cilla, how long is this state of affairs likely to continue? Judging by your earlier comments, the police are no closer to capturing the culprit and, therefore, that state of affairs could remain for a long time to come. Half the residents of the Village could have 'fatal accidents' before he is captured or moves on to his next job and loses interest in us."

"For God's sake, Marion, I don't have a crystal ball," Cilla snapped. "There are no rules in this game. Like any other game – cricket, for instance – it's up to you how you play it. If you choose to tough it out and throw caution to the wind, that's up to you. But, I caution against it and urge you to think hard about what's been said."

"Cilla, how soon are you likely to receive a further update from Richard?" Rod asked quietly. "Will you hear from him on some sort of regular basis, or only when there is something to report?"

"Probably the latter, Rod. Richard is a busy man. The investigation of this crime isn't happening just locally. In fact, any major developments will likely come from somewhere far from here, and he, like the rest of us, will need to be patient until information filters through to him."

"Rod," I started tentatively, "how soon is the Village likely to obtain its own bus?" He looked perplexed by my question, so I rushed on. "It is just that, when the bus arrives, various excursions will occur, even if they're only associated with the bowls interclub competition. Are our residents on the bus likely to be in greater danger when they leave the Village?"

Startled by my question, Rod looked to Cilla for an answer. She appeared to consider the question for a moment before shrugging and replying.

"I'm afraid I've got much the same answer for you. I don't have a crystal ball and am capable of only the same wild guesses as the rest of you. But, yes, that might be a possibility … Just as every other imaginable situation might be a possibility.

Look, I asked you here today because I believed you needed to know what is happening and that the risk still exists. At the same time, I was reluctant to discuss it with you because I knew it would create concern. So, I'll reiterate: take every precaution possible and be alert for anything that looks out of place.

By the way, Rod, did you come away from your meeting this morning with any clear indication of if and when the board will purchase a bus?"

"Although nothing definite was said in the meeting, casual conversation later revealed quotes have been obtained and potential delivery dates negotiated. If my assessment of the situation is correct, a bus is likely to arrive here sometime within the next ten days."

"So the board is capable of making decisions and taking action when it suits them," I said with a heavy dose of sarcasm. "Earlier, you spoke of the meeting outcomes being both good and bad news. If purchasing a bus is the good news, perhaps you should prepare us for the bad news."

He looked uncomfortable when he answered. "I suspect our group will figure large in the bus's operation. And, I suppose that means it might be time to enlighten the rest of the group."

"Are we only going to warn them about the bus? Or, should we also warn them to be on the lookout for any suspicious behaviour around the place that might result in serious consequences for some of us?"

I needed to know what could and could not be mentioned at future gatherings of our group, and I was also concerned about them being kept in the dark about the possibility their lives could be in danger. Again, Rod looked to Cilla.

"Best not to concern them unnecessarily at this stage," she suggested. "No point in having everyone nervous and looking over their shoulders when nothing might happen. Let's wait and see how things pan out over the next little while before we drop more bad news on them. The arrival of a bus and our likely involvement in its operation will give them enough to think about for now."

"And there is the election of a new management committee for the bowls club to occupy their thinking," Rod added before announcing, "Okay, I'm off. See you this evening at happy hour."

Rod and I walked together in silence to the end of Cilla's driveway before going our separate ways home.

Chapter 10

Over the next few days, life in the Village didn't allow much time for peering over shoulders or being nervous about whether something nasty might befall one or some of us.

The first event of some note was the opening of the new pool. Some beautification works on the pool's surrounds still needed completion, but the pool was open for bathers at last. After a few weeks of listening to residents moan about how long they had to wait for a swim, swimmers were in short supply when it finally opened. It probably had more to do with the weather than a lack of interest.

After a night of unseasonal heavy showers, the weather remained blustery and cold for several days. Any excuse is good enough to warrant a social event, and opening the pool qualified in spades. The symbolic throwing open of the gates of the pool enclosure by the board's chairman was followed by a well-catered morning tea. Perhaps it's as well no one came prepared for a swim. Given the truckload of cakes and what-have-you consumed at morning tea, attendees would have been better advised to go for a long walk before considering a dip in the pool.

'Bleak' would appropriately describe the weather for the next few days after the opening. Except for a couple of hardy souls with a point to prove, the pool remained devoid of swimmers. The lack of use of the Village's newest facility came in for much discussion at a happy hour a few days later.

"It's a bit sad to see that lovely new pool not be used," Janet Furlong lamented. "All the residents were so keen to have a pool, and we worked jolly hard to raise the cash for it, and now nobody seems to want to swim in it."

"Have you tried it out, Janet?" Cilla asked.

"Me? No, not yet. It's been far too cold for me to think about taking a dip."

"Well, there you are then. Do you think the weather might have something to do with why there has been a lack of interest in the pool since it opened?" Cilla barked.

Fed up with listening to people moan about the pool's lack of use, Cilla lost patience. Janet just happened to be the last one to comment on it before Cilla made her feelings clear. Poor Janet received the sharp edge of Cilla's tongue. Ted sprang to his wife's defence.

"Really, Cilla, there was no need for that. All Janet did was state what the rest of us had been thinking. And the follow-on question from Janet's is, have we, the residents, invested in a white elephant?"

"I think it's far from being a white elephant," Frank said. "If there is a problem with the pool, it is just that it became available as we head into winter. I wouldn't expect to see the pool used much until the weather warms up again after winter."

"Maybe we should have thought about installing a heated pool so it could be used all year round," Luigi suggested.

"Strange you should think of that," Rod snarled. "It is heated. If no one is using the pool because the water is too cold, it means the heater hasn't been turned on. Has anyone tested the water to know what it is like?"

The only response was silence. Rod found himself surrounded by a group of sheepish-looking people with shaking heads.

"No? It seems no one can say for certain whether the pool is cold or if it is just a common assumption that it is cold. I suppose it is up to me to investigate the matter. I'll do that in the morning." Rod finished with a dismissive flick of his head.

"You are not being fair, Rod," Maria said quietly. "It appears you also don't know what the water is like because you haven't tested it either. I don't think your comments were fair given that the rest of us didn't know the pool had a heater installed."

What has happened, I wondered. I've never seen Rod so cranky before. Is there more to the pool story than I know about? Maria made a valid comment. We weren't aware the pool water might be pleasantly warm, because none of us knew it could be heated. Is he just cranky with himself for not having kept us informed? While I wanted that to be the case, I knew it wasn't. Nevertheless, whatever the reason for them, Rod's comments brought the evening to a speedy conclusion.

Ted and Janet were first to leave … after I saw Janet signal Ted that she wished to go home. Maria said she would go with them. Luigi promptly offered to walk Maria home as she lived further along the street from the Furlongs. That was all the excuse Frank needed to leave with them.

"As Luigi and I live opposite one another in the new section of the Village and have further to walk than the rest of you, I'll join you so I can keep Luigi company on the last leg of the journey," Frank announced.

We stood on Rod's doorstep for a while, watching the others making their way home along the footpath. Then Cilla sighed and said, "I think I'll call it a night as well. After I deal with dinner, I have some things to prepare for a meeting with my team early tomorrow morning. Not exactly a 'happy' hour this evening, was it? We might not please all the people all the time, but it would be nice to get a few runs on the board occasionally."

Attempting to avoid looking as though I was deliberately lingering, once Cilla left, I busied myself gathering up glasses and plates and loading them into the dishwasher. I grew increasingly concerned as I went about it. There was nothing but silence from Rod.

He pushed all the chairs back around the table on his back deck and generally tidied the area without attempting to make conversation. I replayed in my mind everything that had happened during the day, searching for anything I did or said that might have upset Rod. Although I found nothing, it was obvious he would have preferred I had left with the others.

With no valid reason to hang around any longer, I knew I should leave. I also knew such an icy parting would keep me awake wondering all night. Better to have it out now and see where that takes me, I told myself.

"Rod, if I have upset you somehow, please do me the courtesy of telling me what I did."

"What? Who said you had upset me? I don't understand the question or why you would ask it."

"Well, you just gave me an example of why. You have hardly spoken to me. When you have, you've snapped and snarled. I can only assume I've done something wrong… and want to know what it was. No, I *need* to know."

"Oh, I am sorry. I apologise if that is how I've come across today. There are a couple of things on my mind that I'm trying to deal with, and with little success so far. I probably shouldn't subject other people to my company now."

"Is there anything I can help you sort out?"

As it became clear Rod wasn't about to discuss whatever was on his mind, let alone let me help him in any way, I took my leave. On my short walk home, I tried unsuccessfully to think of anything to do with the Village that might be causing Rod's concern. Looks like I'm still in for a restless night.

Feeling decidedly below par when I finally scrambled out of bed this morning, I opted for a long walk to find something akin to feeling human. It made no appreciable difference, but I had little time to mope about it.

The election of a new management committee for the bowls club was set down for this morning. By ten o'clock, people were wandering across to the clubhouse. They might have the right idea, I told myself. If attendance is the same as at the last meeting, it will be wise to arrive early to secure a seat.

I joined the 'early birds' heading for the bowls club A few minutes after ten o'clock. Cilla soon caught up with me, and together, we walked into a room already almost full with mostly women!

"Now, this is interesting," Cilla murmured as we grabbed the first available chairs. "A lot of skirts but not many shirts … not so far anyway. The meeting isn't supposed to start until 10.30am, so there is still plenty of time for the blokes to arrive."

"You don't think the men have decided to boycott the elections, do you?"

Cilla answered my question with a shrug before scanning the attendees to count the number of 'shirts' already present.

"It's starting to look as though you might be right. Apart from our men, the chairman, and another couple of his board members, no other men are here. If it is a boycott, I can't imagine what they hope to achieve by it."

When 10.30 finally rolled around, the room was packed. Extra chairs were scrounged from various places to accommodate the large crowd. I swivelled around on my chair to scan the room behind me before nudging Cilla in the ribs.

"About another four or five men have turned up since you checked earlier. So, overall, it still looks as though it's a deliberate no-show by male club members," I whispered to her.

But there wasn't time for further comment. Our manager, Tanya Jellicoe, called everyone to order before handing the microphone to the chairman to welcome everyone. Then, the meeting got underway. The chairman, after reminding everyone they knew why they were there, and how important having an elected management committee was to the successful operation of the club, he went on to apologise for the short timeframe allowed for nominations to be received.

"In the past," he went on, that is, in the case of the previous management committee, there were seven elected members: three executive members plus four ordinary members. It is proposed that this new committee maintain that make-up."

He called for any objections to the proposal, but none was forthcoming. Tanya hastily scribbled something in a notebook, and I assumed she was tasked with taking the minutes. Then Tanya sprang up off her chair and stood beside the huge whiteboard.

The chairman announced the names of the members nominated for the committee, and Tanya dutifully wrote the names on the board. There were only five. All were women. The chairman reminded the attendees that there were seven positions to be filled and announced that further nominations would be accepted from the floor if others wished to nominate.

A deathly silence filled the room as we waited. No hands were raised. The buzz of murmuring flooded the room as attendees discussed the situation with their neighbours. After allowing a few moments, the chairman again called the meeting to order.

"Right," he continued, "as only five nominations have been received for the seven positions, it appears no voting is required to determine the new management committee members. I confirm all five nominees duly elected." He called the new committee to join him out front.

Someone in the audience asked who the office bearers were. I sat up. It was something I also wanted to know. The only two nominees I knew personally were Cilla and Stella, and I knew Cilla wouldn't want to be on the executive. Stella might be a good choice, though. The chairman hesitated about answering the question regarding the office bearers and needed a brief discussion with Tanya before doing so.

"We will leave it to the new committee to decide which position each will hold. There is only one other thing I must emphasise at this point.

The Merivale Retirement Village Bowls Club is now one of the few bowls clubs in this country run by its women members. Congratulations on breaking yet more new ground, but I would suggest the new committee adds at least one male recruit to its ranks – or two if two are willing to come forward. It might prove easier for everyone if one of the male club members is on the committee to take charge of the men's games committee."

With the meeting closed in almost record time, the sound of chairs scraping across the floor was deafening. Rod and I hung back as a mass exodus surged from the building. Cilla noticed we remained sitting in the almost deserted hall, and as soon as the chairman and manager departed, she approached us.

"Is everything all right?" she asked. "I thought you would be as keen as everyone else to go home for lunch."

"No, we preferred to wait and walk home with you," Rod said.

"Aah, sorry about this, but you'll be on your own. The new management committee is about to have its first meeting, and I must be here for it. God knows what I might get lumbered with if I wasn't here to say 'no thank you' to anything they try to shove my way. I'll see you both for coffee this afternoon if you are available."

Of course, we will be available. "I'll bring something to have with coffee," I offered before Rod and I joined the exodus.

"Those women must be keen on their new jobs to have their first meeting now. I thought they would leave it a day or so before getting stuck in," I suggested to Rod as we walked home.

"Well, they can't really afford to do that. If nothing else, they need to decide who will look after the games subcommittees until a men's games subcommittee is in place. And the draws for next week's interclub competition must be done as soon as possible to avoid chaos next week."

"Who is going to look after organising all the games stuff? I don't imagine the men will be too happy about the women organising their games."

"Probably not," Rod said and giggled. "I can just picture the fuss that might cause for some, and I don't imagine the women want to have responsibility for the men's games either. There is still a way to go before this mess is sorted out properly."

At happy hour that evening, Janet drew Cilla aside for what appeared to be an involved conversation. I thought something heavy was being discussed. Cilla's furrowed brow seemed fixed in place throughout their conversation. It wasn't until Cilla and I were cleaning up after the others had left that I discovered the nature of Janet's conversation.

With the dishwasher loaded, Rod suggested a nightcap before Cilla and I left.

"That would be good," Cilla replied. "Something has come up, and I would like your opinions on the matter."

My mind immediately flew to the body in the paddock. I felt my stomach becoming a squirming mass. Cilla demonstrated great restraint if she managed to withhold whatever the bad news was until after everyone went home. My anxiety proved premature.

"Janet pulled me aside to talk to me this evening, and I'd like your opinion on her proposal," Cilla began. After Rod and I nodded enthusiastically, Cilla continued.

"Janet is such a mousey personality. She couldn't suggest this at the meeting and waited until tonight to talk to me about it. Because we are still two short on the bowls club management committee, and none of those elected appeared keen to take on any executive positions, Janet proposed she take on the secretary's position."

"But she's not a committee member," I exclaimed. "Can she take on such a position when she isn't a member?"

"Actually, that is the question I was hoping you might help clarify for me." Cilla snapped. "What would be the process if the committee wanted to accept Janet's offer?"

"Well, you said two positions on the committee remained vacant. Couldn't Janet fill one of those and then take on the secretary's role?" It seemed a straightforward solution to me.

"We, the committee, that is, hoped at least one of those positions might be filled by one of the men. Ideally, we would like both vacancies filled by men. That way, there would be a bloke to run the men's games subcommittee. While I would be happy for Janet to come on board, I don't want to cruel our chance of getting a couple of the chaps involved."

Rod went to say something and then stopped. After a moment of what appeared to be deep thought, he tried again.

"While I don't pretend to know the scope of the secretary's role, I imagine it could be extensive during busier periods of the year. I wonder …. Yeah…. Might it be possible to split the job into two discrete roles? One to take care of all the usual correspondence and stuff, and one to act as Minute Secretary?"

"Okay, but how does that help solve the problem?" Cilla demanded.

"My thinking is that the secretary would be an elected member who handled all the correspondence and other paperwork associated with running the club. The minute secretary doesn't need to be an elected member. She – or he – could be a member *appointed* by the committee to fill that role. That way, the minute secretary doesn't occupy one of the vacant positions on the committee while providing a valuable service to the club and the committee." After Rod finished speaking, silence prevailed while we considered his suggestion.

"Hmmm… that might work, I suppose," Cilla conceded. "Janet is meticulous enough to do an excellent job as minute secretary. But, she is heavily involved in other events at different times throughout the year. She might not be available to attend all the meetings."

"Does it have to be Janet?" I asked. "Seeing as she has offered, it would be rude to appoint someone else instead. But you make a valid point, Cilla. Janet might not be able to attend all the meetings. How do you work around that situation?" Both Cilla and I looked to Rod for an answer.

"Although I don't know about her availability, I imagine it would be possible to appoint a proxy minute secretary who could stand in whenever required."

"Thanks, Rod." Cilla heaved a sigh of relief. "At the next committee meeting, I will suggest we appoint Janet. In the meantime, I will suggest we try to find a stand-in proxy for the position so Janet and the proxy can be appointed at the next meeting."

"How do you rate your chances of having at least one bloke on the committee sometime soon?" I asked almost as an afterthought.

"Not too highly, I suspect. But once the dust settles and the new committee gets down to business, you never know, we might get lucky. Just one to look after the men's interclub stuff would help."

With nothing more to be said about the committee, Cilla and I took our leave. Walking home, I pondered the magnitude of change that can occur over such a short time. A few weeks ago, none of us would have predicted women would run Merivale's new bowls club.

I found myself hoping this new 'Petticoat Government' didn't cause too much resentment in the ranks of the male club members.

Chapter 11

Rod was correct in predicting a bus would soon arrive at Merivale Village. Just over a week after he made that prediction, the board chairman and our manager took delivery of a shiny new bus out front of the Admin building.

Cilla was returning from a morning ride on Black Bess and saw the bus arrive. Rod had invited me for coffee, and I was about to open his gate when Cilla roared along our street. Abandoning her bike on its sidestand on her driveway, she bounded across the road to join me as I opened the gate. Rod, standing on his doorstep, looked as surprised as I was by Cilla's actions.

"Something has you excited, Cilla," he said as we strode towards him. "Should I prepare myself for good news or bad?"

"As I think you once said, that 'depends on your point of view'. A gleaming white bus parked out front of the Admin building is currently being fussed over by our chairman and manager. It would appear the Village's new bus has arrived."

"Jesus, they didn't waste any time. Perhaps we should go and pay homage to the new acquisition… before the gloss wears off it," he suggested, tongue firmly planted in his cheek. "By the time we return here, we might need something stronger than coffee. If we need them, how will stiff drinks go with your container of cupcakes, Marion?"

The adoration of the new bus continued when the three of us strolled up to the Admin building. The acolytes had moved to the vehicle's interior, and the chairman and the manager were oohing and aahing about the bus's comfortable seats as the salesman extolled the virtues of its safety features.

"Ah, Rod – and ladies," the chairman chirped as he sprang out of his seat. "Good of you to come for a look at our latest acquisition. Come inside and try the seats. They are wonderful.

I doubt there'll be many complaints from residents about our purchase."

A car parked beside the bus as the chairman was speaking. The salesman became a ball of business and began retrieving various bits of paper he had scattered on one of the seats.

"My ride back to work has arrived. So all that is left to do is to sign a couple of documents, and the bus is all yours."

With his face almost split in two by a smile from ear to ear, the salesman marched down the bus and shoved the relevant documents and a pen at the chairman. The necessary signatures secured, the salesman waved to us as he exited the bus and climbed into the waiting car.

"So, what do you think?" The chairman asked. "Not too bad, eh?" he added as he gestured across the interior.

Cilla sniffed audibly and then cleared her throat. "Hmm, I rather suspect that will depend on what happens next," she said sharply.

"Well, the next thing is for it to start being used by the residents. Surely, you can't have a problem with that."

"No. As you say, I don't have a problem with the bus being pressed into service. I just wondered what that service might look like. What it might include and how soon it might begin. As manager, I assume you have drawn up plans," Cilla said, directing her last comment to Tanya.

"Well… Err, actually…." Tanya spluttered as she pinned the chairman with a hard look.

"Yes, well, that's something we were keen to discuss with you, Rod. But, as the three of you are here now, if you have the time, perhaps we might go to Tanya's office to discuss this bus's future use." The chairman fixed Rod with his best version of an encouraging smile before flashing the same at Cilla and me.

Tanya did not appear thrilled by his suggestion, but heaved herself off her seat and started for the door.

"If you will excuse me, I'll go and organise coffee in my office for all of us… unless anyone has to go and can't stay for it."

She looked hopeful as she looked at the three of us. We all indicated that we would be staying for coffee. She didn't look overly thrilled by that, either. Nevertheless, when the four of us strolled into her office to join her a few minutes later, extra chairs were there. Coffees and a plate of plain biscuits arrived soon after.

Before we had taken our first sip, Rod made something of a show of checking his watch. It did not go unnoticed by the chairman.

"Right. Yes, let's not waste time," the chairman began. "I'm sure we all have other things planned for today. Your arrival to check out the new bus was fortuitous. It saved me the trouble of calling Rod to organise a suitable meeting to discuss the development of what might be termed a 'social program' for residents."

"As we already have what amounts to a solid social program here at Merivale, in this instance, should we interpret 'social program' as meaning 'bus usage schedule'?" Cilla demanded.

"Well, yes, if you want to think of it that way. I'm sure just about everybody will have ideas about how the bus might be used to benefit them and their fellow residents.

Rod, as you seem to have your finger on the Village's pulse, you might already know residents' thoughts on this. It goes without saying that you and your group are better placed to collect and collate such opinions than either Tanya and her staff or me." The chairman paused briefly to beam at us again before continuing with what we knew was coming.

"What is important in drawing up any plan for the operation of the bus is that residents feel they have been consulted and had an opportunity for input. Now, how that occurs is entirely up to you," he said, fixing Rod with a hard look, "but that Facebook thing you have going might be an ideal way to glean residents' thoughts on the subject. The only thing that I and my board see as important is that the bus usage is as wide and varied as possible.

The only other thought I might offer is that the bus needs to be used as soon as possible. I know I don't need to explain that to you. Having even a draft plan as quickly as possible would be most welcome. I leave how you go about it up to you, but do you have any questions?"

While I was too stunned to think, let alone speak, Rod did ask a couple of basic questions, which I'm sure didn't need to be asked, but he appeared determined to go through the process. Having answered Rod's questions, the chairman virtually dismissed us.

"Well, if there is nothing else, I won't take up any more of your morning. So, thank you for your time, and if you have any questions or problems, please feel free to talk to Tanya."

While we weren't exactly thrown out of Tanya's office, we certainly weren't encouraged to linger and were soon on our way to Rod's place for another coffee – or something stronger – while we considered our position.

"Bloody cheek…!" Cilla exclaimed as soon we were settled in Rod's lounge room. "Not a *by your leave* or anything else, just an expectation that we would take on the job of organising his bloody bus."

"We knew it was coming," Rod said quietly. "So I don't suppose we should be too outraged by it. If nothing else, the chairman was correct when he said every resident of this Village would expect to be given a say in how the thing might be used. And, as he suggested, our Facebook page probably is the best way to gather residents' thoughts."

As he finished speaking, Rod clambered out of his chair and went to his desk. On his way back to his chair, he gave a notebook and pen to Cilla and me.

"Okay, ladies, how will we use this new chariot the Village has been blessed with? Ideas, no matter how left-field they might appear, are required forthwith, so share your thoughts, please."

"The only things I can think of are those we mentioned in our earlier discussions about the bus: trips to the shopping centres and travel associated with the interclub bowls competitions," I volunteered.

"What about social outings?" Cilla asked. "You know what I mean, trips to the beach or a museum. Those sorts of occasional excursions."

"All those things have to be built into this schedule we're supposed to be developing, but we need to incorporate more information," Rod said as he scribbled a note before continuing.

"If we ask residents for their input, I'm sure all those things will be mentioned… And we will end up no further advanced. I believe we need a draft schedule before we canvass residents' opinions. That way, we would be two steps ahead, but our program would require only minor adjustments and additions in line with the feedback we receive."

"Yeah, it would be good to have a plan before we seek input," Cilla agreed. "It might make it possible to direct residents' thinking in a more structured way."

"I'm not sure what you're suggesting, Cilla," I said. "Are you suggesting that instead of asking what might be included, we should post a draft schedule and ask them to comment on it?"

"No-o, not at all, but it's not a bad approach," Cilla conceded.

"Right; in the interest of moving forward, let's work with what we have to create a draft," Rod suggested. "Let's start with trips to the shopping centres. Which shopping centres, how often and on which days?"

My stomach rumbled. My watch confirmed it was lunchtime.

"Rod, it's gone noon. Should we do something about lunch and leave the schedule until after we've eaten?" I asked.

While Rod and I put together a salad using whatever was in his fridge, Cilla dashed across the road to grab some cold chicken from her fridge to put with the bit of ham Rod had. It was a pleasant lunch. The temptation was to dawdle over it, but Rod kept the clock on us and made sure we didn't. Soon after one o'clock, armed with our notebooks and pens, we adjourned to Rod's back deck. Then, discussions began in earnest.

My tiny mind was foolish enough to think that coming up with days and times when the bus might take people to various places would be a fairly simple exercise. It wasn't. Deciding how often, on what days, and to which shopping centres, generated enough discussion to occupy us for the best part of two hours. Although we agreed almost from the outset that two trips to shopping centres should be scheduled each week, how to achieve that and on which days was a stumbling block.

With two days each week removed from the equation due to the possibility of trips to other bowls clubs, it didn't leave too many other days to play with. Scheduling those extra 'social' excursions was challenging.

Where could we go? How many residents might be interested in those places? How often should they occur? On which days would it be best?

In the end, we took the coward's way out. Instead of detailing such trips in our draft schedule, we left it as a list of suggested places of interest worth visiting. By then, it was late. I only had time to go home, shower, and prepare a plate of nibbles before returning to Rod's place for happy hour.

I figured this evening's happy hour might continue longer than usual. The last thing we agreed on before our 'think tank' broke up this afternoon was to share the news of the new bus's arrival with the rest of the group and seek their comments on our draft plan. I'll be surprised if the discussion it generates doesn't stretch on for a while and possibly becomes a bit tense. The group's reactions didn't disappoint.

It always surprises me how suggesting anything new always meets with an avalanche of negativity. Why does the Village need a bus? Who will ever use it? What's it going to cost to run? … And so the list went on until Rod brought it to an abrupt end.

"Thanks to the board of directors' generosity, the Village now has its own 22-seater bus. After all the whinging that has gone on in recent times about how they never provide anything for the residents, it's probably not in our best interests to complain about the arrival of this proverbial 'gift horse'. The bus has arrived. Its presence here is a reality.

We have two options: sit around being negative and moaning about it, or accept it and consider how to maximise its benefit to the residents. Which do you want to do?"

"There's no need to be cranky about it, Rod," Frank snapped. "While I accept this group didn't need to be consulted about acquiring a bus, I am concerned about what it might mean for us. Your draft plan suggests it will mean more work for our group without much, if any, compensation."

Murmured support for Frank's comments was accompanied by embarrassed shuffling of feet as everyone avoided direct eye contact with Rod. I felt I should step in to help diffuse the situation, but I couldn't think of what to say. Rod let the silence linger on while continuing to regard those around him with an unmistakable look of disdain. And thus, the situation continued for almost a full minute before Maria broke the prevailing icy chill.

"Now that I think about it," she began, "some residents, such as my neighbour, Mrs Withers, will welcome the bus with open arms. Mrs Withers doesn't drive, never has, and depends on taxis or the kindness of other residents if she wants to leave the Village. I know she is quite embarrassed by her reliance on others to take her places. There probably are other residents in similar circumstances or, even if they do drive out of necessity, would prefer to take the bus."

Suddenly, everyone seemed to know of at least one other resident whose situation was similar to that of Mrs Withers. It appeared Cilla and I were the only ones who didn't know anyone. Various residents were mentioned, and their circumstances discussed. Rod let it continue without comment, but I witnessed him becoming more exasperated by the moment. It was a relief when Luigi rescued the situation.

"Yeah, Old Ernie, who lives just up from me, would be a prime example of someone who will make the most of the bus.

He even has his groceries delivered, so the only time he leaves the Village is when he must go into the city, and then he calls for a cab to collect him.

When I've been going to the markets, I've asked him if he would like to come along. He is not interested in the markets as such, but grabs the opportunity for an outing."

"Perhaps, just as an outing, there could be a trip to the marina, and maybe it could include lunching at the sailboat club bistro," Janet suggested. "I know it's not any sort of exotic destination, but it would be nice to wander along the esplanade or just sit and watch the boats coming and going … and the seagulls will always make a fuss of you."

"A new gallery recently opened the valley, and I believe they will put on morning tea for a busload of visitors," Alice told us.

"That's an idea," Ted agreed. "Then, after the gallery, we could continue up the valley to that pub that does a lunchtime special, or go right to the top of the valley and have lunch at the restaurant in the resort there."

"What about the shopping trips?" Cilla asked. "Where should they go, and how often?"

"Shopping trips are likely to become the main use for the bus," Frank mused. "Most people taking the bus into town will do their grocery shopping and visit the large variety stores in the centres. The Christmas and Easter periods are likely to see increased demand for trips to the shopping centres."

"There are two main shopping centres. Which one would the bus go to?" Janet asked. "And what happens if someone wants to go to the other shopping centre?"

"It doesn't matter which one you choose, there is bound to be some who are unhappy because they only shop at the other centre," Maria added.

"Couldn't the bus drop off at both major centres?" Luigi asked. "It could make like a circular trip dropping off at each of the two places and then, later, do the same circular trip again to collect people to return them to the Village."

"How long… I mean, how much time would they have for shopping?" Ted asked. "There are one or two logistical issues to be sorted out before any shopping sprees are implemented.

The bus couldn't leave the Village too early in the morning. Some women will struggle to be ready much before ten o'clock."

"If the bus doesn't leave here until about ten o'clock, that introduces the question of lunch. Do they have time for lunch in town before they are collected and brought back to the Village?" Cilla suggested. "I imagine some of them will want to have lunch at one of the eateries in the shopping centre, while others will want to be home in time for lunch."

"Might we leave the finer details of shopping trips in abeyance for now, please?" Rod asked, exasperation in his voice. "Surely whatever happens in that regard needs to be determined by the residents and isn't something to be imposed by us."

"Yes, but how do we find out what they want?" Janet replied. "I'm sure everyone you ask will have a different idea. Then what do we do?"

"Thanks to our wonderful Village Facebook page, we have the perfect tool for gathering the residents' ideas. That's what we will use," Rod growled. "To receive the input we want, we do need to ask the right questions, and in a way that doesn't allow them much leeway to be too creative with their replies."

"So, how do we do that? I mean, how do we do it without upsetting everyone?" Janet asked.

"We post a rough outline of possible bus trips and excursions on our Facebook page, along with a list of possible responses for them to choose for each item.

For example, under the heading of 'shopping trips', we would list possible multiple-answer questions. Respondents would select the answer that best suited them individually," Rod explained.

"What sort of questions? I'm sorry, Rod. I don't mean to be difficult, but I can't see this working out well at all, and we will be no wiser at the end of it." Janet was shaking her head as she spoke. Murmurs from a couple of the others suggested they shared her view.

Rod audibly inhaled a deep breath before heaving a sigh of resignation. "I know this is a lot to take in without time to consider it beforehand, but can we just think about a draft list of uses for the bus? If we can agree that much, I will devise a list of suggested questions to accompany it and bring it back to you for refinement."

"If you want to do it that way, Rod, that's fine. But I'd be happy for you just to go ahead and post a draft list of bus outings and the relevant questions we need answered. We can always do another post later if we think of anything else we need to ask the residents," Frank suggested.

A supporting chorus of 'yeah' went up from those around Frank. Rod thanked them and said he would produce something for Facebook tomorrow. The others must have felt as wrung out as I did. Within several moments, they had either left or were on their way to the door. This evening's happy (?) hour had come to an end.

As usual, Cilla and I remained behind to clean up and help Rod return his back deck to its usual order. When Rod joined us after seeing the last of the group on their way, Cilla exploded.

"Bloody hell! They don't get any better, do they? I expected some uncertainty, even the usual slight resistance to something new, but they outdid themselves tonight."

"It was all too much for them to take on board, and they didn't hide the fact they did not want to discuss it further. In the end, all they wanted to do was escape before they were asked to contribute further to drawing up a workable schedule," I exploded before continuing.

"As it appears you've received all the help you're going to get from the others, Rod, how do you plan to tackle this?" I asked.

"Ah, no, Marion. The question is, how do WE tackle this situation? Unless you both have something else scheduled for tomorrow, please come at ten o'clock tomorrow morning for coffee and a couple of hours of hard slog as we try to pull something together for the Facebook page."

Neither Cilla nor I could honestly claim a prior engagement. After our rants about the attitude of the rest of the group, there was nothing for it other than to accept Rod's invitation.

Chapter 12

We dutifully gathered at Rod's place at ten o'clock as requested. This morning's coffee was a subdued affair, with convivial conversation in short supply. I didn't know about Cilla, but all my last night's thoughts about a bus schedule hadn't produced much to offer this morning. I guessed none of us looked forward to the hard slog ahead. But Rod is a hard taskmaster and kicked off our think-tank before we finished our coffee.

"Right; at the risk of being howled down, did anyone come up with anything creative after last night's happy hour?" Rod asked in a brisk, expectant tone.

Both Cilla and I gave him a you-must-be-kidding look but remained silent.

"As I thought…." He gave us a disappointed look. Then continued in a more business-like manner. "Okay, let's start with the shopping expeditions. Any thoughts at all? Anything will do. Just throw it out there for us to think about."

After hesitating, I took a deep breath and dived in. "I must admit I saw some merit in Luigi's suggestion that the bus could make a circular trip to drop off at both major shopping centres. What the bus driver might do to fill in time between dropping off passengers and collecting them again remains a mystery to me."

"Maybe his shopping…. I suppose he can do anything he wants to – except go to the pub. Come to think about it, the lunchtime thing at a shopping centre could end up being a group affair," Cilla suggested. "And that's good, but I don't know what we do about those who insist they want to have lunch back here in the Village."

"We're never going to please everyone. Some residents will have to accept the reality of the situation and learn to live with it – or do without." Rod appeared to consider his comment for a moment before continuing. "I think we will need firm arrangements in place once we sort things out, and we will need to stick to them rather than try to accommodate every request for exceptions.

Now, what about which days to allocate to shopping trips?"

"Well, I did give that some thought last night," I said tentatively. "Tuesdays and Thursdays seemed 'safe' days."

"The bowlers will want their say on this one," Cilla said.

"Yes, I thought about that too," I replied. "The men don't play bowls on Tuesdays, but like the rest of us, they still might need to do some shopping occasionally. The men bowlers could shop on Tuesdays without mucking up their bowls routine."

"A similar situation would exist for the women bowlers if the second shopping days were Thursdays," Rod added.

Without much more discussion, it was agreed shopping days would be Tuesdays and Thursdays each week. Deciding the timing of such trips took a little longer. Before we even looked at the timings, the problem was pick-up points for intending passengers. The one thing we agreed was that there would be no collecting passengers from their front doors. Passengers would only be collected from designated bus stops.

"Right… How many bus stops will there be, and where will they be located?" Cilla asked. "I agree we can't have the bus driving all over the Village to collect intending passengers, but there will need to be a number of strategically located bus stops. There are any number of residents who use mobility aids of some sort. We can't expect them to go too far from home to reach a bus stop."

"No, you're right," Rod agreed. "We need a clearly defined bus route through the Village with many pick-up points along the way. Maybe this is something the men of our mahjong group might work on while the group's women consider the requirements from a woman's perspective."

"What about in wet weather?" I demanded. "We can't expect women to wait out on the footpath for the bus when it is bucketing down."

"Good point, Marion," Rod agreed. "This sounds like it calls for a number of discrete bus stop shelters along the bus route to keep people dry during wet weather and out of the sun on other days."

"Yeah, I agree, but who pays for and erects them?" Cilla demanded. "I don't think any of us feel inclined to take on another fundraising project yet."

"Sounds like you might be having another chat with our esteemed board chairman, Rod," I suggested. "Surely it is the board's responsibility to ensure its residents are dry and safe while using its new bus."

"Another good point, but one best left until after a bus route is mapped out and agreed," Rod said. "Now, back to the possible timing of these shopping trips, what are your thoughts?"

"I like to be there almost as soon as the shops open their doors, but I know most of the residents don't find first gear in the morning until much later," Cilla replied. "All that aside, if we aim to drop passengers at the first shopping centre by ten o'clock, they should have plenty of time for shopping… and lunch if they want."

"That would mean those going to the other shopping centre wouldn't be dropped off until at least 15 minutes later. Is that likely to cause a problem?" I asked.

"It shouldn't," Rod said. "But I suppose, if we wanted to avoid the second batch feeling short-changed, we might have to consider collecting shoppers in the same order as they were dropped off."

"And they would need to be back in the Village by not much after one o'clock," Cilla added.

"Why so specific about the time they return?" I asked.

"Most of them have a nap in the afternoon. They will want to be home by their usual nap time. If they are not back by then, they'll be falling asleep on the way home."

"Okay. From ten o'clock to one o'clock allows three hours for shopping and lunch. Is that long enough, too long, or just about right?" Rod queried.

Cilla was losing patience with this scheduling lark, and her tone when she next spoke made that clear.

"Well, if the bus is going to run twice a week for shoppers, it's not like they have to do a month's shopping every time they leave the place. They could stagger their shopping. Buy groceries one day and do other shopping on their next trip to town. After all, the next trip would be only a couple of days later," she snapped.

"Wouldn't our best approach be to suggest times on our Facebook page and see what the residents think?" I suggested.

At last, we could move on from shopping trips … and onto the equally thorny problem of 'outings'. There was no question about it. The bus had to be used for other events besides shopping trips. Again, the main discussion point was which days would likely be most suitable for residents, while also ideal for various venues.

In the end, we agreed we would suggest a list of possible destinations to consider for either Mondays or Fridays. All three of us appeared keen not to have the bus scheduled for anything on weekends other than in exceptional circumstances.

As a last comment on excursions, Rod brought up something we hadn't considered.

"Of course, once the current interclub bowls competitions are over, those days currently reserved for the competition would become available for other outings – if residents felt so inclined."

"Have we overlooked one small matter?" Cilla asked a bit cheekily. "Who is supposed to drive this bus? And are they available on the days we have suggested?"

"Oh hell, I hadn't thought about that," I yelped. "It sounds like something else Rod needs to discuss with the chairman before we go any further."

"Ah, well, no. I intend to do only as much as I was asked: to put something up on the Village's Facebook page to gather residents' thoughts on how the bus might be used. And, Ladies, that is what I will spend the afternoon trying to do."

"Will you at least float it past our happy hour group tonight before you post it to our page?" Cilla suggested.

"Hmm… It probably would help avoid creating a wee bit of tension within our ranks. I'll think about it between now and six o'clock this evening."

Tonight's happy hour was a lot of things, but it wasn't dull. Rod had spent the afternoon working on a draft bus schedule and questionnaire he intended to post on the Village's Facebook page. In line with our discussions this morning, he handed out copies of the material to the happy hour group.

Stunned silence was the first reaction, quickly followed by an avalanche of questions and negativity. Everyone saw something they found unpalatable, and everyone found at least one aspect of the questionnaire to criticise. So much of it was rubbish, resulting from no one having read the document carefully enough to understand it. They all adopted the same approach: *one passing glance before throwing their arms up in horror.*

Rod was fast running out of patience, partly due to the group's response but also because he was a bit strung out after working on the documents all afternoon. Cilla read the same warning signs as I did, but she acted immediately.

"Right, you lot, have any of you actually read the bits of paper you were given? If I asked questions now, how many of you feel confident you could tell me – accurately –what's in those documents? Come on, hands up… Nobody…? So why are you all carrying on like pork chops about something you haven't read?

Well… Now we are going to work through it line-by-line."

And that's what happened after Cilla handed over to Rod to lead us through it. Some questions were forthcoming along the way, but they produced positive outcomes. At last, the assessment of the material was complete, and silence reigned for a few moments before Janet's tiny voice asked a vital last question.

"You've put a lot of work into producing this, Rod, but there is another question. I know it's not something that needs to be in this paperwork, but I am curious about it."

Rod encouraged Janet to 'spit it out so we can deal with it', and she continued.

"I know the bus is now a reality, and your pages outline the proposed way the residents will utilise it, but who will drive the bus? Does the manager propose to hire a driver, or what other arrangement is in place?"

"Good question, Janet," Cilla stepped in to answer and take some of the heat off Rod. "To date, we are unaware of the arrangements for a bus driver. It is one of a couple of issues Rod will discuss with the chairman in the near future.

In the meantime, we have been tasked only with ascertaining the residents' opinions regarding the bus's potential usage."

"As a first step in this process," Rod interrupted, "I will post this schedule and questionnaire on our Facebook page later tonight to start gathering residents' thoughts on the matter."

Further moments of silence followed before being broken by Luigi loudly clearing his throat.

"Ahem… reluctant as I am to suggest this, I will mention it here tonight." He paused and looked around the group to assess their reaction before continuing. "In the interest of allowing residents to start using the bus, I hold a permit to drive a 22-seater bus."

"You're a builder. Why would you need a licence to drive a bus?" Maria asked.

"Many of our jobs were located some way out of town, so I leased a bus and drove my work team to the building site each day. I've continued to renew the licence whenever it comes due."

"Okay… I also need to own up," Frank said sheepishly. "I've held a bus driver's ticket for years. I used to do a lot of volunteer work with a junior sports club. The rep team often had to play at other centres, so I became the bus driver."

"Well, I might as well come clean," Cilla added. "I also can drive the bloody bus if we need a driver."

In the space of the next few seconds, both Ted and Rod admitted they held permits to drive the bus.

"We might keep all those confessions within these walls for now," Rod suggested with a knowing wink. "Let's see what the board plans to do before we consider any drastic action like driving the bus ourselves."

His suggestion met with unanimous support, and happy hour ended on a positive note.

Earlier than usual, I strode out for my walk with renewed vigour this morning. It probably was due to leftover positive vibes from the end of last night's happy hour. Somehow, I felt more enthusiastic about what the new bus might bring to the residents of Merivale Village.

It was one of those glorious mornings, pleasantly cool, with no breeze to speak of and a beautiful clear sky. The birds were in full voice as I strode through the park. Luigi and Frank, on their way to the community gardens, shouted a cheery 'good morning'.

What a wonderful start to the day, I thought as I turned the corner and headed along my street towards home. I shouted good morning to Mavis as I strode past her house at a slightly stepped-up pace so she wasn't tempted to delay me for a long chat. But that's when the first cloud darkened my day.

Cilla's place was up ahead, opposite Rod's house. No one was outside at either her house or Rod's. But a strange car parked on Cilla's driveway caught and held my attention. It wasn't there after happy hour last night, so Cilla must have an early morning visitor. Odd to have someone drop by at breakfast time, I thought as I strode along.

"I… know… that vehicle," I murmured. "I'm sure it's familiar somehow. Oh, Christ, I think that's Richard's car."

The recognition caused my pulse to step up a notch or two. Why would Richard Wilson, the district's top cop, visit Cilla so early today? Despite initially being just curious about it, reality soon dawned on me.

"His visit probably is to deliver an update on the body in the paddock," I murmured to the universe as my gut became a squirming mass.

It could only mean bad news. If there were good news to share, he most likely would have phoned to share it with Cilla rather than dropping by at such an inconvenient hour. Suddenly, I felt exposed and vulnerable out on the street. I quickened my pace to just short of breaking into a jog.

After a shower, I was back at the kitchen window to keep watch on what was happening at Cilla's place. In reality, nothing happened for about half an hour. Then Cilla walked someone, who I thought looked like Richard, out to the car on the driveway and stood there talking to him through the car's window. After what seemed like an interminably long conversation, the vehicle finally drove off, and Cilla disappeared back inside.

"Now what?" I asked the universe. "How do I find out what that was all about?"

My curiosity was at a self-destructive level, but short of thumping on Cilla's door and demanding to know, I couldn't think of any *acceptable* way of finding out about Richard's visit. My only alternative in the meantime was to try persuading myself that, had Richard delivered an update on their body in the paddock investigation, Cilla would share it with Rod and me… particularly if it were bad news from our perspective.

The agony dragged on until just after nine o'clock when Cilla called to invite me to join her and Rod for morning coffee. Although there was barely enough time, I made a quick batch of scones to help pass the time until ten o'clock.

Armed with a basket containing scones and pots of jam and whipped cream, I marched to Cilla's place. I reached her driveway as Rod crossed the road, so I waited to go in with him.

"Any idea what this is about?" I whispered before we stepped up onto the driveway.

"Not really, but I think Richard Wilson was here earlier. I imagine it probably is about that body."

Rod's comment did nothing to quieten the troupe of tap-dancing hippos in my chest. If my pulse kept hammering away as it was, I wondered if it might damage a rib. Even if it didn't, it can't be good for it to persist for too long. But we had reached Cilla's front door, and she was ushering us in. I handed over my basket and dutifully followed Rod through to sit, fidgeting, in her lounge room while waiting for Cilla to deliver her bad news.

Once we were set up with coffee and scones, Cilla enlightened us about our invitation to coffee. I mentally congratulated my gut for being right on the mark again. Of course, she didn't have any good news to share. Although I expected it to be bad, I wasn't prepared for what we were told.

"Richard Wilson paid me a visit this morning," she began. "He came to update me on their investigation into the body we found in the neighbouring paddock. I suppose it's fair to say most of the investigation is occurring at other places a long way south of here, but it doesn't mean we are not involved."

"Is this your way or working up to the bad news, Cilla, or does it suggest there is nothing for us to be concerned about?" I demanded. Her waffling on about nothing was starting to wear thin.

"No. Unfortunately, we do need to be concerned. Richard's crew have detected something of an influx of 'undesirables' over the last few days. While they have identified only about six so far, he is not sure that's all who have arrived and whether more might be on their way here too."

"By 'undesirables', I assume you mean people who might somehow be associated with the demise of the bloke in the paddock," Rod suggested.

"Yeah… All those identified in town are well-known to the police, both here and south of the border. Some, if not all, are known members of an OMC (Outlaw Motorcycle Club). As yet, they haven't given any indication of why they are here or what they might be planning. It goes without saying, I suppose, that Richard was concerned the undesirables might see us as loose ends to be tidied up."

"Even if we weren't involved and don't know anything other than we found the body?" I asked.

I struggled to see how anyone could consider us a threat. A threat of what? We arrived late in the story. The bloke was already dead for some time before we became involved. And what did we know anyway? None of us had ever laid eyes on him before. I didn't know his name or anything about him, and I was pretty sure Rod didn't either. I managed to convey those sentiments to Cilla in a fairly indignant tone. Rod sat silent throughout my outburst but nodded at appropriate points.

"While I know it's difficult to understand, it all comes down to how this mob operates. Their body count to date is quite impressive, and it is believed many of those bodies were in no way involved in whatever was going on. It is just their way of ensuring there is not even one possible loose end that might prove troublesome. That's how they have managed to stay ahead of the game – ahead of the police – for so long."

"So, exactly what does all this latest update mean for us? What should we do… or not do?" Rod asked.

"This will sound inadequate and almost like a fob-off, but it is not meant to be. We need to be extremely vigilant until this situation is wrapped up, or until we receive an indication it is safe to resume 'normal activities'. Stick with crowds. Don't go anywhere alone or with just one other. Anything out of the ordinary – no matter how insignificant or innocuous it might seem – needs to be reported.

I've told Richard I will liaise directly with him to avoid information not getting through to the right people in time. So, anything you notice, or think you saw, needs to be relayed to me immediately."

A sudden thought cut across Cilla's dialogue and blanked her out for a moment. I wondered: Was this a good time – an appropriate time – to mention something I should have mentioned previously? The little voice in my head shrieked in horror as that idea passed by. It counselled that saying nothing was the safest option. That little voice advocated that *I know nothing* was the safest position to adopt if I was asked.

"Richard also suggested he might have more information for me in the next day or so. While he didn't expand on what it might be, I suspect they expect to make a breakthrough on some aspect of their investigation. Whether it will be good or bad news from our perspective remains to be seen.

Look, I know this is not the most uplifting way to start the day but, if it helps keep us safe and alive, it's probably worth it," Cilla suggested.

"None of this is exactly comforting news, is it?" Rod mused. "But, I suppose it is better to know than to be kept in the dark."

There were no cheery goodbyes or light-hearted comments as Cilla farewelled us. Even Rod and I didn't exchange words until we reached Rod's gate, and he suggested he should escort me home. I was having none of it. After all, I had to walk past only two houses before I was home.

With my basket held in front of me in a white-knuckle grip, almost as a makeshift shield, I strode home along the footpath.

Chapter 13

After a tense day of keeping watch on the street from my kitchen or bedroom windows, I found myself at a loose end after dinner this evening. As most of our group had other commitments, there was no happy hour tonight. I called Rod and suggested Cilla and I join him for a drink anyway, but he was adamant we should stay home. Although it was only a short walk to Rod's place for both of us, Rod insisted our current situation demanded we stay safe indoors, especially at night.

Disappointed and with nothing better to do, I settled in for an evening in front of TV. After sampling a succession of boring shows, I dozed off in my lounge chair. I might have remained there until sunrise, if a car cruising our street a little after midnight hadn't woken me. Of course, it could be a Village resident, one of our group even, returning after attending a show or some other event this evening … or so I tried telling myself.

While it sounded plausible, my gut wasn't buying my reasoning. It insisted I switch off the lamp next to my chair, the only light on in my house. Obediently, I reached out and switched it off and suddenly felt quite vulnerable in the impenetrable darkness surrounding me.

My pulse rate achieved an alarming increase in a matter of seconds. Loud enough to drown out all other sounds, or so I thought, I willed it to settle down and become quiet. But it seems it wasn't as loud as I thought.

As I concentrated on regulating my breathing and relaxing the more rigid parts of my body, there it was again. A car cruised slowly along our street. In an otherwise deathly silent Village, it sounded loud and close. Forget breathing and relaxing, I told myself as I shot up out of my chair… and almost died of fright.

124

At that precise moment, my phone played its tune loud and demanding. I froze mid-stride. Who else would be awake at this hour of the night? Why would anyone be calling me? When your phone rings in the middle of the night, you know instinctively it's bad news.

The little voice in my head took charge. 'Answer the bloody thing,' it demanded. Compelled to obey, I almost dropped the phone while trying to pick it up. Then, I noticed the caller ID.

"Cilla, why are you calling me at this hour? Has something happened? What should I do?"

"Well, you could shut up and listen to me instead of blathering on."

I apologised and managed to slip in one more question. "What has happened?"

"Nothing has happened as such, not yet anyway. I just wanted to alert you to a strange car patrolling our street. It may prove harmless enough, but it pays to be aware and maybe watch to see what it might be up to."

"Might this be a situation that calls for safety-in-numbers?" I suggested. "Would it be better if we were all together in one place?"

"Hmm… mightn't be a bad idea," Cilla conceded after pausing to think about it for a moment before replying. "Rod's place might be best. I'll call him to organise something. I'll get back to you as soon as we work it out."

Apparently, Rod's immediate response was: *No, not at my place.* Cilla admitted later it surprised her, but she approved his alternative proposal.

They would join me at my house. Rod would cross the street to collect Cilla, and then they would walk to my place. In that way, no one would be out alone. Like so many well-laid plans, that's not how it happened.

When recounting the story afterwards, Cilla laughed at Rod's insistence he should escort her to my place. She claimed that, *as an ex-police officer, she probably should have been the one doing the escorting.* Later, Rod quietly told me he hadn't been so worried about Cilla crossing the street alone. His concern was my safety if I walked alone from my house to his.

Cilla was indignant at Rod's suggestion she needed an escort. Before he knew what was happening, Cilla had bounded across the road and knocked on his door. Then, as they were about to leave Rod's house to come to mine, that car cruised along the street again. They decided to wait and time the period between laps to work out when to make a dash for my place. But it wasn't so simple.

The car continued cruising the street, with only a brief time between laps. Rod and Cilla, impatient to be on their way, realised, to their dismay, that the car now only travelled to the end of the street before turning and travelling back along it. Realising they were pinned down at Rod's, they had to find another route to my house. They resurrected one utilised on a couple of previous occasions. My first knowledge of what was happening came via another call from Cilla.

"We're coming to your house. We'll go over Rod's back fence and come along the dirt track before climbing over the fence again into your backyard. Open your backdoor for us. We're leaving now."

"Okay, so there's going to be safety in numbers at my place," I confirmed for the universe as I rushed out onto my back deck.

Pushing one of the chairs from my deck ahead of me, I carried on at top speed to my back fence and positioned the chair against it.

"That should make the descent a bit easier," I murmured as I stood back to briefly assess my handiwork before rushing back to cower inside.

In the stillness of the night, the car's relentless laps of the street seemed to be increasing to an almost deafening level. Perhaps it was just my imagination, but I was sure it had become noisier than earlier. And what was taking Rod and Cilla so long to gallop past two houses along the track before scrambling over my fence? Every few seconds, I checked that no one had leapt over my fence while I wasn't watching.

"What the…? How did that car get around here so quickly? I'm sure I just heard it go past along the street again," I whispered to the universe.

Lights crept along the dirt track behind Merivale's perimeter fence. I was a bit slow on the uptake, but I worked out that those lights belonged to a second car and not the one lapping our street. That second car wasn't speeding, but it wasn't exactly creeping along either.

"Where the hell are Rod and Cilla?" I hissed at the night. "They were supposed to be on that track by now." No enlightenment was forthcoming.

My stomach was now far beyond the squirming mass stage and had formed into a lead ball. I stared at my phone's screen as I clutched it in a white-knuckle grip.

"Come on, tell me what's happening," I hissed as it stubbornly maintained its silent vigil.

A vehicle slid past my back fence, no more than a darker shape in the night. It was average size and running with only its parking lights turned on. Nothing interrupted its progress along the track.

Maybe Rod and Cilla saw it start along the track and had delayed their departure from Rod's place. I tried hard to convince myself that was a feasible explanation but without much success.

A few moments later, urgent sounds emanated from behind my side fence. Then, a figure bobbed up from behind the fence and was quickly joined by a second figure.

In Rod's usual chivalrous style, he hopped over the low fence before offering Cilla a helping hand. She demonstrated she was in no need of such assistance by following him over without his help.

The sounds I'd heard on the other side of the fence had lured me out onto my back deck. By the time people popped up from behind the side fence, I had ventured onto the grass and was standing about halfway between my house and the fence.

Once in my yard, my two guests continued, without hesitation, towards my back deck and my open backdoor beyond it. As they raced past me, they each grabbed one of my arms and dragged me along with them.

"Come on, Marion. Don't hang about out here. Let's all just get inside," Cilla growled at me.

It probably wasn't until we were all back inside that I realised how foolhardy I had been to venture out to investigate the noise emanating from my neighbour's yard. For a brief moment, the three of us stood still and silent in the darkness of my loungeroom, straining our ears to understand what was happening on the street… and wondering what had happened to that other car on the track.

"Whoever they are, they appear to be looking for something somewhere along this street. Whatever it is, it's taking them a long time to find it. I can't think what they might be looking for," Cilla murmured.

"*Us…* that's what they are looking for," I hissed at her. "Why else do you think a strange car – no doubt with ill intent – would be prowling our street? And now they've called in reinforcements.

What are we going to do? We don't know how many people are in those two cars, but they are bound to find us soon. Then what happens? Cilla, shouldn't you alert Richard Wilson about our precarious situation?"

"And tell him what?" she demanded. "And no, I don't think they are looking for us. Ours is a short street of about fifteen houses, with our three homes clustered towards this end of it. It wouldn't be hard to work out from which end to start rousing the residents from their beds until they found us.

No. I suspect they are looking for a particular thing… probably one specific house they have now determined is somewhere along this street."

"Yeah, that fits their behaviour pattern so far," Rod agreed. "Initially, they drove around the Village for a while to familiarise themselves with the place. Then, having decided what they were looking for was located in this street, they narrowed their search to here."

"Hmm … Hmm … Yeah, maybe…." Cilla mused. She appeared to be thinking aloud. But she provided no clues about what was on her mind other than tonight's influx of strange cars prowling the Village.

"What, Cilla? What are you thinking?" I demanded in frustration.

"We-ell… it might be a bit of a longshot, but has anything changed in this street lately… possibly while I was still away in Sydney?"

Although I was invisible in the darkness, I shook my head vigorously in reply. Rod started to say something and then stopped.

"Spit it out, Rod. What were you going to say?" Cilla encouraged him.

"I was about to say nothing has changed here for ages, or at least not for some months anyway. Then I remembered that's not quite right. There was a change of occupants in the last house on this side of the street. The one on the corner where you turn to go to the nursing facility."

"Yes, I know the house you mean, but what about it?"

"It probably has no relevance, but a month or so ago, a new couple moved into that house after the old bloke who had been living there moved out. Mick, I think was his name. He lived there alone after his wife passed away about eighteen months ago. Anyway, everything had become too much for him, so he moved to a care facility down south somewhere close to where his daughter lives."

"As you suggested, that's hardly relevant," Cilla snapped.

"Perhaps not in itself, it's not. But I heard that, about two or three weeks ago, the husband of the new couple left. The story was that he went south to deal with some family matter.

Again, I would agree there's nothing too suspicious about that. But the husband hasn't returned, and something I heard last weekend suggested he would not be returning."

"So, he has abandoned his wife at this late stage of their lives. What a fine, upstanding sort of bloke he must be," I spat at Rod.

"Ah, no, I don't think that's the case. Scuttlebutt has it that the husband passed away while he was gone," Rod added quietly.

"And his wife is still here on her own?" Cilla asked. "Did she even go wherever to take care of his affairs or attend his funeral?"

"Not that I'm aware of.… It's all a bit strange, but I don't know more than that about it. There has been nothing official about it … nothing on our Facebook page … nothing. That's why I can't swear any of it is true."

"Maybe not, but what you heard fits with a scenario I have in mind. What do we know about the missing man's wife? Even a name would be a good place to start."

"Zorka.…" I replied.

"What?" Cilla snapped. "What does Zorka mean?"

"How would I know? But that's her name, the woman who lives in that house. I don't know her surname, but Syd, the chap who delivers the mail, commented on it when I encountered him slipping an envelope into her letterbox."

"First time I think I've ever heard the name Zorka," Rod mused. "Did you get a look at her when the mail was delivered, Marion?"

"She didn't come down to the mailbox to collect it while I was there, but I didn't stop to chat. I was just on my way home from my walk and needed a shower.

I think the woman was home, though. I vaguely recall some sort of movement inside the house … like she might have been watching the mailman put the envelope in her mailbox.

Sorry, but I can't tell you any more than that."

"Perhaps that's enough," Cilla replied. "I think I might give our top cop a call."

I thought I detected something in Cilla's voice, possibly excitement – or triumph. At that same moment, something else occurred to allow Richard Wilson a few extra moments of uninterrupted sleep.

"Listen!" Rod hissed. "That car has gone … or stopped. I can't hear it now."

In my opinion, *gone* was good. *Stopped* was not. Now I really was nervous. And it seemed I might not have been alone in feeling that way. For me, the big question was, if the car remained on our street but had stopped, why had it stopped and where? And more importantly, where were its passengers? Were they still in the vehicle, or were they now roaming the neighbourhood on foot?

A crashing sound suddenly shattered the stillness of the night and caused several screams.

"What was that?" I yelped. "Ow-ah, I don't like the way this is going. Cilla, is Richard sending the cavalry?"

"Shhhh… just shut up and listen. Maybe if we listen, we can work out what's going on," Cilla snarled.

"That's all well and good, but that noise sounded like someone's door being smashed in," I fought back. "How soon before they break down my front door, eh? And then what do we do?"

"Please just listen, Marion," Rod pleaded. "That sound we heard came from some distance away, possibly the other end of the street. Let's stay quiet until we better understand what is happening out there."

Before I had time to settle into full sulk mode, all hell seemed to break loose further along the street. How many doors does a car have? Even allowing that there might have been two cars involved, the number of car doors I heard slammed suggested each vehicle must have had at least ten. It was like the 1812 Overture without the quieter bits.

After a few moments, shouts and screams mingled with slamming and crashing. I stood frozen to the spot in sheer terror. Were we also in line for a dose of whatever was happening out there? No one spoke, so I don't know how the other two sharing my loungeroom felt about the situation.

An ex-police officer, Cilla probably was well-used to such events and taking it all in her stride. I wasn't so sure about Rod.

Although, as a journalist who had worked in many parts of the world in his time, he probably experienced similar occasions.

While I stood there in the dark, paralysed by fear and on the verge of being physically ill, things changed abruptly. Another flurry of slamming car doors heralded the change. Then, following in quick succession, came the sounds of revving an engine, the squeal of brakes, and the roar of a car flying along our street. Moments later, a second car followed it out of the Village, although at a somewhat more sedate pace.

Following the departure of the vehicles, a thick, almost impenetrable silence seemed to blanket the Village. Still, no one in my lounge room spoke. No one moved. It was about a minute later before Cilla shattered the silence.

"Where the hell is the light switch in this room?" she demanded. "The show's over, or so it seems. So let's have some light in here."

On my way to switch on the lounge room lights, I almost suffered a coronary occlusion when Cilla's phone suddenly came to life and played its tune at full volume.

"Richard… How goes it? Everything under control?" I heard her say as she answered it. "Right… Right… well, I'll wait to hear from you when you know more. Any idea of the damage done? No… No, of course, it's too soon to know the full extent… Okay, and thanks."

Listening to Cilla's one-sided conversation with her caller, who I assumed to be Richard Wilson, was frustrating. I wondered how much of that conversation Cilla would elect to share with us. I didn't have long to wait to find out.

"You both may start breathing normally again," she announced soon after her call ended. "Don't know any details yet, but Richard says the recent threat has been neutralised – for the moment anyway."

"What does that mean in real terms instead of police talk," I demanded.

"Eh? What do you need explained? It simply means the police have taken a number of people into custody – no, I don't know who or how many – but they have yet to interview them. So, for now, that's as much as any of us knows.

For us, that means whatever was happening here in the Village is no longer a threat, and we should relax and return to normal. Does that explain it for you?"

Now the lights were on, a simple nod would suffice as a response. But I had a couple of other questions nagging me. So, after actioning Rod's suggestion for 'a drop of something to settle our nerves', I took the first opportunity to ask the first of my questions.

"Would one of you please explain why, when I was expecting you to climb over my back fence, you hopped over my side fence? It's as well the house next door is still empty. I don't know how anyone living there might have reacted to strangers skulking about in their yard."

"In such situations, you have to think on your feet, make quick decisions and change plans," Cilla said airily. "And that's exactly what we did."

Rod cleared his throat. "Ahem… in all fairness, Cilla, that's not exactly how it happened. But the bit about thinking on our feet was right," Rod said with a grin. Then, with a brief pause, he appeared to marshal his thoughts into order before continuing.

"We waited until the car went past and was further along the street before quickly scrambling over my back fence. As soon as we hit the ground on the other side, we heard the car coming back. There was no way its occupants would have seen us go over the fence, but we were being cautious. We crouched behind the fence until the vehicle went past again before we started down the track toward this place.

Everything seemed to go according to plan until we were almost behind your neighbour's house. That's when we saw lights swing onto the far end of the track. The car didn't have its headlights on. They wouldn't have picked us up at that stage, but soon would be able to see us."

"So, you had to devise an alternate plan on the spur of the moment," I interjected.

"Yeah, we realised we had to take evasive action and quickly," he continued with a grin. "So, we just dived back over the fence and landed in whoever's yard was on the other side. As it turned out, it was the yard next to yours."

After Rod finished his story, we sat in silence and drained our glasses of the single malt I had doled out to help return us to normal. I felt as though I had descended into some form of stupor, and probably would have sat there staring into space for goodness knows how long if Cilla hadn't sprung into action.

"Time to make a move," she announced as she hauled herself out of her lounge chair. "You two might be happy to sit up for the rest of the night, but at my age, I need all the beauty sleep I can get. So, I'll bid you both goodnight. I'll let you know as soon as I hear anything from Richard."

Rod followed her to the door, and I soon stood alone behind my securely locked front door. I knew there was nothing for it but to go and fall into bed ... but I also knew I had little likelihood of sleep.

Chapter 14

With virtually no further sleep possible after the strange cars departed the Village last night – or, more correctly, early this morning – I started the day not at my sparkling best. Heeding advice not to go anywhere alone and not feeling brave enough to tempt fate, I was facing a day confined indoors at home.

Rod's call at nine o'clock suggesting he might come to my place for coffee this morning lifted my spirits no end. Nevertheless, the fact that he was inviting himself to my place, rather than the other way round, didn't go unnoticed and niggled me for most of the next hour while I rushed about baking muffins.

Punctual as usual, he knocked on my door at precisely ten o'clock and soon sat at my kitchen bench, chatting with me while I made coffee. It was no surprise that the prime topic of conversation today was last night's events.

"I was surprised at how badly last night left me frayed around the edges," I admitted as we tucked into muffins with our coffee. "It wasn't a surprise when I couldn't sleep afterwards, but I am amazed at how jumpy I remained this morning. Usually, once the sun comes up, the world is a much less frightening place. Sunrise didn't quite do it for me today."

"As you say, it's not surprising. It's to be hoped our top cop has some encouraging news to share with Cilla, and the earlier today, the better."

"I don't know how he could have anything to tell Cilla. The police were conspicuous by their absence when everything was happening last night. Cilla did try to call Richard at one stage, didn't she?"

"Yeah, she spoke to him… or somebody instead of him. And I'm not sure we should discount the police's involvement just yet."

"Well, I didn't see them arrive when things were pretty hairy last night." I was surprised Rod was being so positive about the police's involvement when I hadn't seen anything to indicate they were even in the least bit interested.

"Perhaps we didn't see them come last night when it was all happening, but plenty of them are here this morning. And I saw what I think was Richard's car pull onto Cilla's driveway as I left home to come here. Maybe we will hear some news later today."

Rod's comment sent me scurrying to my kitchen window for a look at Cilla's place.

"It looks as though Richard might be just leaving Cilla's. Perhaps we will receive calls shortly," I suggested.

Moments later, Richard's car drove past, and almost simultaneously, Rod's phone played its tune. I heard him say good morning to Cilla before confirming he was having coffee at my house. I eavesdropped on a brief one-sided conversation before the call ended, and Rod announced Cilla would be along shortly to join us for coffee.

As soon as Cilla arrived at my kitchen bench, Rod asked her a question that surprised me – but appeared perfectly normal to Cilla.

"Any word on what's happened at that end house to have so many coppers beavering away up there?"

"That's what last night was all about, or so it seems," Cilla replied without as much as a sideways glance at Rod. "The thinking is that they had to search for the right house before they could carry out their intended business."

"What?" I yelped. "Are you saying it was the police cruising our street trying to find that house last night?"

"Eh? No. Where did you get that idea from?"

Cilla genuinely looked confused and looked to Rod for clarification. Rod just shrugged and shook his head, and then I saw him have a 'lightbulb' moment.

"No, Marion. Cilla wasn't suggesting it was the police terrorising us last night. She was referring to the bad guys that Richard had warned us about."

Okay, now I do feel stupid. Of course, she wasn't suggesting it was the police acting like hooligans on our street. I tried to think of something intelligent to say that might explain my silly comment and help me regain some dignity. Before I could think of anything, Rod continued speaking.

"It seems we might have been closer to the truth than we realised when Zorka's name came up last night. And it only deepens the mystery… unless you have something, Cilla, that sheds some light on this development."

"Rod, what does Zorka have to do with last night, or the body in the paddock, for that matter?" I asked a touch more tartly than I intended.

Instead of a reply, all that happened was Rod arched his eyebrows at me in surprise while appearing to ponder the question. Cilla saved him from too much mental anguish by growling a reply at me.

"*Everything* is the short answer, Marion. In fact, it seems Zorka could be a key player in the whole affair. And, if you were at all observant, you would have noticed all the police activity this morning is at her house.

According to Richard earlier this morning, there is a strong indication Zorka was forcibly abducted last night. It appears all that crashing and banging we heard in the latter stages of the incident resulted from our unwelcome visitors smashing their way into her home."

"For the life of me, I can't understand the threat an old-aged widow might pose for a gang or murderous criminals," I said in disbelief. Why would they….? I mean, what could she possibly have to do with the body in the paddock? She hardly ventured outside since moving into the Village."

"Well, I admit the police are still to determine the full extent and nature of it, but it appears she had a close connection to the body we found. The police believe it was that of her husband.

Okay, 'husband' is one of those points yet to be confirmed, so let's just stick with 'partner' for now."

"Huh, Rod, it looks as though the scuttlebutt you heard about her husband supposedly passing away was correct," I quipped.

I knew the comment was uncalled for, but it slipped out amidst my state of confusion. No matter how hard I thought about it, I could not comprehend how a little old lady at the end of my street and her husband (or partner) could be mixed up in something so ugly that it would result in his gruesome death and her abduction.

Then another thought with another couple of questions attached slammed in. What was Zorka's part in whatever the gang considered them guilty of? And, following her abduction, what was likely to happen to her?

It didn't take much thought to come up with an answer to the second question. I couldn't go there, so I shut my mind to the only obvious answer and instead indulged in a mental prayer: Please, God, don't let her also end up in the paddock for us to find.

Try as I might, I couldn't summon up a mental image of Zorka. Surely, I must have seen her around the Village at some time, but a scan of my memory banks came up empty. I felt compelled to voice my shortcomings.

"Has either of you seen Zorka around the Village? If I have seen her, I can't picture what she looks like."

"Can't say I've ever seen her," Cilla replied. "But, if they moved in while I was in Sydney, I would have missed seeing her then. If I had encountered her around the Village since my return, I wouldn't have known who she was. So I am unable to put a face to the name now."

"Your chances of running into her somewhere in the Village were remote. I don't think either of them ventured outside the house the whole time they were here. Although, I suppose the partner must have been outside at some point to have ended up dead in the neighbouring paddock," Rod told us.

"Maybe they were playing it safe, and he only ventured out after dark," I suggested.

"What about shopping and stuff?" Cilla demanded. "They couldn't have lived on fresh air and water the entire time they were here. At some point, they would have needed to go out for food at least."

"No, I don't think even the need for food was enough to lure them out of their hermit-like existence. I've noticed a supermarket truck delivering groceries there a few times. I think they must have ordered online and had it delivered," Rod told us.

"How good is your relationship with Tanya Jellicoe?" Cilla asked Rod.

"I'm not sure I have anything resembling a relationship with Merivale Village's manager. Why do you ask?"

"If you say so, but how would you rate your chances of winkling Zorka's surname out of our erstwhile manager?

I have a Zoom session with my Special Tasks group later today. A surname would be useful for that." Cilla confided.

"Well, I can give it a go, I suppose. Don't hold your breath, though. I can't imagine why Tanya might be inclined to be so obliging."

"Didn't Richard give you any clue as to the identity of the body you found?" I asked. "I mean, was he able to give you a name? Surely, even if you only had the bloke's name, that would be enough for your team to establish who Zorka is?"

It all seemed like a fairly straight forward situation to me. I couldn't understand why Cilla would need information about Zorka from Tanya.

"Yes... and no, is the simplest answer to your question, Marion.

Richard thinks the forensic mob down south have narrowed down the body's identity, but there is nothing definite yet. It doesn't surprise me. If it is the bloke I and my team believe it to be, he had a list of aliases as long as a phone directory. Zorka might or might not be a part of one of those. Until we establish beyond doubt the body's identity, it's not wise to assume too much about Zorka."

"Okay… So, it is now up to Rod to see what he can achieve from Tanya. But what about us? What is our situation now? If they came specifically for Zorka and now have her, what does that mean for us? Are we now safe to resume our normal lives?" I wasn't too interested in the others' identities. All I was interested in was whether we could consider ourselves safe now or not.

"Of course not," Cilla snapped. "Nothing has changed for us. Why would you think it had?

Last night's activities were likely only one stage of their plan. They would seek first to eliminate everything they saw as their most serious risks. Then come the 'cleaning up' activities. It's reasonable to think we might be considered a potential loose end, so dealing with us may be relegated to the 'cleaning up' phase."

The world Cilla inhabited for all those years as a member of the police service, and still does to some extent, is very different from the one I know. She doesn't appear rattled by any of what has happened. Her only concerns seem to be keeping us safe and ensuring we understand the implications of our present situation. Although I won't say so, I could assure her I do understand, and it terrified me.

Cilla's visit didn't last much longer. She wanted to be at home in case Richard should call with further information. As she stood up to leave, Rod had a couple of last questions to throw at her.

"Do we know what Zorka's current situation is? I mean, do we know if she was still alive when she left here?"

"Nothing I've heard so far suggests otherwise," Cilla replied.

"Hmm… so what do you think her probable outcome is likely to be?" he asked quietly.

"Argh, she might not end up in that same paddock, but she likely is destined for the same fate. I think it's unlikely to have any other outcome … unless there is a miracle, or Richard's men have a major dose of good luck."

Cilla gave both Rod and me a hard look as she finished speaking. I felt a chill run through me as my mouth swung into action before my brain had time to prevent it.

"You mean, she might already be dead?" I yelped. "Why would they take her away if they were just going to kill her? They could just as easily have killed her here and saved themselves some trouble." I blurted out.

I received something akin to a pitying look from Cilla as she delivered almost a rebuke.

"Think about it. I'm sure you'll be able to work it out," she spat at me.

After she left, Rod showed no signs of needing to be elsewhere. Instead, he suggested another coffee would go down well. So, for the next little while, we sat with our coffees in the heavily depressed ambience of my kitchen. I couldn't work out the exact cause of my depression, but it could have been the thought of what might have happened or was about to happen to Zorka. Or perhaps it was that we remained unable to resume our normal lives.

Maybe it was both those things… or everything associated with the whole rotten body-in-the-paddock incident. A casual thought wandered through my mind: How will I fill in my time and get on with my life if I'm not game to leave home? I sighed and looked over at Rod, who had remained silent since suggesting another coffee.

He sat staring into his empty mug, clutched firmly in both hands. He didn't seem troubled, but it wasn't like Rod to be sitting like that. It got the better of me. I had to break the silence and make sure he was okay.

"Should I comply with the adage and offer you a penny for your thoughts?" I asked in a bid to lighten the atmosphere.

"They probably aren't worth the expense," he laughed. "My main thoughts were about whether or not we should continue with our happy hour each evening. Would anyone be safe walking through the village at night? Then, my mind went off in another direction.

"What did the others in our group make of last night's events? The ones living on and around this street must have been aware of the vehicles tearing around, even if they weren't aware of the possible danger.

They likely dismissed it as hooligans again trying to unsettle the elderly residents. After all, it's not the first time we've had strange cars tearing around the Village.

And, as the others weren't involved with finding the body and are removed from the implications now associated with that, they won't be feeling the same degree of stress and insecurity as we are."

"True…. So, Marion, what are your thoughts about our happy hours? Should they continue or not?"

"Dunno… that's probably something you should have asked Cilla while she was here. I'm sure she would have definite ideas about it."

My last comment probably was uncalled for, but it was out before I could stop it, and it proved enough to plunge the room into silence again. In line with the old saying that 'you can only be hanged once', and as I had already aired my negativity, I decided to push-on in the same vein. I wasn't enjoying sitting in silence anyway.

"Rod, what are your thoughts on the explanation of last night's events we were given?" He looked mystified by my question, so I rephrased it. "I mean, what does your journalist's nose tell you about what happened to Zorka?"

"Funny you should ask that," he said, glancing sideways at me. "My nose is twitching violently at the moment… Must be something I heard that's causing it.

Why do you ask? What are your thoughts on what we've been told?"

"I'm still struggling to sort it out in my mind, but here goes. I guess, for me, the question is whether the explanation Cilla gave is a true picture of what happened. That's not to suggest I'm wondering if Cilla has taken up creative storytelling as a hobby. But I can't help feeling the line we were fed this morning might have been concocted between Cilla and her friend, Richard. Somehow, it just doesn't ring true for me."

"Ri-ight… What is it about the story that you are finding hard to swallow? I'm not being negative or trying to put you under pressure in any way. I'm just interested in hearing your 'take' on it."

"Let's go back to basics. Zorka is an old lady who has been living alone here in the village since her partner died. Although none of us can claim to have seen her, it stands to reason that Zorka is elderly. You have to be elderly to move into the Village. If you don't meet the minimum age requirement, you can't move in.

Before you argue, yes, I know it's possible Zorka's partner met the age requirement. So, although Zorka might not, the couple were still eligible to live here. Regardless, as we know the situation – or think we know it – for the last little while, Zorka had been living alone."

"While I don't disagree with your reasoning so far, I'm waiting to hear the rest of your thoughts."

"In my mind, how the events played out doesn't fit what we have agreed so far. For me, the real problem lies in the way the abduction supposedly was carried out."

Rod nodded and gave me a 'give me more' gesture to continue with my explanation.

"Well, up to a certain point, I can accept that the first vehicle that arrived had to search for Zorka's house and that involved tearing around the Village like hooligans. But, after focussing their attention on our street for a while, how did they identify which was Zorka's house?"

As Rod hadn't argued against or criticised anything I had suggested to that point, I was encouraged to air more of my thoughts.

"While we don't know how many people were in that first car, I think there would have been the driver and his offsider. So, two people… more than enough I would have thought to overpower a little old lady."

"Yeah, I agree there probably were two people in that vehicle, and two determined people should have been enough to carry out the job. What else do you have to offer?"

"Okay… this is the bit I find really confusing. Why did the first car need backup assistance from whoever was in the second vehicle? And why did the second vehicle arrive via the outside dirt track instead of driving up our street straight to Zorka's house, where the other vehicle was already waiting?"

"Good questions, Marion. Do you have any answers to go with them?"

Rod's tone and demeanour told me he wasn't rubbishing my thinking. He looked genuinely interested in my comments. But, as for answers, I didn't have any yet – just more speculation.

"Argh; I have lots of *what-if* scenarios rattling around in my mind, but none leads anywhere logical."

He encouraged me to talk them through, so I did. I was surprised how some of them started to take on credibility.

"Why would a couple of presumably skilled practitioners require assistance to carry out what amounted to a routine operation for them? Did they forget to bring their sledgehammer and need someone to fetch one for them? Then, there is a totally different possibility.

What if the occupants of the second vehicle weren't reinforcements to assist with the abduction of Zorka but were racing to her assistance to prevent it?"

"Oh, you do ask the most interesting questions. And, in my opinion, you have effectively refuted the story we were given about last night's events. I find it fascinating how alike our thinking is on this matter.

And you are right, but not only is my journalist's nose twitching, it's also detecting a strange and unpleasant odour about the whole incident. The only difference is, unlike you, I'm not so sure the story we were given this morning wasn't a concoction created by Richard and Cilla. I doubt it was something Richard fed to Cilla to pass on to us to keep us quiet.

Cilla is no fool and would have seen through such a ploy. But she might have gone along with it had she been directly involved in developing the story."

"Well, we haven't progressed very far, have we? I mean, we don't really know more than when we got out of bed this morning – not real facts, anyway. What do we do about that state of affairs? And what about the original question: do we continue with our regular happy hour ritual, or do we cancel them until we know it's safe again?"

"Safety is my prime concern," he admitted, "particularly as happy hours involve some people walking alone through the Village to participate and then return home. I'm not keen on that, particularly as you would be one of them.

It's why Cilla and I ended up here last night instead of everyone congregating at my place. I did not want you walking alone along the street to my house. Given what supposedly happened last night, will it be any safer now for people to be out and about on their own at night? And I guess that leaves your original question about continuing with happy hours still up in the air."

Rod admitted he didn't have any answers or any new thinking to offer. He said he would go home and talk to a few 'friends' to see if that might give rise to some positive thoughts. I knew the 'friends' referred to were journos and other people in positions where they 'know things' that the rest of the public might not. By 'talking to friends', he was referring to mounting an information-gathering quest.

As for happy hours, he thought he might be too busy with other matters to host them for a while.

My mind wandered to what I had in the fridge. It was almost lunchtime. Good manners dictated I should invite Rod to stay for lunch. But what to feed him? My fridge was a bit light on for cold cuts, although I could manage a salad. Then, a powerful thought blasted in to obliterate further thought about lunch.

"Please don't take this the wrong way, Rod, but should you still be sitting here talking to me? Wasn't Cilla hoping you would winkle Zorka's surname out of Tanya Jellicoe before she held her Zoom meeting with her team? I half expect that at any moment, Cilla will demand to know why you're still sitting in my kitchen."

"Jesus, I'd forgotten about that. I don't hold much hope of success anyway, but I shall be off to see what I can do."

As I walked him to the door, I had one last question. "Do you really believe Cilla, and probably also Richard, have no idea who Zorka is or what her surname might be?"

He gave me a sly grin and dropped me a mock salute as he stepped outside and headed for the footpath. I wasn't sure whether he was going home for lunch or to the admin building to interrupt Tanya Jellicoe's lunch.

Chapter 15

As Rod shut my gate behind him, Charlie, the head groundsman-cum-handyman in his work buggy, came around the corner and onto our street. A large sheet of plywood protruding from the back of the truck caught our attention. Rod dashed out and flagged him down. Sensing an interesting conversation was about to occur, I rushed out to join them.

Charlie was in no hurry to be wherever he was going. He happily climbed out of his truck and stood beside it to talk to Rod – and me when I trotted up to join them.

"What's with the lumber in the back of the truck, Charlie? Are you going into the construction business?" Rod asked by way of opening the conversation.

"Seems like some fun and games went on around here last night, and I now have a few temporary repairs to make," Charlie replied before adding a contemptuous sniff.

"Ah, I see," Rod replied solemn-faced. "Well, I had better let you get on with whatever you have to do."

"No chance of that yet by the look of things. I won't be able to go near the place until the cops leave."

It seemed like a good opportunity for me to contribute to the conversation.

"What sort of repairs are required? Is there something major, or just a few bits and pieces to tidy up?"

"Not sure exactly what I'll find until I have a look, but I'm supposed to board up the front entrance until a new front door is delivered in a couple of days. Then I'll have to come back to remove the temporary arrangement and fit the new door. There's bound to be other stuff needing attention, but it should only be minor."

"Well, I don't suppose you have to make such repairs every day, so think of it as a new experience. It must have been some party they had at that house if the front door needs replacing," Rod suggested, trying to elicit further information from Charlie.

"Party? There was no party as far as I'm aware. The manager seemed unsure about what had happened when she told me to go and do whatever was necessary to secure the place until a new door could be installed. Whatever it was, I don't think it had anything to do with a party.

Come to think of it, I don't imagine the old lady who lives in that house will be too pleased about having her front door boarded up for a while. Still, I suppose it will be better than having a gaping hole there for a few days."

"Hmm… maybe she will opt to stay somewhere else until the damage is fixed. Anyway, we shouldn't hold you up any longer, Charlie. Good luck talking to the cops about when you might be able to start work there."

As Charlie drove off, Rod and I exchanged looks before Rod asked, "What did you make of all that?"

"A couple of things struck me as odd. It appears nobody told Charlie that the occupant was no longer in residence and wouldn't be in the least inconvenienced by having the front door boarded up. And I gained the impression that maybe Tanya didn't know quite what had happened last night either. Surely, if she knew, she would have enlightened Charlie a bit more."

"Running into Charlie on his way to Zorka's house might prove handy when I talk to Tanya. I can use my interest in what is happening in our street as a way to explore what she does know. That should lead to mention of Zorka, at which point I will claim temporary amnesia regarding Zorka's surname. What do you think?"

"Worth a try, I suppose," I replied, although I didn't feel confident about the likely outcome.

For a moment, I stood and watched Rod stroll down the street to where all the activity was still happening at the end house. After I watched him stop and chat briefly with one of the police officers at the site, I went back inside. Frustrating though it was, I accepted it would be much later before I learned more about that house and its residents.

So, still confined to barracks, so to speak, for the foreseeable future, how to occupy myself exercised my thinking. As much as I tried to avoid it, the one thing that came readily to mind was housework. But, by dawdling over lunch and then falling asleep in front of the TV, I successfully reduced the time available to devote to such drudgery.

Scrubbing the shower and cleaning the bathroom handbasin required no concentration and allowed my mind to roam free. I suppose it was inevitable it would eventually settle on Zorka… and it landed there accompanied by the big question: Was she still alive?

From there, my mind replayed my review of last night's events I had shared earlier with Rod. Nothing new emerged from the murky soup of my thinking on that matter, other than I became even more convinced the story Cilla had given us was nothing more than a load of malarky.

Why? Why had she done that? Was it her idea, or was it something cooked up between Cilla and Richard? And that brought me back to the original question: why would they do that? Or, perhaps the real question should be, what are they covering up? Why would they see the need to fabricate such a flimsy story? Although the questions kept coming thick and fast, answers were nowhere to be found, not by me anyway... or so I thought.

Then, a sliver of inspiration sliced through the fog clouding my mind. My house was almost at the start of our street. While the three of us cowered here last night, the main action took place at the other end of the street. Someone who lived near Zorka's house, perhaps a nextdoor neighbour, would have viewed it from a 'front row seat'. Who did I know well enough along that end of the street to casually drop by for a coffee?

Mavis! Mavis Grimshaw lives next door to the house in question. If I went for a walk past her place now, I suppose it would be too much to expect her to be out in her front yard. She always manages to be there when I'm hurrying home after my walk, but I suspect she won't be there today. Ooh, but I could knock on her door to check if she was okay after what I heard happening at her end of the street. Might be best to check the cops have gone before I wander up there, I told myself as I headed for my front door.

People scrambled into what appeared to be the last police vehicle as I watched from my gate. Charlie's truck was already backed up and stood waiting on Zorka's driveway. As I watched, Charlie hauled the sheet of plywood out of the buggy and carried it to where the front door used to be.

I fortuitously found a couple of weeds to remove from the garden bed inside my front fence, and made a show of dealing with them and not being interested in the police vehicle as it drove past. Right, now the coast is clear, I can stroll along to Mavis's house without looking too obvious about my visit.

As I was about to lace on my walking shoes, a thought slammed in from left field to halt operations. Many Village residents indulge in an après-lunch nap, and it was likely Mavis was one of them. Should I postpone my visit? It was lunchtime. I didn't want Mavis to feel obligated to ask me to stay for lunch. But, if I left my visit until later, she would likely be having a nap.

It presented me with two options: go now and think of a reason why I couldn't stay too long or leave my visit until sometime after three o'clock when she should be up and about again after her nap. Bugger that idea. I'll die of curiosity if I wait until after three o'clock to talk to her.

Decision made; I went back to lacing on my walking shoes. A few minutes later, I set a brisk pace along the footpath towards Mavis Grimshaw's house. It felt great to be out walking again, and it wasn't until I was about to pass Rod's place that it hit me: *As a safety measure, the three of us were not supposed to leave home alone.*

That's a complication, I reminded myself as I slowed my pace to give me time to think. I doubted there would be any risk here on our street, given that the police had just left. But that might not be the case in the rest of the Village.

If I used an appointment with the hairdresser or the gym as an excuse not to stay for lunch if Mavis invited me to, it would mean having to continue to those venues and then hang about there a realistic period before I could head home again. The thought of being so far from home and alone made me nervous.

By the time I reached Mavis's gate, I had resolved not to fabricate an excuse. I would simply say I couldn't stay. Ah, well, we all know what can happen even to the best-laid plans.

Mavis wasn't gardening today, but she had come out to check her letterbox just as I reached her place. And, yes, she was keen for a chat. Come to think of it, I've never known Mavis not eager to chat, but usually about her family members. Taking control of the conversation seemed prudent if I didn't want to be stranded there for too long.

"Hello, Mavis. Did you manage to get much sleep last night?" I chirped as I strode up to her.

"I feel as though I didn't have any sleep at all. I stayed up late watching the tennis on TV, and then, not long after I went to bed, that terrible ruckus broke out next door. Even after things went quiet again, I was so nervous, I wasn't game to close my eyes. I'm looking forward to a long nap this afternoon."

"From down my end of the street, whatever was happening here sounded pretty horrific. I was concerned about whether you were all right, but then I saw the police cars at your neighbour's house and became even more concerned. What on earth went on here last night?"

"You're right. It was frightening. There was so much screaming and shouting, and things being smashed. I wasn't game to sneak a look out my window. I don't know what happened but it was confined to the house next door. I was relieved when I heard the last of the cars leave. The police didn't arrive until after it was all over. I see that groundsman fellow is over there now barricading the entrance. I suppose it's going to require a new door at some point in time. They can't leave it boarded up like that for too long."

"What about the people who live there, Mavis? Do you know them at all?"

"Not really; they didn't seem keen on making friends and spent most of their time indoors. I saw the husband out in the backyard a handful of times. He only nodded at me when I called out hello. I don't think I ever saw either of them out in their front yard except when she checked their mailbox on mail delivery days.

He struck me as being a strange fish. I can't say I got to know her either, but she was a little more friendly than he was."

"Well, I don't imagine they will enjoy living in that house with the front door boarded up like that, even if it is only for a few days. Perhaps they will look at staying somewhere else for a while. Maybe the police will organise some alternate accommodation for them." I knew my suggestion was rubbish, but I hoped it might prompt her to share more about last night with me.

"Marion, I don't know what happened there last night, but I don't think anyone is there this morning. They would have had to move out anyway while the police tramped through the place. I think she was there on her own when it happened.

He just seemed to disappear a couple of weeks ago. Not that I ever saw much of him, you understand, but he hadn't been outside for a while ... and there have been no men's clothes hanging on her clothesline lately."

"It's terrible to think of an elderly woman home alone being attacked by a mob of hooligans. I hope she is all right. Have you seen her at all this morning?"

"No, and I'm trying not to dwell on what might have happened over there. I heard screams, you know, muffled screams. It sounded like they were trying to keep her quiet, to stop her screaming too loudly.

After that, the next thing I heard were car doors being slammed shut. By the sound of it, that vehicle must have had a lot of doors, and they all were slammed twice."

"That poor woman. I have to admit I don't know anything about her, but it is still frightening to think about what might have happened to her. Do you know anything about her at all? I'm pretty sure I've never even heard her name mentioned."

"We had a brief conversation one day when I was on my way home from the hairdressing salon. An envelope had fallen out of her letterbox and was lying on the footpath. As I was about to shove it back into her box, she came out to collect her mail, and I handed it to her. I introduced myself. I suppose she felt obliged to do the same.

She told me her name was Zorka Weinhardt, but that wasn't the name on the envelope I picked up. Although it was only addressed to an initial and a surname, it wasn't the same name she gave me. I supposed the name on the envelope was her husband's … or maybe they weren't married."

Mission accomplished; it was time for me to leave Mavis to have her lunch.

"Goodness! Look at the time. I'm sorry, Mavis. I've been keeping you from your lunch. I really only came to see if you were okay. I should go now so you can have lunch and a good long nap to make up for all the sleep you missed last night."

If I hadn't been insistent, I might still be standing talking to her over her gate. But I eventually managed to 'disconnect' and headed home. My stomach rumbled all the way to remind me I also hadn't had lunch yet.

As I reached Rod's place, I slowed and then paused a moment to consider whether I should go in to share what I had learned from Mavis. The little voice in my head counselled against it, and I had started to move off again when I heard my name being called. Rod was heading home, presumably after meeting with Tanya Jellicoe.

"Have you had lunch?" was his opening line when he caught up with me. I shook my head. "Good; if you're up for cold chicken and salad, come in and join me."

Cold chicken and salad sounded wonderful, and my stomach also voiced approval with a particularly loud and embarrassing grumble. Everything happened fast with both of us involved, and minutes later, we took our plates and glasses of wine out onto Rod's back deck. It was show-and-tell time. I encouraged Rod to go first and share what he had learned from the Village's manager.

"Well, as Tanya doesn't live in the Village, she was more interested in gathering details of last night's events than sharing information. My assessment of my meeting with her is that it was almost a complete waste of time.

After checking the file, she told me the residents in that end house on our street were Franco Tonelli and his wife, Zorka. I queried whether the wife's surname also was Tonelli. Tanya stated she thought it would have to be 'if Zorka was his wife'."

"Did she offer any further information about the husband?"

"Yeah ... sort of... She remembered hearing that he had gone away for a while to deal with some family business. So, to summarise, she confirmed the scuttlebutt I'd heard and provided a surname for the couple."

"My source also tended to confirm the husband's absence, but without any mention of his death. I was told he appeared to have been absent for a couple of weeks."

"There's no news in any of that stuff about the husband, given that the police seem to think the body in the paddock is the bloke from that end house. As soon as we finish lunch, I need to tell Cilla what I discovered about Zorka's surname."

"If you tell her that Zorka's surname is Tonelli, you will give her inaccurate information. Tonelli is not the name Zorka goes by."

"So your source is an authority on that, too?" Rod snarled, leaving me speechless for a moment or two.

"I don't think anyone thought they were an authority on any of this but, when Zorka introduces herself, she doesn't use that surname."

"Sorry…. So might I be allowed to know what surname she does use?"

“Weinhardt… She introduces herself as Zorka Weinhardt.”

It might have been fortuitous that Rod’s doorbell interrupted our conversation. We were both still some way from being our usual relaxed selves. But the doorbell had announced the arrival of someone I was less than happy to hear Rod invite to join us.

“Cilla… I just said how I need to go across to see you,” I heard Rod welcome the new arrival. “We’re out on the back deck. Would you like to join us for lunch?”

Damn! The woman must have some special kind of radar that alerts her every time Rod and I manage to spend five minutes alone together. She never fails to materialise and turn a cosy twosome into a polite threesome. As they made their way from the front door to the back deck, I heard Cilla respond to the invitation to lunch.

“No, thanks. I had an early lunch to get it out of the way before my meeting with my team.

Now, did you do any good with our esteemed manager? Did she give you a surname?” Cilla asked.

“Well, yes… and no,” Rod began. “She told me the husband was Franco Tonelli, and his wife’s name was Zorka.”

“Tonelli…? That’s not one I know. It must be one he’s dug up exclusively for life here in the Village. If the body is the bloke we think it is, he’s gone by several names in the past but never Tonelli before, as far as I’m aware. Still, I suppose it makes sense to create a new identity if you are trying to set up a new life.

You were a bit indecisive when you answered. What was that about?”

Rod raised his eyebrows at me before answering. I shrugged, waved him onto the ‘virtual stage,’ and gestured for him to continue.

“Uhmm… Yes, there could be a problem with that information,” Rod began hesitantly. “That may well be the name the husband was using, but information from a separate source since then indicates that might not be Zorka’s surname.”

“What? Oh, for God’s sake, get on with it. What does this ‘other source’ suggest is Zorka’s surname?”

Rod indicated I should answer, so I did.

"Weinhardt…."

While I didn't feel it necessary to lengthen my reply, I was intrigued by the response it received from Cilla.

"Weinhardt? Weinhardt… Why does that name ring a bell?… Argh, Christ, yes. I do know why." Cilla glanced at her watch before continuing. "Look, I have something to do before my meeting, so I'll leave you two to enjoy the rest of your lunch."

With that, Cilla turned on her heel and strode back through the house and out the front door. Rod was left standing there with his jaw hanging slack. After Cilla's hasty departure, a shocked silence lasted a few moments before I felt obliged to do something about it.

"I didn't know I possessed such incredible power," I quipped.

"Eh? Power to do what?" Rod demanded.

"Such is the strength of my power; I can make people disappear by uttering just one word. You just witnessed a demonstration of that ability."

"See if frequent practice might strengthen your ability. I can think of any number of occasions when application of your 'gift' would be an advantage," Rod said between giggles.

"All joking aside, Rod, mentioning Zorka's surname seemed to hit a nerve for Cilla. What do you make of her reaction to it?"

"It's obvious she is familiar with the name. Who knows? Maybe it will expedite a breakthrough with their investigation of the case surrounding the body she found."

The few minutes it took Rod to conjure up a pitcher of iced tea provided me the luxury of time alone with my thoughts and to generate a whole raft of questions on a new subject to put to him.

Chapter 16

"While I admit it has been hard to think about much else over the last few days, in between times, I have wondered about the Village's new bus. Have you had much response to your post about it on our Facebook page?" I asked by way of moving the conversation away from anything to do with the body Cilla found.

Rod blinked at me a couple of times before replying. I guessed my segue to the bus had caught him off guard. He took a moment to reorganise his thoughts.

"It hasn't been quite as I expected. I thought there would be an immediate rush of *good advice* offered that would be of no help whatsoever. That's not what happened. The response was slow initially, and I wondered whether I should redraft the post and try again. But the residents have come good, and there's been a lot of comment in just the last couple of days."

"What's our next move, Rod? Should we start analysing the information coming in? Maybe create a spreadsheet or database to keep track of it as it comes in so it doesn't become a massive job later?"

"Hmm… Do you have anything planned for this afternoon?" I shook my head. "Good, if you don't need to go home, we could look at what's come in so far and maybe work out how to deal with it."

Of course, I wasn't in a hurry to go home. There was nothing but housework waiting for me there – and time alone with Rod was far preferable. It took only a couple of minutes to have a processing operation up and running.

Rod printed each of the responses to his post. I retrieved the printouts and tried to sort them into groups along the kitchen bench. The sorting part of the operation wasn't at all satisfactory, and it became obvious almost immediately that a better way of recording the information was necessary.

"This isn't working, Rod. Sorting stuff like this will not be of any use to anyone. We need to stop and think about it a bit more."

"There are only half a dozen responses I haven't printed yet. I'll print them out, and then we'll think about what to do with it so it makes sense."

We gathered up all the printouts and took them out to the table on the back deck. They made a substantial pile of paper. One by one, we examined each of the first fifteen sheets in the pile.

After about five minutes, Rod took the ones we had looked at and spread them out in front of him.

"A spreadsheet would work. It would require a number of columns to gather the data in a meaningful way. And it will take a bit of thought about how to handle the various responses to limit the number of columns without damaging the integrity of the data produced."

Oh, good; so long as one of us knew what that meant, I decided we probably would be okay. Then, my education in collating a wide range of information via a relatively simple spreadsheet began.

Several sheets torn off a pad were crumpled up and thrown away before Rod was reasonably happy with his draft layout for our spreadsheet. Even in Rod's rough scribble, the planned design looked perfect to me, but Rod wasn't quite so sure.

"Once we start inputting data, we might discover we need additional columns. We can add them as we encounter the need. It won't stop us starting with just this basic layout."

We discovered a big lump of the afternoon had slipped away while we were busy designing the spreadsheet. It was decided coffee should be the next thing on the agenda before actually creating the spreadsheet. Sitting sipping coffee, I was startled when Rod suddenly shot upright on his chair and checked his left wrist – his bare left wrist. He wasn't wearing his watch.

"Marion, what's the time, please?" he asked and then, before I could answer, murmured, "Geez, I hope I haven't missed him."

I told him the time and watched him relax. Although I was dying to know what his panic had been about, I decided to wait to see if he told me. The few moments before he did explain seemed to stretch on for hours.

"A colleague I've been trying to contact might be available in about ten minutes. It seems he is working on a delicate assignment, and I'll only be able to talk to him while he is in his car and driving to his next surveillance location."

"Good luck with your call. I'll be off now, but I'll take all this with me to set up and make a start on our spreadsheet."

Although I kept checking over my shoulders and felt as nervous as a teenager on a first date, it was good to be out of the house and on my own again. Nevertheless, my pace was a notch or two faster than normal as I strode along the footpath. Once my front door closed behind me, I heaved a sigh of relief.

On my way through, I turned on my computer to boot up while I made another coffee. I justified having coffee so late in the afternoon by reminding myself I hadn't even drunk half the one Rod made me before I hurried home.

Then, it was time to attack the dreaded spreadsheet. Of course, I had used spreadsheets in my working life, but all that had ended some time ago. Since then, I hadn't felt the need to reacquaint myself with the program… until now. And I needed to do a good job on this one.

Almost overwhelming was my self-inflicted need to prove to Rod that I was not just another old biddy slowly losing whatever meagre abilities she might once have possessed. So, with a lack of confidence and a load of trepidation, I sat at my computer and spread out Rod's draft layout of what we required to record the residents' thoughts about the bus.

After about ten minutes, I felt almost delirious about my achievement. The spreadsheet was created, checked, and awaiting data input.

"Best I get on with it then," I told the universe as I grabbed the top printout from the stack of responses. And that's when progress slowed to a crawl.

Each printout had to be read carefully, and its responses to Rod's questionnaire assessed and considered in relation to how they might fit the spreadsheet layout. There appeared to be an endless range of variables submitted, including a few rude suggestions. How to accommodate them on the spreadsheet was the challenge. I abandoned the computer to think about the problem as I checked what was in the fridge that might make a quick and easy dinner.

When I returned to the computer, I knew I would have an omelette for dinner, with a side salad perhaps … and that I needed to add another couple of columns to my spreadsheet. Right then, get stuck in, I told myself as I again turned my attention to that first printout.

Six o'clock came and went and was fast on its way to seven o'clock before I realised it was dark outside, and perhaps I should take a break to do something about dinner. Before I headed for the kitchen, I took a moment to scrutinise the work I had done. Pride almost had me dance my way to the kitchen.

In fact, I felt so buoyed by my efforts that, after bolting down my omelette and salad, I rushed back to my desk to deal with the remaining printouts.

Having entered the last comment from the final printout, I slumped back in my chair to again admire my efforts. A car's headlights flashing across my windows as it turned onto my street brought my self-indulgent moment to an end. It was almost nine o'clock. Village residents tend not to be driving around at that time of night – except for Cilla, and occasionally Bernard and James.

My stomach immediately went into spasms. Were we in for a repeat of last night? While I hadn't completely forgotten the danger we might be in, somehow, I had relaxed a bit today. Perhaps it was being able to pursue normal behaviour for a while that had done it. Now, the reality of our situation returned with a vengeance with those headlights. A return visit by last night's undesirables could only mean it was our turn tonight.

Being so convinced of it, I went rigid with fright when my doorbell rang. It rang again. That mob from last night wouldn't ring the doorbell, I told myself… and tried to persuade myself I was right. When the bell rang for a third time, I had to answer it. Still stiff with fear and filled with trepidation, I almost fell off my chair as I tried to stand.

"Marion, are you all right in there?"

"Yes. Yes, I'm coming," I shouted as I rushed to the door to open it for Rod.

"When I turned onto this street, I noticed your lights were still on, so I thought I might drop in for a nightcap or something. Are you sure you are okay? I didn't wake you, did I? You had me worried when you took a while to answer the door."

"No, I wasn't asleep. I was just finishing one last thing on the computer. No need for concern. All's good here. But I like your idea of a nightcap."

Armed with a platter of cheese and crackers and our nightcaps, we adjourned to my loungeroom. Curiosity about where Rod had been tonight was getting the better of me, and I'm sure he knew it. After a couple of minutes of conversation about nothing of importance but dealing mainly with the sort of day it had been, Rod put me out of my misery.

"Yeah, after all the last twenty-four hours delivered, I felt I needed to get out of the place, so I went for a drive. I wasn't going anywhere in particular, but after driving around for a while, I found myself near a wine bar I hadn't visited in ages. Nostalgia drew me in, and it was just as I remembered it: quiet, low lighting, few patrons, and still with a good cellar.

Just one drink wouldn't have taken long, but Fate took a hand in things. A familiar face came towards me as I wandered over to a vacant table. He greeted me like a long-lost friend and was in the mood for a chat. So that's what we did. It only took a matter of moments before we were discussing the body in the paddock, last night's events, and our current situation."

"Who the hell did you run into? I didn't think anyone in town would know what was happening here. So, come on; who was it?"

'Ah, didn't I say? It was Richard Wilson."

"Our top cop, Richard Wilson?"

"The very same. Before you ask, he had no fresh information to pass on, but I might have helped him."

"I don't know that Cilla will be too happy about that. I think she might see Richard and everything that's happened here as hers and hers alone. I doubt she'll appreciate your shoving your way in and maybe stealing her thunder."

"Funny you should say that. Richard as much as said Cilla had been trying to lord it over him. She used her knowledge from her previous days in the New South Wales Police Service for some one-upmanship. And, she now seemed to be treating him like a lesser copper since he handed over much of the investigation to his southern masters."

"Oh, surely not our Cilla…," I murmured in mock horror. "So, how were you able to help him with his investigation."

"It seems part of Cilla's game is to keep us apart from Richard, although he had asked several times to talk to us."

"Well, I suppose it's hard to achieve one-upmanship if everyone is in on the game. She would lose some of her importance and superiority if Richard talked to anyone else. But what didn't he know that we do?"

"Mainly all the information we discovered today regarding last night and Zorka's identity. Don't worry. I made sure you received the credit for your sleuthing efforts. Despite Cilla's having a meeting with her team this afternoon and, no doubt, passing on everything to them, she hadn't shared any of it with Richard."

"Ouch, I don't think you will be Cilla's favourite person after tonight."

"Maybe not, but we have established new lines of communication. Richard will now share any new information with me – and you – first. I've agreed to dig into a few things for him with some of my former colleagues. He will send me some information, and then you and I will have more sleuthing to do".

There it was again, that troubling pang of guilt. If we are now to be liaising with Richard, should I come clean? Should I mention to him what I saw? The little voice in my head and my gut both counselled against it. Rod saved me from further exploration of my guilt by resuming his conversation.

"So, while I've been out drinking with our top cop, what have you been doing to keep you up so late? I can see you weren't watching TV."

Beckoning him to follow me, I led him to my computer, brought up my spreadsheet, and left him to study it while I refilled our glasses.

"Ah hah, I see you have been busy. This looks great. Very impressive… It certainly helps make sense of the responses to the bus questionnaire. With just one quick look, I can see a few clear trends emerging. Maybe asking for input from the end users will prove more useful than I thought.

We'll keep the spreadsheet updated for another week or so. By then, it probably will be time to make some decisions, so the bus becomes operational as soon as possible after that."

"The interclub bowls competitions still have a few more weeks to run. Will that influence how soon the bus is up and running?"

I foresaw a great ruckus if bus trips were scheduled on competition days. I don't imagine the board would be too happy to see one great initiative (the interclub bowls competition) disrupted by the introduction of the next great thing (the bus schedule).

"It shouldn't be a problem, even if trips are scheduled on Wednesdays or Thursdays, the two interclub games days. Men who play bowls on Thursdays can do their shopping on the other day of the week when the bus does a shopping run. Likewise, if Wednesdays were scheduled shopping days, women bowlers could shop on the other shopping day of the week."

"Yes, I realise nobody needs to miss out on going shopping, but I still think whatever days are scheduled, it's likely to cause howls of protest."

"Hmm…," Rod murmured as he scanned the spreadsheet. "It seems Tuesdays and Thursdays are leading the pack as preferred shopping days. Oh well, I'm sure management and the board will be able to weather the storm."

"I'm not worried about them. My concern is for us and the backlash we will likely receive from those who don't agree with our decisions."

"But they won't be *our* decisions. I intend it will be the board issuing the scheduling information … after I've sold them on what we develop."

Now, why didn't I think of that? Of course, Rod would distance us, as much as possible, from any fallout from the scheduling. And, as the board is keen to have the bus in service as soon as possible, they will accept anything Rod puts before them.

While continuing to scan the spreadsheet, he added, "Anyway, as it is unlikely the first bus trips will occur for another three or four weeks, the interclub games will be at the pointy end of the competition and probably will have only a couple of weeks left to run."

"Christ…Whatever you do, don't do anything to mess up the semi-finals and finals games," I cautioned him.

It was late, and with little more about the spreadsheet to discuss, Rod went home. All evening, I thought how surprising it was that I didn't feel particularly tired or sleepy tonight after so little sleep last night. That only lasted until I cleaned up after Rod left. Then it hit me full force, and at about the same time, I realised I hadn't had a shower this evening.

About fifteen minutes after I dragged myself off for a quick shower and fell into bed, I wasn't aware of anything more until the next morning.

The sun was up a long while before I was this morning. What does it matter? I asked myself as I tried to ignore the clock on my bedside table. I don't have to go anywhere or do anything today … or most other days, if the truth be told. Wasn't that supposed to be one of the joys of being retired – and old?

I did a poor job of convincing myself I didn't have to bound out of bed just because I had woken up, and eventually managed to haul myself upright. My eyes were open, and I was on my feet, but my brain remained wrapped in the fog of slumber. *Coffee*, the little voice in my head shouted at me, and I somehow managed to get the process underway.

Still in some sort of semi-stupor, I sat at my kitchen bench and sipped what I knew would be just the first of many coffees this morning. Then something from last night elbowed its way through the fog to have me on my feet again in a flash.

Although I wasn't sure what it was, I knew it had something to do with last night's spreadsheet. I felt my stomach tightening as I waited for my computer to boot up. What had I done wrong? Why was that little voice in my head telling me I had stuffed up?

"Well, I can't see anything wrong with it," I told the universe after a cursory scan of my work.

Nevertheless, something kept telling me to look harder. There was a problem with it. The thought of having to review each of the printouts to check I hadn't entered something incorrectly was just about enough to bring me out in a cold sweat. But my eyes kept being drawn to one particular section of the sheet.

"Argh, hell… why didn't I notice that before?" I yelped. "Now it stands out like the proverbial. I had better let Rod know about it."

My immediate reaction was to reach for my phone to call him, but the time displayed on the home screen reminded me he would probably be out for his morning run. Given our current safety concerns, was he still adhering to his routine of long morning runs alone? Knowing Rod as I did, he probably was. So, instead of calling him, I strolled back into the kitchen and made breakfast.

It doesn't take long to eat a light breakfast and sit a while dawdling over a second mug of coffee. Impatience got the better of me. I retrieved my phone and called him. He answered almost immediately.

"I was just thinking about you," he answered. "A few more questionnaire responses have come in overnight, probably as a result of the post I put on the page after I came home last night.

What do you want to do about the spreadsheet? Do you want to maintain responsibility for updating it, or do you want to hand it over to me to work on?"

"I don't mind working on it if you keep feeding me the printouts. The spreadsheet is the reason I called you. There's a problem with it. At least, I think it might develop into a problem." I didn't have a chance to say more.

"Right; I'll be right over," Rod announced. "Are you decent, and have you had breakfast yet?"

"Almost…. Give me about ten minutes, please."

Breakfast might be over, but sitting here in a housecoat was hardly 'decent'. I giggled as I dashed to the bedroom to pull on some clothes. Although Rod had seen me in a lot less, I probably wasn't appropriately attired for the conversation we were about to have.

I doubted it was ten minutes later before he was ringing my doorbell. He inhaled deeply as he came in.

"I smell recently brewed coffee. I'll have one if there is any left," he said as he beamed at me.

"And will you be wanting breakfast to go with it?" I sniped.

"Ah well, now you're asking… yes, that would go down a treat."

"I'll make it while you sit there and consider what I'm going to show you on the spreadsheet," I told him as I gestured for him to sit at the computer.

"Yep. These are the days residents have indicated they prefer for shopping trips once the bus is operational. I can see that, but why should I be concerned about the information?"

"Think about it while I make fresh coffee – and your breakfast," I told him as I flounced off into the kitchen.

Despite banging things about in the kitchen, I heard Rod murmur, "Obviously, not at my brightest this morning." That was before he ran up the white flag and called out to me.

"Take pity on me. I've studied the part you indicated, but I still don't see anything to be concerned about."

"To date, by far, the preferred days for shopping trips are Tuesdays and Thursdays. Tuesdays are for ladies' social bowls, and Thursdays are the men's competition bowls days."

"I can't see that being a problem. The bowlers should be able to work around that without too much trouble. Unless they want to go shopping twice a week, in which case they are going to have to miss out on bowls for at least one day a week."

"It wasn't the fact that it might interfere with bowls days that worried me. Tell me again, who is going to drive this bus?"

"There are about four of us, I think: me, Luigi, Ted, and perhaps Frank as well."

"Rod, you are all members of our mahjong group. So, every Tuesday and Thursday morning when we play mahjong, at least one of you will be missing, and possibly more if others in the group go shopping."

"Oo-oh, yeah. That could be a problem. I'll need to think about it for a while.

Let's not dwell on it for now. I've given them until the end of the coming week to respond to the questionnaire. Once that cut-off occurs, I will have another look at it. In the meantime, I'll think about what we might be able to do. Of course, we could always fudge the figures."

"What? Lie about what people had indicated their preferences were? We'll need to keep this spreadsheet under wraps if that's what you plan to do. It's the evidence that might get us hanged if it doesn't back up the story we're telling. I'm not sure I feel comfortable with that solution."

"Don't go getting twitchy just yet. I'm sure it'll work out okay."

Chapter 17

Silence kept us company as Rod dispatched his breakfast, and I sipped yet another coffee. I'll be bouncing off the walls after so much coffee so early in the day, especially as I'm still not going for my daily walks to wear off some of the caffeine. After about five minutes of sitting like that, the silence was shattered when Rod's phone played its tune.

One glance at the caller ID had him up off his chair and heading for the door with his phone in one hand while his other hand desperately tugged at a small notebook in his pocket. I rushed ahead and opened the door for him.

Then, brushing his free hand aside, I wriggled the notebook out of his pocket and slapped it into his outstretched hand. I stood for a few moments, watching him talking animatedly on his phone as he strode along the footpath towards his house. The caller's identity had me intrigued. I would have given anything to know who it was. Whoever it was, their call certainly excited Rod. I couldn't help but wonder whether it also should interest me.

Although I carried my phone around all day in anticipation Rod would tell me about this morning's call (or was it just hope?), my phone remained silent. It was nearly five o'clock when he called, and then it was only to ask if I would be coming to happy hour. I hesitated before answering.

Was it wise for me to be outside alone in the evening? Had the supposed danger we were in changed somehow during the day? If it had, why hadn't I been told? The temptation was to tell Rod I didn't think I'd be safe out alone, so I would not be joining them. Fortunately, common sense snapped in before I delivered my terse reply.

If I told Rod I didn't feel safe walking to his place on my own, he would make a fuss and insist on escorting me. In the end, I decided what the hell and said, of course, I would be there. That sent me scurrying to the kitchen to come up with some nibbles to take with me.

In the hope he might feel expansive and inclined to share something about the call he received this morning, I made a point of arriving a little early for happy hour. I made the excuse I had come early to help him set up, only to be told he had already done that. So, with nothing to be done, he poured us a glass of wine, and we sat in his lounge room while we waited for the others to arrive.

Six o'clock, our usual happy hour start time, came and went with no further arrivals. Rod suggested it was a nice night outside, and perhaps we should relocate to his back deck. I followed him out and then stopped suddenly. Something was not quite right. It took a moment to work out what it was.

Attendees at these happy hours usually numbered somewhere between seven and ten. Extra chairs were brought out from inside, and two tables were pushed together to accommodate everyone. Only one table and no extra chairs were set up for tonight. Obviously, Rod wasn't expecting too many to show up.

"Uhmm… Did the others know there was a happy hour tonight?" I asked. "Is there a better option I was unaware of on offer somewhere tonight?"

"No. No, we're set up and ready for everyone who is expected. One of us is running a bit late, as she indicated she might, but she should be along soon."

"I take it the 'she' you mentioned is Cilla?" I asked – perhaps a little too sharply.

Rod nodded, and disappointment invaded me. When I realised the whole mob wouldn't be here tonight, I thought Rod might have intended a quiet night alone for the two of us.

How silly of me. It seems we still can't do anything without Cilla also being involved. I mentally reprimanded myself for allowing the green-eyed dragon to emerge again. I thought I had laid to rest those feelings of resentment about Cilla seemingly encroaching on my territory. *My territory!* What a joke. How long had it been since Rod and I spent time together, let alone spent the night together?

Right; if I want to know about his call this morning, it seems I need to take the initiative and ask about it now before Cilla arrives.

"So, Rod, that call you took this morning, the one that sent you rushing back home, was that anything I should know about?"

"Good question…. I'm not sure yet whether the information I received means anything or not. I passed it onto Richard Wilson, and I hope he might have something more to add sometime soon."

"Am I correct in assuming the information you received is relevant to the situation we find ourselves in as a result of the body in the paddock and Zorka's disappearance?"

"Correct… well, it seems that way. Bear with me while I tell you what I discovered, and I want to do that before Cilla arrives. So, best not to interrupt with too many questions at this stage."

Although a bit taken aback and affronted by being told not to interrupt, I nodded my agreement and gestured for him to get on with it.

"The call was from a colleague from a long while ago. He has amazing contacts in some interesting circles. Yesterday, I fed him the names Tonelli and Weinhardt and asked for anything he knew or could discover about either of those surnames. This morning's call was his feedback."

"And how did that go? Did he have anything useful to offer?" I demanded.

I was losing patience with the conversation. It was beginning to feel like swimming through treacle. And I was developing a sneaking suspicion he wasn't going to share what he had learnt –not all of it, anyway. As a result, my questions had been a bit sharp. I hoped they sent the message that I wasn't about to be fobbed off.

"Yeah, it was an interesting call. He had a couple of major points to share, as well as some speculation, but he didn't have much to offer on the Tonelli name.

It seems the Tonelli family are small fry, no more than a speck in the 'underbelly' world everyone seems interested in these days. His assessment of them is that they are small-time players, who wanted to be somewhat more if they could, but have limited opportunities to make it happen."

"Okay… so not a real scary mob. They don't sound like the sort who go around murdering people and leaving their bodies in an abandoned cow paddock.

What about the Weinhardt name? Did that ring any bells for him?"

"Ah, yes. He is well familiar with the Weinhardt name. It seems they are big-time players in the underworld. They basically are a family organisation, but some of its many 'branches' operate under other names.

They have been around for about three generations, and as he describes them, this mob would have no hesitation in providing us with a body to find. My reference to Zorka Weinhardt specifically brought an interesting insight."

"This doesn't sound like it is going to be good news. For him to know Zorka's name, she must play a major role in the family's operations."

"Not so much a major player as the head of the family. The Head of the Family position had come down much as you would expect through the male line to Zorka's father. When Zorka was in her thirties, her father was seriously injured in a gangland shooting that left him wheelchair-bound and struggling to maintain his position within the family. Zorka stepped in to become his right-hand man and became the power behind the throne, so to speak.

That situation continued for about twenty years until her father died. Then, as his only child, she officially took over the reins and has been running the family's operations ever since. But, it appears she doesn't run the show from a back room or an office somewhere. Law enforcement agencies have quite substantial files on Zorka as she has played an active part in many of the family's operations it ran over the years. She is still considered an active player rather than just a figurehead."

"Geez, how did she end up here in Merivale Retirement Village? It hardly seems like somewhere a key player in the southern underworld would want to spend time."

"My colleague thinks something that occurred upset a few people, and as a result, Zorka took a 'holiday' to allow things to cool down – or while the family 'hosed' things down."

"Perhaps running off with that bloke Tonelli might not have endeared her to some people.

So, is it likely then that Weinhardt family members eradicated the problem by eliminating Tonelli?"

"Nah, I suggested that too, but my colleague hadn't come across anything to suggest that was the case. He suspects that the couple, Tonelli and Weinhardt, had pulled off a job along the way, and whatever that was, had incurred the anger of other players.

He did have an interesting footnote to add. A few days ago, one of his contacts became aware of something interesting happening in the Weinhardt family. Three or four members were seen leaving town in the middle of the night, and they appeared to be in a rush to get to wherever they were going."

"Were they on their way here, do you think?" Suddenly, I felt nervous again.

"That's one of the things we speculated about, but there is no evidence, not even rumour, about where they might've been heading."

It was predictable the comments about the Weinhardt family, and particularly about Zorka, would invite speculation. Although they had been dismissed by his colleague, Rod and I revisited a couple of scenarios regarding the Tonelli/Weinhardt situation that Rod had previously suggested. I was inclined to agree with his colleague's assessment of those suggested scenarios – and I made the mistake of saying so.

Rod was not impressed and demanded I come up with a better suggestion. After some thought on the matter, I managed to round up a few loose ideas floating around in my mind and massaged them into a sort of cockeyed theory.

"Uhmm…. Well, yes, maybe I do have the makings of a theory.

What if two groups were involved in what happened here the other night?"

He shook his head in disbelief, but before he could say anything, I proceeded to talk through my idea.

"What if one of the groups was on a payback mission for something that had happened back home? Maybe whatever it was ultimately led to Tonelli's death and Zorka's subsequent abduction."

"Okay, I'll humour you for a bit longer. If that was one group, who was the second group in this theory of yours? And what makes you think there were two groups anyway?"

"Thank you for your patience. I'll try to explain," I said with a heavy dose of sarcasm before rushing on with my theory. "The first mob that came, the ones who tore up and down the street for so long before making a move, I think they were the group on a payback mission. Having dealt with Tonelli as they saw necessary, they then were lining up to dish out Zorka's just retribution also.

Then, the second group arrived and became involved. They were in the dark vehicle that arrived via the dirt track on the other side of the back fence. I grant you, they might've been reinforcements coming to assist the first group if they ran into difficulties, but I doubt that was the case."

"Hmm… If they weren't reinforcements, why were they here? Why were they interested in anything happening at Zorka's house?"

"Oh, now that's a good question. Were they interested in Zorka? Do we know if that car they arrived in also went to Zorka's place? It could have gone anywhere in the village. Maybe I need to talk to Mavis again."

"Or let's stick with your original thought. Who were the second lot, and why were they racing to Zorka's place when another group was already there?"

"Don't laugh, but my original thinking was that the second group might've been to protect or rescue Zorka.

What if they were part of the Weinhardt family, and Zorka had summoned them after Tonelli was killed? That would fit with a group of Weinhardt family members setting out on a secret mission, as mentioned by your colleague."

"That's worth thinking about. It's a plausible scenario," Rod agreed but remained deep in thought.

Not wanting to interrupt his thinking, I allowed him to think it through in silence, but after a few moments, his phone shattered that silence. As soon as he answered it, I knew the caller was Cilla. It wasn't a long phone call, but it caught my attention when I heard Rod ask her if she thought she would be safe. Rather than wait to be told, as soon as the call ended, I demanded to know what was happening and why Rod might be concerned for Cilla's safety. After all, if there was some level of risk for Cilla, were we at risk as well?

"She doesn't seem to think she is in danger. She called to say she wouldn't be joining us tonight. She is on the early morning flight to Sydney and has some work to do tonight in preparation for her meetings tomorrow. Given our current situation, it seemed risky to me, but she didn't expect any problems at this end or on the flight, and someone from her team would collect her from the plane in Sydney."

"You don't have to be a genius to work out that this trip to Sydney is probably a direct result of the Zorka incident the other night. Did she give you any clues about that?"

"I've given you everything she told me, but I agree that her sudden trip is closely related to what's happened here in the Village."

"Rod, have you passed on all the information you received from your colleague to Richard Wilson?"

"Yep, and he seemed a bit excited by it. I suspect he won't pass it on to his superiors down south. They appear to be trying to take over the investigation. I think he will follow it up himself. He has agreed to keep me informed of anything he discovers."

"It's so tantalising, isn't it? We know more than we did before your colleague passed on his information, but they are such tiny clues as to what might be happening. While it's great to find out as much as he told us, it's opened another can of worms and brought forth a whole truckload of other questions – and speculation.

Was there anything else of interest your colleague had to offer?"

"Uhmm… There was one other thing, but I don't know if I should mention it."

I jumped in to put a stop to that thinking before it became a problem. Unless it was personal to Rod, I wanted to know about it.

"All right, settle down. I wasn't being funny about it. It's just that I'm not too sure about its accuracy.

My colleague suggested the Weinhardt name might reopen old wounds for Cilla. No, not physical wounds, more like memories. I was told she had several run-ins with the family during her police service days. On one particular occasion, the rumour was that things went badly pear-shaped, and Cilla lost one officer, and another was permanently injured. The story has it that her career took a beating for it."

"That would explain her reaction when I told her Zorka's surname. Oh hell, what if those visitors from the other night know Cilla lives here now? And that she was the one who found Tonelli's body? Perhaps we should continue looking over our shoulders for a bit longer," I suggested.

Rod didn't argue with my suggestion, and we spent the next few minutes speculating on what the future might bring for those of us still here in the Village, and what things might be like for Cilla in Sydney. The night was slipping away. Our 'happy' hour had extended way past its usual time.

"How do you feel about chops for dinner?" Rod asked out of the blue, taking me by surprise.

Chops sounded wonderful, and we both bolted for the kitchen to prepare dinner. It wasn't the most elaborate feast, just chops and vegetables, but it was a long, wonderful meal. We ate inside, added a great wine, and followed up with thick slices of a Sarah Lea cheesecake for dessert. But best of all, there was just the two of us for dinner.

After we cleared the table and loaded the dishwasher, we took coffee and glasses of port through to the lounge room and settled down to what developed into a lovely long session of pleasant conversation. It had been such a blissful evening, I was dismayed when my watch told me it was gone midnight.

"Goodness, look at the time. I'm sorry, Rod, I hadn't intended to stay so long. I'll be off so you can catch some sleep before the sun comes up."

"I don't think that is going to happen. I am not having you walking along that footpath at this hour of the night, even with me as your escort. Have you suddenly developed some form of allergy to spending the night with me? It seems far too long since we've done that."

Well, I couldn't argue with it having been too long … and I certainly hadn't developed any such allergy…. So, what else was I to do except to spend the night?

The aroma of coffee brewing and something baking assailed my nostrils as I gently coaxed my eyelashes apart. Suddenly, I was wide awake, my eyes darting around everything within viewing range. Strange bed. Strange room. Where the hell was I?

Then, my brain finally fired up, and I remembered not going home from Rod's place last night. I squinted at the window, too bright for anything more than a squint. The reality of my situation hit me. The sun had been up for some time by the look of the light streaming in through the bedroom window. The little voice in my head repeatedly suggested that I should join the sun – and Rod – that I should become vertical and make a start on my day.

Oh, argh, how much wine did I drink last night? It must have been a lot because, since I sat up, 'high tide' had been slamming around between my ears. "Gently does it," I reminded myself as I eased up into the vertical position… and then stood there for a moment, waiting for my head to stop pounding. Yep, definitely too much wine!

After climbing back into last night's clothes, splashing water over my face, and rinsing my mouth, I felt brave enough to investigate the aromas wafting from the kitchen.

Rod hummed something unidentifiable as he set out mugs and plates. Condiments already occupied the kitchen bench in readiness for breakfast. A quick peep through the oven's door glass told me croissants were on the breakfast menu. Croissants and coffee, just the thought of it almost had me drooling.

"You should have woken me," I complained as I sat at the bench. "By sleeping so late, I've wasted half the day."

"Some people don't wake easily or well. I didn't know what you might be like if I disturbed you. When in doubt, do nothing; that's my motto."

"Often have to decide whether to wake the strange woman in your bed or let her sleep, do you?" My tone was a little too sharp, probably due to my pounding head rather than anything else. "Anyway, Rod, what's on the agenda for today? Do you have any plans?"

"I didn't have until last night, but now that Cilla is away, I'm inclined to attend today's bowls club meeting."

"Are you expecting trouble? You aren't normally interested in bowls club meetings unless something is happening."

"There isn't anything happening that I'm aware of, but I haven't attended a meeting since the election of the new committee. I've relied on Cilla to give feedback on anything of interest. I just have a feeling that the men might be becoming restless, so I want to be there.

The meeting will also provide an opportunity to talk to people about the new bus service and maybe spur along anyone who hasn't responded to the questionnaire. If I get lucky, you might end up with a whole lot more data to input in the next little while.

What are your plans for today, Marion?"

"Well, I have a hairdresser's appointment just before lunch, and I should return my library book before it becomes overdue.

Do you think it would look strange if I drove around to the hairdresser's salon today instead of walking there? The recent information we've received has me feeling more than a little vulnerable again about being outside alone."

A haircut and the library would not take up much time. That left housework as the only other means of filling in my day. After a few reassuring words from Rod about being reasonably safe to walk about the Village in broad daylight, I reluctantly headed home to face my day of drudgery.

Chapter 18

With the washing done and on the line to dry, I thought I'd earned a coffee... until Rod called and suggested I accompany him to the bowls club meeting scheduled for ten o'clock. Of course, I'd go with him, but I would have to leave soon after eleven o'clock for my hairdressing appointment.

As well as Cilla, one other committee member couldn't attend the meeting. Rod and I arrived a few minutes early and planned to use the time to talk to people about the new bus. When the meeting opened, there was no more than a handful of observers there, including Rod and me. About three minutes after it started, a group of four blokes hellbent on disrupting the meeting arrived.

They came in talking at the top of their voices and shouted greetings at other observers. Adding to the disruption, they dragged chairs around, talked and laughed between themselves, but at full volume. Stella tried to continue with the meeting, but it became impossible. Frustrated, she slammed a book down hard on the table. The sound it made startled the rowdy blokes as well as the rest of us.

"Silence…. That is quite enough of your disruptive nonsense, thank you," Stella bellowed. "Either take your seats and be quiet, or leave now." One of the men laughed, and the other three also started to twitter.

While this was going on, my attention was focused on Rod. When the four chaps first walked in, I saw Rod pull his phone out of his pocket and start texting. At first, I thought he must be responding to a message that he received. I hoped it might be something more from Richard Wilson. Now, I wasn't so sure he was responding to anything. Whatever the reason, he was still frantically working his phone when Stella called for silence.

The situation showed signs of turning ugly – very ugly – and it had my pulse and breathing rates on the rise. What were these loud-mouthed blokes capable of, and what was the intention behind their attendance today? Would they become violent? Unlike the rest of us there that morning, they didn't look quite so ancient. All four had walking sticks. Were they simply mobility aids, or was there a more sinister purpose for them? Surely, the men wouldn't resort to violence after all that had happened in the recent past. At least, that's what I tried to tell myself.

My stomach was tying itself in knots. Stella again called for silence, and several other women echoed her request. Movement at the other side of the observers' gallery caught my attention. A frail-looking lady with a walking frame struggled to her feet and headed for the door. I wished I could go with her. As she approached the door, she stopped and shuffled a little off to one side.

Tanya Jellicoe, followed by three burly grounds staff members, strode through the door and past the woman with the walker. With so few observers today, only the front row of chairs was occupied. Tanya continued around to stand in front of the four men in the audience. The three staff members did not. They marched straight up to stand behind the four blokes. Rod quietly slipped out of his chair and joined the staff members.

"You four… Leave this meeting now," Tanya shouted.

Before she could continue, one of them shouted back, "Or what? You going to chuck us out?"

"Me… chuck you out? Goodness, no. But the men standing behind you are about to help you on your way. They will see you all the way to your homes. By then, the security officers will be in place and will stand by while you pack your belongings.

The police have been notified. If you are still in this Village at five this afternoon, the police will evict you and possibly arrest you."

"Where are we supposed to go at such short notice," one of their number demanded.

"To hell would be good," a female voice replied.

Ignoring the woman, Tanya responded, "What you do and where you go when you leave here is your problem and not one that concerns me at all." Then, addressing her staff members and Rod, she added, "Gentlemen, if you would assist these men to leave and see them home now, thank you...."

Within moments, the 'problem', now lacking its earlier bluster and bravado, was obediently on its way to the door. With the matter now dealt with, after inviting Stella to resume the meeting, Tanya bade us all good morning and left. I sat slack-jawed and stunned for some time after the meeting got underway again.

After checking my watch yet again, I was just about to leave when Rod returned and plonked down on the chair beside me again.

"What time are you supposed to be at the hairdresser's?" he asked.

"I was just about to leave. Is everything under control with those four blokes?"

"Yeah, all under control now. The security company's officers turned up almost at the same time as we delivered the blokes to their homes. You had better go now, or you will be late. When you are done, come back to mine for lunch. By then, this meeting will be over, and I'll be at home waiting for you."

For once, Bianca Porter, my hairdresser and Mavis Grimshaw's granddaughter, was running on time. I almost did a 'hot seat changeover' with the client before me. Bianca is a good operator, but clients book in for something, and when the time comes, they also want something extra done. The salon is so busy that it doesn't take much to have it running behind schedule. Today, it was refreshingly on time. It meant I was shampooed, trimmed, dried, and out of there in what felt like record time. I headed for Rod's place and lunch – and hoped he was home by the time I arrived.

Bianca's salon is on the far side of the administration building complex. Returning home involved walking to the end of the complex and around it to be on the same side as where I live. It was a nice day outside, and after the disturbing incident at the bowls meeting this morning, I found the stroll around the complex somewhat settling. At least, it was for a short time.

As I strolled along the opposite side of the complex from the hairdressing salon, I heard a car somewhere in the distance. Although it registered with my subconscious, it didn't perturb me… until I was about to cross the road and start along my street. The house on the corner opposite where I was standing was the site of the 'Zorka incident' the other night. I hesitated as I was about to step off the pavement. Seeing that house revived vivid memories of the fear and terror of that night.

Then, the screech of brakes cut through all else to grab my attention. The vehicle was close, much closer than before, and it was coming my way. We had been warned against being out alone, but there I was, standing right out in the open on my own.

I don't remember any conscious thought being involved, so it must have been pure instinct that kicked in. I found myself standing in the gym's small entrance foyer. Footsteps were coming my way. Suddenly, the poster on the wall listing the different sessions and the various times they ran became riveting reading. The trainer found me intently studying the list when he bounded into the entrance foyer.

"Sorry; I didn't mean to disturb anyone. I just dropped in to check what was available and when," I stammered as a lame excuse for my presence. He was keen to sign up a new client. Resorting to rudeness as my only hope of escape. "I only dropped in to look at that list," I said, pointing to the poster on the wall. "but I'm expected somewhere for lunch and need to be on my way."

He appeared taken aback by my outburst. I didn't care. It stopped him in his tracks and allowed me to turn and dash out of the building. Without even hesitating to check for oncoming vehicles or listen for any traffic, I dashed across the road and started down my street at a pace just slightly slower than a jog. And after maintaining that pace all the way to Rod's gate, I arrived sweating and out of breath. Rod saw me arrive and, noting my condition, dashed out to meet me.

"What are you trying to prove? Did you run all the way from the salon? I didn't have a set time for lunch. The plan was to have it whenever you arrived. Come inside and sit down before you collapse."

Once I was seated at his kitchen bench, the questions began again.

"Now, come on. Tell me what happened to have you arrive here in such a distressed state."

"Nothing actually happened, Rod. I suppose I'm the product of my imagination. After leaving the salon, I was on my way here when I heard a car coming. We don't often hear cars driving through the Village at this hour of the day. But it sounded as though it was coming my way, so I dashed into the entrance to the gym to hide from the vehicle. When the trainer came out to see who was there, I pretended to be interested in the sessions the gym was running. He was all for drumming up business and signing up a new client.

After eyeing me up and down, the trainer seemed to consider me a worthy challenge. As I tried to escape, he followed me, asking personal questions about my weight, how often I exercised, what I ate and drank, what my sleep patterns were like, and if I had any existing health problems.

Anyway, I ended up having a helluva job getting away from him, and then, just as I was back outside again, I heard the screech of brakes. Nobody screeches their brakes as they drive through the Village. Those sorts of speeds are not allowed. I remembered our warning not to be out alone. I panicked and raced the rest of the way to here. Did you see a vehicle at all?"

I had to wait until Rod controlled his chuckling before I received an answer.

"Yes, I did catch a glimpse of it as it raced out along the main drive."

"It raced out…? So, it wasn't coming in, it was leaving?"

"That's correct. Neither of us was in any danger. As it happens, I saw the vehicle while I was on a call to Tanya for an update on this morning's incident. The car you heard leaving the Village ties in with the aftermath of that event.

It all goes back to that major incident when a group of blokes from the 'old brigade' decided women shouldn't play bowls or be members of *their* bowls club. None of us will forget the open hostility that boiled over into actual violence against at least one woman. The ringleaders were thrown out of the Village, and three or four other residents were put on what amounted to good behaviour notices, or they too would be sent packing."

"Is there a connection between what happened then and this morning's disgusting performance at the bowls club meeting?"

"Those who had been given a second chance after the earlier debacle decided everything had settled down sufficiently now for nobody to be watching too closely. They decided the time was right to mount another offensive."

"But, surely they knew what the consequences would be if they tried anything like that again. It wouldn't matter how covert they were. Everyone would be keeping an eye out for any little thing out of the ordinary."

"Oh, yes, they were aware, all right, but the punishment handed out last time appears only to have made them more determined. This time, they adopted a different approach that they thought would allow them to deny any involvement should things go pear-shaped. They brought their sons in to do the dirty work for them."

"That explains a few things for me. I didn't recognise any of those four blokes. I couldn't remember ever seeing them before. Somehow, they looked a bit too young to be residents, but these days, just about everybody, other than the residents here, looks young. It comes from now being so old.

The other thing that intrigued me was the walking sticks they carried … *carried* being the keyword. They *carried* those walking sticks, but never once did any of them use theirs. They never even looked like they might need to use them. Do you think they might have intended to use those sticks as weapons if they didn't achieve what they wanted by other means?"

Rod rubbed his hand across his face as he appeared to give my question a moment's thought before answering.

"I'm not convinced they would have used them. I think it more likely the mere fact that they had brought the sticks to the meeting was meant to intimidate rather than threaten real violence."

"Were they violent in any way when you escorted them home?"

"Not at all; in fact, one of them seemed more concerned about the reception he might receive when he arrived at his father's place under escort. It was never a problem anyway. By the time we were in the residential area, the security chaps were already waiting to take over from us."

"So, what was the outcome of this morning's debacle? Are there likely to be repeat performances in the future?"

"No, there is no fear of that at all. By this evening, there will be two additional vacant houses in the Village. The sons were seen off pretty well straight away. The security guards gave them their marching orders, and then the police arrived. They made sure the ring-ins left. The two fathers involved have been given till five o'clock to move out and be gone. I understand the police have been engaged to ensure they do.

In hindsight, the two exiting the place today probably should have been chucked out along with the first lot when they were given their marching orders. They were all part of the same faction."

"Four sons of residents were disrupting the meeting this morning, but you say only two residents have been evicted. What was the relationship between all the players?"

"One resident had called in his three sons, another resident had one son join him, and it seems there was a third resident involved, but he pulled out of the deal in the latter stages of planning the event. Nevertheless, management was aware of his earlier involvement, and he has been notified to find somewhere else and be gone by the end of the year."

"The whole situation involving the bowls club since its opening is almost beyond comprehension. How can such situations develop here in a quiet retirement village? How did those men end up being residents here in the first place? It's hard to believe that men with tendencies to violence and obstructive behaviour would want to live in a sleepy retirement village, as opposed to remaining in their own home in town somewhere."

"From what I've heard, I gather that at least some of those evicted were not locals to begin with and only moved here when they managed to secure a place in Merivale Retirement Village.

Unlike most other retirement facilities, Merivale has virtually no vetting process for aspiring residents. It appears that some of those who have been evicted, because of their somewhat dubious operations in the past, would not pass the vetting process at most other retirement facilities. So, when word gets around that Merivale isn't too fussy about who lives here, all sorts apply and are accepted."

"That could also apply to Zorka and Franco Tonelli. It sounds like they weren't locals before they moved into the Village. How many others like that might be living here?"

"We don't know, and nobody might ever know if they keep their heads down. I believe new guidelines regarding vetting processes and procedures for applicants to reside in the Village are being drawn up. Although it might be a bit late coming, it might go some way to preventing a repeat of recent incidents."

Despite not having given much thought to it all morning, I found myself wondering whether there had been any change in our situation. I didn't doubt the police were doing whatever they could to sort out what was going on, but the only thing that interested me was how soon I could resume a normal lifestyle. I didn't enjoy being on the sidelines to whatever was happening – if anything was happening. I was sure Rod would pass on any information he received but, when there are so many other things happening around you, it's easy to forget you haven't yet shared something.

"Rod, in amongst everything else that happened today, has there been any word from Richard Wilson or Cilla regarding our situation? I wouldn't know Zorka Weinhardt if I fell over her, but I do feel concerned for her."

"While I know it's pointless to say this, I will do so anyway. Don't waste too much time and energy worrying about Zorka. She will either be okay and with her mob, or it will be too late to worry about her anyway. Apart from that, you need to remember Zorka is not just another little old lady living alone in a retirement village.

Zorka was something else entirely, whose life was based in a different world a long way from here. Like the others we've been discussing, Merivale Retirement Village was a convenient bolthole for Zorka and Franco. A place that didn't ask too many questions and was a universe away from the world they normally inhabited."

I knew Rod was right, but that didn't stop me from wondering about Zorka. Perhaps it was the not knowing, rather than any real concern, that niggled me. And I'm certainly questioning the adage about no news being good news. There's plenty of *no news* at the moment, and I don't find anything good about that at all.

We eventually ate a late lunch before I went home with a handful of the latest responses to the bus questionnaire. Rod suggested he might let the members of our group know the happy hour 'curfew' had been removed and invite them all to resume meeting at his place from six o'clock tonight. He also suggested that, if I had a chance to update the bus schedule spreadsheet this afternoon, I might bring a printout of it to tonight's happy hour. That ensured I would work on the spreadsheet this afternoon. And why not? The only alternative I could think of was housework.

While I fully intended to go straight to my computer when I arrived home, my library book lying on the end of the kitchen bench caught my attention. I paused and picked it up. It had been there for two days, patiently waiting for me to return it to the library. Perhaps I should take care of that before I start work on the spreadsheet.

As we are still largely confined to barracks, I'll need something to read to keep me entertained. There has been nothing on TV, and I tend to fall asleep in front of it anyway. Yes, I should return this book and find something else to read… And that idea was all well and good, except it involved a walk to the library. After one hair-raising experience today, am I foolhardy enough to risk the longer walk to the library?

It really isn't such a long walk, I tried to convince myself. After crossing the street out front, the remainder of the trip is across an open grassy area for the rest of the way to the library. I admit it took me a few minutes to persuade myself and summon the courage to venture out again, but then common sense prevailed. It was broad daylight. If anyone was determined to harm me, or worse, they probably would choose to do so under the cover of darkness.

After a couple of deep breaths, I resolutely strode out my front door with the library book tucked under my arm… only to hesitate briefly at my gate. "You're more vulnerable standing here than when crossing the grassy area, so get a move on," I muttered to myself.

There's nothing that stirs your motivation more than a few stern words. Pulling the gate closed behind me, I marched across the street and onto the grassed area. Nothing untoward happened. The sky didn't fall in. No vehicles were heard. Nobody jumped out of the bushes to grab me. It was all something of an anticlimax.

With my breathing returning to normal and my pulse rate descending rapidly to a more acceptable level, I walked – briskly – across the grass to the library.

Chapter 19

Joan Pembroke raced out of the library. Tears streaming down her face, and almost bowled me over in her rush to leave the place.

Had something happened? Was an evacuation now in place? The little voice in my head urged caution. Stunned, I remained anchored where I stood outside the library door for a few moments, watching Joan's retreating figure stumbling its way across the park. I saw the retreating woman trip and tumble to her knees before picking herself up again and continuing on her way.

A stray thought drifted past as I watched: Someone Joan's size should not be rushing about like that. A tumble was inevitable, and it could trigger something worse. Still, she seemed okay, I consoled myself as I watched Joan continue at almost a jog until houses blocked her from view.

That's when I became aware of something unheard of in the past happening in our library: loud, angry voices. More importantly, it was our librarian, Marjorie Bosworth's, raised voice. I'm sure none of us thought mousey Marjorie was capable of such anger, let alone a raised voice. It sounded as though she was reading the riot act to one of the library patrons.

Intrigue had a firm hold on me. I stepped up off the path and reached for the door. Again, I was almost knocked over. The library's door was flung open, and Bernard Stuart-Parnell stormed out. He stomped the standard route across the grass, to also soon disappeared from view.

"Interesting," I murmured to the universe. "Looks like serious trouble in paradise."

For quite some time, Bernard and Marjorie were considered 'an item' by the rest of our group. Apart from one minor upheaval some time ago, it appeared to be a constant and consistent relationship until recently. While Bernard appeared more than happy with his new relationship with the enigmatic, recently-arrived resident, James, Marjorie had taken her 'discarded' status particularly hard.

So, I was shocked to find her standing flushed and angry at a table in the corner after having delivered Bernard what was probably the most traumatic verbal whipping of his life. The three members of the book acquisition committee who remained seated at the table looked stunned and in a state approaching suspended animation. Although my first inclination on entering the library was to ask what had happened, I hastily changed my mind. I wanted information, but I was interested in facts rather than a load of long-winded dialogue.

"Congratulations, Marjorie," I chirped as I approached the table where the incident occurred. "That was an impressive forceful stand you took in dealing with the situation here." Marjorie looked surprised but nodded her thanks, and I continued. "I'm a little concerned about Joan Pembroke. She was in such a state when she left here. Do you think she will be okay after what happened? Should someone look-in on her on their way home, perhaps?"

Nodding heads and murmured agreement filled the space around the table until Iris West found her voice and responded directly to my question.

"You're right. Joan was in a state, and we should show our support for the way she stood up to Bernard. None of us was game enough to do it. I'll call on my way home to see how she is."

Adelaide Ballard said she would accompany Iris. That prompted the last member of the book acquisition committee, a woman I only know as Sandra, to throw her lot in with the others and go with them. With all three of them now committed to checking on Iris, they decided to do so straight away and left. That left Marjorie and me standing at the table like two pigeons on a fence.

"Come on, Marjorie. Let's go out the back. I'll make us a cup of tea."

She shook her head and appeared to be about to argue as she looked over at the volunteer on duty behind the desk.

"No, don't argue, Marjorie. The library is in good hands. Your library assistant can handle things in here, and if anything that she's uncertain about should crop up, we will only be out in the back room. She can call you."

I spoke loudly enough for the assistant to hear. As I finished speaking, she confirmed my comments with a nod. Then, with my arm firmly around Marjorie, I shepherded her through to the back room and put the kettle on.

As I reached for cups from a tiny overhead cupboard, Marjorie announced, "I prefer coffee, please. I only ever drank tea because that's what Bernard said he liked."

Good God, what was it about that obnoxious, supercilious man that allowed him to exert such a demoralising influence over Marjorie? Yes, I had thought her devoid of a personality – a mouse – but that was before the previous brief parting of their ways. On that occasion, Marjorie had morphed into a totally different person with a vibrant and outgoing personality. But it didn't take Bernard long to drive it out of her again once their 'differences' were mended.

This time, the wounds from the breakup appeared to cut much deeper. They resulted in Marjorie's avoiding contact with any of the residents outside of the volunteers who assisted in the library. It took a determined effort to drag her back to our mahjong sessions, and then only succeeded after strenuous reassurance Bernard no longer played. Despite her return to the mahjong table, Marjorie had not become quite the same vibrant person she had been during their last break-up.

As we sat sipping our coffees in silence, I noticed Marjorie's colour had returned, and she now looked more relaxed. I judged it was now safe enough to ask questions about the earlier event, but I needed to do it in a way that suggested I knew more about it than I did. I needed to take her back to the inciting incident that resulted in the uproar.

"Marjorie, how did Bernard manage to create such havoc today? I realise book acquisition meetings are always tricky and often involve working through a degree of disagreement and fuss and bother. To an outsider, today seems to have been the worst there has ever been.

"Oh, it was nothing new. As usual, it was deciding which books to purchase that caused the fuss. Bernard was being particularly argumentative and offensive this time."

"Did something in particular trigger it, or did he arrive spoiling for a fight?"

"Well, no, I wouldn't say he came spoiling for a fight exactly, but he was being obnoxious from the moment he arrived, worse than usual. He claimed he couldn't understand why he had to waste time on a meeting to discuss books with people who didn't know the first thing about literature. He demanded to know why people with no knowledge of literature were allowed a say in which books were bought for the library.

The insults went on from there. They were personal insults directed at the other committee members. I suppose it all became too much for Joan. She took him to task about it. It wasn't the wisest of moves. She received the full force of his vitriol, and quite frankly, had he said those things in any other forum, she would have just cause for legal action against him."

"What a bastard! I suspect part of the problem is that he knows he can get away with it. He must've been shocked when Joan took him to task for his comments. Still, I'm a little surprised it affected Joan as harshly as it did. She is made of fairly stern stuff, not easily moved to tears."

"You're right, Marion, but Joan has been a bit fragile for the last week or so. Her sister died about a week ago. She was Joan's only remaining family member, and they had always been very close. Not only did losing her come as a shock, but the way she found out about it almost knocked her off her perch. When she made her regular phone call to her sister, one of the nieces answered. She told Joan her sister was dead, and they had just returned from the cremation service. I can't begin to imagine what a shock that must've been for Joan."

"Had her sister been ill or anything beforehand?"

"Not that Joan was aware of, but it appears she became ill about six weeks beforehand. Then, she became critically ill about three weeks before she died and was placed in care. Joan and her sister spoke to one another on the same day every month. Although the family knew that, nobody bothered to let Joan know what was happening. If she had known about the illness, Joan said she would have gone to London to be with her sister and would have stayed with her to the end. I think that was the really hurtful aspect of it, that she had been deprived of the opportunity to say goodbye to her sister.

Almost as a postscript to the whole rotten affair, during that horrible conversation with Joan, the niece told her she believed her mother had left Joan something in her will but, as the will wouldn't be read for at least another couple of weeks, she didn't know what it was."

By the time she finished telling me the story, Marjorie also was in tears. Not surprising, I suppose. I felt much the same way myself. Joan was one of this world's good people. There was no way she deserved such treatment. I wondered aloud what the sister might've left Joan in her will and how difficult it would be to take possession of it – whatever it was.

Marjorie was thoughtful for a moment before responding. "I wonder if it might be that property in Melbourne that her sister owned.

During their last phone call, the sisters somehow talked about the terrible homeless situation in both their countries and the high cost of rental and real estate that was contributing to it. Apparently, the sister told Joan she couldn't believe how the value of the property she owned in Melbourne had escalated over the last couple of years. I don't think Joan knows whether the sister still held it when she died, or if she'd sold the property since that phone call."

"While it wouldn't make up for the loss of the sister, the bequest of a Melbourne property would go some way to easing the pain, I would think… Particularly if it meant the snotty niece didn't benefit from it."

We talked about nothing in particular until we finished our coffee, and I went to rinse our mugs. Without giving the matter any thought, I asked the question that had been floating around in my mind since we sat down with our coffee… and immediately wondered if I might've overstepped the mark.

"You probably don't know the answer to this question any more than I do, Marjorie, but I'll ask it anyway. What is going on with Bernard these days? He's always been obnoxious, but lately, there seems to be an added 'something' mixed in with it that renders him really unbearable. Do you think it's James's influence that's to blame?"

"At the risk of sounding spiteful and bitchy, yes, I do think the changes somehow are down to James, but how that's come about is a mystery to me as well."

It was close to the library's closing time. I hadn't returned my book or selected a new one, so I left Marjorie alone in the back room and went out front to take care of what I'd come to do. Marjorie hadn't reemerged by the time I'd finished, so I left without talking to her further. Nevertheless, our conversation gave me plenty of food for thought and succeeded in exercising my mind all the way home.

My quick trip to the library had taken up more of my afternoon than I intended. It was late, and I still had material to enter on the spreadsheet before happy hour. So, as soon as I was home, I went straight to my computer and brought up the spreadsheet. There wasn't an enormous amount of work required, but by the time I had completed the data entry and printed out enough copies, it was almost time to head to Rod's place.

After a quick shower, and carrying a container of store-cupboard nibbles and a stack of printouts, I managed to be the first to arrive for happy hour. The first of the others came almost the minute I was inside with Rod, so there was no time to discuss the printouts or what had happened at the library earlier.

Although he hadn't given the printouts more than a cursory glance, after allowing a few minutes for latecomers to arrive, Rod called the assembly together. Assuming it would be a long session based on stuff I was already familiar with, I dragged out a chair and sat down at the back of the group.

Rod's first move was to provide an overview of what had happened since he posted the bus questionnaire on our Facebook page. He then explained the fairly urgent need to give the Board of Directors the residents' views regarding the use of the Village's new bus. Before progressing further, he asked if all those present had responded to the questionnaire. I wasn't even mildly surprised when there were a few sheepish negative responses.

Having taken them to task for not responding, Rod then moved on to discussing the spreadsheet we had created and the emerging trends it indicated. After stressing that they were not to go any further, Rod handed out the printouts of the spreadsheet. There was a short silence as people studied the document they'd been given before Rod called for the group's thoughts on what it contained.

The discussions (or should that be a debate?) between the group members, excluding Rod, took care of the next twenty minutes or so. By then, Rod was a little short on patience … and I was becoming fed up and irritable. At that point, Rod called them all to order again and demanded to know what their main problem was with the trends so far.

"Well, there are several things on this sheet that…," Janet began.

"No," Rod shouted. "I want to know the *most offensive* thing about the data collected so far. I don't want to hear a list of things you don't like or can't agree with. What is the *biggest problem* with what's indicated on this sheet?" he demanded, waving a copy of the printout at them.

After a moment of shocked silence, Ted cleared his throat. "Ahem… It seems we all have a problem with trips to the shopping centres scheduled on Tuesdays and Thursdays. Those are our mahjong mornings, and that's how it has been for a number of years. None of us wants to give up mahjong to drive people to shopping centres."

"Okay, so what are the alternatives?... No, no. No, that was not an invitation to start discussing the matter. Listen up! … I will give you the only alternatives to consider.

Option 1: trips to the shopping centres are moved to Mondays and Fridays … regardless of what the trends indicate. It might not keep the majority of the residents happy, but it wouldn't interfere with our mahjong mornings."

"What about bowls?" Luigi interjected.

"Please wait until you have heard all of the options. Right, thank you. Now then….

Alternative 2: none of us drives the bus for trips to the shopping centres, regardless of what days they are scheduled.

Does anyone have any other practicable alternatives to suggest?" The invitation was greeted with silence, so Rod continued. "Right, let's hear your arguments for and against those alternatives.

"If we don't drive the bus, who will?" Frank demanded. "We're the only ones with permits to drive the thing. It's just another example of the Board's lack of planning. They should have thought about a driver before they bought the bus."

"We don't know if some members of this group are the only ones holding permits to drive a bus of that size. Aside from that, who drives the bus to the shopping centres is something the Board must sort out once they are aware we are not available."

"Might it mean there will be no shopping trips if a driver isn't available?" Janet asked.

"Oh, I hardly think the Board will let that happen. The shopping trips were one of the key arguments for purchasing the bus." Rod looked smug as he shared that piece of information.

"Well, what about bowls?" Maria asked in a timid voice. "It doesn't matter whether the shopping trips are on Tuesdays and

Thursdays or Mondays and Fridays. People play bowls on those days. Anyway, residents will not find Mondays and Fridays suitable. They are just not the days when people want to go shopping."

"I can see how you could work around the bowls thing regardless of which days are scheduled for shopping," Frank said and then went on to explain how both men and women bowlers could still go shopping on the bus without giving up their bowls days. His suggestion came in for some discussion before there was general agreement that it might work.

"Rod," Ted began tentatively, "does this mean we might not be required to drive the bus at all?"

"No, I don't see it that way. My thinking is that we would restrict our services to driving the bus for some outings. And, yes, I know 'outings' could cover many types of events, but I suspect we will be organising the outings and choosing when it suits us for them to occur."

As I sat watching and listening to the to and fro between the various members of the group, I didn't get any real feel for where it was heading. It wasn't until after Rod's response to Ted's last question that I relaxed, and my breathing returned to normal. The chatter that followed was excited, not contradictory. The happy hour group were now positive about potential bus operations. But I felt sorry for Rod.

He works so hard for the benefit of us all, and then those closest to him give him a hard time about what he's trying to achieve. There's not much about life that is fair. I couldn't help but wonder what the evening might have been like had Cilla also been there. I don't think I've ever heard her express her opinions on any of these matters, but as she likes to play Devil's Advocate, I'm sure she would have argued every point brought up. We would have still been there at midnight. Sometimes Fate is in your corner....

Cilla remained stuck fast in my thinking. We hadn't heard from her since she left for Sydney. While there was nothing unusual in that, this time, her absence has some relevance to us.

It was obvious this trip was to work with her team on the Franco Tonelli/ Zorka Weinhardt business. Logical thinking suggested they hadn't made any progress with the case, or surely we would have heard something from Cilla or Richard Wilson.

Come to think of it, our top cop, Richard Wilson, also appeared to have nothing worth reporting for the last couple of days. I found myself struggling to convince myself there wasn't some conspiracy of silence in place out there.

Contentious issues regarding bus scheduling having been resolved, the group didn't linger long and were soon heading home. With no Cilla there tonight, it was Rod and me left to clean up after they left. I gathered up as many glasses as I could carry safely and was packing them in the dishwasher when, over on Rod's desk, his phone played its tune.

He rushed in to answer it. To afford him privacy, I returned to the back deck and resumed cleaning up. How late was it, I wondered as I pushed chairs back under the main table. My watch told me it was only just gone seven o'clock, not late enough to read anything into Rod's call. It wasn't a long call, but I had finished all I could do before the call ended, so I dragged out a chair and sat down to wait for Rod to reappear.

About ten minutes later, Rod wandered out onto the deck. He seemed preoccupied, and for a moment, I thought he had forgotten I was there. I startled him by reminding him of my presence when I stood up and started gathering up the last of the glasses and plates to be washed.

"My call was from Richard Wilson. He didn't have a lot to say, but he expects to have more definite information for us in the morning. Depending on how things go overnight, he has arranged to call me around ten o'clock tomorrow morning. If he hasn't called by eleven o'clock, it will mean their operation is still in progress, and he will call later when it's over."

For someone who didn't have 'a lot' to say, it took him a long time to say it, I thought as I stacked the last things into the dishwasher... but I elected to keep that thought to myself.

"Did he at least sound positive?" I asked, "Or was he just feeding you that old 'no news is good news' line?"

"No, he sounded fairly upbeat – well, upbeat for Richard. He said they had a bit of a breakthrough earlier today and were able to capitalise on it. I got the distinct feeling there might be a bit of one-upmanship in the wind at the moment, with 'our' boys determined to show their southern counterparts how to do it."

"Huh… or is it more a case of Richard trying to trump Cilla and her team? Anyway, I don't care who outshines whom. All I want is my normal life back again."

"Yeah. Let's hope tomorrow goes some way towards that."

There was nothing more for me to do at Rod's place, and for some strange reason, I suddenly felt quite weary. I was about to take my leave when I remembered the walk home alone along a dimly lit footpath lay ahead of me. Of course, I would be all right. I tried convincing myself, but I didn't entirely believe that. Still, it was time to go home….

"Okay, let's see what tomorrow brings. I'll be off home now. Good night, Rod."

"Where the hell do you think you're going?"

"Like I said, I'm off home."

"Not alone, you're not. I intend to walk you home. If you are ready, let's go."

I didn't need a chaperone. Nothing untoward happened. But, having walked me home, it was only good manners to invite Rod to stay for dinner. After a pleasant meal, he didn't appear to be in any hurry to go home… not before breakfast anyway.

Chapter 20

It wasn't until after a long, lazy breakfast that Rod went back to his place this morning. As I stood watching him striding along the footpath, I saw him answer his phone – and quicken his pace.

Was it our top cop delivering exciting news? Richard Wilson had said he would call around ten o'clock. Was 9.30 close enough to ten o'clock, or was it some other caller? If Richard was Rod's caller, I expected Rod to either rush back or call me to share whatever news he had received. But that caused me something of a problem.

Until I heard from Rod, I would be virtually holding my breath. What if I didn't hear from him? Would that be an indicator of bad news, or just that the call was of no consequence to me? Regardless of how it played out, I knew I was in for a long, unsettled morning. With my ears finely tuned to my phone and the doorbell, I tackled various minor domestic chores to help pass the time.

Somewhere between eleven o'clock and lunchtime, my phone finally demanded my attention. It was Rod. He asked if he might come to see me now or if I would prefer he left it until later. Silly man; I'd only been waiting all morning. Why would I want to wait any longer?

"What a morning…." Rod announced as I held the door open for him, and he rushed past me.

"First, there was a call from Richard Wilson as I was on my way home from here. Then, a former colleague, chasing up information for me, called to give me what he had found so far. I was all set to call you after the chat with my colleague, but Cilla called before I could do that."

"I hope all the calls were to deliver the information we want to hear and not more of the stuff we don't want to hear."

"Uhmm, yeah. I'd say it was all positive news."

"Maybe if you were a little more convincing in how you said that, I'd be inclined to believe you. Let's not pussy-foot around it. What did they all have to say? And was there any news on Zorka's fate?"

"Well, Richard's call dealt mainly with the Zorka situation. He didn't have any definitive information, but they now believe she is likely still to be alive. It seems she was the prize being fought over by two rival factions the other night.

The first lot, that stormed the house after touring the Village for a while, was the mob associated with Franco Tonelli's untimely demise. They planned a similar fate for Zorka. But then the second contingent arrived and scuttled the first mob's plans. That second lot was from Zorka's operations, and they had come to rescue her."

"So, which group does Richard think was successful? Did that second lot of arrivals manage to save Zorka from the first mob, or is it still unclear who ended up with the 'prize'?"

"No, he seemed sure Zorka was rescued by her own team. His problem is, they don't have any hard evidence to confirm that, and they don't know where she is now... Although, he thinks she has been taken back across the border into what is basically their 'homelands'."

"Okay, I suppose we have to take that at face value and accept that Zorka is no longer in this state. What I don't understand is what it means in terms of our safety. Does it mean it is now safe for us to resume our normal lives, or do we still have some risk hanging over us?"

"Dunno... not exactly anyway. I think Richard's call was to give us some degree of confidence that we would be all right from now on. Although I asked him to explain what his information meant for us, I didn't receive the definitive answer you want. I didn't receive a 'yes, you're now safe' answer... or a 'no, continue as you have been' response.

Before you ask what that means, I reiterate: I don't know. To me, it tends to suggest *proceed with caution.* Perhaps it might be best if we adopted the approach that felt most comfortable for us individually."

"Right, so not a lot of reassurance or boost to confidence from any of that lot. Now, what about Cilla's call? It's unlike her to call when she is working. So, did she have something important regarding the investigation to pass on to us?"

"It's been an interesting morning, if for no other reason than the insight it provided into the interaction of the various police services.

Although Richard's call stopped short of telling us we were safe now, his message had a positive pitch that tended to indicate it might be the case. On the other hand, Cilla's message was virtually the opposite of that. She delivered a gloomy 'nothing new to report' message that tended to suggest the status quo should be maintained."

"Was she implying they haven't uncovered any new leads and still haven't determined Zorka's fate?"

"Argh, I suppose that was the gist of the call. She suggested there had been a lot of activity detected amongst the various underworld groups in that state. What they hadn't picked up was any definite leads connecting it to events up here in the Village. Don't ask.... Why Richard is telling one story while Cilla is telling a completely different one also mystifies me."

"What about that call from your former colleague? Did he have anything relevant to our current situation to offer?"

"Not really. I had asked him for some background information, particularly regarding recent activities. His call was to tell me he was putting together some stuff to send me."

It was lunchtime. I still had more to discuss with Rod, so the obvious thing was to ask him to stay for lunch. He accepted the invitation, and I almost went into a meltdown as I tried to work out what we might have. After a raid on my fridge, we sat down to cold meat and salad and washed it down with iced tea.

As soon as our plates were empty and we were sitting sipping the last of our iced tea, I felt it safe to begin the conversation I wanted to have, but my problem was how to lead into that conversation. In the end, I decided to dive straight in and see how it panned out.

"Rod, what do you know about that James, who Bernard appears to have attached himself to in some almost inseparable way short of surgery?"

"Funny you should ask that. On the last occasion I visited Tanya Jellicoe's office, I decided our manager might be just the right person to provide some background information on James. Of course, I knew I couldn't just come straight out and ask. I needed to adopt a more subtle approach if I wanted her to talk to me about another resident. So, I decided to pitch my query from the angle of what skills James might bring to the Village, and how we might involve and best utilise him in some of our ongoing projects."

"Sounds like a fair enough approach to me. How did she respond?"

"Initially, I thought I was in for a disappointment. She claimed James was something of a 'dark horse' and that she didn't know too much about his background at all. But, once she got talking, it was obvious she did know quite a bit about him, and none of it changed my opinion of him."

"That is disappointing. I suppose I hoped James had some redeeming features that Tanya might reveal. I find it strange that I can so thoroughly dislike someone who I know so little about. Perhaps it's the way he has about him – his demeanour – that gets up my nose. He gives the impression he is so superior to the rest of us, and we are not fit for him to develop any involvement with us."

"If it makes you feel any better, that's also about how he made Tanya feel. She did tell me something about his academic background, but there was nothing in it that made him superior to the rest of us. It's surprising Bernard is so smitten by him. Academically, Bernard outstrips him by miles."

"But they're fairly evenly matched personality-wise. Argh, the relationship, whatever it might be, doesn't really bother me. It's just that since they have paired off, Bernard has become more obnoxious than ever… More obnoxious and hurtful than I would have thought possible even for Bernard."

Having laid the groundwork for the conversation I wanted to have, I felt the time was right to recount the story of Bernard's performance at the library yesterday. So, I launched into my account of the incident I encountered and how it made Joan Pembroke so distraught.

"It sounds a bit over the top, even for Bernard. Did you find out exactly what triggered it?

"Only in a superficial way. While it is a standard occurrence at every one of that committee's meetings, yesterday's debate about which books to acquire and which ones were considered unsuitable seems to have been fiercer than usual.

Then, it turned personal when Bernard started hurling humiliating insults at the other members. It became so intolerable, Joan Pembroke found it necessary to take Bernard to task for his behaviour. That just resulted in her receiving 'special' attention for her trouble."

"How was it resolved?"

"I don't know that it was resolved. I know Marjorie stepped in to sort out Bernard. A couple minutes after Joan left, Bernard was booted out of the committee and told to leave the library. From the committee's point of view, it's probably a relief that he's gone, but I am concerned about the potential for some form of spiteful retribution."

"Hmm, I suppose that might be a possibility. It would be Bernard's style to try to humiliate the committee members in retaliation, particularly Joan.

Maybe we should adopt a wait-and-see approach, at least for a couple of weeks, until we see if anything further develops."

"While I accept that Bernard is free to develop whatever liaisons and relationships he wants, I'd hate to see the members of our mahjong group being subjected to the same treatment as was dished out to Joan Pembroke. How do we handle Bernard if he attacks us?"

"Again, let's wait and see. We don't know what's going on in his life right now. Yesterday's performance might have been a consequence of a combination of perhaps minor, once-only incidents happening simultaneously in Bernard's life that came close to tipping him over the edge. I'm not condoning his behaviour. I'm simply suggesting we wait to see if yesterday was a response to a certain combination of events or if it becomes a constant attitude.

And I'm certainly not suggesting anyone needs to put up with it. Anyone subjected to such unacceptable behaviour is entitled to give back as good as they are given and then some. Stand up to the poor excuse for a man."

"You're probably right about adopting a wait-and-see approach, but I still want to know more about James. What's his surname anyway? I don't think I've ever heard it mentioned. Did Tanya mention his surname when you asked her about him?"

"Bellinger…. I had never heard it mentioned either until Tanya, at some point in our conversation, referred to him as Mr Bellinger. I'm not familiar with the name. I don't know whether it has local connections or not. I don't know why he ended up here, anyway, if there wasn't some prior connection to this locality."

Rod didn't stay much longer after we discussed James. It appears recent events here have inspired Rod to write an article about Zorka and her family's operations over the years. While I look forward to reading it when it's published, its potential to stir up further trouble for us has me worried.

It was Friday evening again, and the tension had been building all afternoon to the point where I now felt in danger of being physically sick. Before he left this afternoon, I had asked Rod whether, given our current circumstances, we should front up to help run our regular Friday night pizza and karaoke evening. I was inclined to stick with our current cautious approach to life and stay home rather than being out and about after dark. Rod didn't share my view.

"I can't see why we wouldn't be okay. It's not like we would be wandering around outside by ourselves. Before and after the event, we will be with the other members while setting up and then cleaning up afterwards. Then, once the night kicks off, there will be plenty of people around us all the time. I think we will be fine.

Besides, with Bernard being otherwise engaged these days, if we don't turn up and it's another full house tonight, they will be too shorthanded to cope."

His comments made sense, and for the rest of the afternoon, I kept reminding myself of his reasoning. It didn't quell my fear. Usually, Cilla and I walk over early together to set up for the night. Then, the blokes arrive a bit later to set up the tables and chairs and the karaoke gear. But Cilla was still in Sydney. This evening, I would have to walk over on my own. Although I knew it would still be daylight when I made the trek, it didn't help calm my nerves.

Of course, nothing happened on the way to the Rec Room this evening, and nothing happened during the evening. Once again, we had a full house for our pizza and karaoke night, with even all the outdoor tables filled. It goes without saying that, without Cilla and Bernard helping out, those of the mahjong group who were there were rushed off their feet.

At the end of the evening, we seemed collectively to collapse in a great heap in the Rec Room kitchen. After a glass of wine, I would have been happy to stretch out on the floor for the night rather than face the walk home. But, as the conversation became brighter and more interesting, and was helped along by another glass of wine, I seemed to find a new burst of energy.

Somewhere on the periphery of my consciousness, I heard Zorka Weinhardt's name mentioned. It helped refocus me and draw me back into the here and now. I became aware Ted was asking questions about Zorka's fate.

"Well, whatever it was that happened there the other night, it didn't sound good. And, as Zorka hasn't been seen since, I don't think things went too well for her. Has anyone heard how she is or what happened? No one I've spoken to has seen her since that commotion the other night."

"That's not really surprising, though, Ted," Maria suggested. "I mean, even before that, no one ever saw Zorka around the place, or her husband, for that matter. Now that their front door is boarded up, you don't even know if anyone is home, let alone if they are okay or not."

"Yeah, strange fish, the pair of them," Luigi commented. "Fancy spending your whole life indoors and away from everyone…! What was wrong with them anyway? Was one of them ill or something that they didn't leave the house at all?"

I glanced at Rod, who was studying his hands resting on his thighs. I knew that look. I knew he was wrestling with his thoughts … and I thought I knew what they were about. He would have been tossing up whether or not to share what we learned about Zorka with the rest of the group. Or, perhaps more accurately, what the current thinking is about Zorka's fate.

Rod and I only know what we've been told, and to me, it sounded like the stuff of fiction novels. I suspected Rod wouldn't share anything with the others, and by the time the evening drew to a close, I knew I was right. He hadn't shared anything we'd been told, and I commended him on it as we walked home together after he locked the Recreation building. As usual, and in one group, the others left before us. With Cilla missing from our usual trio tonight, Rod and I could speak more freely than we might have otherwise.

"When she called you, did Cilla give you any indication of when she might be returning?" I asked as we started for home.

"No, but while there was no indication of her movements over the next while, I don't imagine she will be back until after this whole Zorka thing is put to rest."

"That could take ages – if they manage to sort it out at all. From what we've heard, the police have been trying to shut down that mob's operations for years. Why would they be more successful now than in the past?"

"Good question, but I don't have the answer. Anyway, I suspect Cilla is enjoying every minute of being there with her team. She will be right in her element again and lapping up the challenges of this case."

"Honestly, Rod, what do you make of it all? Do you think we'll have to keep looking over our shoulders until the police wrap up their investigation and neutralise Zorka's family's operations?"

"It's a possibility. I mean, it's possible we might have to wait until the police complete at least this current investigation before we start living normal lives again. And, before you ask, I don't know what might constitute successfully wrapping up their investigation.

Even if everything starts to look and feel normal again around here, we would be foolhardy to let our guard down."

"Nothing for it but to grin and bear it, eh?" I said and added a sigh of resignation for dramatic effect. I was about to whine about having to live in fear when something stopped me in my tracks.

"Rod, listen. There's a vehicle … and it sounds close. It sounds like it is here in the Village. What are we to do? Come on, Rod… Run!"

He grabbed me and held me back. "Shhh, listen. Yeah, it is somewhere here in the Village. Come this way." I felt myself being dragged over towards the nearest house. "We won't be noticed if we take cover in the shadows of those fruit trees growing along the outside of the fence line."

With my brain and feet finally in sync, I no longer needed to be dragged. I raced beside Rod to stand in the shadows of the trees… and not a moment too soon.

A speeding car raced around the corner and onto our street before reducing its speed to a crawl. Sometimes, you can be lucky. The vehicle had entered at the other end of the street, the end where Zorka's house is located. Had it come in from this end, the light shadows cast by the fruit trees would not have been sufficient to hide us from the car's powerful lights.

The house behind where we huddled in the shadows was the first house at this end of the street – and it was in darkness.

"Is the house behind us unoccupied at the moment, or are its occupants asleep already?" Rod whispered to me through the darkness.

"It's empty. No one has lived there for a couple of months."

"Good; before that vehicle reaches this end of the street, we are going over the fence to hide behind the rear of that house. Are you right to go? Right, let's go… Now… Marion, run."

No second invitation was required. I hopped over the low fence and raced to the rear of the house. Puffing and panting, and with my pulse playing a dangerous tune, I flattened myself against the wall in the darkest patch of shadow I could find. It took me a second or two to realise Rod wasn't there with me.

"Rod…," I whispered. No response….

I tried again, this time hissing a little louder. Still no reply. Panic set in. I tried calling his name again, but my throat spasmed, resulting in my effort producing no more than a strangled croak.

"Shush! Shut up. Just keep quiet and watch," he spat back at me.

The harshness of his voice didn't go unnoticed, and it did the trick. Shocked at being spoken to in that way by Rod, I was stunned into silence. And just in time…. Rod had just finished delivering his message when the car idled past the house we were hiding behind.

In my peripheral vision, I saw Rod turn to face the wall and huddle in close to it. Intrigued by what he was doing, I craned my neck to see what was happening. I saw him whip out his mobile phone. Although I couldn't see his phone's screen, I heard a number being keyed and then the soft sound as it dialled.

I hoped he had God or some other miracle worker on his speed dial.

Chapter 21

While waiting for his call to be answered, Rod slid further away from me along the wall, making it impossible for me to hear even the odd words of his side of the conversation. But Rod's phone call didn't command my focus for long. Something happening out on the street demanded my attention.

The car that had crawled past had only gone as far as the corner at the end of our street and now sat there idling. Was it waiting for someone or something? It had to be waiting for something, or why else would it sit there out in the open like that? But what was it waiting for? Although I had no logical answer to that question, it had started my stomach churning.

That's when it finally registered. How thick can I be? The vehicle was now being driven without lights. Not even its parking lights were turned on. Until it reached the corner, the car had been nothing more than a darker shape moving through a dark night broken by only dim, occasional street lights. But now, the two street lights on either side of the corner highlighted the vehicle like spotlights. It was obvious the vehicle's occupants were not concerned about being seen in the vicinity.

After idling there for a minute or so for no apparent reason, the sedan moved off, but still without lights. Although I couldn't see it, I tracked its sound as it headed towards the Village's main ring road intersection. So, it must be leaving… Surely, if the vehicle was heading for the ring road, it intended to leave the Village. I breathed a sigh of relief that proved somewhat premature. My relief quickly evaporated, and my stomach continued forming itself into a lead ball.

With my ears straining to capture any variation in the sound of the vehicle's progress, I realised it wasn't departing the Village, but merely making another circuit of the place. A soft buzz from Rod's phone cut across my concentration. Again, he moved further along the wall to speak to the caller. A couple of furtive glances he gave me during his call were disconcerting. Then, he started moving towards me again, although it was obvious his conversation was ongoing.

I raised my eyebrows at him in question. It produced no response. Stupid move anyway, I told myself. How was he supposed to see my eyebrows when we were standing here in the dark? Whatever the conversation was about, it had captured Rod's undivided attention. As I stared at him through the darkness, I realised he was either listening intently to the other speaker or waiting for something to be said. Ah, no, definitely waiting for something, I decided.

Distracted by Rod's call, I had stopped listening for the vehicle. Suddenly, I realised that when I last heard it, I thought it sounded like it was about to turn onto our street again. So, where the hell is it now? I couldn't hear it any more. I was plastered, unmoving against the wall and barely able to breathe as I strained my ears for any sound of the car.

There it was. I finally picked up the sound of it again… But something was wrong. Something was different now. Yeah, that's what it was. The vehicle wasn't moving. It sounded as though it was stationary, parked but still idling. And it was somewhere close by. I had kept my eyes on Rod in the hope some gesture or facial expression might provide a clue about the call that continued to occupy him. Okay, no, it wasn't easy to see his face, even in the glow from his phone, but there was nothing about him transmitting any clues as to what was happening. Then I heard his almost triumphal response to something from his caller.

"Yep… Right, we'll remain here until I hear from you… Cilla? … No, as far as I'm aware, she is still away… That's correct, both of us are here."

Interesting… but not particularly informative. Why would whoever the caller was ask Rod about Cilla? And why would Rod need to confirm that *both* of us were hiding behind this house? That comment had caused me some discomfort, and I felt a degree of vulnerability sneak in. What's the point of hiding if you tell people where you are?

As soon as Rod's call ended, I was inclined to demand to know who he had been talking to and what was going on. But Rod's demeanour gave me pause. Although his call had ended, he still clutched his phone with its now darkened screen firmly to his chest. He stared intently at it. Was he willing a call to come and light up the screen again? Instinct warned me not to interrupt but to wait until Rod was ready to share with me.

It was almost simultaneous. Rod's phone lit up almost at the same time as an incident of some sort occurred out on the street. Rod's call was brief, no more than a couple of sentences at best. But my attention was focused on the shouts I heard from out on the street.

"Stay back. Don't be stupid. I mean it."

I didn't recognise the voice. The words, while worrying, were difficult to interpret without some other reference. Then, a voice I did recognise boomed out over a loudhailer: Richard Wilson's voice.

"Put the weapon down... Put your weapon down on the ground and step away from it... It's over. Put the weapon down now –before they're given the order to shoot."

A shot rang out. Someone yelped. The loudhailer cut across everything.

"Fire at will... Take him down."

This time, a strangled scream followed almost immediately after those instructions were issued.

Paralysed with fear – and with shock, I suppose – I crouched hard up against the rear wall of the house we hid behind. Although unable to move and barely able to breathe, my eyes were fixed on Rod, a darker shape in the gloom a couple of metres further along the wall from me. I couldn't see his face, but I thought I discerned a tension in him as he also pressed hard against the wall. He still held his phone up in front of his face. What was he waiting for? Who did he expect to call him?

The sound of an approaching vehicle registered through the soup of terrifying thoughts filling my head. Although not physically possible, I pressed myself harder against the wall when I realised its sound was coming our way. I was so focused on the sound of the approaching vehicle that I jumped and struggled to stifle a yelp when Rod's phone buzzed impatiently.

"Right... Right... Okay, thanks."

As far as one-sided conversations go, Rod's response to his caller was both frustrating and unhelpful in the extreme. Was it the call he appeared to have been waiting for? I had no way of knowing whether the call was good news or a concern.

Then, as I pondered his call, I watched Rod flex his shoulders and slip his phone back into his pocket. He took a couple of steps away from the wall and stood there flexing and moving various body parts. I was so engrossed in his performance that he startled me when he spoke.

"Come on, let's go out front to see what's happening."

"Are you mad? I would prefer to stay here and be safe, thanks. Well, as safe as possible, I suppose."

"It's all over bar the clapping. Come on... let's go and applaud the efforts of our boys in blue."

He took me by the arm. After gently peeling me away from the wall and into a fully upright stance, he led (maybe that should be 'dragged') me from behind the house and out onto the footpath. I stopped abruptly and shook his hand free of my arm. The scene on the street a little further ahead was beyond my comprehension.

"Rod, that's in front of your house," I gasped. "What happened here? Given whatever is happening there, is it safe to be out here on the street?"

"Yeah. Richard says the situation is under control now, and it's safe for us to go home."

"Okay, that's good to know, but exactly what went on out here? And, when Richard says it's under control now, what does he mean? Is it under control for now and until the next time it happens? Or should we read something more final and long-term into his comments?"

"Marion, I don't have a definite answer for any questions you might want to ask tonight. All I can tell you is what I have told you so far, and it's because that is all Richard has given me. I'm sure more will be forthcoming and that it will probably answer at least some of your questions, but I don't know when that will be.

Now, I suggest we wander along the street to see for ourselves what has been happening. You never know. We might even receive some answers while we're about it."

Our first real view of the scene was of a herd of people going about their business around a vehicle parked in the middle of the street. Several figures clad in white forensics suits crawled all over the car while a number of uniformed police officers kept watch. As we approached the scene, I spotted a bloke with a loudhailer dangling from his shoulder, talking to a couple of the police officers. Richard was still on the scene. Maybe we would get some answers tonight after all.

We remained on the footpath and a little way from the scene to avoid interfering with the work happening around that car in the street in front of Rod's place. Despite our being as unobtrusive as possible, Richard spotted us and made his way over to speak to us.

"It will probably be a little longer before we are finished here," he informed us. "Rod, can you stay somewhere else for a while rather than going home? It would be best to stay out of your place for a while. Perhaps until morning would be best."

"He can stay at my place," I volunteered. "If you should want to speak to us later, that's my house over there," I said, pointing across the street.

"Good; I'll be over for a chat as soon as I finish here. I suspect we will all need a coffee, or something stronger, by then. I should be able to wind up my part of the operation in about twenty minutes, and I'll come to your place then."

Although Rod didn't argue with the arrangement, he didn't seem particularly pleased. As soon I let us into my house, I asked him what was wrong and why he wasn't happy about spending the night at my place.

"No, it's nothing like that. I'm not unhappy about spending the night at your place. It's just that I would have preferred to stand in my yard and watch what was happening out on the street in front. Put it down to the journalist in me if you wish, but I need to know what is happening and why."

"Yes, I do understand that, and if Richard comes to speak to us as he suggested he would, maybe you will end up even better informed than if you stood watching what was happening.

Richard was right about needing a coffee or something. What would you like, coffee or something stronger?"

We settled for a coffee and glass of port, and I raided the cupboard for some crackers to put with an unopened camembert I had in the fridge. Richard rang my doorbell as we were about to settle down in the lounge room with our late-night supper. Partaking of our feast was delayed a few minutes while I organised another coffee and port for Richard … and Rod engaged him in small talk to prepare him for the questions we would be asking later.

Richard proved he was one step ahead of us. He knew the questions we would throw at him, and he set about answering them before we asked them.

"I don't doubt it will take you both a day or two to recover fully from tonight's adventure, but from my point of view, it has been a successful evening… thanks to you, Rod. When I say successful, it was that, but it also has been disappointing. And, I don't know what your mate, Cilla, will make of it.

For the last week or so, I've had a niggling suspicion that not all is right in my camp. Initially, just a couple of minor funny things caught my attention. While they were really nothing in themselves, they didn't seem quite right. I now know they were a mere hint of much wider activities."

"Do these incidents – the minor hints and the wider activities – have anything to do with events happening here in recent days? I mean, are they connected with Tonelli's body and

Zorka's disappearance?" Rod asked. "I suppose what I'm really asking is, were those suspicions of yours linked with what I believe was intended to be an unpleasant evening for us tonight … and for Cilla, had she been home?"

"Unfortunately, yes. Believe me when I say there was nothing I could do to prevent tonight from happening. At the time, I did not know to what those things I thought a little strange might be linked, or the scope of the problem.

The occupants of the vehicle that kept you pinned down behind the house were two of my officers. At this stage, I don't know their intended target this evening, but from where they pulled up in the middle of the street, their target could have been on either side of the road – you, Rod, or Cilla. As Cilla is still away, they probably would have settled for you. Then they might have gone after Marion as well to tidy up as much as possible in the one operation."

A cracker loaded with cheese froze in transit to my mouth. Not for one minute did I doubt Rod and I were in danger tonight, but having it spelled out like that stunned me. Maybe it was some form of self-preservation device, but my brain had not allowed me to fully comprehend the magnitude of tonight's events from a personal perspective.

Now I realised that, without Rod's intervention and quick thinking, tonight, we might have joined Franco Tonelli in going to meet our maker.

Calling it a sobering realisation would be the understatement of the year. The little voice in my head kept shouting, *why? Why us?* But, although I didn't understand their reasoning, I knew why we were being targeted … and it still didn't make any sense to me. There wasn't an opportunity to ask questions. Richard pressed on with his story.

"It pains me to confirm the two occupants of the car that cruised the Village tonight were two of my officers. One was a detective, and the other was a senior constable. When my uniformed officers boxed in the vehicle and ordered the occupants out, the detective came out brandishing his weapon. He forced the officers in front of his car back a short distance and tried to have them move their vehicle so he and his companion could drive off. The other occupant was a little slower clambering out, but he emerged armed and threatened the uniforms from the police vehicle that had them boxed in from the rear.

Extra uniforms came in over your back fence, Rod, and on my command, they stormed out to wrap things up. You probably heard me on the loudhailer. That was the cue for those in your yard to come out. They were armed and wearing full safety gear, so a very different ending was possible."

My mind was reeling as it struggled to process Richard's information. When Richard finished speaking, silence prevailed for a few moments. I seized the opportunity it presented.

"At the risk of appearing dumb, Richard, please clarify something for me. Were those two officers you just told us about somehow part of what happened here? I mean, did they have something to do with Tonelli's death and the attack on Zorka's place the other night?"

"Oh, yes, they were involved. I'm not saying they were responsible for the killing, and I'm still not sure whether they played an active part in the attack on Zorka's house. But indications are that they had a hand in both of those incidents. From my point of view, there are even wider implications. It appears those two men have been operating as part of an underworld organisation for some time. I don't know how far back their involvement goes. I suspect they have been able to remain a mainly covert information resource until the recent events brought the underworld closer to home."

"Richard," Rod started hesitantly, "what do we know about Zorka's current situation? Was she abducted and might have met with a horrible end, or was she whisked away to safety by members of her own mob?"

"We believe some of her own people rescued her in the nick of time and spirited her away from here. There have been some developments south of the border that tend to confirm that situation.

Our counterparts in the southern state have nabbed three men who were driving what we think was the rescue vehicle used here to transport Zorka to safety. While that suggests Zorka got away from here okay, the fact that she wasn't with those three men when they were picked up poses new questions."

"So, Richard, are you saying that Zorka is now back on her home patch safe and sound after her mob rescued her from here?"

"No, that's not what I'm suggesting at all. All I'm saying is that it is likely Zorka was with those men when they crossed the border and that she probably is now back home with the rest of her mob."

I glanced at Rod to see if he was about to pursue further his line of questioning. He was staring off into the distance, and I could almost hear his mind churning through the details Richard had provided. Something about Rod's demeanour told me that something Richard said troubled him. It was probably a couple of minutes later, a couple of long minutes of absolute silence in my lounge room, before Rod spoke.

"Are you convinced about any of that?" he asked without turning his gaze to Richard, who simply shrugged and shook his head in response.

"What about if that's not the case? What if… Zorka didn't go home? … What if … she was dropped off somewhere before her rescuers crossed the border? … What if… maybe she did cross the border with those three men… but then… somehow … She crossed the border to return to this state?"

"Am I right in assuming you are proposing a scenario that suggests Zorka might be alive and well and still somewhere in this state?" Richard asked, and Rod shrugged but didn't deny it.

"Right then," Richard continued, "I'm interested in hearing your reasoning behind this assumption. More than that, I need to know if you're privy to information I haven't received."

Richard's tone had become hard, and it left no room to doubt who was in charge of our conversation. I wasn't impressed with the way he looked at Rod or the thinly veiled accusation he aimed at him. I felt my pulse step up a gear. There was a real possibility this could become unpleasant at any moment. But, at that point, Rod focused on Richard, cleared his throat, and spoke in a low, measured voice.

"I resent the inference in your last comment, but I will make allowance for it – for the moment. It has been a difficult night for all involved, particularly for you, after the harsh reality you uncovered.

Unfortunately, I don't have a sixth sense or some incredible information source. I'm simply trying to apply logical thought to the possibilities that might exist regarding Zorka's current whereabouts. Your reaction to such rational thoughts has me intrigued. In fact, I suspect my comments cut close to the bone. Perhaps there is more you know, but you have decided not to share it with us."

Rod's words had me squirming in my seat. Rubbing Richard up the wrong way was not a good move. I liked having him in our corner. And I would much prefer he remained a willing informant and friend who was interested in our continued wellbeing.

It seemed as though Richard paused to take stock of the situation for a moment or two before continuing. When he did, his tone had returned to normal, and I saw Rod settle back again in his chair. Ruffled feathers appeared more or less settled again.

"You might be right, Rod. And that might be a fairly astute assessment on your part. It lines up with others' thoughts on this matter.

Some reasonably reliable intelligence we've received suggests Zorka didn't cross the border, or if she did, she quickly returned to this state. So far, we haven't been able to verify it, but it does seem a strange move – if it is true."

"Yeah, I agree it would be strange – if that is what's happened. I figure Zorka would have to be desperate to forgo the comparative safety of her home base to seek refuge in Queensland. If her rescuers from the fracas that happened here the other night are now behind bars, the question then is, who does she have with her? I don't like her chances if she is back on this side of the border alone," Rod suggested.

"If she has come back to this side of the border … And if she is alone…," Richard added. "She might not necessarily be alone if she crossed back into this state. I'm beginning to think she might have a solid core of supporters on this side of the border, and she might consider herself safer here than back at her home base."

"What's your next move, Richard? I mean, regarding your two rogue officers. Are you convinced they were two lone operatives, or might there be more of them interspersed through the service?"

"Again, some astute thinking on your part," Richard began before pausing briefly.

He appeared to consider whether to continue with what he was about to say or to leave it at that. In the end, he continued speaking, but whether it was what he originally intended to say is unclear.

"My two rogues will be safely locked away by now, out of sight and incommunicado. I've had a quick call to my superiors to alert them to the situation we uncovered here and to suggest they explore the rest of the service for similar problems. Knowledge of our two bad apples will be restricted to this location and my officers.

Unfortunately, we can't assume those two were the only two operating on the wrong side of the law. So, while my precinct is in a virtual lockdown, every person associated with it will be rigorously investigated over the next few days.

I trust I can count on you not to release any articles for the next little while that might impact the undercover investigation we will be undertaking."

"Of course, you can rely on me not to jeopardise your activities, but I would appreciate a nod when it is safe to do so, and I would appreciate an 'exclusive'," Rod told him.

The matter dealt with, the conversation took on a lighter note as it wound down towards time for Richard to be on his way. We said our goodnights on the doorstep, and Richard was about halfway down my path before halting abruptly.

"I would appreciate being kept informed should you hear anything from Cilla over the next few days," he told Rod before continuing to his car. It didn't sound so much a casual request as a demand, but Rod just nodded sagely and agreed.

Not much of the night remained by then. Activities continued in the street between Rod's and Cilla's houses. We agreed there was little point in Rod going home. The lights and action happening on the road weren't conducive to sleep.

So, we agreed there was nothing else to do but go to bed and try for at least some sleep before the sun came up.

Chapter 22

It was two days later before I caught up with Rod again. First thing after he went home on Saturday morning, after spending a large chunk of Friday night cowering behind a house over the road from my place, Rod cancelled our regular happy hours until further notice. No real explanation was given, and we had to be content with 'something had come up'.

Although tempted, I didn't seek further information. I knew I was still unsettled after Friday night's adventure, and I guessed Rod would be too. I knew I wasn't inclined to spend an hour or two with a group of other people, and I suspected Rod felt equally reluctant to host a horde of people.

If Rod had received an update from Richard or Cilla, he made no move to share it with me. That meant I didn't know whether it was safe yet for us to resume our normal lives, or if we were to continue looking over our shoulders. I decided to play it safe until I had confirmation we were out of danger. After two days of remaining indoors, I was suffering a major bout of 'cabin fever'.

Monday morning found me awake at my usual time and struggling to ease into yet another day of being confined to barracks. After about twenty minutes of procrastination, I sat up and swung my legs over the side of the bed.

"Damn it! I'm going for a walk. To hell with living caged up in fear of what might happen if I venture outside alone," I told the universe … and in a voice loud enough to also alert the neighbours.

Minutes later, I strode out onto the street and headed for the little park beside the Village where I always walked. It took no more than about twenty paces before my bravado began evaporating. After hesitating briefly, I mentally took myself by the scruff of the neck and dragged me across the grass towards the park. It was a false show of defiance. I might have been striding along resolutely but, internally, I felt like a bowl of jelly.

No one jumped out at me… No one tried to abduct me … I saw no one and spoke to no one but the trees and the birds. Absolutely nothing happened… except the park worked its magic on me yet again.

This morning, the world seemed a glorious place and that included for Merivale Retirement Village residents. A sparkling clear blue sky coupled with a light breeze made for pleasant walking. Later in the day, once the morning breeze disappeared, the heat would crank up, and the day would become hot and humid.

As I strode through the dappled shade of the paperbarks and eucalypts, the birds voiced their displeasure at my intrusion into their world. But, they are a forgiving lot and, having recognised me as their former regular visitor, soon filled the air with their song as they went about their business.

It was as though the rest of the world hadn't yet come to life today, and that suited me fine. Even after I left the park and entered the Village again, I encountered no signs of life. It felt odd, eerie even. By this hour of the day, there were always people about. Other residents would be strolling through the Village. Some would be out tending their front garden or washing their car on their driveway. If it wasn't for the occasional sound of a TV or a yapping dog as I passed, the place might have been deserted.

Rod returning from his run at the other end of my street was a welcome sight. Although I knew nothing was wrong, today, the Village seemed strange, and I had an almost overwhelming urge to ask the universe where everyone had gone. Perhaps, terrified by Friday night's events, they had all up and left the Village over the weekend. But, there was Rod, setting the world aright for me again as he usually did.

"Your timing is perfect," he called out as he approached. "Are you up for a juice and a coffee? And can you put up with my being all hot and sweaty?"

"If you would prefer to have a shower first, I'll come back and join you for coffee after I have a shower," I offered.

He accepted my suggestion, and I continued the rest of the way home alone. The good thing about returning to Rod's place later was that I might be lucky enough to avoid being offered juice. Hopefully, he will have his juice before I join him, and I will only have coffee with him. It's not that I don't like the occasional long glass of cold juice. It's just that I have seen some of the stuff he drinks… thick green gloop whizzed up in his blender. Just the look of it is enough to make me race home again.

Only coffee was on offer when I returned to Rod's, and for that, I was grateful. It was inevitable that conversation almost immediately focused on Friday night's incident and its aftermath. And it was equally predictable that I would demand to know if Rod had heard anything more from Richard or Cilla.

"I had intended to catch up with you this morning, so this has worked out well," he told me. "Cilla called me late yesterday afternoon, and then Richard called around dinnertime last night. Neither of them had anything earth-shattering to report, but they did provide updates."

"My hope is that, sometime soon, someone is going to tell me the world has returned to normal, and I can now resume my former life," I told him. "I suppose it is too much to hope that their latest updates amount to any of that?"

"Well, not exactly; no, but they were encouraging nevertheless.

Cilla says she might return tomorrow or the day after at the latest. She says her team has – to use her words – 'neutralised' a significant part of the operations of the mob they were targeting. Although her team will still have some mopping-up to do, she should be able to come home."

"She is talking about Zorka's family's operations, I presume, and I suppose that is good news as far as it goes. It doesn't exactly tell us we are now safe, though, does it?"

"No, but I suppose it tells us we are a lot safer than we might have been if Cilla's team's campaign had not been successful.

Now, Richard's update was interesting. He found another bent copper somewhere in the region that comes under his control. I asked what was happening with those coppers. All he would tell me was that they had been moved covertly to a secret location a long way from here as an interim measure, and they would soon be moved to prisoner facilities in other states."

"Why all the secrecy? Does he think someone might try to break them out of goal?"

"That's not his primary concern. He is more worried that the mob they worked for might try to 'tidy up' those loose ends before they have a chance to say too much.

He also reported that, subsequent to his alerting Brisbane to the situation here, a number of other 'bad apples' had been apprehended in the southeast corner of the state. His superiors told him they now have fairly reliable information that Zorka is somewhere in the Brisbane area. Richard thinks a splinter group of the family's network has operated out of the southeast corner of our state for some time. While they have largely been dormant for much of that time, they have been called on to assist the family on the odd occasion."

"Doesn't it seem strange that they have been there for a while without doing anything? Wouldn't you think their connection with the Weinhardt family's operations would fade away if they weren't doing anything?"

"Oh, they were doing their bit, but it was mainly intelligence gathering and alerting the family whenever the situation here might be about to become troublesome for their operations.

The only other item of interest Richard had to share was that he believed we were now out of danger."

"Are we safe to move about freely again? Is that what he was saying?"

I needed confirmation to help me take in what Rod had said. It almost seemed too good to be true. There probably was some sort of caveat attached to it, I told myself, and again questioned the information Richard had given Rod. He was almost exasperated by the time I finally accepted what I was being told, and I sent up a loud cheer.

Cilla arrived home late on Tuesday night. I didn't manage to catch up with her until happy hour at Rod's place on Wednesday night. Our world slowly returned to normal this week. Our regular evening happy hours at Rod's had resumed. And, with Rod and me again free to be out and about and Cilla now home again, we would have our full group once more for mahjong mornings.

As might be expected, during Wednesday night's happy hour, the discussion turned to mahjong. There appeared to be a collective uplifting of spirits when Rod announced he could see no reason not to reinstate our mornings.

"Oh, that is good news," Janet purred. "It hasn't felt right lately. I felt completely out of touch with everyone. What with no mahjong and no happy hours, it was like living in isolation."

Rod and I exchanged a look. That's exactly what we had been doing for some days: living in isolation. While it developed into a lively evening, Cilla remained somewhat subdued and a bit withdrawn. Usually, at the end of a happy hour session, Cilla and I stay behind to help Rod clean up and return everything to its proper place on his back deck. Tonight, Cilla was one of the first to leave.

"Any idea what that was all about?" Rod asked when he returned to the back deck after seeing the last of them off. "Did someone say something to upset Cilla tonight, or is it just us she is offside with us for some reason?"

"Dunno, but it was obvious she wasn't enjoying herself tonight. Do you think she might be offside with us for talking to Richard Wilson while she was away? Although, I suppose it is possible she still might be a bit strung out from whatever she was involved with in Sydney… and then there was the late flight home last night."

"Yeah. She might be feeling a bit worn out. It might be just as well they all agreed to leave resuming mahjong mornings until next week. I don't think I was quite ready to start again tomorrow."

I had to agree with Rod. I wouldn't have welcomed having to rush about tomorrow morning to produce something for the mahjong group to have with morning coffee. Maybe recent events have taken more of a toll on me than I thought. Perhaps I do need a few days of long, solitary walks to find my equilibrium again.

The next few days were a slow wind-down, a release of tension built up over the previous couple of weeks. They saw a return to doing 'normal' things – like shopping in the city and buying groceries at the supermarket.

During our period of being confined to barracks (as I like to think of it), the few groceries I needed were delivered to my door. Everything else I needed, like a haircut, for instance, was available in the Village. But, if I'm honest, it was the companionship of others that I most missed: playing mahjong, happy hours, chatting with people I encountered on my walks. Slowly, I slipped back into my old life.

On my way into the city on a shopping expedition, I cursed the traffic lights turning red as I pulled up at them. These were set with particularly long sequences favouring traffic going in the other direction. I heaved a sigh of resignation and allowed my mind to roam free while I waited for them to change. Like a hammer blow, a stray thought slammed in uninvited.

"That bloody bus…!" I yelped. "We still have to finish that schedule."

All thoughts of the new bus and its schedule we had been working on had completely vacated my mind over the previous couple of weeks. Rod hadn't mentioned anything about the bus, so it probably wasn't occupying his thoughts either. As the lights changed and I drove off into the city, I resolved to speak to Rod about the bus as soon as I returned home.

Shopping trips often don't go as planned. Today was no different. A visit to one of the big department stores resulted in an encounter with an acquaintance I hadn't spoken to in some time. We arranged to meet for lunch at a coffee shop on the north side of town. Then, while waiting to be served in another shop, I was tapped on the shoulder by a friend who runs a produce stall at the various local markets and often drops off any leftovers from the markets at my place. As she was also a friend of my lunchtime companion, I asked her to join us at the coffee shop.

An enjoyable lunch followed. It was so enjoyable, it dragged on for over two hours. I still had to visit the supermarket, and by then, it was 'after school time'. That time of the day when mothers and their kids they have just collected after school invade the supermarket on their way home. Today turned into one of *those* days for me. The supermarket was crowded, and kids of all ages seemed to swarm, unsupervised and uncontrolled, throughout the store.

After spending the best part of an hour continually bleating *excuse me please* as I tried to manoeuvre my trolley up and down the aisles, I finally made it to the checkout – and took my place fourth in the queue behind trolleys loaded to overflowing. When I arrived home, I was tired and cranky – and I still had the groceries to unpack and put away. Bus schedules were a long way from my mind by then.

They didn't pop back into conscious thought until we were cleaning up after happy hour that night. Cilla stayed behind for a few minutes to help load the dishwasher but had gone home by the time bus schedules came to the fore.

"Argh, Rod, before I forget again, what is happening with the bus schedules?"

"The what…? Oh, yes; bus schedules…. Well, I confess nothing is happening because they had slipped completely from my mind. Come to think of it, it's surprising no one has been screaming for them before this. I'll check tomorrow to see if any further responses have come in. There won't be time to do anything. Being Friday tomorrow, a big chunk of the day will be taken up with preparations for pizza and karaoke night.

Tomorrow, I'll print any new responses and get them to you to add to the spreadsheet. Then, we'll need to set aside some time over the weekend to finalise a draft schedule I can take to Tanya on Monday. I think the board of directors meet this coming week, so it will be timely to have something out to them prior to their meeting."

True to his word, Rod printed out the few new responses to his questionnaire and delivered them to me around mid-morning. As I was about to make a coffee, he stayed for morning tea with me. As soon as he left, I added the new data to the spreadsheet and printed several copies of it to use when we worked on the schedule. While the afternoon was the usual blur of activity preparing for Friday's pizza and karaoke night, I did manage to slip Rod and Cilla a copy of the spreadsheet to take home with them.

"Thanks, Marion," Rod said as he glanced at his copy. "How about we meet at ten o'clock tomorrow morning at my place? We could kid ourselves that we can knock over this schedule thing by lunchtime, but realistically, we're likely still to be working on it after lunch."

Both Cilla and I volunteered to bring something for lunch and told Rod he could provide the chilled white wine to go with it.

As I drifted off to sleep that night, my lingering thought was about how pleasant it had been walking home after the pizza and karaoke night with Rod and Cilla. In reality, it was nothing, but somehow, it made the world seem right again… and tomorrow's workshop at Rod's would confirm life was back to normal.

Saturday morning developed into a bit of a rush. After taking myself off for a long walk, I faced the problem of what to make to take to Rod's for lunch. There was no question we would be having lunch together whether the schedule had been completed by then or not. But I had no doubt our work would be far from done by lunchtime, and if we continued working after lunch, we were likely still to be there when it was time for afternoon coffee. All of that meant I needed to prepare something for lunch and bake something to have with coffee throughout the day.

I was almost hyperventilating as the morning slipped by. But five minutes before the appointed hour, with a folder containing all the bus schedule information under one arm and a bag full of food in the other hand, I strode along the footpath to Rod's place. Cilla saw me coming and crossed the street to meet me at Rod's gate. Between us, we carried enough food to feed an army, not three people.

After the obligatory coffee and cake immediately after our arrival, we adjourned to the table on Rod's back deck to begin what we knew would be an arduous task. As we had noticed earlier, the residents' responses to Rod's questionnaire produced few clear preference trends. Initially, we thought choosing the most preferred option in every case would be a simple matter.

It didn't take us long to realise that approach wouldn't work. There was only one bus, and it could only be in one place at any given time. By selecting the most preferred options in every case, we would have needed at least three buses to meet the requirements. To help with problem-solving, Rod ruled a large sheet of paper into seven columns and labelled each column with a day of the week. At last, we began to make progress. Nevertheless, the debate continued to rage until lunchtime.

By the time we left Rod's place after a mid-afternoon coffee, I felt brain-dead, but we did have a draft schedule.

Although it took us until nearly three o'clock to refine it as much as possible and to the point where all three of us were happy with it, I knew that wasn't the end of the story. As we sat sipping our coffee in an exhausted silence, my battered brain came to life in response to a question from Cilla.

"So, what happens now, Rod?" she asked. "We've always referred to the schedule as a draft. Does that mean it has to be approved or endorsed by others before it can become operational?"

"Yep, the board has to decide whether to accept and implement it or not."

"Right… so what is the process to get that to happen, and what happens if they choose to reject it?"

I knew Cilla was, to some extent, playing Devil's Advocate, and her questions were real enough, but I judged us all to be too mentally exhausted to deal with them then. Nevertheless, Rod rose to the occasion – while I remained semi-comatose and slumped in my chair.

"I'll tidy it up tomorrow and then take a copy to Tanya first thing Monday morning so she can send it out to the board to read before their meeting later in the week. After that, we wait to see what happens next."

Rod sounded weary as he spoke, but Cilla wasn't put off by it.

"Okay. So, it's discussed at the board meeting, and then what? I mean, what happens if they reject it, or they don't like some of the content? Will they use our efforts as the basis for a new schedule that the board will develop instead?"

"For Christ's sake, Cilla, use your common sense," I snapped. "You know as well as I do that the board won't exert themselves over a bus schedule. If they don't like something about it, our draft will be returned for remodelling according to their recommendations. So, yes, that might mean we will be having another session to create a new version of our draft schedule.

And, Rod, unless I misjudge him, I'm almost willing to bet the chairman will insist on your attendance at this week's board meeting."

"Why would they need Rod if they already have the draft schedule to consider?" Cilla demanded. "It's up to them to decide what they want."

"Hang on, Cilla," Rod chided her. "We both know how things work around here. Marion is probably right. I fully expect to be called to speak to – maybe I should say *explain* – our draft schedule. And, of course, I will be more than happy to do that."

"Before you get too bogged down in explaining how the schedule will work, maybe your first task should be to ask who will drive the bus," I suggested. "For what it's worth, I think it unacceptable that, every day of the week, one of our team should give up his time to drive the damn thing for the benefit of the other residents. It's up to the board to make proper arrangements for the operation of its bus."

"Good point," Cilla claimed. "While one of our group might be prepared to drive it occasionally, say, for special excursions, there should be no expectation that we will supply a driver on all occasions."

"Are you sure you pair wouldn't prefer to front the board meeting instead of me?" Rod asked.

His sarcastic intervention successfully ended the discussion. A minute or two later, Cilla and I took our leave and headed home. We had achieved a lot, but it left me feeling drained and not at all looking forward to a happy hour this evening. During the short walk home from Rod's place, I managed to convince myself I had nothing more important to do for the remainder of the afternoon than to have a nap. And that's what I did.

As soon as I was home, I turned back the cover, crashed on my bed, and stayed there until my phone woke me. It was Rod demanding to know where I was and why I wasn't coming to happy hour tonight. I swung my still blurry eyes in the direction of the bedside clock. It was 6.30pm … and happy hour would be half over. Within a few heartbeats, I was off the bed and splashing water over my face. A couple of minutes later, at a pace just short of a jog, I was on my way to Rod's.

With no apology for my late arrival or for arriving empty-handed, I marched past Rod when he opened the door and continued to the back deck. As I joined the group, Ted thrust a glass of wine into my hand. Instead of moving into the midst of the group, I drifted around behind them and stood a little way off. Rod rushed over to me. He had a strange look on his face.

"What are you doing? Are you all right? You didn't have to come if you preferred to stay home tonight. I was just about to introduce the mob to our draft schedule and thought you would want to hear their responses to it."

"I do want to hear what they have to say. It's just that I was asleep when you called, and I'm still trying to wake up enough to be capable of intelligent conversation. Anyway, I didn't think you would have the draft finished until tomorrow."

He chuckled and leaned in close to whisper in my ear. "I thought it might be worthwhile giving it a 'dry run' tonight. They will be caught off-guard now, but I'm sure they will return with plenty of good advice tomorrow evening."

After refilling his glass, Rod banged an empty wine bottle on the table to gain everyone's attention. As he delivered a bit of an introductory speech, I slipped inside to his desk and grabbed a pad and pen before returning and settling in a chair behind the group. By the time I was seated, Rod had handed out copies of the draft schedule and provided a brief explanation.

Silence descended like a heavy blanket. For the next couple of minutes, not a murmur was heard, although I did see Janet nudge Ted in the ribs and direct his attention to something on the schedule. Ah, wait for the first of the arguments, I warned myself, as I wondered what had caught Janet's attention.

Chapter 23

Janet and Ted surprised me. I was sure one of them would raise a query, or worse, about whatever was in the draft schedule that had caught Janet's attention. Luigi was quicker off the mark.

"According to this, something is happening every day of the week. That's five days," Luigi announced. "There are only four of us who can drive the bus. I think we might have a problem here. I don't want to drive the thing more than once a week, and not every week either, if possible."

"Yeah, I agree," Frank snarled. "I don't mind helping out occasionally, but I'm damned sure I'm not going to spend my time chauffeuring other residents around the place."

Ted quietly added his support to the comments already made. I had my head down noting what was said and who said it. Cilla's voice made me stop and look up.

"Might your thinking be a bit premature, do you suppose?" she asked. "I haven't heard anything about how the bus will operate, including who the driver will be. Should we perhaps wait to see what the board's plans are in this regard before we become too outraged about it?"

"Cilla's advice makes good sense," Rod said. "So, if we could leave the matter of the driver in abeyance for the moment, please focus on what is being scheduled, when, and how that might fit with the rest of life here in the Village."

As expected, the issue of shopping days clashing with bowls days was brought up and debated at some length, along with carting players around to the various bowls clubs for the interclub competition. The latter issue died a sudden death when Rod reminded them that the finals of the interclub competition were to be played next week and, after that, the bus would no longer be required on those days.

It goes without saying that happy hour that night extended past its usual finish time of seven o'clock. By the time the last of the group left, it was after 7.30pm. I started gathering up the glasses to take through to the dishwasher while Rod began restoring the furniture to its rightful place. About to dump empty wine bottles in the bin, Cilla called for our attention.

"Unless you pair have better plans, there is a large casserole keeping warm in my oven. I'd be happy for you to come and help me dispatch it."

How could we refuse? The aroma drifting across the street from her house had started my stomach rumbling the best part of an hour earlier. No time was wasted finishing up at Rod's place before we crossed the street. For a few glorious moments after we sat down to eat, no one spoke. The silent interlude was wonderful. Rod and Cilla used the time to rest their vocal cords after having dealt with all the queries and arguments generated by the draft bus schedule, and all three of us rested our ears after what had been, at times, a heated debate. As expected, once conversation resumed at the table, the draft schedule swept all other topics aside.

"Well, that went well, didn't it?" Cilla said with sarcasm dripping off every word. "Was there anything positive or constructive to come out of tonight's discussion of the bus schedule?"

I shook my head in response. Rod stared off into the distance for a moment before answering.

"Uhmm… Aw, I think things went as intended. There's always a negative reaction to anything unexpected you throw at people. That was the thinking behind giving them the draft tonight instead of tomorrow night. They all behaved exactly as I expected… and we dealt with their reactions as well as possible. Now, they have all of tomorrow to stew over it before happy hour tomorrow night.

Never doubt there will be another hotly debated session tomorrow, but it will be more meaningful and more likely to produce real – worthwhile – input. Regardless, I can't see me making many, if any, changes to the draft schedule before I take it to Tanya on Monday morning."

The subsequent pause in conversation provided the opportunity I'd been trying to engineer all day, so I took it.

"Cilla, is everything all right with you?" I asked quietly and with no particular emphasis, and immediately wished I hadn't.

"With me…? Yes, why wouldn't it be? Why do you ask?"

Her tone was enough to tempt me to drop the subject, but having committed to it, I pushed on – gently.

"You look a little tired, and you've seemed a bit quiet, withdrawn maybe, since your return from Sydney. I was concerned something might have been amiss."

"No, nothing is wrong. Well, nothing much anyway, and nothing any of us can do anything about right now." She glanced up to find both Rod and me studying her intently.

"Argh, it's a combination of things, I suppose, rather than any one issue." Her attempt to dismiss the matter didn't work.

"We're both good listeners," Rod told her. "You never know. Maybe just talking about it will help. Give it a go."

"Look, it's nothing to be concerned about. It's just a combination of things all coming together at the same time… and I suppose I am a bit tired, too.

My time in Sydney was a procession of long, difficult days that did produce results, but not the desired level of success. Although everything turned out well in the end, I have to admit that was largely due to the efforts of the police in this state rather than those of my team. Oh, don't get me wrong. I'm not criticising my team's efforts. It's just that we didn't seem to be receiving the same high level of intelligence as was available elsewhere."

"Did your team not live up to other people's expectations?" I asked cautiously. "Was there some degree of unfavourable comment as a result?"

"God, no. At the end of the day, they received praise all around. But I knew we hadn't performed as well as we should have. I knew there was more we could have achieved. Argh,

I suppose I'm questioning my own ability, and probably my suitability to lead that team.

I felt we lost our edge somehow, and 'special' teams are not allowed the luxury of that. There will be an extensive post-mortem on our performance, but I'll wait a few days before I schedule it."

Rod took a moment to offer reassuring advice regarding the complexity of the situation her team had faced, and emphasised that so much going on across such a wide geographical area hadn't helped.

"So, Cilla, my advice would be not to beat yourself up," Rod counselled her. "Others, who perhaps have a better perspective on your team's operations, appear to be satisfied with the outcome. While it's right to strive for improvement, sometimes we lose sight of what improvement looks like."

"Yeah, I'm aware of all that… And it's not the first time I've sat back and reflected on similar issues. It's just that, this time, it's come at a time when the team and its operations were overshadowed by something of a more personal nature for me.

You remember my friend – Joe, I think we called him.… Anyway, I won't go into details, but there's something about his situation that is causing me concern at the moment."

"As I recall, Joe's line of work was something nobody talked about. For you to be concerned, I think it's safe for us to assume something serious has happened in that regard," I suggested.

Joe was Cilla's Significant Other, whom Rod and I had met on a couple of occasions and spent a few days over one Christmas with him and Cilla. There was no question about Joe being his real name. Both Rod and I knew it wasn't, but we were happy to play along with the ruse. We had never been privy to the nature of his employment, but we were given to understand that it was something hush-hush that required him to operate in some difficult parts of the world most of the time.

If Joe's current situation was causing Cilla concern, there must be a strong possibility something had gone seriously wrong with his recent deployment. I felt my stomach start to squirm at the thought of what that might be and what it might mean to Cilla. I mentally made a vow to be super supportive for a while.

"Okay," Rod began after appearing to consider Cilla's information for a few moments. "You know you have our support in whatever is going on in your life, and by now, you should know anything you tell us is secure with us.

All I'm saying is that we are here and want to support you in any way we can. You should feel safe talking to us should you wish to discuss anything."

Cilla nodded and struggled to produce a lopsided, half smile. "Thanks. I'll keep that in mind, but for the time being, I have this superstitious belief that not talking about it might help prevent worse things happening."

It was a depressing note on which to end the evening, but there was little more to be said and little more Rod and I could do. It brought a rapid end to the evening.

Sunday night's happy hour was almost a scripted event. It unfolded much as Rod predicted, with most of the conversation revolving around the draft bus schedule. Tonight's discussions were much more benign, less aggressive, and even supportive of what was proposed. Discussions actually progressed to the stage where group members suggested possible outings that might be incorporated once the interclub bowls finals were over.

There were still questions, but they were largely issues that rested with the board of directors. Nevertheless, I noted them, and Rod assured the group he would pass all questions on to the board chairman. The people cleaning up after happy hour on Sunday night were a lot chirpier than they were the previous evening … except for Cilla, who remained somewhat tense and distracted.

Rod took the draft schedule to the Village's manager, Tanya Jellicoe, on Monday morning as arranged. Later that day, he cancelled Monday and Tuesday evenings' happy hours without explanation. I suspected it had something to do with the bus schedule, but I couldn't think what it might be. It did worry me, though, that something had gone horribly wrong regarding the bus schedule.

Then, I was almost convinced I was right about something having gone awry when Rod said he wouldn't be attending our Tuesday morning mahjong session. Rod never missed our scheduled mahjong mornings. Although he unlocked the Rec Room before any of us arrived on Tuesday morning and went back later to lock up again after we left at lunchtime, I didn't see or hear from him until Wednesday.

Cilla did come to mahjong on Tuesday, but she arrived later than usual, just as games were about to begin. She was one of the first to leave afterwards. Rod's absence, coupled with Bernard's continued abstinence from the game, meant I looked like missing out on a game for lack of a playing partner. Cilla's arrival at the last minute allowed me a two-handed game with her.

For some unknown reason, everyone seemed to think I should know why Rod wasn't at mahjong and why he had cancelled happy hours until further notice. Every single player there that Tuesday morning asked me about it sometime during the session.

When one player seemed a bit put out when I rather pointedly explained I wasn't privy to what was going on in Rod's private life, I raised my eyebrows questioningly at Cilla to see if she could shed any light on what might be happening. Her answer was a shrug and a shake of her head. After mahjong, I walked home alone, feeling anxious, cranky, and frustrated by being unable to find out what was happening.

The good thing (if there is one) about no happy hours and nothing worth watching on TV is that I can settle down with the new book I borrowed from the library. After settling myself up in my favourite lounge chair with a glass of wine and my new book, I planned a long read. It only took me a few minutes to realise the book was not one of the best choices I'd ever made.

Sticking with the belief that it might get better as it went along, I continued to skim, rather than read it, for about an hour before abandoning it. No, it hadn't improved as I continued with it.

Still way too early for bed, and with my mind in neutral, I returned to surfing the TV channels for anything I might be able to suffer for another hour or so. I eventually settled for a cricket match in which Australia looked like being given a hiding. However, an interesting thought did emerge during that mindless channel surfing.

Perhaps the book I borrowed wasn't all that bad. Maybe it was my state of mind that was the problem. My current outlook on life might mean that perhaps it wouldn't have mattered which book I chose. None of them would interest me. That thought caused a moment or two of soul-searching.

Exactly what was wrong with me at the moment? If I were honest, I'd admit that I had found it difficult to settle to anything over the last few days. Why was that, I wondered. Frustration…. Yes, frustration was the problem. Nothing was happening. It was as though I hadn't resumed my life after being confined to barracks for all those days.

"Whose fault is that?" I demanded of my empty lounge room.

I didn't need to be a genius to work it out. I had to get out and about a bit more to widen my interests and have more interaction with a wider group of people. Having identified the problem, without actually having solved it, I decided to abandon the pathetic cricket match. Although it was still far too early to go to bed, I took myself off anyway, lay awake for hours, waiting for sleep to come, and then woke too early next morning.

My long walk on Wednesday morning was an ideal time to devote thought to the solution I came up with to deal with my frustration. If I needed to be out and about more and mixing with a wider group of people, what opportunities existed for me to do that?

Inspiration hadn't provided any answers by the time I was striding down our street towards home. Apart from a cheery good morning to Mavis in her garden as I passed, nothing new or exciting had happened so far today. Over breakfast, I remembered the final games of the ladies' interclub bowls competition were being played on our rinks today. Although I normally wouldn't have bothered, I would be a spectator today.

Cilla also had elected to be a spectator, but then she was a committee member and probably felt some obligation to be there. Almost like iron filings to a magnet, I gravitated to her side. She was talking to Stella Winters, our club president, and a couple of other women I had never met. As it was a few minutes before the day's events were due to begin, we drifted inside the clubhouse for a coffee and cake to fill in time.

The conversation was lively and interesting. I was enjoying myself immensely until a kerfuffle outside brought things to a halt. Stella gulped down the last of her coffee and scrambled off her chair.

"Sorry, ladies. Duty calls. I must don my official hat and go out there to kick off today's big event," Stella said as she pushed her chair back under the table and headed for the door.

The two women, Doreen and Gwen, who I hadn't met until this morning, followed Stella's example and rushed outside. Startled by their sudden departure, I raised my eyebrows in question at Cilla.

"Officials….," was her unhelpful reply, and she could see I was confused. "Our club has to provide the officials – scorers and things – and Doreen and Gwen volunteered to help out. We should follow their example and head outside to find a decent vantage point if we want to watch the games."

As I followed Cilla out of the bar area, I almost fell over Rod wandering along outside the building and also in search of a decent vantage point from which to watch play. By the time we had untangled ourselves, Cilla had disappeared amongst those milling around the end of the green.

"Might have left it a bit late to find a good spot," Rod commented as he surveyed the gathering crowd. "How do you feel about sitting inside instead of out here? The bar area is elevated. If we sit at the windows, we should have a reasonable view of the rinks."

What was there to argue about with that? We dragged a couple of those high bar chairs over to the windows, ordered long cold drinks, and settled down to watch play. At a break between ends, I risked asking the question I had been struggling not to ask ever since I ran into Rod this morning.

"I'm almost not game to ask this, but has there been any reaction to our draft bus schedule? I assume Tanya managed to get copies to the chairman and board members in time. When is their board meeting anyway? It is supposed to be sometime this week, isn't it? It will be just our luck if they already have a full agenda and don't have time to study the draft before the meeting. Discussing the bus schedule might have to be deferred until their next meeting."

"Oh, Ye, of little faith, when did you become so cynical? No, don't answer that," Rod chuckled. "For your information, the board meeting was last evening, and, yes, the bus schedule was discussed.

Tanya emailed all the board members a copy of the schedule as soon as I gave it to her. The chairman called me almost immediately and requested a meeting at six o'clock Monday evening to discuss the draft. It gave me a golden opportunity to get some points across before the board meeting. As it turned out, I shouldn't have worried. He insisted I attend the board meeting as *he was sure there would be many questions that only I could answer.* He wasn't far wrong either."

"Well…? Come on. What was the outcome?"

"Uhmm, no definite outcome yet. No, relax… They were left with a couple of issues requiring decisions. I assume they dealt with those after I left the meeting. I haven't heard from the chairman today, so I don't know if decisions were made or not. I assume the chairman will be here at some point today. I intend to try to drag him aside for a couple of minutes to find out what happened after I left last night."

Loud clapping and cheers drew our attention back to the state of play on the rinks. It was a close-run game, and competition was fierce not only amongst the players, but also the spectators. Even inside the clubhouse, I could almost feel those on the sidelines willing their team to win. But the game – and the competition – must have been nearing its finale.

A small table was set up in front of the building, with pride of place on it given to the winners' trophy. Other small tables were strategically placed around outside and in the bar area behind us. Lynda and her catering staff bustled back and forth from the kitchen to put covers and other essentials on all the tables. Every time the kitchen door opened to let someone in or out, the aroma of food wafted out to tease my nostrils. A couple of the Merivale club members came in and started rattling around behind the bar. Frank and Luigi came in and began tinkering with that terrifying coffee machine that produces the most exquisite brew.

"Looks like we are about to be overrun," Rod murmured as he watched the action playing out behind us. "As soon as the game is finished, the chairman will take centre stage to wax lyrical about the competition (for far longer than required) and then present the trophy to the winning team – again, with more words than needed. And then we will be inundated by a stampede through here as there is a mad rush to the bar for drinks or coffee."

"Don't be too hard on the chairman, Rod. He is allowed to feel pretty chuffed about this competition, and he doesn't get too many opportunities to wave the Merivale flag, so to speak. Anyway, the mob out there is becoming restless. I doubt they will allow him to prattle on for too long. They will be more interested in sustenance and hydration than long speeches."

"You're probably right. So, if you will excuse me, I will go and position myself somewhere strategic and close to the presentation site. I want to nab him as soon as he finishes the official part of the event."

I watched Rod gently elbow his way into position next to the table holding the winners' trophy. While I wasn't paying attention, a second item had been added to that table. It was a fancy stained timber shield with silvery-looking mini shield attachments. I assumed it was some sort of perpetual trophy that would have the winner's name added to a miniature shield each time the competition was run. It would certainly help break the monotony of the bare walls in the bar area of the clubhouse.

As Rod had predicted, the chairman had come prepared to praise at length the brilliance of the Merivale Bowls Club in organising the interclub competition before finally presenting the trophy. But the crowd became restless. A couple of spectators, fed-up with the dialogue, had to be physically prevented from entering the clubhouse when they tried to opt for alcohol instead of speeches.

At last, it was all over. The winners' photographs were being taken – with the chairman – on the now almost deserted clubhouse's front patio. Rod leant up against the wall, patiently waiting for the last of the official part of the day to end. Then, the photographer was packing up his equipment, the winners were making a mad dash for the bar, and Rod had cornered the chairman before he could escape.

From the vantage point of my perch above them, their conversation appeared relaxed and devoid of any obvious tension. It wasn't long before, smiling, the two men shook hands, and the chairman made a beeline for the bar. Rod spent the next few moments alone on the patio. He appeared deep in thought, so I didn't speak as I approached him. Nevertheless, he was a bit startled when he looked up and saw me standing close to him.

"You can't hear yourself think in there," I quipped, pointing over my shoulder towards the bar area, "so I thought I'd come and join you in comparative solitude out here.

Is everything okay? How did it go with the chairman?"

"Everything is better than okay, I think. It's all good news… unless I've overlooked something along the way. Look, the silence at my house will be positively deafening after this place. Why don't we go back there to test it out over a quiet coffee or a drink while I tell you where we are at with the new bus?"

What's not to like about that suggestion? We weren't far from the clubhouse when Cilla caught up with us... And, yes, thanks, she will join us for a coffee at Rod's place.

Chapter 24

Wednesday evening's happy hour was interesting. Contrary to my expectations, Rod's big announcement about the new bus fell a little flat.

"I managed to catch up with the board's chairman after today's finals of the women's interclub bowls competition. He filled me in on decisions the board made regarding the bus after I left the meeting last night.

The good news is that the board has endorsed our draft bus schedule. Although they made one or two minor suggestions, the draft we put forward will be actioned unchanged."

My disappointment must have been obvious to everyone. I had expected applause and maybe even a cheer following Rod's news. Instead, the response was a heavy silence that lasted a few moments until Luigi shattered it.

"What about the driver?" he demanded. "I'm telling you here and now, I have plenty of other things to do with my life."

"If you had let me finish, you wouldn't have had to ask that question," Rod told Luigi. "I did point out our concerns regarding a bus driver, and it seems the board accepted our position on the matter. The plan is to engage a driver who will help the maintenance team when he is not driving the bus. The board also is happy for us to drive the bus from time to time for special excursions or whatever else. Does that answer your question, Luigi?"

Suitably chastised, Luigi shuffled on the spot and gave Rod a curt nod.

"Good; now for the finer details…. It is intended the bus will begin servicing the Village as soon as a driver is available. There is some suggestion that might occur as early as next week. It appears a bus driver already is available, and the board just has to find a replacement for that person in the maintenance gang to free him up to start driving the bus."

Having delivered all the news he had to share, Rod swept a beaming smile across his audience and then sat down to signify he had no further information to give them. Again, I waited for a reaction from the group.

Nothing happened. It was as though no one had spoken. After a couple of heartbeats, I couldn't control myself any longer and was about to demand to know what was wrong when, all of a sudden, the tide turned. A loud babble broke out as everyone tried speaking over the top of everyone else. It appeared the common topic was possible excursion destinations.

"There's that new gallery that's opened in the valley," Maria suggested. "I hear it features great exhibitions, with a part of its space reserved for local artists' work."

"A trip to the marina or one of the other local beaches probably would prove popular," Ted mused, "and also a visit to some of the weekend markets."

"Do the outings just have to be during the day?" Janet asked.

"What did you have in mind, Janet?" Frank queried.

"Well, I was thinking about plays and concerts, but they are usually held at night. For instance, the local university drama students are to stage a play at the end of this month. Even if we could only get tickets for the dress rehearsal night, it would be a nice night out."

Cilla, who had remained quiet until then, decided to add her thoughts to the conversation. "For the Village's keen bowlers, it might be possible to arrange a bowls day at one of our northern neighbours, at one of the clubs that wasn't part of our interclub competition."

Luigi backed Cilla's suggestion. "There are bowls clubs at a few of the beachside communities to the north of us. By the time you allow for travel, it would make for a long day, though. One of the places I'm thinking of is about a two-hour drive from here. So the day would have to include about four hours of travel time."

"And another hour for lunch, plus a few ends of bowls…," Frank added. We would need to get away from here early in the morning and then count on not returning until maybe six o'clock that evening."

"What about a boat cruise to somewhere?" Alice suggested quietly. You know the sort of thing… drive to wherever you catch the boat and then do a day trip to one of the islands."

"Or, maybe just spend the day on the boat cruising around the various islands," Maria added.

Rod allowed the discussion to run on for some time before intervening. I was relieved when he did. I was exhausted from trying to make notes of all the possibilities as they were put forward. Nevertheless, I wasn't sure I favoured Rod's alternate approach.

"Instead of knocking ourselves out trying to figure out what excursions to arrange, shouldn't we let the residents tell us what they would like? I'm not saying we would necessarily have to go along with their suggestions, but it might indicate the kinds of outings we shouldn't bother scheduling."

"What… run another questionnaire?" Cilla demanded. "We all know how that usually turns out."

"Well, I think it would be good to ask the residents for their input," Janet said. "And, as Rod pointed out, we don't have to stick with what they suggest.

There is something else I think we should consider when we're planning any such excursions. Apart from what to see and do when we get there (whatever the destination), what about morning and afternoon coffee and lunch? People can't be out all day without some arrangements for those things."

"Good point, Janet. Does anyone have any comments or suggestions in this regard?" Rod asked.

"Dare I say it… But it sounds to me as though there should be a committee – a *small* committee – responsible for organising any arrangements required for a particular excursion. In some instances, it might not be more than arranging for a local coffee shop to handle a busload of oldies for morning tea," Cilla added.

"Are you saying caterers need to be arranged at any destination we might visit?" Maria demanded.

"No. That's not what I meant," Cilla responded a touch sharply. "All I'm saying is that it could be difficult and embarrassing, if we arrive at a certain place expecting to have coffee at the only coffee shop in town, only to find it's a take-away hole in the wall somewhere with no available seating anywhere nearby … and no toilets either."

"Yes, I agree," Alice began, deep in thought. "If there are to be outings of any substance, they will need to be well planned and any necessary arrangements put in place beforehand. How big do you envision such a committee would need to be, Cilla?"

"Does it need to be a committee as such," I asked. "Wouldn't two or three people designated as excursion organisers be enough?"

Alice and Maria volunteered to take on responsibility for such arrangements as an interim measure until the full scope of the role became clearer. There seemed little else to discuss regarding the bus and potential outings, and people started making noises about going home.

Within minutes, Rod, Cilla and I were seeing people off amid promises to see us at mahjong in the morning. But bus trips remained a topic of discussion after the last of them left. With everyone else gone, the three of us got stuck into cleaning up, but it became obvious Cilla's mind continued to deal with issues regarding potential excursions.

"If you are going to post another questionnaire on our Facebook site, Rod, it will have to be quite precise about the information we require. And, the only way we might achieve that is to spell out – in extensive detail – what potential outings might involve."

That was enough to bring work to a halt while we explored Cilla's thinking on the issue. After only a few moments, Rod brought our discussions to an end.

"Look, while our thinking is still focused on this, now might be a good time to put something together for the Facebook page.

Do either of you have to be somewhere else this evening?" Rod asked.

Neither Cilla nor I had any plans for the night, and Rod obviously didn't either, or he wouldn't have suggested staying to work on it. But there was the small matter of dinner to consider. I remembered I had a large tray of pasta bake in the freezer and offered to fetch it. It could thaw out and heat through in the oven while we worked on putting together Rod's questionnaire. Cilla also made a quick trip home to retrieve garlic bread from her freezer. Then, with dinner sorted, we sat down to work. Although it would be a late dinner, we allowed ourselves up to an hour. By then, the food would be ready.

As soon as we were seated with pads and pens, Cilla shared her theory.

"Right… the way I see it is that we want to gather as much information as possible about what residents think they might like in terms of possible outings … while limiting flights of fancy to what's realistic and achievable."

"No arguments so far," Rod agreed, "but how did you have in mind for me to achieve that?"

"We need to narrow their thinking to what is achievable. Ask whether they prefer morning outings or day trips. Suggest the types of outings: visits to galleries and museums, concerts and plays, boat trips, and the markets."

"Isn't that being a bit restrictive? I mean, it might bring Rod under fire for trying to curtail excursions from anything or anywhere not listed on the questionnaire," I argued.

"Possibly… but I think Cilla is right," Rod responded. "And it wouldn't be the first time I've come under fire from the residents. But I agree that, if we don't suggest a wide range of options that might be available, the majority of them won't be able to think beyond shopping trips."

The next few minutes were devoted to putting together words for the post Rod would place on the Village's Facebook page first thing tomorrow morning. At least, that's what he claimed he would do, but I had no doubt the questionnaire would be up on the site before Rod went to bed tonight. I was pleased we were finished dealing with matters relating to the bus.

My stomach had taken on an almost constant rumble as the aroma of the pasta bake and garlic bread in the oven became hard to resist. Although they didn't admit it, I think the other pair might have felt the same way. As soon as a rough draft of the questionnaire was done, Rod herded us through to the dining room for dinner.

It wasn't a long, leisurely meal, but as soon as the dishwasher was loaded, Cilla and I said our goodnights and headed home.

Cupcakes, muffins, or scones….? No time for even a short walk this morning. Although it wasn't late when I went to bed last night, I overslept and had to hit the floor running to produce something in time to take to mahjong for morning tea. I settled for scones.

While the scones baked, I realised that, for some unknown reason, mahjong seemed to have lost a little of its appeal to me. Perhaps the poor attendance on Tuesday, coupled with being reduced to playing a two-handed game with Cilla, had something to do with it. As I strode across the grass to the Rec Room with my basket loosely swinging in my hand, a part of me hoped this morning would be better and I would again enjoy today's games.

Rod and Frank were already setting up the tables when I arrived. As I was setting up for our pre-games coffee, Cilla walked in. She still wasn't herself. Joe's situation seemed to have a firm hold on her. Although she was turning up and joining in everything as normal, there was a certain reserve about her, an aloofness almost. It rendered her uninterested in unnecessary conversation about anything. I made a mental note to ask Rod if he knew anything more about it.

Over the next few minutes, today's other players dribbled in, and we soon stood grouped around the table where morning tea was laid out. Managing a coffee and a scone on a plate without wearing jam and cream down your front was a struggle. Players drifted to other nearby tables in search of somewhere to safely deposit their coffees while dealing with their scones. I wondered if I should change my deodorant when I found myself deserted, except for Cilla and Rod, who remained standing nearby.

Morning tea was almost over, and games were due to start. Some already had taken their places at the tables in readiness. I was returning the leftover scones to their container before joining the players at the tables when I noticed a sudden hush settle over the room. I glanced over my shoulder and noticed everyone was looking towards the open door. I followed their example – and gasped.

Bernard Stuart-Parnell had just walked in and was heading to the morning tea table. Frank and Luigi, standing talking near the door, gave Bernard a cheery 'good morning' as he walked past and received a response devoid of warmth. I was aware of a movement close to me and glanced sideways to see what was happening.

Cilla had stepped forward a pace or two. She was now leaning to one side and craning her neck as if to see something immediately behind Bernard. I was about to ask her what was wrong when what happened next eliminated the need.

"What?" Bernard demanded when he noticed Cilla looking in his direction. "What are you looking at, Woman?"

"Well, I'm sorry, Bernard… but you appear to have lost something."

"Lost something…. What have I lost?" he barked as he patted his pockets and ran his hands down the front of his clothes.

Then, alarmed to realise Cilla was looking behind, and not at him, Bernard half turned to scan behind him and out through the open door. It was as though he half expected the Hounds of Hell to pounce on him from behind. Having found nothing terrifying there, he turned back to scowl at Cilla.

"I have no idea what you are on about, but I assure you I have not lost anything. If you are so convinced I have lost something, perhaps you might be so kind as to tell me what it might be." He ended his request with one of his trademark audible sniffs.

"Uhmm…," Cilla continued hesitantly. "Somewhere between your unit and here… you appear to have lost your shadow."

"My *shadow*! Have you taken leave of your senses? What *shadow* are you talking about?"

"The one you call James. You know the one I mean. The one that is always with you and never leaves your side… Or is it that you never leave its side?"

Bernard's face turned crimson, and his nose pointed a couple of degrees higher in response, but his words were lost in the laughing and clapping that followed Cilla's comments. Brushing it aside, he marched to the nearest table with a vacant chair and plonked himself down at it.

Janet Furlong, already sitting at that table, was stunned. She looked around wildly for some means of escape. On their way to join Janet at her table, Maria and Alice paused briefly mid-stride before veering off towards a different table. Having managed to collect herself sufficiently, Janet leaned across to speak to Bernard.

"Would you like a coffee before the games begin?" she asked quietly, still looking uncomfortable about the current seating arrangements.

"Ah, yes, thank you. Black with one sugar would be fine, and one of those scones to go with it, thanks."

For a moment, I thought the bewildered-looking Janet might topple from her chair, but she managed to recover sufficiently to push her chair back from the table and make her way on wobbly legs to the morning tea table.

Luigi took a couple of steps forward and cleared his throat. "There's no table service here, Mate. Coffee and stuff are over there if you want anything," he announced loudly as he pointed to the morning tea table.

Having seen his wife leave her table to respond to Bernard's request, Ted Furlong moved quickly to catch her by the arm as she was about to start making Bernard's coffee. Ted gently led Janet back to the table where he had been sitting and pulled a chair out for her.

I leaned in close to whisper in Cilla's ear. "Should we alert Marjorie to Bernard's arrival this morning? His presence might be a bit traumatic for her."

"Yeah… Uhmm… No… If we tell her that Bernard is here, she won't come. Why should she give up mahjong just because that supercilious sod has decided to return to the fold? Let's just prepare to gather around Marjorie to support her when she arrives … if she arrives. She is running a bit late. Maybe she already knows he is here."

"Maybe I should just duck into the library to see if she is going to join us this morning, but I won't mention Bernard. What do you think?"

Before Cilla could answer, Marjorie bustled in from the library. Looking a bit harassed, she made straight for the morning tea table.

Bernard remained parked at the table where he had spoken to Janet. Seemingly, the fact that Janet was not about to bring him coffee hadn't yet registered with him. It wasn't until he started looking around to see why Janet and his coffee were taking so long to arrive that he noticed Marjorie's presence. His eyes fixed on her, and he started to rise from the table.

"You won't mind if we join you at this table, will you, Bernard?" Frank asked as he and Luigi, dragging Maria along with them, approached an ostracised-looking Bernard at his table.

As the trio clattered about dragging out chairs and settling themselves at the table, Bernard heaved a resigned sigh and settled back on his chair. Although he managed to respond in kind to the chorus of 'good mornings' from his fellow players, Bernard's eyes never left Marjorie, who remained corralled by Cilla and me at the morning tea table. We had moved quickly to stand close behind her and engage her in the usual welcoming pleasantries as she made herself a coffee. But that move could last for only so long before she must become aware of the reality of the situation that awaited her. Cilla took the initiative in a bid to lessen the shock.

Once Marjorie had armed herself with coffee and scone, Cilla stepped in to block her path as she was about to turn and move away from the table.

"Marjorie dear, please put your coffee down for a moment while you listen to something I need to tell you.

Bernard has turned up for mahjong this morning. No… Relax and don't pay him any attention. What you must not do is bolt back to the library. What you are going to do is carry your coffee and scone back to our table with Marion and me, and then you will spend the morning playing mahjong at our table."

I saw Marjorie blanch and begin wringing her hands. She swallowed hard a couple of times and tried clearing her throat.

"Is James here too?" she croaked in not much above a whisper.

"Nah… Mahjong and mahjong players are not to James's taste, I don't think. Anyway, there seems to have been some form of parting of the ways for James and the one mahjong player who briefly held his interest." Cilla paused and looked over her shoulder to check our table was still free before continuing to encourage Marjorie.

"Come on, old girl. Don't let us all down. We are about to let him know he doesn't run this show, and we need you to be a part of that. Ignore him as you accompany us to our table, and don't as much as cast a glance in his direction."

We didn't exactly drag Marjorie to our table, but she did need encouragement and help to make the short trip. Cilla made sure Marjorie was seated with her back to Bernard. I wasn't too confident about that strategy. I figured that if I were in Marjorie's shoes, I would feel vulnerable seated with my back to Bernard. I would probably think I could feel his eyes boring into my back all morning. Rod completed the foursome at our table, and Marjorie appeared to become more relaxed as play progressed.

The morning wasn't a complete success, though. We had hoped that, after the games finished, Marjorie would linger with the rest of us at least for a few minutes of chatter before everyone departed the Rec Room. That wasn't how it panned out.

As soon as 'mahjong' was called on the final hand at our table, Marjorie sprang up off her chair and bolted for the library.

"Bugger," Cilla murmured. "I had hoped she would stick around for at least a minute or two to help reinforce the 'up-yours' message to Bernard. Well, there is always Plan B."

"Plan B? What the hell is that, and do we have one?" I asked.

"Listen and learn," Cilla replied with a knowing wink. "Walk with me to the morning tea table – via Bernard. Play along if you feel inclined."

While Cilla appeared completely relaxed about the whole exercise, I wasn't sure I felt comfortable with whatever she planned to do. But I seemed to be swept along by her as we strolled towards the table … passing Bernard so closely that Cilla almost brushed him on the way past. As we approached Bernard, Cilla spoke in a loudish voice as though she was continuing a conversation started at the end of our games.

"…Yeah, it is a shame she couldn't stay. But, I suppose if something is happening in the library that needs attention, she does need to be there to deal with it. We'll miss her lively conversation today. Maybe next time, she will be able to stay and chat for a while."

We had slowed our pace as we neared Bernard. By the time Cilla finished speaking, we were almost past him. I felt compelled to play along but managed only a lame contribution.

"I agree. It's good to have her keep us up to date with what's happening library-wise. Maybe after next Tuesday's mahjong session, we will hear about whatever today's drama was."

By the time I had added my few words to the ruse, we had left Bernard trailing in our wake and continued to the morning tea table. Nothing more was said on the matter until Cilla and I were alone washing the coffee mugs and plates in the kitchen.

"Did you notice any reaction to our little role play from Bernard?" Cilla asked.

"No, but I wasn't game to even glance in his direction in case I gave the game away somehow. You know, I almost feel sorry for him."

"What? What we said wasn't so brutal that you need to feel sorry for him."

"Of course not. I wasn't suggesting it was. All I'm saying is that I feel a bit sorry for how he seems to have been shunned, almost ostracised, by the group this morning. I'm not saying he doesn't deserve it. But he is entitled to do what he likes with his own life and doesn't need to ask our permission or answer to us for his actions."

"Even if it involves traumatising one of our own….? No, I suppose you are right, but the way he always treated Marjorie doesn't sit well with me.

By the way, was there any comment at all this morning about where James was, or about what might be happening in that department?"

"Not that I heard, but the blokes might have picked up something. If nothing else, Bernard's presence today – *sans* James – will give us something to speculate about at tonight's happy hour."

"You don't think he might turn up at happy hour, do you?" Cilla looked slightly appalled as she asked the question.

"Who, James…? Aw, I doubt our happy hour would be to his taste."

"No, not James… I meant Bernard."

Now, that possibility was something to ponder – and discuss at some length as we walked home accompanied by Rod.

For a moment, as we passed the library, the temptation was to call in to see how Marjorie was faring after this morning's shock of seeing Bernard. Rod counselled against it, suggesting it might be best to allow Marjorie some space to deal with it in her own way in the first instance before rallying around her any further.

Chapter 25

Over the next couple of evenings, any fears we might have held about Bernard joining us for happy hours (or worse still, arriving with James in tow) were put to rest. But Bernard also didn't show up to help with Friday's pizza and karaoke night.

As we sat in silence sipping a wine after yet another frantic Friday night, Ted voiced an observation.

"It appears Bernard's appearance at mahjong on Thursday morning was a 'once only' event. I was hoping he would be here to help out tonight."

"Perhaps Thursday's session was enough reminder of how 'ordinary' we mahjong players are, and maybe we're a bit too uncouth for Bernard's life in a more refined academic world these days," Frank suggested.

"Come to think of it, I haven't seen Bernard and James together for a few days now," Janet said. "I often saw them going to the gym or at the pool together, but I haven't seen either of them around the place, apart from Bernard's appearance at mahjong on Thursday, of course." After a brief pause, she continued. "Does anyone know how Marjorie is coping? It can't have been easy for her seeing Bernard at mahjong the other day, not after the way he treated her."

The only responses Janet received to everything she said were shrugs and headshakes from all those around her. But, for me, she had raised an interesting point. Had Bernard and James had a bit of a spat last Wednesday that resulted in Bernard's unexpected appearance at mahjong the next morning? If that was the case, was it a once-only event, and they had now made-up again? Or was it something more monumental?

Whatever the situation, Janet's words caused me a massive guilt attack. I had been meaning to check on Marjorie to make sure she was okay, but somehow, I still hadn't managed to do so. Tomorrow was Saturday. Although the library does open for a couple of hours in the morning, Marjorie rarely is there on the weekend. Not wanting to call her or to rock up and knock on her door, a more casual approach now would have to wait until Monday.

Happy hour on Sunday night was brief and ended almost half an hour earlier than usual. As the last of the group chorused their goodnights as they left for home, I found myself wondering what I might do with an extra half hour to myself on this Sunday evening. It turns out I shouldn't have bothered thinking about it.

"Do either of you ladies have anything pressing to do tonight," Rod asked as we tidied his back deck after happy hour.

"Apart from dinner and then falling asleep in front of TV? No, nothing else on my agenda," I replied while Cilla simply shook my head.

"Good… the Village's bus service is about to become a step closer to a reality," Rod continued. "I've been summoned to attend a meeting tomorrow morning to create guidelines for the driver for shopping trip days. As far as I'm aware, the only ones attending the meeting will be the chairman, our manager, me, and the intended bus driver.

In the interests of the briefest possible meeting, I would like to attend armed with concise but detailed operational instructions for the driver. Your input in formulating that document is required."

Both Cilla and I agreed to help but, anticipating the work might take some time, asked about dinner – with a view to maybe raiding our fridges for the necessary fixings to put together a meal.

"Well, I have a casserole that I am about to put in the oven to reheat," Rod announced. "Then, as soon as we finish tidying up out here, we can make a start on the driver's instructions while we wait for dinner to be ready to eat."

It sounded like a fairly straightforward task to be followed by a pleasant meal cooked by someone else. I couldn't find fault with that. A few minutes later, dinner was in the oven reheating, and the three of us were perched around the dining room table with pads and pencils at the ready. That's when reality seeped in. What I anticipated would be a short, simple exercise turned into something akin to rewriting the American Constitution.

Rod obviously had devoted some thought to the matter beforehand and, although there was no written list, he was well prepared with difficult questions about the simplest aspects of the shopping trips to the city.

"Okay, I think we will all agree that the bus can't drive all over the village, going past every residence, in case there might be someone there who wants to hop on the bus to go shopping. So, how do we streamline the pickup of passengers for these shopping trips?"

"The same way as other buses pick up their passengers," Cilla suggested. "Intending passengers wait at designated bus stops and flag down the bus as it comes past. Isn't that how it works?"

"Yep, that's how I understand it works," I agreed. "All we need to do is to come up with a simplified, straightforward route through the Village, with a number of designated pickup points along that route. Is that a summary of the task ahead of us?"

"Perhaps...," Rod murmured, "but let's make a start and see how we go. The bus is to be garaged at the admin building, so that will need to be both its starting and end points on shopping days.

So, when it leaves the admin building in the morning, in which direction does it go? Bear in mind that the bus route should be one smooth, continuous trip through the Village and out onto the highway. Having the bus double back on itself as it moves through the Village should be avoided. Right then, your thoughts on the matter, please."

Ouch! I felt reality bite before we even got off the mark. Stunned silence followed for a few moments before Cilla announced, "A plan of the layout of the Village would be helpful about now."

Rod promptly gave a great performance of someone who just remembered something important. He smacked his forehead before bounding up off his chair and dashing over to his desk. Moments later, he was back at the table and spreading out a drawing that just happened to have been lying on his desk. After anchoring all four corners of it with saucers hastily fetched from the kitchen, the three of us pored over a map of the layout of the Village that also included the new area. It took me a while to get my head around it sufficiently to be able to identify where the admin building and other strategic points were located. Chuffed with my achievement, I thought to inform the others.

"Right… So, that's the admin building where the bus will be at the start of the day, and over here is where the ring road joins the main road outside the Village," I pointed out, and the others nodded in agreement.

Flushed with success so far, I continued by tracing with my finger what I considered to be a straightforward route from the admin building, through the Village, and out onto the main road.

"I can't see too many difficulties being encountered with that. It would have everyone collected and on their way into the city quickly and efficiently. What do you think?" I asked and waited for the anticipated praise to flow.

It didn't. In fact, all I heard for a few moments was silence. Then, I was brought back down to earth with a thud as the questions began to flow.

"What about the residents who live in one of the streets behind the route you indicated?" Cilla demanded. "Are they expected to walk all the way out to stand on the side of the designated bus route to wait until the bus comes along? Some days, the bus could stop at every house along the way. It could be a long wait on the side of the road. On other days, it might stop at only a couple of places. If people weren't in position and waiting for it well ahead of time, it might go without them."

"Hmm… I suppose you have a point," I conceded. "And another thing to consider is the number of people who might want to go into town on any particular day. It could be half the Village residents or only a handful. The bus only seats 22. By the time it was halfway through the Village, it might be full."

"Good point, Marion," Rod said as he reached for his pad. "Maybe there needs to be some form of booking arrangement in place. Anyone wanting to go shopping needs to book a seat for the required day. How are bookings to be made?"

"Just a phone call to the office would do. Maybe Tanya needs to make one of her staff the designated booking officer," Cilla suggested.

"Might work… if Tanya doesn't think her staff are too busy already to deal with the bookings," Rod said. "The only other alternative might be for residents to book online. Perhaps it might be worthwhile having a word to Steve Parish about how that might be done… just in case Tanya says no."

"If there is some booking arrangement in place, the driver would be able to collect a list of intending passengers before heading out each day," I suggested.

"And that might then determine the route through the Village for that day," Cilla added. "The driver would know on which streets people would be waiting to be picked up and route his trip accordingly. What do you think, Rod?"

"Can't say I like the idea much so far."

Not off to the most promising start, this aspect of shopping trips took some discussion before agreement was reached on how best to advise the board. In the end, we agreed on designated bus stops located strategically within easy walking distance on each street. Intending passengers would need to book either online through a new section of the Village's Facebook page, or via a physical form dropped in at the admin office.

"What about if it is raining," I asked – just as we were starting to feel relaxed about having sorted out the collection of passengers.

"So, passengers will need an umbrella and/or a raincoat. Why is rain a concern?" Cilla demanded none too politely.

"You're right, I suppose. Passengers will need at least that much protection if they have to wait on the side of the street for the bus to arrive," I admitted. "Wouldn't it be better if there were some sort of bus shelter for them to wait in and be undercover?"

It didn't take much discussion before my suggested need for bus shelters was added to the advice to go to the board. A couple of further points were discussed before we finalised our recommendation to the board.

Drop-offs at the shopping centres should alternate, with alternate centres being the first drop-off point each week. And then there was the thorny question of whether passengers should pay for their shopping trips.

"Whether bus passengers need to pay or not is a matter for the board to decide," Rod believed. "While it's not for us to provide advice on this matter, I don't doubt it will come up during my meeting with the board, and I'm bound to be asked for my thoughts on it."

"I don't think it should be a free service and, knowing our board as I do, it won't be offered as such," Cilla suggested. "Perhaps a token payment would be acceptable. Something like $2 per passenger for the round trip wouldn't be considered excessive by residents, and it might at least pay for the fuel used."

As well as agreeing that $2 was a reasonable charge, we also decided that it would not be put forward with our other suggestions and would only be put forward if Rod was pressed for his thoughts on the matter. Rod had the final word on the subject.

"There does need to be some fee for passengers. If the bus is to be used to take residents on various outings, there will be a cost for the use of the bus, and the board will need to see some income offsetting those costs."

Finally, all matters relating to the use of the bus were dealt with. Rod was equipped with the advice he would give to the board the next day. We could have dinner, and then Cilla and I could go home.

As there wasn't a happy hour on Monday night, I didn't see Rod again until we were setting up for mahjong on Tuesday morning. It goes without saying that my prime interest then was Rod's meeting with the board regarding the operation of the bus. He claimed it went well, and everything he recommended was endorsed – including Rod's 'reluctant' suggestion of $2 per passenger per trip.

My curiosity regarding the bus now put to rest, it was time to focus on other issues I wanted to discuss with Rod before the other players arrived.

"Tell me if I'm misreading the situation, Rod, but Cilla still seems to be decidedly frosty towards me. I know she has worked okay with us on all the stuff we've been doing lately, and she seems to talk to you all right, but not to me.

I am unaware of having done or said anything to upset her and put her offside with me, but her attitude is starting to wear a bit thin with me. I don't know what to do about it. Any suggestions?"

"Well, it's not just you that she is keeping at arm's length. I don't know what's happened either, but she is not the Cilla we knew before she went to Sydney the last time."

"Do you think it might be PTSD? You know, all the stress of finding the body and then worrying about our safety. And who knows what she might have encountered in Sydney when her team went after Zorka's mob?"

"Marion, she was a copper for a lot of years. Cilla would have seen her share of bodies and worse in the past. I doubt anything she experienced in the last couple of weeks would rattle her, but you are right about her not being herself since her return. To me, it appears as though she has something on her mind, possibly nothing to do with anything here."

"So, what do we do? Should we just put up with it and let it run its course – and hope she comes good soon?"

"That would be my suggestion. Cilla is a private person. I wouldn't recommend asking questions, even if they didn't sound like you were prying."

The appearance of the first of this morning's other mahjong players brought our discussions to an abrupt end, but I knew Cilla's current attitude would continue to niggle me. As the others all stood around, tucking into coffee and muffins, my concern for Cilla deepened. She still hadn't arrived and, while she wasn't always among the first to arrive, she wasn't usually this late. My concern was proved ill-founded a few moments later when Cilla arrived with Marjorie in tow.

"Look who thought she might give mahjong a miss today," Cilla chirped as she shepherded Marjorie to the morning tea table.

Despite Bernard's presence, Marjorie seemed more settled than she did at last Thursday's session. The morning's games proceeded much as usual for the first hour … until all hell broke loose.

"You cheated!" Bernard shrieked. "You did not have that pair of tiles before the third one was discarded to the centre. You should not have been able to pick it up and claim 'pung'. Come on; tell me how you miraculously managed to have a pair when I know you only had one of those tiles."

Maria, the target of Bernard's accusation, looked mortified and about to burst into tears. Luigi's chair shot back from the table as he sprang to his feet.

"Take that back and apologise," Luigi demanded. 'How dare you call her a cheat. If anyone is cheating, it is you, Bernard, or how would you know how many of those tiles Maria had?"

By the time he finished speaking, Luigi was leaning over the table and shaking his fist in Bernard's face. Bernard gave Luigi a dismissive toss of his head before fixing him with a disdainful glare. I felt my eyebrows race to my hairline as I turned to Rod in panic… But Rod lounged on his chair, apparently unmoved by recent performances. It was Cilla, her hackles well and truly up, who jumped in to control the situation.

"Oi, you two… Gentlemen, please settle down. We are not playing for sheep stations here. Your behaviour is completely uncalled for, Bernard. And, Luigi, calm down, please.

"Bernard, you have been sniping at people all morning. It was uncalled for, and we are not going to put up with such behaviour. Now, it was obvious to me that you arrived here this morning with something on your mind. Whatever it was has done nothing to enhance your disposition. In fact, you have been thoroughly obnoxious the whole time.

We are not going to pry into whatever your problem might be but, if you can't behave appropriately, take yourself and your problem home – now."

Applause rang out around the tables. While Luigi moved to rest a comforting hand on Maria's shoulder, red-faced and primed to deliver an abusive tirade, Bernard spun around to face Cilla. She fixed Bernard with one of her deadly stares, and he instantly deflated.

"If a truce has been reached and World War III avoided, perhaps some apologies might be in order before we leave here today. In the meantime, unless some of you are so committed to your current games, you cannot drag yourselves away, I suggest we call mahjong concluded for today," Rod announced.

"I really didn't cheat, Rod," Maria said with tears brimming. "I did have a pair. I just hadn't realised it and hadn't placed them side-by-side on my board. That's probably why Bernard didn't know I had a pair."

Marjorie startled just about everyone when she sprang up off her chair and snarled, "Oh, yes, Bernard owes you an apology, Maria, but he also owes this group an apology for his reprehensible behaviour. And he will apologise… if he intends to continue to play mahjong with us in the future.

Such behaviour might be acceptable when playing chess with James but, Bernard, it is not acceptable here."

'Hear, hear' rang out from around the table, and was quickly followed by a scraping of chairs as people abandoned their games and began packing up their tables.

As Luigi brushed past Bernard, I overheard him murmur, "You ever insult Maria again, and unlike you, I might just forget I am a gentleman. You could end up measuring your length on the floor."

People didn't hang around for another coffee before they headed home, and Marjorie returned to the library. As Cilla and I washed and dried this morning's coffee mugs in the kitchen, I thought I heard hushed tones emanating from out front. Logic said someone had stayed behind to speak to Rod, but I thought it strange that it sounded a bit clandestine. It wasn't until the three of us walked home together that Cilla and I found out what had taken place, but it took a bit of coaxing for Rod to open up about it.

"All right, all right. I know I won't have any peace until you find out. It was Bernard who stayed behind for a few moments to talk to me. Happy now?"

"No!" Cilla and I chorused in unison.

"That seems a bit off after his performance this morning," I commented, "unless, of course, he was apologising for this behaviour."

"Yeah, and why would he apologise to you personally and not to the rest of us?" Cilla asked.

After a bit more 'encouragement', we managed to extract the entire story from Rod.

"Look, you two, Bernard's conversation with me was both private and personal. I'll share it with you as long as you guarantee it will remain confidential."

Of course, we agreed and promised on 'scout's honour' not to repeat a word of it.

"Right. Well, it appears as Bernard was leaving to come to mahjong this morning, he found a note in his letterbox. In essence, the note told him that James was moving out of the Village early this morning, and it was Bernard's fault that he was leaving."

"For it to have upset Bernard so much that he acted like a prick all morning, whatever was between him and James couldn't have been all over as we thought," Cilla suggested.

"Hmm… you might be right," I agreed. "But the way it played out seems a bit odd, don't you think? Although, I suppose we can't make too many assumptions about what happened between them, because we don't know anything about the nature of their relationship, not the real nature of it."

"Apparently, Bernard didn't know what it was either," Rod said with a wry smile.

"Eh? What do you mean, Rod," Cilla demanded. "If Bernard was one of the parties in the relationship, how could he not know? Ah, did his moment of enlightenment come via the note he was left? Come on, Rod. The whole story now, please. What was the nature of their relationship?"

"It seems James believed it was more than a friendship, and he accused Bernard of having strung him along before abandoning him with callous disregard for James's feelings."

Rod searched our faces as he finished speaking. Not having found any signs of enlightenment there, he pressed on – as delicately as possible.

"James sought a sexual relationship, but Bernard was…"

"Ooh, a sexual relationship…," I repeated. "Well, I think we could have set James straight on that one, couldn't we? I never saw any evidence he was that way inclined."

"I thought the only close and personal relationship Bernard had was with himself and his ego," Cilla muttered. "So, James's revelation was what upset Bernard and caused his wonderful performance this morning?"

"So, it would appear," Rod agreed. "Bernard went to great lengths – and to my discomfort – to assure me he was straight and had never considered James, or any other chap, in that way. He genuinely was devastated by the contents of James's note and, after apologising again for his behaviour, he asked to be allowed to continue with our mahjong group."

"And, of course, you told him he would always be welcome, as would anyone else who wished to join us," Cilla responded a bit tartly.

"My concern would have been for Marjorie if Bernard was to become a regular player again, but after her performance this morning, I think she might be okay. But Bernard still owes her a major personal apology for the way he has treated her," I said.

"Amen…" Cilla added.

"Both of you will be pleased to know that a move in that direction has occurred. Of course, I have no way of knowing the outcome, but Bernard did go into the library after speaking to me outside the Rec Room."

The Bernard situation kept my thought processes entertained all afternoon and still lingered as I walked to Rod's place for happy hour this evening. I still couldn't work out whether to feel sorry for the bloke or to feel satisfied that, for once, Bernard might have received just comeuppance.

Cilla was ending a call as she caught up with me at Rod's gate. The set of her jaw warned me she was not in the best of moods, and her first words by way of a greeting confirmed it.

"That bloody bowls club!" she exploded. "I can't think whatever possessed us to imagine it would be a good thing for the Village. The president of the bowls club, Stella Winters, just called to warn me we could be in for another torrid bowls club meeting tomorrow."

"Not more trouble from the duffers of the 'old brigade'?" I asked cautiously.

"Oh, Christ, no. We now have all of them licked into shape or gone. No, this time, the culprit appears to be *the cutest ever canine furball,* to quote Stella. Don't ask…. I don't know any more than the dog belongs to some bloke over in the new section. It's been going to bowls with its owner, and somewhere along the line, it developed a way of filling in time while it was there: chasing bowls down the green."

I tried not to laugh, and the strange look on Rod's face when he met us at the door erased all traces of mirth. Even Cilla noticed Rod's look.

"We are supposed to be here for happy hour tonight, aren't we?" she asked.

"Yes. Why do you ask?"

"You looked a bit stunned when you opened the door and found us there."

"Come in. I'll explain… and you too can be stunned."

After Cilla and I exchanged a look, we followed Rod in silence through to his back deck. That was about as long as either of us could wait to find out more, and we let Rod know.

"Okay, okay. Well, Bernard called just as you two arrived. He wanted to know if we were having a happy hour tonight, and if it would be all right if he and Marjorie joined us."

"Bernard *and Marjorie*," Cilla echoed. "Well, that was slick work; I'll give him that."

I stayed mute and immediately set about dragging chairs over to the big table. Rod's prediction was right. I was stunned, too stunned even to comment.

Chapter 26

Rod's bombshell about Bernard and Marjorie joining us for happy hour had me wondering how that would go down with the rest of the gang. Almost from the outset, once everyone had arrived, predictably, it looked like it was shaping up to be a tense night.

While I felt for the 'renegade' couple, the way Marjorie was being treated particularly upset me. The couple almost were being ostracised. Marjorie didn't deserve that. As soon as I finished putting the last of the nibbles out on the table, I intended to take Marjorie under my wing.

Janet must have been suffering similar feelings. She beat me to implementing the 'mothering' role when she strode up to Marjorie and engaged her in conversation. I joined them, and Cilla copied my example as soon as she could disengage from a conversation with Maria and Alice. A couple of minutes later, it was interesting to note the men followed our example. Before too long, both Bernard and Marjorie were returned to the fold, and the evening's earlier tension had disappeared.

I commented on it as I helped Rod and Cilla clear away after everyone had left. I was flushed with a certain pride in the way the group had put the past behind them and welcomed Bernard and Marjorie back as if they had never been away. Cilla was quick to scupper that feeling.

"Good God, really, Marion? What did you think we were going to do? Nobody brought tar and feathers. Good manners dictated they should be treated as our guests, and that's what happened."

"Well, it didn't initially, Cilla. It wasn't until the women gathered around Marjorie in support that the blokes made a move to do likewise. The way the evening started, it looked as though the couple would be left out in the cold until they felt embarrassed enough to leave."

"You do talk such rubbish sometimes, Marion; such emotional stuff. It's as though you've been sheltered from reality for the whole of your life."

"What…? Okay. Here's a bit more emotional stuff for you to deal with. What has been wrong with you since your return from Sydney? If I have done something to upset you, let's have it out in the open and talk about it. I am sick of being constantly sniped at by you, and I believe I'm entitled to know why."

"Ladies, please…." Rod began.

"Stay out of this, Rod," Cilla snarled. "You just carry on being everyone's friend and go-to person while I sort this one out," she added with a jerk of her head in my direction.

"No, Cilla. I won't stay out of it. I feel exactly the same way as Marion does about your behaviour since your return. So, if it is due to something we are responsible for, we have a right to know.

And, just so you are aware, I do not appreciate your personal insult." Rod stood, hands on hips, glaring at Cilla… while I wished I could slide under the tiles, and that I had never brought up the issue.

Cilla appeared to wilt before my eyes. She reached for a chair, flopped down onto it, and rested her elbows on her thighs. For a moment, she sat there with her head in her hands. I felt panic rising in me and cast a frantic look at Rod. He looked as bewildered as I felt, and I thought it wise not to seek guidance at that point. There was no time to do anything anyway.

A deep, agonising groan came from Cilla. Startled, I spun around to face her but then didn't know what to do next. Should I say something? Should I rush to wrap an arm around her? All I managed was to stare dumbfoundedly at her.

It probably was no more than a couple of heartbeats later when she lifted her head and looked up at us. My heart broke. How could I do this to someone I considered a friend? Agony and pain were etched on Cilla's face and in her eyes. She had no tears, but I struggled to hold mine back.

Finally, my brain – instinct or whatever it was – clicked into gear. I rushed to throw my arms around her and held her tight until she seemed to regain her composure.

"I'm sorry, so sorry. I didn't realise I was taking it out on you two. I thought I had a tight rein on it."

Cilla looked so devastated. It tore me to pieces. It was obvious that whatever personal issue she was dealing with was huge. I went to speak, but nothing would come. I tried again and managed a few croaky sounds before the words finally came.

"Is it everything that's been happening here? Finding the body in the paddock, being confined to home, and then the supposed abduction of Zorka and probable murder of her husband… Has all this finally climbed on top of you?"

"Eh…? Christ, no. That stuff was all in a day's work for me and probably still is in some ways. No, this is an issue much closer to home. Do you remember my friend, Joe?"

"Let's see… is he the one whose name probably isn't Joe and whose job we can't be told about?" Rod asked in an almost whimsical way. It brought an attempt at a wry smile from Cilla.

"Yeah, that's the one."

"The one who works in funny places in unsavoury parts of the world?" I asked tongue in cheek.

"Yep, you've nailed him. Before we drag this charade on any longer, here is a headline: *Joe is missing.*

He seems to have disappeared and hasn't been heard from since before I left Sydney to return here. It does not look good for him. That's all I know, and now you know as much as I do."

"Can't you find out more from his employer… I mean the mob he works for, whoever they are. Don't they know more about what's happened?"

"Huh, chance would be a fine thing. 'The Firm' doesn't even know I exist – not officially anyway. A couple of his mates within the organisation pass on what they can whenever they can. People like Joe aren't supposed to have private lives. They are not supposed to develop close attachments to anyone or any place. It would make them too vulnerable, you see."

"While it might seem a bit trite, remember the old saying about trouble shared… Don't keep us at arms' length. Let us help. While I don't know how we might do that, perhaps just talking about things sometimes might help," Rod offered by way of advice.

The evening ended on a brighter note. Bridges had been mended. Cilla seemed a little brighter in herself, although the worry she was suffering at the moment was something none of us could take away from her. Cilla's situation remained uppermost in my mind as I made my way home. It's almost impossible to know the depth of someone else's anxiety.

I tried to imagine how I would feel if I suddenly discovered Rod had gone missing under suspicious circumstances in some God-forsaken part of the world. It wasn't the same. I knew Rod was safe at home and probably tucking into his dinner about now. My experiment to put myself in Cilla's position just didn't work. As I toyed with my steak and pushed my salad around on my plate, an unpleasant thought elbowed its way to the fore.

How long does hope persist? It was a disturbing question but one that wouldn't go away. In a case such as Cilla's, how long would you hold on to hope that your partner would be safe and sound, and would come home to you again? Common sense told me it would be a long – *long* – time. My heart went out to Cilla, and I felt a monumental dose of frustration at not being able to do anything to help her.

First thing tomorrow morning, I will try to set up a meeting with Rod to discuss Cilla's situation. Should we try to lighten her load a bit here in the Village, or would it be better to try to keep her as busy as possible to take her mind off other things? By the sounds of it, tomorrow's bowls club meeting will give her plenty of other issues to think about.

Although I don't usually attend bowls club meetings, I was half inclined to sit in the gallery today. This break with normal practice, if it occurred, would be down to Cilla's mention last evening that today's meeting could prove interesting. As it transpired, an early morning phone call from a friend I hadn't heard from in months delayed my early morning walk. It wasn't until after I returned from my walk that I remembered the bowls club meeting and realised it was about to start. The other thing I realised, as I locked the door behind me, was that I had forgotten to call Rod to set up a meeting to discuss Cilla's situation. Oh, well, too late now, I told myself as I strode out for the bowls club.

By the time I settled on a chair behind the other few observers there today, the committee was completing the mandatory routine stuff that happens at the start of every meeting. Then Stella, in the chair, announced 'General Business'. My ears pricked, and I sat up ready to be entertained.

"The first item on the agenda is the matter of a small dog currently creating havoc on the rinks during games," Stella announced with appropriate solemnity. "Keith, the dog's owner, was invited to join us to discuss the matter, and I believe he is here somewhere."

Someone in the front row of the gallery, presumably Keith, waved a hand in the air, and Stella continued.

"Thank you for coming. Now, what are we to do about your dog's making a nuisance of itself for bowlers? The one thing that is certain is that it must not continue. Keith, would you care to explain how this situation has come about and share any thoughts you might have on how to rectify the problem?"

Keith was not a happy chappy about being summoned to attend the meeting, and was indignant about the accusations being levelled at Snowy, his dog. He told the gathering in no uncertain terms that Snowy went everywhere with him, including the bowls club, and that it would continue to include the bowls club. In a final dramatic flourish, he threatened to cancel his membership of the club if he were prohibited from bringing Snowy to bowls with him.

Cilla cleared her throat. "Through you, Madam Chair… Keith, that might be the best thing for you to do, especially as you don't appear prepared to contemplate any other solution. It's a shame, but you must do what you think best for you and Snowy."

For a moment, Keith looked as though he had been delivered a punch to the solar plexus. He spluttered and stammered a couple of times before finally regaining the power of speech.

"It's not that I wouldn't consider alternatives, but I don't know of any that might work for all involved. Obviously, my interest focuses on Snowy and me. If something doesn't work for us, then it won't be considered."

He went on to admit he knew the havoc Snowy was causing and how upset the other bowlers had become about the dog's presence at the bowls club. But there was a finality in his words that suggested, if Keith were to continue with bowls, Snowy would be at the bowling green with him.

In desperation, Stella threw the meeting open to suggestions on how to deal with the problem. About five suggestions were put forward, each one being shot down almost as soon as it was delivered. Then, Alice Logan raised a tentative hand to catch Stella's attention and was invited to speak.

"As I see it, there are a couple of options available to remedy the problem. Snowy could be granted the wonderful peace and quiet of some time alone at home when Keith comes to bowls."

Before she could continue, Keith leapt up and announced that was never going to happen. Unphased, Alice continued.

"Right then, as I was about to say… Anyone who knows anything about dogs will tell you the problem with Snowy is a lack of training. He needs to be taught to obey a few simple commands. If that happens, he will be easily controlled and will no longer be a problem when he is at the bowls club."

"How dare you say my dog is untrained," Keith shrieked. "He is a loving, gentle, well-behaved animal – and I defy anyone to prove otherwise."

My admiration of Alice leapt way up the chart as she continued to stand, looking apparently unmoved by Keith's outburst.

"Well, Snowy is here with you now … And is becoming quite upset by your shouting and carrying on. Perhaps you and Snowy might move out to stand in the space out front of us."

Keith scoffed and was about to sit down again when Stella intervened.

"No, Keith, don't sit down. Please bring your dog and stand out the front for us … Good … Thank you. Now, Alice, what were you going to suggest should happen next."

A scowling Keith and a slightly anxious Snowy were not at all happy with their present situation, but Alice seemed unaware of Keith's hostile glare. Sensing things were not good, Snowy was beginning to prance about agitatedly. Alice again took charge.

"Now, Keith, Snowy is upset and becoming agitated. Please try to reassure him."

Keith shook his head to signify he didn't know what Alice wanted him to do.

"Tell him to sit. Give him the SIT command, Keith."

"Oh, ah hah," Keith said, laughing, and then bellowed, "Sit!"

All that happened was that Snowy stepped up its prancing on the spot and appeared to expect something to happen.

"Okay; strike one," Alice said quietly. "Right, Keith, now I want you to return to your seat … No, wait … I want you to tell Snowy to stay where he is while you return to your seat. Would you do that, please?"

The confused look on Keith's face suggested he had no idea what he was supposed to do. Someone in the front row of the gallery hissed 'STAY'. Keith's face lit up, indicating he understood. Obviously, Snowy didn't. Despite Keith's bellowing 'stay' a few times, Snowy attenpted to go with Keith every time he attempted to move away.

Finally, Alice had proved her point, and Keith accepted that perhaps Snowy could do with a bit of training. But Keith wasn't quite done yet.

He rounded on Alice and growled, "You bring your dog here. So, where's...."

"Yes, there is a difference, Keith. Chester does not chase bowls and has never even thought about trespassing on the green. And, should he ever be tempted to do any of that, he would quickly be called back into line."

The result was that Alice volunteered to babysit Snowy for the next little while whenever Keith went to the bowls club, and she would implement a training program whenever he was with her. It was agreed there should be a short period before the babysitting began for Snowy to get to know both Alice and her dog, Chester.

Stella declared the matter 'resolved'. A sigh of relief went up from many of those present, but the meeting was far from over. The other item on the agenda for today's meeting was a complaint from women players about the men trying to muscle in on the women's Wednesday playing days.

It appeared that now the interclub competitions were finished, some of the men were of the opinion the women didn't need their Wednesdays. It caused an uproar from the (mainly women) observers.

While many women seemed to prefer something of a full frontal attack to sort out the problem, an alternate approach – when it was finally outlined – received full support. But, before the matter could be discussed in detail, Keith and the male committee members were asked to leave. Once they left the meeting, and a check confirmed they had left the building, a 'more devious plan' was unveiled.

"This is like *déjà vu*," one of the committee members exclaimed. "Every time we think we have sorted out the men, they try something else to take over the greens."

"Instead of having a row with them every time, let's adopt a more sneaky approach," Cilla suggested. "Thursdays were their interclub games days. They don't have interclub games on Thursdays any longer. So, why don't a group of women players front up on Thursday and take over at least some of the rinks?"

"It will cause a helluva row," another committee member responded.

"Yeah, won't it! It probably will result in a minor skirmish at the time, but I doubt it will escalate," Cilla suggested. "Stella, as president of the club, you need to be there. When they become unpleasant, you should remind the women that Thursdays are not their playing days, and they should go home."

"Are you suggesting we should just cave-in to the men?" someone in the gallery demanded.

"No, of course, that's not what I'm suggesting. If you let me finish, you will understand the nature of the whole operation.

Right; when Stella tells you to go home, you should object and complain about the men taking over your Wednesdays, and so you thought it would be fine for you to invade their Thursdays. You will be told that's not the case … and then you will leave. But before you actually go, you will hear Stella warn the men that any further incursion on Wednesdays will result in Thursdays being designated open days for all players. The men would be reduced to having only Fridays and Sundays as men-only days. How does that sit with everyone?"

A cheer went up from both the committee members and the gallery. I wasn't sure how effective Cilla's plan would be, but I did fancy being a fly on the wall when it was enacted.

After the meeting closed, Cilla stayed behind to discuss some club matters with Stella, so I walked home with Alice and Maria. I was intrigued by Alice's offer regarding training Snowy for Keith and decided to delve further into it while we walked.

"Alice, are you sure about taking on training Snowy? He's not a puppy any more. I imagine it might be difficult to train a mature dog that's had no previous training."

"Oh, I am sure. Snowy will respond to a bit of tough love. It might take us a bit longer, but he will be fine by the time I'm finished with him. It's sad to see such a lovely little fella given no training, but I am going to fix that."

"What's this tough love you are talking about? And is Keith likely to approve?"

"It doesn't involve anything brutal, just a tap on the snout when he gets it wrong and a treat when he gets it right. You don't whack them. You just tap them on the nose with a folded-up newspaper when they don't do as they are supposed to, or they do the wrong thing, and you tell them 'NO'. That way, they learn two commands at the same time: the command for whatever you want them to do, and 'no' when you don't want them to do something. And, of course, we give them a reward of a biscuit or some other titbit when they do well."

I remained sceptical, but Alice seemed quite confident of achieving the outcome she wanted for the challenge she had taken on. But we had arrived at my place. I left the other two to make their way up the street to Maria's house together while I rushed inside to call Rod. I was determined to do it before I forgot about it again.

Our conversation was brief. After I explained what I wanted to discuss, he invited me to his place for coffee at three o'clock.

"Uhmm… No, Rod, I don't think that will work. If Cilla sees me arriving at your place in time for afternoon coffee, she will invite herself along to join us. Perhaps it might be better if you came here for coffee with me," I suggested.

As soon as he accepted the invitation, my mind quickly detoured from what to have for lunch to what to make to have with coffee this afternoon. Scones with jam and cream, I decided, before opting to leave making them until after lunch so they would still be warm when we had them with our coffee.

In his usual way, Rod rang my doorbell at precisely three o'clock, and we indulged in small talk about nothing of any consequence while we waited for the coffee to be ready. In the end, we had a lovely afternoon tea of coffee and scones, but there was little else to report from the event.

Just as we were finishing afternoon tea and I was all set to open discussions on the subject of how we might help Cilla through her current troubling time, Rod's phone demanded his attention. After a glance at the caller ID, Rod told his caller he would call him back in a couple of minutes.

Then came a few words by way of a lame apology, and Rod was out my front door and striding along the footpath towards home, leaving a stunned me standing on my doorstep.

Later that evening, when I arrived a little early for happy hour, he again went through the apology routine.

"Apologies for dashing off like that this afternoon. That call was one I had been waiting for since Monday. It was paramount I talk to the caller. I will explain why, but not right now. If I didn't talk to him there and then, God knows when he might be available again."

For the moment, that was the best I was going to get. Although I knew not knowing would gnaw at me until I found out more, there was nothing more I could do but wait for the rest of the story whenever it was offered.

Anyway, the others had started arriving. There was no chance for further discussion as happy hour got underway.

Chapter 27

As I was leaving Rod's place last night after Cilla had already gone home, Rod suggested we reschedule yesterday's aborted meeting for nine o'clock this morning, again at my house. He suggested that, if I didn't mind his being a bit sweaty, he would call in on his way home from his morning run.

Of course, I didn't see any problems with such an arrangement when it was put to me. Why would I? But later, as I waited for sleep to arrive, I realised it might be a bit trickier than I thought. I would either have to cut short this morning's walk or leave earlier in order to be home, showered, and ready for Rod's arrival at nine o'clock. I settled for an early start and set my alarm – just in case….

The alarm did its thing, but I immediately dozed off again. It wasn't for long, but it meant the extra time I had allowed myself was cut in half. Leaping out of bed and dashing about with the speed and agility of a gazelle, I made up a minute or two of lost time. That was until I went to put on my sneakers.

A broken lace was not something I needed this morning. Of course, for just such emergencies, I always keep spare laces on hand – somewhere. Exactly where I thought they should be was precisely where they weren't. Well, they were really, but they took ages to find because they had slipped into a packet containing other things.

So much for an early start. I resigned myself to a short walk and promised myself a long walk this evening to compensate. Then, on the way home, Mavis Grimshaw, out deadheading the roses in her front garden, stopped me for a chat. I was forced to be rude to escape before almost jogging the rest of the way home. In the end, all the planning and rushing about was to no avail. Rod rang my doorbell while I was still removing my shoes. And so, it was two sweaty people for breakfast this morning.

When I opened the door to Rod, I noticed something interesting happening further along the street. It seemed only right to mention it to him. Well, it was over the road from his place.

"Did you notice anything interesting when you came down this street just now?" I asked. He shook his head.

"I received a text message as I came around the corner into our street. I was reading that until I was at your gate. So, no, I didn't notice anything."

"There's an interesting car parked on Cilla's driveway."

"Don't get too excited. I'm sure she didn't have overnight company. There was no vehicle there when I went for my run. Well, I don't think there was. What's so interesting about it anyway?"

"It wasn't there when I came home from my walk. I haven't heard a car go past since I've been home, so I don't know how it managed to be there without us knowing about its arrival."

"Perhaps it came in along the other side of the ring road from where I was running. Anyway, what about it?"

"Well, I'm not sure, but it looks like Richard Wilson's vehicle."

"Oh, I see… I think… You do mean Richard Wilson, our top cop?" I nodded. "Hmm… are they likely to kiss and make-up, or at least declare a truce? Richard has been a bit scarce around here since he and his team gazumped Cilla's mob's investigation of the Zorka case."

"Be serious, Rod. You don't think Richard's visit might have something to do with Joe's disappearance? I mean, you don't think he might be here to deliver bad news, do you?"

"Hardly likely, I would say. Even Joe's own mob supposedly don't know of Joe and Cilla's connection. So, our state's police service is unlikely to be aware of it, are they?" he said with a knowing nod.

"Intriguing! Perhaps we should invite Cilla to join us for afternoon tea today. What can we use as an excuse for a get-together?"

"Bus trips… Yeah, there's been a lot of feedback to my post about proposed trips. We need to set a date for the first shopping trip and settle on where our first major outing will take us. Let's ask Cilla to join us at two o'clock, and then have Maria and Alice (if they are available) join us for coffee at three o'clock.

Maria and Alice will have to do the heavy lifting involved in planning our first excursion."

Time seemed to move slowly today as it made its way from breakfast to afternoon coffee. Five minutes before our scheduled meeting with Cilla, and swinging a basket loaded with afternoon tea cupcakes, I attempted a nonchalant stroll to Rod's house… only to manage a brisk walk instead. As seems to be the routine way of things these days, Cilla bounded across the street to meet me at Rod's gate.

I sensed a change in her, nothing I could put my finger on, but she seemed different somehow. My assessment was confirmed when Rod opened his door to us. Cilla bounded inside, giving Rod a cheery 'good afternoon' as she went past. He raised his eyebrows questioningly at me. I responded with a shrug. But, we didn't have long to wait to find out what had brought about her amazing – and rapid – transformation.

As soon as we took our places around the table on Rod's back deck, Rod outlined what he hoped to progress over the next couple of hours and announced that Maria and Alice would join us for coffee later.

"That's great news," Cilla sighed. "At last, things are coming together… And today has been a great day all around."

Rod and I exchanged a look but said nothing to discourage Cilla from continuing and to enlighten us about her 'great day'– which she did without further ado. A coy-looking Cilla shared her good news.

"One of those blokes who works for the same mob as Joe contacted me. Obviously, he couldn't say much and was quite guarded about what he did say, but there are indications Joe might still be alive."

I let out a yelp of delight. "Have they found him? Is he coming home?" I blurted out without thinking.

"No. No, there's no indication of that, but 'The Firm' appears to have strong intel regarding his present whereabouts. I know there is a long way to go before he is back here with me, but this is a start." I thought I detected a waver in Cilla's voice as she finished delivering her good news.

"That is great news, Cilla," I said and rushed to hug her. "I know it is a weight off my mind, and I can only imagine how relieved you must be."

While Cilla continued to look as though her grin might split her face in two, Rod made appropriate comments and gave her a quick hug as well.

"And that's not all the good news," she announced, still beaming. "I had a visit from Richard Wilson this morning. I hadn't heard or seen anything of him for a while, so his visit this morning came as a surprise."

"If it was good news, I assume he didn't come to tell us we were confined to barracks again," I suggested.

"No. He came to give me an update on the situation with Zorka and her mob. It appears Zorka, along with four of her henchmen – bodyguards, if you prefer – must like the weather up this way. They are holed up a bit south of here but still in this police region, so they're on Richard's turf."

"Are they going to do anything about them?" I couldn't believe the police would allow them to just sit there without trying to round them up.

"Richard has them under constant surveillance while he waits for the right moment to make a move. They will round them all up, but they need to pick a time when there is the least chance of officers being damaged. Anyway, he will be keeping me in the loop.

Because… The other surprising news is that I have been offered a consultancy contract with this state's police service's special operations team. Basically, it amounts to much the same arrangement as I have on the other side of the border."

"Will you be able to manage both contracts without running yourself into the ground?" Rod asked.

"Oh, yes. Unlike my southern contract, this new one will only involve me in major operations, although I will be working closely with Richard across this region on an ongoing basis. But, yep, it's do-able, and I have to admit to being quite excited about it."

"Good to have the old Cilla back with us," Rod announced. "Now, can we talk about bus trips, please?"

Rod was right about the level of response to his latest post about the possible use of the new bus. It seemed like half the Village expressed an interest in using it to go shopping, and there was also quite a long list of suggested excursion destinations.

By the time Maria and Alice joined us for coffee, the three of us had agreed the regular shopping trips should commence from next Tuesday. That gave Rod a couple of things to do later today. Steve Parish had created an add-in for the Village's Facebook page for residents to book seats on various bus trips as they were scheduled. The booking site now needed to go live as soon as possible so residents could secure seats for the first trip in five days. Rod also had to update the Facebook page to inform people about what was happening, when, and how to book.

Once all five of us were settled around the table with coffee and cake, Rod distributed a list of residents' suggested excursions. Alice and Maria made comments on each of them where they could before the hard decision-making process began. By five o'clock, a proposed schedule of three excursions had been tentatively agreed, pending further information from Maria and Alice on what the venues had to offer. It was further agreed not to mention excursions on the Facebook page until further planning had occurred.

Then a mass evacuation occurred as all four of us women rushed home from Rod's to freshen up and prepare to return to Rod's at six o'clock for happy hour.

The following day, I dragged Rod along with me when I met Richard at the coffee shop as I had arranged, to give him the information I had withheld for so long.

"Richard, I owe you an apology for not speaking sooner, but I think I know when Tonelli's body was dumped." I mentioned the date as I remembered it, and then continued my story.

"Rod, you might recall, we had no happy hours for a few days around that date as everyone had other things on their social calendars. There was nothing on TV that night, so I went to bed early… and lay awake for ages. I remembered I saw mail delivered that morning but hadn't collected it from my letterbox. As there was a hint of rain in the air, I wandered out to collect it then.

It was a bit after midnight and it was a glorious, cool night outside. I wandered around the yard, finally coming back into the house through the backdoor. During my wanderings, I noticed lights – quite small lights – like maybe, torch lights – moving about in that paddock. At the time, I thought it was teenagers probably up to no good. I remember hoping whatever they were doing didn't set the place on fire. Bearing in mind everything that's happened since then, I realise it could have been Tonelli's body being dumped."

Silence reigned for a moment before Richard spoke. "Hmm… that date fits with when the body was likely to have been dumped … and it fits with my two officers being involved."

There wasn't much else to say on the matter and Richard looked anxious to leave, so we left the coffee shop together. Richard went back to his office and Rod drove me home.
I don't remember much of that day after our meeting. I think I was in a state of euphoria now that the burden of guilt, carried for so long, was gone.

Days morphed into weeks with nothing out of the ordinary occurring to cause concern or brighten our lives. It was nearly three weeks later when Cilla quietly told us as we cleaned up after happy hour that the news she had received earlier about

Joe had now been confirmed. He was alive, and it was likely a bid to rescue him would be made in the next few days.

Cilla also suggested she might not be available, or even around much, for the next little while. She planned to return to Sydney to do some work there with her team, instead of trying to manage it from home. We didn't need her to point out that already being in Sydney would be handy if Joe were suddenly returned to Australia.

We saw nothing more of Cilla before she left. Questions kept being asked about her absence, and various people wanted to know when she might return. Rod and I fended off the many enquiries until Fate stepped in to ease the situation. Various personal commitments outside the Village for a number of our gang resulted in a postponement of happy hours until further notice.

I couldn't have been happier. Rod and I spent our evenings alone together, either at his place or mine. We discussed what we might be able to arrange for the four of us to do once Cilla returned with Joe and we knew more about Joe's condition.

Life almost felt idyllic. The shopping trips were working well. No further rows erupted at the bowls club. Alice reported Snowy was ready to be allowed back to the bowls club without fear of his causing further havoc… but he would not be allowed back until Keith had completed *his* training. It was now up to Keith to know how to control his dog.

Two full busloads enjoyed successful outings, one to a new gallery and one to a seaside hamlet a little further north along the coast.

Somehow, it was a bit like waiting for the other shoe to drop. Life was too perfect, too ordered and calm. As I dawdled over breakfast one rainy morning, I thought something had to come along to wreck it soon. That 'something' came along a few days later. Janet Furlong reminded us the annual High School plays competition was due to open in a couple of weeks. As all the plays are staged in our theatre, and we look after all the bookings and ushering of people to their seats, life was about to become hectic again for a few weeks.

When we next spoke to Cilla, I warned her the busy season of dealing with the High School plays competition was almost upon us again. Her response was much as I expected.

"High School plays… God helps us. As I've said before, life in Merivale Retirement Village is a procession of one thing after another … or maybe that should be one crisis after another. Whatever happened to the concept of being concerned about how one might occupy oneself during their retirement years?"

And in our latest communique, on a more positive note, Cilla hinted she would be returning soon and bringing with her an extra pair of hands to help out with this year's plays.

The End

Other Books by the Author

Sonoma Whittington series:
An Ancient Solution
A Public Service
Missing!
Connections
A Different Obsession
Shattered Illusions
After The Ball
Unholy Secrets
Fateful Reunion
A Dark Place
Layers of Deception

Merivale Retirement Village series:
Close to Home
Growing Pains

About the Author

Neive Denis is the creator of the series featuring the Private Investigator, Sonoma (Sonny) Whittington. Neive Denis is the pen name of a writer who was lured from her usual genre to focus on the mystery and excitement that are a part of Sonoma Whittington's world. She came into being specifically for this series and, for the moment at least, intends focusing mainly on stories from Sonny's case files.

This series tells of the intrigue and scrapes – some on occasion life threatening – that are part of the life of Sonoma Whittington, an Australian Private Investigator, based in a Central Queensland coastal city. However, Sonny doesn't confine her escapades to Australia, and that provides Neive with an opportunity to weave some of her other areas of interest into Sonny's hair-raising adventures on occasion.

One Thing After Another is the third book in Neive's new series set in the Merivale Retirement Village. This series takes readers on a light-hearted trip through the world of a group of mahjong playing retirees who are not about to spend their final years being bored.

See more about Neive Denis and her work at

www.eaglemountbooks.com.au/neivedenis

or contact her at

admin@eaglemountbooks.com.au

www.ingramcontent.com/pod-product-compliance
Lightning Source LLC
Chambersburg PA
CBHW061055100726
47911CB00012B/246